IRON CITY

Other titles in The Northeastern Library of Black Literature
edited by Richard Yarborough

IRON CITY

a novel by

LLOYD L. BROWN

with a foreword by Alan Wald

NORTHEASTERN UNIVERSITY PRESS
Published by University Press of New England
Hanover and London

NORTHEASTERN UNIVERSITY PRESS

Published by University Press of New England
One Court Street, Lebanon, NH 03766
www.upne.com

First published 1951 by Masses and Mainstream
Northeastern University Press edition 1994

Printed in the United States of America 5 4 3 2

ISBN–13: 978–1–55553–206–2
ISBN–10: 1–55553–206–3

Library of Congress Cataloging-in-Publication Data
  Brown, Lloyd L. (Lloyd Louis), 1913–2003
      Iron City : a novel / Lloyd L. Brown ; with a new foreword
  by Alan Wald.
          p.   cm. — (The Northeastern library of Black literature)
      ISBN 1–55553–205–5 (cloth : acid-free)
      ISBN 1–55553–206–3 (paper : acid-free)
      1. Afro-American communists—Fiction. 2. Afro-American
  prisoners—Fiction. 3. Afro-American men—Fiction.
  I. Title. II. Series.
  PS3552.R6935I76   1994
  813'.54—dc20   94–17812

for LILY

    whose devotion made this story possible

FOREWORD TO THE 1994 EDITION

*"Don't think I'm being nationalistic, folks, but it's
just that I know my own people so much better."*

Henry Faulcon, *Iron City*

Lloyd L. Brown's 1951 novel *Iron City* is a
compelling testament of his love and loyalty to a fellow African-
American worker he had known ten years earlier. Twenty-seven
at the time, he became friendly with twenty-six-year-old William
("Willie") Jones in the spring of 1941 while Brown was serving a
seven-month sentence in Pittsburgh's Allegheny County Jail
during an early version of the anti-Communist witch-hunt.[1]
Jones had been framed for murder the preceding fall, and would
be executed eighteen months later on November 24, 1941, at
the state penitentiary in Bellafonte, Pennsylvania. Brown's novel
thus has documentary and testimonial qualities. These bind it to
a tradition of African-American "resistance culture" dating back

to oral tales and stories transmitted by West Africans kidnapped and imported to the North American continent as chattel slaves starting in the fifteenth century. Like nineteenth-century progenitors of this tradition such as Frederick Douglass in his *Narrative of the Life of Frederick Douglass* (1845) and Harriet Jacobs in *Incidents in the Life of a Slave Girl* (1861), and twentieth-century examplars such as Arna Bontemps in *Black Thunder* (1936) and Richard Wright in "Bright and Morning Star" (1938),[2] Brown systematically unmasks the physical and ideological mechanisms of a repressive system. His aim in *Iron City* is to depict strategies of defiance through representative protagonists who are imaginatively rendered even when they are biographically and autobiographically based. Moreover, from a literary point of view, the behavior of these protagonists is intended to express the authentic patterns of Black life and culture.[3]

The thirty-eight-year-old Brown was also a devoted Communist, fully conscious of the main policies and historical practice of his party. His desire to write fiction stemmed from personal, not doctrinal, compulsions; but the analytical categories and political lessons acquired from more than twenty years of activism and study informed the artistic construction of the prison and urban setting. They also shaped his recreation of the unfolding psychological drama of the last months in the life of Willie Jones, who was renamed "Lonnie James" in the novel. Moreover, as a managing editor of the Party-sponsored weekly *New Masses* magazine in the postwar era and an editor of its monthly successor, *Masses and Mainstream,* in the McCarthy years, Brown relentlessly campaigned against what he saw as the tendency of writers such as Richard Wright (starting with *Native Son*) and Chester Himes to represent African-American characters primarily as victims.[4] *Iron City* was in some respects intended as a corrective.

Beyond this, the moment of publication of *Iron City* was a singularly tense one in U.S. political history. The year 1951 was a crucial juncture in the Cold War witch-hunt. A second set of arrests of the leadership of the U.S. Communist Party under the

Smith "Gag" Act, for allegedly advocating the violent overthrow of the U.S. government, had occurred that June.[5] A number of crucial anti-racist defense cases were also under way on behalf of Willie McGee, the Trenton Six, and others.[6] In recreating the events of 1940–41, Brown could not help but be aware of parallels to both the political repression and anti-racist struggles of 1950–51.

Contemporary readers of *Iron City* may also be surprised to discover that a "lost" novel of nearly forty-five years ago focuses on issues that preoccupy radical activists of the 1990s. These include the racist criminalization of the African-American population in the mass media, systematic police brutality against Blacks, and the inherent bias of the judicial system. With a distressingly high percentage of African-American males currently in prison, and the Rodney King beating and outrageous acquittal of the police in the first trial barely out of the headlines, the story of Lonnie James may be dated in details but not in essence.[7] The capture of Lonnie in a racist police dragnet, the forced confession, the incompetent legal representation, and the futile battle against the judiciary suggest that the novel would have served well as required reading over the past decades for anyone wishing to be informed of some of the fundamental truths of racist capitalism in the United States.

Nevertheless, Brown and *Iron City* were consciously erased from U.S. cultural memory by the press and ersatz literary histories. Mostly ignored by the mainstream white media, *Iron City* received favorable notice in a number of left-wing and African-American papers, but was bizarrely denounced as having been based on "improbable circumstances" by the African-American scholar Margaret Just Butcher in *Phylon*.[8] Robert Bone's influential history of the African-American novel anachronistically described *Iron City* as "a propaganda tract inspired by the Foley Square trial."[9] Granville Hicks, a former Communist who was at that time an influential book reviewer for *The Saturday Review of Literature*, drafted a review essay in which he conjectured that, if *Iron City* had been written fifteen years earlier, it would have been published by a major press and praised in leading periodicals—but Hicks's article didn't appear.[10]

Perhaps the factor most complicating a contemporary appreciation of *Iron City* is the change of political climate and in the culture of the U.S. Left in the decade following its publication. The 1960s witnessed a dramatic shift in the style and strategy of African-American political and cultural leadership under the impact of the new Black Arts and Black Power movements. Among the results was that the African-American Marxist political tradition represented by Brown, and expressed in *Iron City* through the complex articulation of both class and nationalist themes, became misunderstood and then pilloried as a version of liberal integrationism or even assimilationism.[11] Thus the lines of continuity between Brown's revolutionary political commitments—particularly in the areas of national pride and militant resistance—and the struggles of the African-American radicals who followed were unfortunately obscured.

The Return of a Lost Generation

Indeed, by 1969, the political and cultural terrain of the African-American freedom struggle had shifted so dramatically that *Negro Digest,* a leading intellectual publication with considerable authority, was in the process of changing its name to *Black World* so that it would not be outdistanced by the very movement it aspired to lead.[12] That June, editor Hoyt Fuller ran a short piece in a column headed "Dissent," by Lloyd Brown, who was identified only by his name. Brown's essay, called "A Middle-Aged Negro Tells It *As* It Is," addresses the new generation of African-American militants, bluntly and ironically, but with humor and sympathy. Although Brown's epistle to the next generation comes late in the decade that is most famous for producing a new brand of revolutionary politics, it has some features of an African-American counterpart to white sociologist C. Wright Mills's "Letter to the New Left" nine years earlier.[13]

Brown begins by taking the young militants to task for their reliance on "obscenities from the speaker's platform." The use of such profanities is "not in the Black cultural pattern," he observes. "It is merely a steal from the revolutionary white kids, especially the upper-middle-class white kids . . . now that you won't let them play with your revolution." Don't "call me a brainwashed Negro," Brown warns, "but if you call me a *mouth*washed Negro—well, you are *so* right."

Brown then quotes the chair of a recent Black Power seminar who interrupted a speaker to admonish that "no Black person who ever respected his blackness would ever refer to himself as a Negro." In refutation, Brown provides an impressive compendium of quotations and book titles demonstrating that, throughout the last two centuries, the terms "Black," "Negro," and "Colored" had been, at various times, appropriated by freedom fighters and renegades alike; no term in and of itself guarantees moral and political superiority.

Turning to the issue of "armed struggle," Brown recalls his own initiation in the tradition of self-defense as an eighth-grader in the 1920s, when he trained with a real Winchester rifle against imaginary gangs of Ku Klux Klan members. He was inspired by reading newspaper reports about Ossian Sweet, an African-American doctor in Detroit, who shot a member of a white racist mob assaulting his house. Dr. Sweet and a dozen Black friends and family members charged with murder were acquitted after several trials in which they were defended by Clarence Darrow and the NAACP.[14]

In the 1960s, Brown ruefully observes, it appears that rifles are not merely an instrument of self-defense but the magic key to seizing state power. Moreover, "it now seems [as if I] should have been banging away not at the attacking Klansmen but at the main enemies of our race—the majority of Negroes (both in and out of the NAACP) who believe in self-defense but not self-destruction; and also white liberals like Clarence Darrow who defend them."

In a grand finale, Brown warns that the preachment of any form of racial superiority or inferiority, even if traditional roles are inverted, is nothing less than the manifestation of the Western European doctrine. Racism, originally disseminated to rationalize colonial conquest, is "the most antihuman ideology ever to inflict mankind"; it reaches "its depth of depravity in Hitlerism," which Brown describes as "a Ku Klux Klan in power." Racism, Brown implores, "is not a weapon that we can snatch from the hands of our enemy for use against him." It must be fought by creating its antithesis, values expressed in W. E. B. Du Bois's call for a "pride of self so deep as to scorn injustice to other selves," and in words from Malcolm X's last formal speech: "The Negro revolution is not a racial revolt. We are interested in practicing brotherhood with anyone really interested in living according to it."

The ultimate purpose of Brown's intervention in this debate—where, because of his age and vocabulary alone, he was likely to be ignored, if not traduced—was summarized poignantly in a concluding paragraph. To the new militants, acknowledged as inheritors of his lifelong political struggle, he advises more humility regarding ancestors: "You did not invent the concepts of self-respect and race pride. You did not start the struggle for liberation and survival. But those concepts and that struggle are your heritage—a heritage to be cherished and to be fulfilled."[15]

There is no evidence that Brown's impassioned plea influenced the political strategy of the African-American Left in the following years, any more than did the admonitions of white veterans of earlier struggles shape the direction of the newly radicalizing white college students. The preponderance of each rebellious generation strives to make a fresh mark in its own way, often by misreading and then dismissing those who came before. After all, the failures of predecessors seem apparent, since racism, class exploitation, and the waste of human potential persist in spite of the advance of technology and thus the increase in our capacity to relieve suffering.

Still, there come moments eventually in the anti-racist and other struggles when interest in taking a longer view begins to grow; when connections are made, ancestral links are acknowledged, and what was once regarded as ephemeral if not irrelevant suddenly takes on fresh meaning in a new context. Since the 1980s, in fact, a steady effort to reconstruct the U.S. radical traditions, including that of the African-American Left prior to the 1960s, has been in progress, with a special emphasis on ways in which earlier rebels anticipated what were thought to be contemporary problems. Before the late 1970s, studies of the history of African-American Marxism tended to emphasize what was dead, irretrievable, or undesirable, especially in books such as Wilson Record's *The Negro and the Communist Party* (1951) and *Race and Radicalism* (1964), and Harold Cruse's *The Crisis of the Negro Intellectual* (1967). The publication of Richard Wright's bitterly anti-Communist and, at times, wildly inaccurate *American Hunger* (1977), was met with national acclaim, while little attention was devoted to Benjamin Davis, Jr.'s *Communist Councilman from Harlem* (1969), William L. Patterson's *The Man Who Cried Genocide* (1971), and Philip Foner's edition of *Paul Robeson Speaks* (1978).

In the late 1970s, however, a new direction was augured by much discussion on the Left of Harry Haywood's *Black Bolshevik* (1978), although it was printed by an obscure radical publishing house, and Hosea Hudson's *The Narrative of Hosea Hudson* (1979), produced in collaboration with the African-American scholar Nell Irvin Painter under the imprint of Harvard University Press. These were augmented by impressive works of research such as Abby Johnson and Ronald Johnson's *Propaganda and Aesthetics: The Literary Politics of Afro-American Magazines in the Twentieth Century* (1979), Mark Naison's *Communists in Harlem During the Depression* (1983), Cedric J. Robinson's *Black Marxism: The Making of the Black Radical Tradition* (1983), Gerald Horne's *Communist Front? The Civil Rights Congress, 1946–1956* (1988), and Robin D. G. Kelley's *Hammer and Hoe: Alabama Communists During the Great Depression* (1990).[16]

Yet none of the recent published works touches significantly upon left-wing literary activity of the period of the Cold War and McCarthyism, the years just prior to the Black Power and Black Arts upsurge. Thus, the resurrection of the career of Lloyd Brown, including the republication of his unique and well-crafted novel of African-American political prisoners, *Iron City*, has the potential of assisting a new assessment of the history of U.S. literary radicalism in general, and the continuity of the African-American cultural Left in particular. The integration of Brown's contribution to these two overlapping narratives of culture and politics will hardly settle or exhaust the topics; equally important are the restoration of the achievement of John O. Killens and other writers associated with the Harlem Writers Guild, the left-wing African-American theater movement of the 1950s, the Cold War cultural activities of W. E. B. Du Bois and Shirley Graham, and many other subjects. But the republication of *Iron City* and a consideration of Brown's views on African-American culture and politics may help stimulate a more favorable climate for such studies by initiating further debate, discussion, and reflection among the communities of scholars devoted to the theory and practice of political and cultural emancipation.

Dialectic of Class and Nation

The world outlook of African-American writers, like that of all other writers, is forged not in isolation but through participation in subgroups of various kinds. These start with family units or other circumstances of birth and early childhood, but usually evolve more selectively into networks of relatively like-minded thinkers.[17] The mature literary work of many mid-twentieth-century left-wing African-Americans might be theorized as developing in an important (although certainly not exclusive) dialogue with the political and cultural practice of a relatively specific current of political ideology. For the most part, this was the Communist movement and the anti-racist, anti-fascist, and union struggles that it led from the time of the Russian Revolution to the advent of new left-wing leadership in the 1960s.

Such an approach does not, of course, preclude other major influences.[18] However, many African-American Marxist writers knew each other personally, participated in the same literary clubs, nurtured and mentored each other, read and reviewed each other's works, followed the same publications, and shared many of the same political positions for periods of time.[19] Even where there developed sharp hostilities and rivalries, many of the issues dividing them tended to be associated with that shared Communist tradition. Of course, at the present time, research on the forty or so writers who might constitute this politico-cultural school of African-American literary Marxists is still in its infancy. Indeed, owing to McCarthyism or disillusionment, many left-wing writers have never even gone on record about the details of their ideological and organizational commitments. Lloyd Brown, however, is unabashedly proud of his record as a Communist militant, and his life is testimony to the quality of intellect and political commitment among the cadres of what now must be regarded as the most effective activist organization ever built by radicals in the United States.

Lloyd Louis Brown was born in St. Paul, Minnesota, in 1913 to an interracial married couple. His mother, the German-American daughter of a Union Army veteran, died while he was in infancy. His father, a Louisiana-born African-American, worked as a dining car waiter and Pullman porter. Since there were no Black orphanages, and white orphanages would not admit Black children, Brown was put in the Crispus Attucks Home, a residence for elderly Blacks, with two sisters and a brother. Thus, he was raised by African-Americans in their seventies and eighties, some of whom knew firsthand about slavery. The result was a lifelong respect for these elders and their folk and religious culture, which he saw as dignified and highly moral. Brown's short story "God's Chosen People," which was based on that childhood experience, was listed in the O'Brien collection of *Best Short Stories of 1948*.[20]

Self-educated after a year of high school, Brown read voraciously. Everything he laid eyes on seemed to radicalize him, from the *American Mercury* of H. L. Mencken to the *Rubaiyat* of Omar Khayyám. Even before joining the Young Communist League in 1929 in St. Paul, he knew about Toussaint L'Ouverture, John Brown, and Spartacus, and considered himself a revolutionary. After a period of YCL activity and a visit to the USSR in 1933–34, he became a YCL organizer in New Haven and Pittsburgh, where he also worked as a CIO organizer. Like other African-American Communists of his generation, Brown was convinced that the Soviet Union under Stalin was advancing toward socialism and then communism, and that it had instituted policies for national minorities that promoted political and cultural autonomy. This conviction about the success of the Soviet Union, seemingly verified by firsthand visits and discussions with others who traveled there, served as a key component in Brown's political outlook regarding international events, even though the sources of his anti-capitalist radicalization were entirely homegrown.

As a writer, Brown received his first serious training by working as the editor of the YCL newspaper, *Young Worker*. In 1937 he married Lily Kashin, to whom *Iron City* is dedicated, a member of the Young Communist League who was born of Polish-Jewish immigrants to Quebec and recently a student at Hunter College. Through World War II, when he served more than three years in a Jim Crow squadron of the Army Air Force, he produced only political journalism, although in the early 1930s he had unsuccessfully submitted a poem to the *New Masses*. His view throughout the Depression decade was that most writers were not serious about revolutionary politics. When *Native Son* appeared in 1940 while he was in Pittsburgh, he hated the novel for its portrait of Blacks, believing that left-wing critics were insufficiently critical of it because of Wright's public Party membership.[21]

In the postwar era, he was politically close to Black Party leader Ben Davis, and was influenced in literary and artistic matters by the Marxist critic and poet Charles Humboldt. In addition to *Iron City*, Brown published about a half-dozen short stories in the 1940s and 1950s,[22] a great deal of political journalism, a dozen critical essays, and, in later years, articles on Paul Robeson, some contributions to *Freedomways*, and many letters to the editor of the *New York Times*. Moreover, he completed a second novel but, owing to sharp criticisms of friends such as Humboldt, decided to keep all but one chapter from publication.[23]

Brown remained publicly a Communist Party member until

1952, when he went to work for the great singer, actor, and pro-Communist activist Paul Robeson, writing many of his speeches, columns, and articles and greatly assisting with Robeson's book *Here I Stand* (1958). He stayed with Robeson until Robeson's passport was restored so that he could leave the country to resume his career, which had been destroyed in the United States by McCarthyism. Although Brown never rejoined the Communist Party, his association with Robeson in the 1950s was consistent with his earlier views, and he has maintained a socialist outlook. In the early 1970s, he visited the USSR a second time and was again enthusiastic about developments among the national minorities.

Much has already been written about the development of the Communist political program to assist in the liberation of the African-American population. As has been well documented, part of the thinking was initiated in the leadership of the Third International with input from U.S. Black Marxists.[24] However, the practical activity of the Party took on a life of its own as it linked up with powerful trends in African-American life in ghettos and rural areas.

What characterizes Brown and most African-American Marxist writers is that they saw themselves as a cultural wing of a social movement that struggled against both racism (white chauvinism, in particular) and class oppression. A narrow, all-class Black nationalism was rejected, but solidarity among African-Americans and recognition of a semi-autonomous African-American cultural tradition were regarded as prerequisites for an interracial class alliance. Wright's 1937 "Blueprint for Negro Writing"— which Margaret Walker believes to have espoused the collective view of the Chicago South Side Writers' Group[25]—is a key text because it expresses a common set of concerns felt broadly among African-American Marxists about race and class. "Blueprint" 's perspective is one of going through the national struggle from a proletarian perspective to reach internationalism. While most artistic creation can be neither explained nor controlled by political loyalties, specific issues of form and technique were often discussed and debated within this framework of the dialectic of class and nation.

This development in Marxist theory has the potential of breaking what is often seen as the integrationist/separatist dichotomy; from the 1930s through the late 1950s, interracial class unity was regarded as possible only through Communist and Euro-American support for Black nationalist autonomy based on the hegemony of the proletariat. In literary thinking, following the approach of Wright's "Blueprint," Communist writers often adapted a famous formula from the USSR: the culture to be supported in the African-American struggle was to be nationalist in form (that is, based on African-American life experiences, and using African-American folk expressive culture), but proletarian in content (that is, communicating values leading to interracial working-class unity). Hence, the cultural work of Black writers had to allow space for Black-specific impulses; yet, in the end, to be compatible with political doctrine, their work should motivate interracial alliances on the basis of mutual interests.

The Black and the Red

Lloyd Brown's novel is entirely worthy of the haunting cover of the original *Masses and Mainstream* edition by Hananiah Harari.[26] Tackling a subject virtually ignored by previous novelists—it is possibly the first Black prison novel, and certainly the first depicting the activities of political prisoners in the United States—and artistically driven by a desire to reconcile his strong emotions about the subject with his powerful political convictions, Brown experimented with a multiplicity of forms and styles that he integrated with a craft that is remarkable for a first novelistic effort.

As *Iron City* unfolds, the Monongahela County Jail relentlessly discloses more and more features that suggest a microcosm for the state-repressive aspects of capitalist society. Step by step, we are inaugurated into the prison system of enforced segregation, supervision of behavior, spying, and censorship. The jail also has at least one other major characteristic of capitalist society—price gouging for necessary goods is perpetrated by those in power among the prison population, just as merchants increase prices for ghetto residents.[27]

The Monongahela County Courthouse, which works in tandem with the jail and is located on the very next block, may claim to provide "justice for all," but its essential weapons are police terror against Blacks and frame-ups against radicals. The same Judge Hanford Rupp presides over the case of Lonnie James, a black worker accused of killing a drugstore owner in a robbery, as well as that of the group of imprisoned Black and white Communists charged with violating election laws in their efforts to get Communist candidates on the ballot. In fact, early in the novel a page from an official guidebook to Iron City is produced, describing both the courthouse and the jail as gifts of industrial magnate Adam T. McGregor; they are hailed as fine architectural examples of Western culture.[28] The notion that the system is a kind of prison for the workers who, if organized to struggle, might be the gravediggers of capitalism, is reinforced by a prisoner's observation that "Half the guys in here . . . have made McGregor steel. . . . We made this here jail for them to put us in."[29]

In a memorable scene, the three Black Communist prisoners survey the cell block across from them; with its gray steel walls and "trellis-work of bars," it resembles "a great ocean steamer, riding high in the water and converging upon them, with all passengers lining the five long decks, facing forward, eager for port."[30] A closer look transforms the block into a fantastic, race-stratified, *Pequod*-like ship of humanity:

> The top three levels were white men, but directly across, running the length like a waterline, the row of faces was dark; and on the next range down which was the bottom. The men on D could see only this one side of Cell Block Two, but they knew that the color line marked this level exactly on each of the five structures.
>
> A thousand men on fifty ranges were standing and waiting—the young and the old, the crippled and the whole, the tried-and-found-guilty and the yet-to-be-

tried: the F & B's [fornication and bastardy cases], the
A & B's [assault and battery cases], the drunk-and-
disorderlies, rapists, riflers, tinhorns, triflers, swindlers,
bindlers, peepers, punks, tipsters, hipsters, snatchers,
pimps, unlawful disclosers, indecent exposers, delayed
marriage, lascivious carriage, unlicensed selling, fortune
telling, sex perversion, unlawful conversion, dips,
dopes, dandlers, deceivers, buggers, huggers, writers,
receivers, larceny, arsony, forgery, jobbery, felonious
assault, trespassing, robbery, shooting, looting, gambling, shilling, drinking, winking, rambling, killing,
wife-beating, breaking in, tax-cheating, making gin,
Mann Act, woman-act, being-black-and-talking-back,
and conspiring to overthrow the government of the
Commonwealth by force and violence.[31]

This fine passage, with its energetic and jazzy rhythms, provides a fundamentally clarifying perspective, but the overall form
of *Iron City* may well have presented Brown with something of
a conundrum. The essence of the plot is the alliance developed
among three African-American Communist prisoners and Lonnie
James, aimed at creating a defense committee outside the prison
to defend the rights that the police and judicial system had
denied Lonnie. In terms of linear chronology, the novel is
organized around specific events in Lonnie's life, starting in
1940. On April 10, there is the killing of a drugstore owner. On
May 4, Lonnie is picked up by police. On May 20, he is officially
arrested and placed in the county jail. On May 21, his confession
(achieved through beatings, torture, and sleep-deprivation) is
declared. On October 13, there is the announcement of his death
sentence. This is followed by an appeal to the State Supreme
Court; and when that fails, a second appeal is made based on his
lawyer's suicide and the location of a crucial witness, Leroy
Flowers, who had disappeared at the time of Lonnie's arrest.
Nevertheless, aspects of the work suggest that Brown aspired to
realize a highly complex agenda.

Iron City, first of all, is aimed at documenting "real" events.
Yet Brown must rely heavily on imaginative techniques to hu-
manize the characters through their thoughts, dreams, and inti-

mate dialogue. While it is a work primarily set in a prison, Brown dramatizes events of the past and future, and of the imagination, which occur in various regions of the United States and also in the Black community just outside the walls of the jail.

Another feature is that there is a large number of characters in the novel (perhaps too many for some readers to remember and absorb) because Brown wants to present a cross-section of the prison population, of the Black Communist cadre, and of the Black community of Iron City. Thus, at least a half-dozen life stories are told to one degree or another (some of them with extraordinary beauty, as in the narrative of Zachary's youth in the South), and fragments of the lives of many more are more briefly depicted.

In accordance with the concerns of his literary essays, Brown aspired to present a counter-model to Black writers who were abandoning Black-specific topics in the late 1940s and early 1950s (for example, Frank Yerby, Ann Petry, and Willard Motley), or who were depicting Blacks as brutalized (in the manner of Wright and Himes).[32] At the same time, *Iron City* must also be understood as an intervention against larger trends in Euro-American culture in the United States. Methodologically, the text is designed to take a stand against what Brown perceived as a retreat from "realism" in literature of the 1950s, typified by Norman Mailer's shift from *The Naked and the Dead* (1948) to *Barbary Shore* (1951).[33] While characters in *Iron City* are often vivified by depicting their fantasies and dreams, the plot is structured to continually bring them back to the material world of hard facts suggested by a frequent use of graphically repro-duced newspaper clippings, prison regulations, and reports on world events.

Finally, the novel aspires to dramatize political lessons learned through experiences such as the 1940–41 Pittsburgh struggle. Among the most obvious is that the rulers of society want through political repression to behead the leadership of workers' movements; this makes it even more crucial to reunite and organize under prison conditions, and to fight back through the creation of alliances and the intelligent use of local opportunities.

Another political lesson is that struggles like Lonnie's are ineffective when undertaken individually; the possibility of success is greatly enhanced when organizational cadres assist. In short, the prison struggle reflects in small the national battle led by leftists against misleaders, police, and stoolpigeons. At the same time, the Communist Party comes in for some criticism in *Iron City* for a tendency to be too narrow politically—the Party members had been so concerned with their electoral fight that they were unaware of Lonnie's life-and-death trial occurring at virtually the same time.[34]

Such a political focus means that *Iron City* is also a novel written against despair, trying to mobilize hope. And such a fighting, militant theme was an act of rebellion against conventional literary subjects of the 1950s, especially those of bestsellers. Moreover, in contrast to works such as *Native Son,* Brown felt he was depicting "real Communists"—people whose revolutionary politics are part of the fabric of their whole person, not merely the mouthing of political slogans.[35]

Above and beyond these specific concerns, however, the novel is stuctured to allow the dramatization of the complex Communist perspective on nation and class. Lonnie doesn't need anyone to tell him to fight; he is already fighting, but alone. In other words, African-Americans don't have to wait for politicos or whites to advise them about their need to struggle; they take charge and show initiative themselves. Still, for ultimate success, a coalition with whites remains essential.[36]

From the beginning, the perspective of the novel is highly Black-specific. Although white and Black Communists are imprisoned, we are led to identify only with the Blacks. Henry Faulcon, the oldest Black Communist and a moral center of the story, introduces the theme of Black Pride to the point where he has to defend himself against the charge of being a narrow nationalist: "As long as they got this Jim Crow it's better for a man to be on this side of the line than with the whites. . . . Don't come accusing me of nationalism, but I'm telling you the *people* here are better. . . . You aint heard nobody Red-baiting us have you? . . . But up on those [white] ranges it aint like that. All kinds of reactionary bastards up there—Coughlinites, Jew-haters, fascists and everything."[37] Among features of the text specifically reflecting African-American culture are the diction and vocabulary of the Black characters,[38] spirituals, folk songs, humor, and "the dozens." However, Brown's Black population is far from idealized. African-American traitors appear both in prison and in the Party, and one of the Black prisoners, Tuxedo, is described as pimping his own wife.

Iron City also embodies Brown's conviction that nationalism must ultimately be transcended for the sake of interracial unity. Thus, we see Lonnie evolve from believing that what landed the Black Communists in prison was their exploitation by white Communists, to collaborating fully with interracial efforts on his behalf. Still, Black unity and an emphasis on Black culture are never abandoned for the sake of this necessary alliance. Rather, Brown dramatizes both components of the ideological tension. On the one hand, for example, we have Henry, a Communist who leans toward nationalism; on the other, we have Paul, who is drawn toward a class-against-class view of the world.[39] Their separate orientations are reflected in an exchange in which Henry reports to Paul a discussion he heard among Black prisoners to the effect that all humanity is Negro and the Negroes are simply the better part. Half jokingly, Henry announces that he is about ready to demand that, since he is among the better part, he and all the other African-American prisoners ought to be on the upper ranges of the cell block, which are warmer and where the food is served first. Paul angrily directs Henry's vision to the top tiers of Cell Block Two: "Maybe you're getting so old you can't see so good any more . . . but those sure look like bars up there to me. Meaning we'd still be in jail just the same, just like the white workers in the mill are still exploited even if they do get a better break than we do." But then Paul realizes that the old man was just "jiving."[40]

Themes of interracial unity are clearly evidenced in many episodes: for example, in the scene where the three Black Communist prisoners learn that white and Black members of the Party are all contributing a day's pay to raise funds for their appeal; in Paul's reminiscences about his Jewish-American friend, Marty Stein, who died in Spain; in discussions of the interracial activities of the International Labor Defense to support the Communists and, later, Lonnie James, after Lonnie's lawyer commits suicide; in the references to an Irish-American union president who supports Lonnie's case; in the return from semi-retirement of the older white Communist leader Archer to work with Paul's wife, Charlene, on the Defense Committee; and in the appointment of the liberal Jewish lawyer Milton Cohen to defend Lonnie.[41] The linkage between racism and red-baiting struggles is dramatized when Lonnie's lawyer, Winkel, tries to get Lonnie to break with the ILD by citing Congressman John E. Rankin's denunciation of Archer as a notorious Communist. When Lonnie learns that Rankin is the representative of the racist state of Mississippi, he refuses in a feisty manner to repudiate the ILD.[42]

"What Can an Old Negro Have to Dream About?"

Subtlety and distinction of characterization are among the artistic strengths of *Iron City*, The portraits of Lonnie James and Paul Harper, who are linked together in multiple relationships of similarities and differences, are fairly detailed.[43] Lonnie is twenty-three years old and grew up in Ohio in an orphanage. Although strongly alert to possible signs and omens that may affect his fate, he is a person of religious faith, frequently reading a Bible, which seems connected to his will to live and fight back.[44] Previously a laborer in a tin plate mill, Lonnie is now housed in C 10. His relations with his main white jailers are contradictory: one guard, Dan, won't mess with Lonnie at all; another, Steve, who himself suffers some discrimination as a "Hunky" but who is politically a reactionary, treats Lonnie with respect; and a third, an older guard named Byrd, has Lonnie terrified.

Paul Harper in some respects recalls the novel's author, Lloyd Brown.[45] He is the leader of the Communists and faces a possible ten-year sentence. Twenty-seven years old, Paul is married to

Charlene, a former Cleveland school teacher, and he is reading Victor Hugo's *Les Miserables*. Significantly, Paul is housed in a room directly below Lonnie, in Range D, Cell 10. He is six feet tall and his physical resemblance to Lonnie is frequently noted. Twice it is remarked that he has the same dark complexion as Lonnie, and three times it is said that they could be kin.[46] Although the most politically single-minded of the Communist prisoners, Paul undergoes a transformative experience in relation to Lonnie because he realizes how easily he could be in Lonnie's place.

Two other Communists, both older than Lonnie, present their life stories in *Iron City*, and their tales are joined by that of another prisoner with whom they become friendly. The Communists, Henry Faulcon and Isaac Zachary, face possible three-to-five-year sentences, since they are regarded as less important than Paul. Henry, a former waiter, is sixty-three years old, has gray hair, a round wrinkled face, and is short and heavyset. He has been imprisoned twice before and is a veteran of the campaign in defense of the Scottsboro Boys. Isaac Zachary, from the country, is big, tall, broad-shouldered, and solemn-looking. Between forty and fifty years old, he has been married for twenty-two years to Annie Mae. His dream since his childhood in Mississippi had been to become a locomotive engineer, but the Jim Crow system restricted him to the job of fireman.

The third life story is that of Harvey ("Army") Owens, who is in jail because he failed to pay alimony. He is the character with most of the features of a folk hero. In a surprising flash-forward in time, we are told what follows his decorated service in World War II. After falling in love with a woman from Georgia, they travel to her home with another couple and all four are killed by racists who believe Army is acting too "uppity."

The most disturbing relationship in the novel is between Lonnie and "Crazy Carl" Peterson. Described as an "idiot," Carl is one of the three whites confined with Lonnie on Murderers' Row, but he is entirely ignorant of racism. Lonnie regards Carl as the "first decent white man I met"[47] and has more close physical contact with him than anyone else, calling him affectionate pet names and even carrying on imaginary conversations with him. Carl, in turn, waits for Lonnie like a puppy, offers him simple words of friendship, and is said to be the only person able to reach the "hidden Lonnie within."[48] Moreover, Carl, on his own, surprises Lonnie with the suggestion that the Communists in prison might be of help. Yet Carl has committed infanticide—he bludgeoned his own son to death, and doesn't even seem to realize it!

If the Dostoyevskian Carl adds some "modernist" mystery to what might otherwise be a relatively "realist" plot, there are numerous other elements that enrich and complicate the narrative. For example, references to various kinds of games are interwoven throughout *Iron City*. The pattern begins with a reference to Lonnie's childhood game of Giant Footsteps; but soon he is depicted playing basketball by himself, and then as part of a baseball team.[49] There are also several episodes involving boxing. One occurs when the prisoners demand to be allowed to hear the Joe Louis fight on the radio; their shouts transform into a cry against white supremacism.[50] Another motif in the novel is ornithological imagery, including comparisons between birds and people—Peterson is compared to an owl; the brutal guard, Byrd, is called a buzzard; and Henry Faulcon's name suggests falcon.

The climax of *Iron City* also defies what one might expect for the conventional ending of a realist or naturalist novel. On the one hand, the accumulation of evidence begins to clarify the dynamics of Lonnie's frame-up. It appears that a new district attorney was anxious to find someone on whom to blame the murder, probably in order to make a name for himself and restore confidence among the white citizens. Big John, the bartender who failed to back up Lonnie's alibi, turns out to be linked to the police commissioner. On the other hand, toward the end of the novel Lonnie has given up all hope , even though the suicide of his lawyer and the appearance of another witness seem to suggest the likelihood of his either gaining a rehearing or having the death sentence commuted.[51]

In a bold move, the final episode of *Iron City* shifts away from

Lonnie almost entirely, into the magnificent dream sequence of Henry Faulcon. On night patrol, the brutal guard, Byrd, peers into Henry's cell and sees "the smooth brown face of the sleeping gray-haired" Henry. The guard thinks: "He must be dreaming . . . but what can an old Negro have to dream about?"[52] The dream that follows is a memorable fusion of folk religion and Marxist politics, an Afro-Americanized utopian socialist vision. Politically and artistically, it is a rather striking counterpoint to the horrific fantasy of castration that is the penultimate section of Ralph Ellison's *Invisible Man*, published a year later.[53] Henry's dream recapitulates much of his life and of events in the novel as the imagery shifts from an urban to a pastoral setting, with a euphoric Henry surrounded by celebrating African-American men. Overlooking the crowd from a platform, Henry sees a row of rich whites hogging the front seats and has them ejected by a group that includes the folk heroes Stackalee and John Henry. Next, the men are joined by throngs of African-American women,[54] and finally, the crowd becomes interracial. Lonnie then appears with Peterson on his arm, and Zachary, the frustrated engineer, is shown at last driving the glory train. Henry himself proposes marriage to his longtime sweetheart, Lucy Jackson.

Then, suddenly, in the last three paragraphs we leave the world of dreams and are back with the aging guard, Byrd, who, this time, is peering in on the sleeping Lonnie on death row before continuing his rounds. Thus, although the fight is far from over, the imagery of Faulcon's dream constitutes a powerful affirmation of socialism—not as an externally imposed abstraction, but as the concrete expression of the aspirations of a people. Socialism's universalizing tendencies are depicted as growing out of national culture and experience. Fused with religion, culture, and the history of class and anti-racist struggle, it is figured as the modern expression of the age-old hope that drives humanity toward freedom, despite the prisons and prison guards of the moment.

In a 1988 unpublished reminiscence called "The Inside Story of

My Novel, *Iron City*," Lloyd Brown reveals for the first time many of the actual names of the individuals who participated in organizing the Willie Jones Defense Committee in Pittsburgh. He also emphasizes the crucial role played by his wife, Lily, in transmitting Brown's messages from the committee inside the jail to the "Outside Committee." Finally, he reflects on the considerable trust that the doomed Jones had developed in his new Communist friends, and the feeling of personal responsibility that this engendered in Brown himself. One can hardly imagine a more inspiring symbol of the committed artist than this relationship of Brown to Jones.

"I like to think that in his last moments he [Jones] knew that we had never deserted him," Brown concludes.[55] The republication of *Iron City* at a time when racism is as virulent in the United States as it was in the 1940s and 1950s is a clarion call to a new generation to be as loyal to targets of racist repression in our time as Brown was to Willie Jones in his.

ALAN WALD

Notes

I am grateful to Lloyd Brown, Robert Chrisman, Lee Freeman, Robin D. G. Kelley, and Richard Yarborough for reading a draft of this essay and offering suggestions, although I alone am responsible for its content.

1. This was at the time of the Hitler-Stalin Pact (August 1939 to June 1941), when U.S. Communists were isolated from their former liberal allies; owing to the Dies Committee Hearings on Un-American Activities, 1938–41, the period is also referred to as the "Little Red Scare." Communist Party leader Earl Browder was indicted on old charges of having traveled under a false passport; the Rapp-Coudert probe of Communist influence in the New York City school system was held; and Communist activists around the country were arrested on various kinds of trumped-up charges. Brown, who was Young Communist League District Organizer for Western Pennsylvania, was arrested along with twenty-seven other Party members for alleged irregularities in attempting to get Party candidates on the ballot. Brown himself

anonymously wrote a pamphlet on the case, *The Conspiracy Against Free Elections* (Pittsburgh, 1941). He received and served a sentence of four months, plus another three months for refusing to pay a fine and part of the court costs. Brown and his colleagues were found guilty on October 31, 1940, one week after Jones's conviction on October 24, in the same courthouse.

2. This first appeared as a pamphlet by International Publishers, before its incorporation into *Uncle Tom's Children* in the new and expanded edition of 1940.

3. The most impressive overall theoretical work on "resistance culture" is Barbara Harlowe, *Resistance Literature* (New York: Metheun, 1987). H. Bruce Franklin's *The Victim As Criminal and Artist: Literature from the American Prison* (New York: Oxford University Press, 1987) draws noteworthy links between the slave narrative tradition and contemporary prison literature by writers of color. Barbara Foley's *Telling the Truth: The Theory and Practice of Documentary Fiction* (Ithaca, N.Y.: Cornell University Press, 1986) has a provocative chapter entitled "The Afro-American Documentary Novel."

4. See, for example, his important review of Chester Himes's *The Lonely Crusade* in *New Masses* (September 9, 1947), p. 18, and a two-part essay, "Which Way for the Negro Writer?" in *Masses and Mainstream* 4 (March, April 1951), pp. 53–63 and 50–59. The latter was a response to the symposium "The Negro in Literature; The Current Scene" in *Phylon* XI, no. 4 (Winter 1950): 296–391. Blyden Jackson responded to Brown in "Faith Without Works in Negro Literature," *Phylon* XII, no. 4 (Winter 1951): 378–88. Another essay expressing Brown's views about the representation of African-Americans is "Psychoanalysis vs. the Negro People," *Masses and Mainstream* 4 (October 1951): 16–24.

5. See Michael R. Belknap, *Cold War Political Justice* (Westport, Conn.: Greenwood, 1967), pp. 152–53.

6. Willie McGee, executed in 1951, was a Mississippi truck driver accused of rape in 1946 by a white woman. The Trenton Six were African-Americans originally convicted for murder in 1948, but the Communist-led Civil Rights Congress managed to get the verdict overturned by the State Supreme Court.

7. According to statistics cited by Cedric J. Robinson, "one quarter of Black men in their twenties are under the control of the criminal courts." See "Race, Capitalism and Antidemocracy" in Robert Gooding-Williams, ed., *Reading Rodney King/Reading Urban Uprising* (New York: Routledge, 1993).

8. See review by Margaret Just Butcher, "Violence and Reform,"

Phylon XII, no. 3 (1951): 294–95. I am grateful to Lloyd Brown for sharing his collection of reviews with me, many of which are not indexed in reference books and would be difficult to locate. In the following list I have provided all the bibliographic information that is available on the materials in possession of Brown. African-American publications: "The High Price of Integration: A Review of the Literature of the Negro for 1951," by Alain Locke, *Phylon* XIII, no. 1 (1952): 7–18; "*Iron City*," by J. Saunders Redding, *Afro-American*, August 4, 1951; "Up and Down Farish Street," by Percy Greene, *Jackson* (Mississippi) *Advocate*, June 1951. Left-wing publications: "A Courageous Challenge to Corrupt Literature," by Milton Howard, *The Worker*, March 4, 1951; "A Gripping, Mature Novel of Negro Struggle," by Robert Friedman, *Daily Worker*, June 22, 1951; "The History of Lonnie James," by I. Dubashinsky, *Literary Gazette* (Moscow), April 17, 1952; "An Inspiring Novel of Negro Life and Struggle," by Richard Walker (probably a pseudonym for John Pittman), *Political Affairs*, August 1951; "Iron Will in the Iron City," by Henry Kraus, *March of Labor*, September 1951; "A New Writer Comes to the Fore," by I. Mikhailova, *Soviet Literature* 5 (1952): 140–43; "A Path-Breaking Negro Novel," by Sidney Finkelstein, *Jewish Life*, September 1951; "Don't Miss *Iron City*," by Sid Gold, *New Challenge*, September 1951; "John Henry's People," by John Howard Lawson, *Masses and Mainstream*, July 1951; "Lloyd Brown's *Iron City* Breaks Cultural Frontiers" by Howard Fast, *Freedom*, August 1951; "Story of a Negro Framed," by Marvel Cooke, *New York Compass*, July 29, 1951; "Without Magnolias—Story of U.S. Negroes," by James Aronson, *National Guardian*, October 24, 1951. Commercial papers: "Communists to See Bad Times" by Rev. L. Gillespie, *Cleveland Plain Dealer*, 1951; "Iron City" by G.A.P., *Springfield Republican*, July 15, 1951. The novel, published in both hardcover and paperback, went through three printings in the United States, and was also published in Great Britain, the German Democratic Republic (in both English and German), Japan, Soviet Union, Poland, Hungary, Bulgaria, Denmark, China (separate editions in Peking and Shanghai), Czechoslovakia (in both Czech and Slovak), and Israel (in Hebrew).

9. Robert Bone, *The Negro Novel in America* (New Haven: Yale University Press, 1958), 159–60. The Foley Square Trial was in 1949 and bears no resemblance to the William Jones case. It should be noted that adverse reactions to Brown's and other left-wing novels are sometimes the result of a failure to see what is on the page, because of political prejudice, virulent preconceptions, or simple ignorance. A startling example of this is the 1986 doctoral dissertation by Sam Gon Kim ("Black Americans' Commitment to Communism," University of

Kansas, American Studies Program), which claims that *Iron City* takes place in the deep South at the same time as the Scottsboro case, on which it is allegedly modeled, and that, as in the Scottsboro case, the defense campaign is victorious in reversing the death penalty. See pp. 173–85.

10. It is undated and can be found in Folder #104 of the Hicks Collection, Syracuse University Library.

11. Harold Cruse's aggressively anti-Communist Party *The Crisis of the Negro Intellectual* (New York: William Morrow, 1967) was a major influence, especially noteworthy as an early attempt to bring some theoretical rigor to the prospects of a cultural nationalist position. For an example of Cruse's harsh treatment of pro-Communist African-Americans, see the section called "From *Freedom* to *Freedomways*," pp. 240–52.

12. Abby Johnson and Ronald Johnson, *Propaganda and Aesthetics: The Literary Politics of Afro-American Magazines in the Twentieth Century* (Amherst, Mass.: University of Massachusetts Press, 1979), p. 193.

13. Mills's piece originally appeared in *New Left Review* no. 5 (September–October 1960) and was reprinted in Mills, *Power, Politics and People* (New York: Ballantine, 1963), pp. 247–59. Mills, of course, was writing on the eve of the 1960s, and his politics was aimed at creating a third way between the "end of ideology" school and those orthodox Marxists who he believed held to a "labor metaphysic."

14. The case is discussed in Wilson Record, *Race and Radicalism* (Ithaca, N.Y.: Cornell University Press, 1964), pp. 47–48.

15. Lloyd L. Brown, "A Middle-Aged Negro Tells It *As* It Is," *Negro Digest* (June 1969): 23–28.

16. This list is only meant to indicate a growing trend; it is by no means an exhaustive inventory of all available scholarship, biography, and autobiography about the African-American Left, nor do I mean to imply that all texts prior to 1980 were hostile and redundant while the more recent ones are uniformly original and sympathetic. A few additional general studies concerning left-wing writers are Doris E. Abramson, *Negro Playwrights in the American Theatre, 1925–1959* (New York: Columbia University Press, 1969); Kenneth Brown, "The Lean Years: The Afro-American Novelist During the Depression (1929–1941)," Ph.D. dissertation, University of Iowa, 1986; Donald Gibson, *The Politics of Literary Expression* (Westport, Conn.: Greenwood, 1981); Sam Gon Kim, "Black Americans' Commitment to Communism: A Case Study Based on Fiction and Autobiographies of Black Americans," Ph.D. dissertation, American Studies, University of Kansas, 1986;

Edward Margolies, *Native Sons: A Critical Study of Twentieth Century Negro American Authors* (New York: Lippincott, 1968); Jabari Simama, "Black Writers Experience Communism: An Interdisciplinary Study of Imaginative Writers, Their Critics, and the CPUSA," Ph.D. dissertation, Emory University, 1978; James O. Young, *Black Writers of the Thirties* (Baton Rouge: Louisiana State University Press, 1973). Some autobiographies and biographies of African-American activists include Faith Berry, *Langston Hughes: Before and Beyond Harlem* (New York: Citadel, 1992 [revised edition]); Martin Bauml Duberman, *Paul Robeson* (New York: Knopf, 1988); Wayne Cooper, *Claude McKay: Rebel Sojourner in the Harlem Renaissance* (Baton Rouge: Louisiana State University Press, 1987); Angela Davis, *An Autobiography* (New York: Bantam, 1974); Michel Fabre, *The Unfinished Quest of Richard Wright* (New York: William Morrow, 1973); Lorraine Hansberry, *To Be Young, Gifted and Black: An Informal Autobiographay* (New York: Signet, 1970); Angelo Herndon, *Let Me Live* (New York: Arno, 1969); Chester Himes, *The Quality of Hurt* (New York: Doubleday, 1972) and *My Life of Absurdity* (New York: Doubleday, 1976); Langston Hughes, *I Wonder as I Wander* (New York: Octagon, 1981); Claude McKay, *A Long Way from Home* (New York: Lee Furnam, 1937); Willard Motley, *The Diaries of Willard Motley*, ed. Jerome Klinkowitz (Ames: Iowa State University Press, 1979); Arnold Rampersad, *The Life of Langston Hughes: Volume 1: 1902–1941, I, Too, Sing America* (New York: Oxford, 1986) and *Volume II: 1941–1967, I Dream a World* (New York: Oxford, 1988); Theodore Rosengarten, *All God's Dangers: The Life of Nate Shaw* (New York: Avon, 1974); Margaret Walker, *How I Wrote Jubilee and Other Essays on Life and Literature* (New York: Feminist Press, 1990).

17. This argument is fundamental to developing a U.S. application of Lucien Goldmann's Marxist theoretical work on the novel. See *Towards a Sociology of the Novel* (London: Tavistock, 1975), where Goldman explores novels as corresponding to the structures of thought of particular social groups.

18. One must consider the specificities of the kind of writing undertaken (fiction, poetry, drama, criticism); the duration and character of the writer's relation to Marxist politics (from ephemeral to lifelong commitment); the region of birth and upbringing of the writer (urban, rural); the writer's class background, education, religious training; significant facts of personal biography (sexual orientation, relation to parents and siblings, marital life); and key elements of literary development (early reading, models and mentors, friendships with other writers, networks of friends and collaborators, activity in the other arts, theoretical views).

19. For example, a significant set of personal relations existed among Richard Wright, Chester Himes (who appears to have had Communist associations, if not a brief period of membership, in Cleveland and Los Angeles), Ralph Ellison (certainly a Communist ideologically for a period and possibly in a Party Writers Unit), and James Baldwin (a Party sympathizer while in high school, a student at the Party-led League of American Writers School, and a *New Masses* contributor). Wright also knew William Attaway, probably a Party member at some point and certainly a longtime friend of the Party, and collaborated with other Party members and leftists such as Theodore Ward, Dorothy West, Frank Marshall Davis, Marion Minus, and Margaret Walker. Another pro-Communist network involved many participants in the Harlem Writers Club and Guild, such as John O. Killens and Julian Mayfield, who worked with Audre Lorde (a member of the Communist youth group), Sarah Wright, Maya Angelou, and others. In left-wing theater circles there were a number of associations among Lonne Elder III, Nat Turner Ward, Lorraine Hansberry, Alice Childress, Ruby Dee, and Ossie Davis, among others. Langston Hughes and Paul Robeson personally knew many African-American pro-Communist writers, such as Lorraine Hansberry and Lloyd Brown.

20. The story first appeared in *Masses and Mainstream,* April 1948.

21. Letter from Lloyd Brown to David Bradley, December 13, 1986.

22. Brown's published stories include: "Jericho, U.S.A.," *New Masses,* October 29, 1946; "Battle in Canaan," *Mainstream,* no. 4 (1947), which was listed as one of the distinguished stories for 1947 in the annual O'Brien collection of short stories; "God's Chosen People," *Masses and Mainstream,* April 1948; "The Glory Train" (excerpt from *Iron City*), ibid. (December 1950); "Cousin Oscar" (excerpt from unpublished novel "Year of Jubilee"), ibid. (December 1953).

23. Jabarti Simama speculates on p. 238 of his dissertation that Brown's novel-in-progress, "Year of Jubilee," may have been "suppressed by the Party." No serious evidence for this view exists; to the contrary, Brown's correspondence with Humboldt in the Humboldt Collection at Yale University indicates that the problems with the manuscript were purely literary.

24. See Robin Kelley, *Hammer and Hoe,* p. 238, note 1. Communist policy differed from the approaches of all earlier Marxists and socialists in the United States. African-Americans were regarded by Communists not simply as an especially-persecuted section of the working class but as a nation within a nation in the U.S. South, a population with a distinct history, territory, culture, and, to some degree, language and cultural expression. Thus, the Southern population of African-Americans

had the right to its own state, as would a colony. However, the ultimate decision as to whether to constitute a state rests with the population itself, as does the form of the state, which could be either capitalist or socialist; otherwise, the notion of self-determination would be a fraud. Moreover, this struggle for national expression of African-Americans, whether or not it took the form of a state, would be most effectively waged if working-class elements came to the fore. However, even though middle- and upper-class elements tended to compromise to save their privileges, these elite African-American groups were relatively insignificant in the South.

Still, in the long run, whatever the dynamics of the national struggle in the South, the Communist view was that the United States as a whole had to be economically reorganized on socialist principles. This couldn't be achieved without unity between the African-American nationality and the white working class, among other allies. In the North, where the Black community was more dispersed among urban ghettos, and more heterogeneous in class composition, the favored Party policy was to form Black organizations to defend political rights (such as the National Negro Congress) as well as interracial unions, political defense committees, and other organizations. Of course, the weight given to each component, all-Black and interracial, varied according to circumstances.

The dual elements of this basic formula for the African-American liberation struggle, national and class struggle, shifted in emphasis in different times. The nationalist component was most aggressively expressed before 1935 and during the Cold War. During the Popular Front and World War II, it was somewhat muted, and there was an obvious softening in regard to middle-class black leaders such as those in the NAACP. Then, because of economic transformations in U.S. capitalism after World War II, the idea of a potential Black state in the South was dropped in 1958. A helpful review of this history and its implications for literary developments can be found in Barbara Foley, *Radical Representations* (Durham, N.C.: Duke University Press, 1993).

25. Margaret Walker, *Richard Wright: Daemonic Genius* (New York: Warner, 1988), p. 77.

26. The cover depicts the industrial operations of a city (Pittsburgh, renamed Iron City in the novel) through the iron bars of a prison (Allegheny County Jail, renamed Monongahela County Jail). Both jailhouse bars and urban landscape are reciprocal, equally weighted but with different iconic forms that overlap and address each other. From the perspective of the cover, with its bold, red block lettering, the city appears as nothing less than social prison; indeed, it could almost be a

group of factories and railroad lines within the confines of a Nazi concentration camp. The overwhelming power of the economic structure is reinforced by the artist's omission of any human workers from the scene. The only activity is the smoke billowing out of factory chimneys, imparting an eerie atmosphere, as if the employees had suddenly died or the machines were being operated by robots.

In contrast, human agency is concentrated entirely in the powerful Black hands on the prison bars, which are drawn to suggest a nexus of intersecting cultural meanings. The round poles of the bars directly resemble the round poles of the smokestacks of the mills below, which, in fact, produce the metal used in the bars. In addition, the hands of the prisoner gripping the bars suggest, in the absence of any workers below, that these belong to one who should be working in the factories. When the cover is turned on its side, the bars also resemble stripes of the United States flag gripped by the black hands of the person they imprison.

27. *Iron City*, p. 36.

28. Ibid., p. 20.

29. Ibid., p. 103.

30. Ibid., p. 31.

31. Ibid., p. 31–32.

32. In fact, *Iron City* has several features of an answer to *Native Son*. Brown starts with an accused murderer in prison developing a relationship to Communist allies, which takes off from where Wright's novel terminated. Moreover, Paul Harper, the imprisoned black district organizer of the Party, is specifically referred to as an example of a "*bad* nigger," a pointed contrast to Bigger Thomas, whose name is a condensation of "bad nigger" and who was said by Wright to have been a composite of various types of the "bad nigger" that he observed in the South. (See Wright's essay "How Bigger Was Born," which appears in most editions of *Native Son*.) Toward the end of *Iron City*, a newspaper article is reprinted that describes a lecture by one "Richard Canfield, noted lecturer and sociologist." Canfield refers to the protagonist of *Native Son*, Bigger Thomas, to explain pathologies of the Black community by analogizing African-Americans to rats in an experiment. The speaker's remarks as well as name recall Dorothy Canfield Fisher's infamous Introduction to the first edition of *Native Son*. That the lecture is to raise funds for "Brotherhood Week" shows Brown's belief that the perspective of Fisher and Wright is an outlook shaped by white paternalism. After reading the article, the Black prisoners laughingly compare themselves to "wild rats" (*Iron City*, pp. 207–9).

33. The literary shift was not unconnected with a political shift on

Mailer's part, from sympathy for Communism to the semi-Trotskyist politics promoted by his French translator, Jean Malaquais.

34. *Iron City*, pp. 122–23. Brown is also attempting to extend the radical tradition of proletarian literature and Popular Front literature into a new period, building upon the past without repeating its mistakes.

35. Brown may well have been influenced by his friend Charles Humboldt's impressive essay "Communists in Literature," which appeared in two issues of *Masses and Mainstream:* Vol. 2, no. 6 (June 1949), and Vol. 2, no. 7 (July 1949).

36. Here it may be useful to note that, in the period leading up to the publication of *Iron City*, much debate about racism and the politics of African-American liberation was occurring inside the Communist movement. At the December 3–5, 1946, plenary meeting of the National Committee of the Party, a resolution was passed strongly reaffirming the view of "the Negro question in the United States as a national question" (see *The Communist Position on the Negro Question* [New York: New Century Publishers, 1947]). At the very moment *Iron City* appeared, the Party was engrossed in an internal campaign against suspected white chauvinism in its ranks. Brown wrote an intelligent article on the issue, "Words and White Chauvinism," *Masses and Mainstream* 3 (February 1950): 3–11.

37. *Iron City*, p. 65

38. In his review of *Iron City* in *Political Affairs*, Richard Walker points out the following about Brown's use of language: "[It shows] sensitivity to the Negro people's idiom and to the *sound* of the language as Negroes speak it. This is a different thing altogether from the customary way of presenting the speech of Negroes as dialect, or as a kind of hodge-podge, distorted, ungrammatical English." In his *Afro-American* review, J. Saunders Redding observed that Brown "has done something quite worthwhile with the race idiom . . . the same sort of thing Ring Lardner did with sport and barbershop idiom—given it elasticity, made it a vehicle not only for speech (dialogue) but of narration and analysis."

39. In this regard the characters somewhat parallel the attitudes of Aunt Sue and Johnnyboy in Wright's "Bright and Morning Star."

40. *Iron City*, p. 104.

41. Cohen is possibly a vague counterpart to Wright's Boris Max in *Native Son*. Another example of interracial unity is the group of students and their teacher, who, inspired by the Dreiser investigation of the violence against miners in Harlan County, Kentucky, in the early 1930s, form a committee to investigate James's case. The suggestion came from a white student; after the committee turns up evidence that strongly supports Lonnie, the white teacher is fired.

42. *Iron City*, pp. 178–79.

43. Some years after Willie Jones's execution, Brown gained access to a number of his letters, which he published in *Masses and Mainstream* as "The Legacy of Willie Jones," 5, no. 2 (February 1952): 44–51. The correspondence between the personality of Lonnie James in the novel and that of Jones as revealed in his letters is impressively consistent.

44. On pp. 17–18 of *Iron City*, Lonnie says, "A man has got to believe."

45. Physically, however, Harper resembles James Ashford, a leader of the Young Communist League and a founder of the Southern Negro Youth Congress. Letter from Brown to Wald, March 11, 1994.

46. *Iron City*, pp. 25–26, 71; pp. 26, 122, 237.

47. Ibid., p. 71

48. Ibid., p. 235.

49. However, the baseball game, like the prison church services, is subverted as Lonnie and his new friends use the opportunity to transmit information about the defense effort on his behalf.

50. *Iron City*, p. 44. Another reference to boxing is when the guard, Steve, knocks out a prisoner yelling quotations from the Bible.

51. Ibid., p. 237.

52. Ibid., pp. 246–47.

53. Brown negatively reviewed Ellison's novel when it appeared in *Masses and Mainstream* 5, no. 6 (June 1952): 62–64.

54. Throughout *Iron City*, issues of gender and sexuality are treated in the conventional and somewhat puritanical manner traditionally associated with male writers on the U.S. Left before the 1960s. For an analysis of the masculinist depictions of the working class and struggle for socialism, see Paula Rabinowitz, *Labor and Desire* (Chapel Hill: University of North Carolina Press 1991).

55. These documentary materials are in the possession of Lloyd Brown.

PART 1

Nobody knows the trouble I see,
Nobody knows my sorrow,
Nobody knows the trouble I see,
Glory, Hallelujah!

. . . Lonnie clapped his hand to his chest and then reached under his sweater and brought out an envelope which he handed to Paul. "The clippings. Now you-all can read about me. And for Christ's sake don't lose them, whatever you do."

There were three items torn from the Iron City *American* and the Kanesport *Morning Eagle*, but the main story was told in the two-paragraph account which had been published October 13, 1940, on the bottom of page 38 of the *American*:

NEGRO TO HANG

Judge Hanford J. Rupp today sentenced twenty-three-year-old Lonnie James, Negro, to be hanged for the murder of Waldo Thornhill, white Kanesport businessman, on April 10.

No date of execution was set pending action by the State Supreme Court on the appeal to be submitted by defense counsel. James was returned to the County Jail where he has been held since last May.

CHAPTER 1

Crazy Peterson was sitting in Lonnie's cell when Lonnie returned to Murderers' Row from the yard. He was a small man and bone-thin, and squatting there on the bunk with his arms wrapped tightly around his knees and his pale eyes large and staring, he looked like an owl on a perch. Only an owl is supposed to be wise, Lonnie thought, and not like this guy who has no sense at all. Doesn't even know why they are going to put him on trial.

"I'm glad you came back," Peterson said.

Lonnie flopped down beside him. "Of course I did, Carl. I told you I can't go nowhere else. Keep telling you that. And I keep telling you that you ought to go out in the yard too. Get some air. Meet some other people. But no, you keep sticking around in here worrying about me getting back!"

Peterson smiled, pleased with the rush of words. He took an envelope from his pocket and offered Lonnie one of the butts it contained. "I like you, Lonnie," he said. "You're a good boy. Yes you are."

Lonnie shook his head. "No I aint, Carl. Look—" he pulled out the pack of cigarettes Faulcon had given him; it was almost full. "I aint no good. Know why? Cause I wasn't even going to let you see I had all these smokes. Go ahead, take one. Go ahead—maybe today is your birthday and this will be like a present. How old are you anyway?"

"I don't know. You know I don't know."

"That is *correct!* And you get nine silver dollars for that one. You don't know nothing cause you're nuts, that's why. Nothing up here. Screw loose. Bugs. Understand? *Crazy.*"

Peterson grinned at him and held up the new cigarette for a light.

"Uh uh," said Lonnie. "Maybe it *aint* your birthday. And don't you go trying to confidence me out of a match. You know good and well that whichever one gives the smoke the other's got to give the light. I aint Rockefeller, you know."

After they had smoked their cigarettes to the halfway point and stored away the butts, Lonnie said: "Now get up off my bunk so's I can stretch out and think."

The white man got up. "Can I stand over here?"

"Sure," said Lonnie, not looking. "Guess where I got the cigarettes. Out in the yard. Reds gave them to me. You know who the Reds are?" He repeated the question and rolled onto his side so he could see Peterson, standing now in the cell doorway. "Well, do you?"

Peterson put one hand over his eyes, pretending to concentrate. Then he dropped the hand and stared up to the ceiling. "I can't remember. Honest to God, I can't remember."

"You're lying, Carl. You never did know so how could you remember? But I know all about them. Last summer it was, while I was waiting trial, and they decided to overthrow the government. Sure wish they had gone ahead and done it, cause maybe they'd have turned me loose. But they got caught before they had the revolution even started good and last week they got put in here. Know how I know all about them things? Cause I read, that's why, and not like you just looking at the pictures. They had a big trial last winter and every day I read about it in the papers. Hell, them Reds weren't so smart—I could have told them all along they didn't have a chance before old Judge Rupp. But at least they had a fair trial and they had their own lawyers—" He sat up with a jerk and jabbed an accusing finger at Peterson who flinched at the violent motion. "How come everybody else can have a fair trial and not me? *Why not me!*"

"I like you, Lonnie," Peterson said softly.

Lonnie laughed. "Keep on saying that and I'll believe you. But you aint supposed to like me. You're supposed to *hate* me. That's right, Carl."

"No."

"Yes you are."

"No."

"I said *yes*. Now look here, Carl"—Lonnie tried to control the anger that always came when Peterson argued like this, stubborn, unreasoning—"Goddamit, don't just stand there saying no. Why not? Tell me why not?"

Tears were rolling down the white man's face now, but still he shook his head. No.

"Stop bawling and come here. I said: *come here!*"

Peterson moved cautiously toward the sitting man. When he was near enough, Lonnie snatched his trembling hand and pulled him down to the bunk.

"Don't be so damned scared all the time," Lonnie said. "I just want to show you something. I'm going to make it real simple, but by God I'm going to show you."

Holding Peterson's skinny wrist, he extended the captive hand and put his own hand next to it.

"See that?" he demanded. "No, don't look at me. Look at those two hands. See—mine is black and yours is white. OK. That's because I'm colored and you're white. Don't you even know that, Carl? Don't you even know *that?* Well, I'm showing you now. That's why you're supposed to hate me."

"I don't hate you, Lonnie. You're my friend."

"Oh, for Christ's sake, man! I know you don't hate me else you wouldn't always be hanging around in here instead of with those other two guys up the range. That's what I'm trying to get through your thick skull: you like me and that's where you're wrong. Hear me? That's where *you're wrong!* Look at those hands again. Can't you see? Can't you understand?"

Peterson pulled away. "You're hurting my arm, Lonnie. You don't want to hurt me."

15

Lonnie threw the hand down. "No," he said sadly, "I don't want to hurt you none. I was just trying to make you see something but I guess it aint no use." He sighed. "Just aint no use cause you're too dumb to understand. I show you right before your eyes, but you still don't see. You still don't see."

Lonnie James's cell on Range C was brightened at night by a beam slanting in from the runway. To Lonnie the light was a comfort; he had moved into that cell because of it. There is no rangeman appointed on Murderers' Row and a man may pick his own cell, especially when there are only a few men on the tier. Another advantage to Number 10 cell is the greater privacy. Range C is on the level of the Hub and because of the way the cell block angles in, the first several cells are always in view from the chief guard's desk.

Lonnie had been pleased when Crazy Peterson moved into Number 11 to be near him. In the long hours from lock-up till morning a man is not so much alone when he knows that on the other side of the steel wall there is a friend. Sleep never came easy to Lonnie: the strenuous exercise in the yard and the miles of runway pacing tired his body, but his mind seemed most alert at night, resisting the oblivion of sleep. Long after the radio had ceased to blare and when the only sounds were the tower-clock striking and men coughing and the squeaking of bunk chains as restless sleepers turned upon their canvas, Lonnie would be awake.

Tonight he had counted again the rivets that climbed up to the ceiling, three rows on each of the side walls and one on the back. Forty rivets to a row, 280 in all. He was satisfied with the count: as long as it comes out right I know I'm not like Peterson.

He rolled over onto his side to talk to Carl. His neighbor could not hear his low whispering through the thick barrier, of course, and besides the poor dummy was sure to be sleeping; but Lonnie would talk like that to him for hours on end. Keeps me from talking to myself, he said.

You know what, Carl? One of these days I'm going to tell

you that I like you and you're my friend. I really am. You're
all right with me and you can't help it cause you're white.
Nobody can help something like that. And one of these days
I'm going to stop talking mean to you like I always do. You
know, I don't know why I do that, honest I don't. It's not
because you're simple, cause you can't help that either. Maybe
it's because I'm not used to being friends with your kind. But
I don't think so, Carl. Tell you why. You don't even know
you're white or I'm colored—oh you poor crazy fool! Like
today. You don't even know that. Know what I think? I think
it's because I'm getting jumpy. Inside, I mean—not outside.
Remember Monday I made fourteen practice fouls in a row
like I told you? Well, you don't know nothing about basketball
either, but let me tell you everybody can't do that! I didn't
tell you I missed the eleventh one, did I? Well, I really wasn't
lying because it rolled around inside the rim and should have
went in and if you'd ever come out to the yard you would
have seen it too, so don't come calling me no liar, see? I'll
punch you right in the nose. Go ahead, man, put up your
mitts! *In this cornah, wearing black trunks, weighing one
hundred and seventy-eight pounds, the world's champeen—
LONNIE JAMES! And in this cornah, wearing white trunks,
weighing ninety-two pounds, the challengah—CRAZY PETER-
SON! . . . and the bell for Round One! Peterson comes out
slowly but Lonnie rushes out like a tiger—misses with a right—
HE'S DOWN! PETERSON IS DOWN! . . . Six! seven! eight!
nine! TEN! . . . The winnah and still champeen of the world—
LONNIE JAMES!* See that, Carl? Didn't even hit you, just
the wind from my fist and you're out cold. You're lucky I
didn't sock you. In fact, you're lucky all the time and maybe
that's why I holler at you so much. You're not only white—
and white is right even if *you* don't know it—but you're crazy
too and old Judge Rupp won't say they're going to hang you,
like he said about me. No, they won't hang you, Carl. *Not me
either!* Not me, no sir. You see me writing all those letters
don't you? And you see me getting a lot of letters back too.
Well, all right then, you got to believe me. A man has got to

17

believe, to believe in everything, just like I'm always telling you. What do you mean, you don't believe somebody will help me? Just look at all those letters up there!

Lonnie turned around so he could see the cigar box on the shelf. Inside were the answering letters and he knew them all by heart. *Thank you for your letter . . . unable at this time . . . hence you will see . . . regret we cannot . . . no doubt your attorney . . . referred your communication . . . the courts will . . . shall pray for you . . . unfortunately . . . with best wishes . . . not in our scope . . . may I suggest . . . only in cases where civil liberties . . . under advisement . . . other agencies perhaps. . . .*

He was breathing hard and clutching the bars of the door where he was standing. He looked over to the bunk where he should have been, but there was only the crumpled blanket. Damn! He released the bars and noticed that he had been gripping them in that wrong place. The shiny place where the paint had been worn off by many hands before him. He wiped his palms on his trouser legs and went back to the bunk, sitting down with his back to the wall and his heels propped upon the rim of the sagging canvas.

That was a bad thing to do, forgetting about not putting his hands on that place. How many men had been in Number 10 on Murderers' Row? And what happened to them? But anyway, he was not like them, whoever they were. With him it would be different. He would not put *his* hands in the place theirs had made; no, and he would not follow their footsteps either. Thirteen steps up, that's how people said it was. Thirteen steps up to the gallows, and maybe their feet had worn a path there too. . . .

The snow-covered field was sparkling blue under the new-risen moon, and no one must walk upon it before the game. The game was called Giant's Footsteps. First, all the kids got in line, one behind the other; and then, following the leader, they ran out in great soaring leaps. Sometimes Lonnie would be first and the glazed surface would give way in big jagged chunks, like pieces of frosting, and there would be a hollow creaking and cracking that you could hear above their laughing. Each boy in turn must leap into the footsteps ahead of him and it was always hardest when long-legged Lonnie was first. Finally they would be across the field and up the slope on the other side where they would gather, puffing and blowing, to look down upon the expanse and see the enormous footprints the Giant had made when he walked across.

Returning, there were other games to play—like Cut the Pie. Still running in single file behind the leader, they would trample out a great circle. Around and around, floundering and sometimes falling, and then the leader would break a path across to cut the pie. They followed him through each stroke and when, to fool them, he angled back sharply at the center instead of going straight across, only the most nimble could keep on his feet. When one of them went down, the game became Pile on Sacks, with all the others throwing themselves upon the fallen one, one upon the other, until all were down in a yelling, yammering, hammering, clamoring pile of frenzied joy.

The last game came when they were too tuckered out to run any more. Standing abreast, ten of them or more, they would throw themselves back upon the snow and, by waving their arms from head to hip, make a row of holy angels.

The flying angels, the battered pie, the giant footprints, the boys and the laughing and the big blue moon and the merry stars and the glistening snow and the wind on your cheeks and the sting in your lungs and the billowing breath and the pounding heart—a dark blue wonderful magic, a winking, twinkling, tingling brilliance of the world that was yours and the bursting, burning deep inside that was *you.* . . .

"Hello," said the guard. He lowered his flashlight and Lonnie saw the warm smile, reflecting his own.

The bastard thinks I'm smiling at him! But he tightened his face to hold the look that had come with the memory.

"What's the matter, Lonnie—can't you sleep?"

Lonnie could hold the smile no longer. "Sure I can sleep!" He flung himself down on the bunk and turned his face to the wall. A second later he jumped up, but the patrolling

19

guard was gone. He ran to the bars and shouted after him:
"Goddam right I can sleep! What makes you think I can't
sleep, you lousy no-good sneaking son of a bitch you! Come
back here! *Come back here!*"

But strangely, for he must have heard, the guard did not
come back.

CHAPTER 2

*"Occupying two entire City blocks, the Cathedral
of Justice, comprising the Monongahela County
Courthouse and the Monongahela County Jail, is
considered by many the finest example of Roman
architecture in the country. Erected in 1887, this
civic temple is another enduring testimonial to
the community spirit of the late Adam T. Mc-
Gregor, who donated the site to the County. . . .
The Courthouse is open to visitors daily except
Sat. and Sun."*

The Official Guide to Greater Iron City
does not mention that visiting hours in that lesser iron city
which is the County Jail are on Wednesdays only from 9:00
A.M. to 11:00 A.M. except on holidays when no visitors are
permitted.

"It's funny," Paul Harper said. "Me pressing my face here
against this wire makes me remember about when I was a
kid down home and when I did something real bad—sassing
her back or fighting with the white kids or something—Ma
would latch the screen door back of the kitchen and make
me stay in."

"It looks like you've been real bad again," she said softly.

He smiled. "Got to go now, hon."

"Three more minutes," she said.

"You're looking real pretty, you know?"

"And you need a shave."

They both laughed, for all they could see through the two tight-woven steel screens was a shadow.

"Well, one good thing," she said, her low voice sounding moist and very near, "your being with Zach and Faulcon."

"You wouldn't say that if I was with Peggy and Ann and Bertha."

She giggled. Then: "Hon. . . ."

"What?"

"Do you? . . . You know."

"Oh, that. You still want me to say it—after five years?"

"Uh huh."

"Besides, they probably got this place wired."

"Well?"

"OK, you got me cornered. I do."

"You do what?"

"Love you. Oh yes, I nearly forgot—when you write me put D ten after my name. That's Range D and Cell Ten."

"D ten?"

"Right. You ought to be glad I'm not on C."

"What's that?"

"Murderers' Row. Right over us."

"Oh . . . anybody in there?"

"Some. I don't know how many. I hear one of our folks is up there."

She was silent a moment. . . . "Goodby, hon. They say half hour's up. I've got to go."

"Goodby sweetheart, and don't forget about the pan under the icebox—every morning before you leave, OK?"

"I love you, Paul." And then she was gone.

He paused on leaving the cubicle and glanced back at the screen; but the pin-points of light were unbroken. He smiled. Always asking me like that.

A week ago when he and the others sentenced with him had been brought here he had not looked at anything until the gate slammed on their range, locking them in. Now, going back along the circular catwalk to the stairs on the opposite side, he walked slowly—but not too slowly—in order to see everything. He did not turn his head, only his eyes, like a spy who knows he is being watched.

There it is, the narrow steel door that opened in from the bridge they had crossed from the courthouse. And this is what they call the Hub. Of course . . . the five oblong cell blocks, rising one, two, three tiers above this level and the two tiers down below, went out from here like spokes. All around the sides was the granite outer shell and high overhead the great bronze dome. They get some sun up there on A and B ranges —at least they can see slices of it coming through the window slits. But not down there where they put our folks. They say the Hole's down there too . . . somewhere.

But now the prisoner had reached the stairs in front of Cell Block One. He went down into the shadow, his steel toe-taps clicking on the metal treads. The sound reminded him that he was happy and he lifted his knees higher to make it louder. *Look out—me and Bojangles!* He pretended to himself that he was dancing down:

> *. . . sa- dly I roam, tappetty tap tap tap tap*
> *still lon- ging for the old plan- tation*
> *and for the old folks at home, tap, tap.*

One flight down to Range D where he stood outside the gate, waiting uneasily for a guard to put him back in.

(2)

The two new men who squatted against the wall were grateful for the shaft of March sun they had found. The last of the marchers, the Negro contingent whose ranks they had left, straggled past, and now they had a clear view of the yard.

The enclosure was shaped like a hollow E: three sides were squared by the wall; the other, opposite them, was broken into three narrow courts by projecting wings of the jail. At the far end of the center court, a hundred yards across from the men, a guard was sitting in front of the door they had come through, tilting his fireman's chair against it. Half the distance closer, a tall young Negro was playing with a basket-ball, shooting at a basket-rim mounted on one of the buildings.

He was playing at top speed, a one-man team, dodging sharply around the puddles as though they were defending players, leaping for the rebounds, dropping the ball and then racing away to catch the imaginary pass.

"The kid's good," said one of the watchers, a gray-haired man whose round, unwrinkled face was a shade darker than the camel's-hair coat he wore. But before the other could reply, the circling line of marchers had swung back across the yard, blocking their view.

Leading the line, some twenty paces ahead of the rest, was a one-legged man on crutches, his coattails flaring in the wind like ragged pennons; a dirty bandage helmeted his head. He stopped several times, waiting for the others to catch up. There were about a hundred out from Cell Block One, shuffling along in twos and threes; a third of them, they noticed, were Negroes. Many of the prisoners were in shirt-sleeves, hunching their shoulders and hugging their bellies against the chill.

The two watched in silence, and when the last stragglers had passed, they looked again at the player. He was still going hard, but now, as he faked a pass, the wet ball slipped out of his hands and came bounding across to the men in the sun. One of them half rose to meet it, but it stopped dead in a large puddle a few yards away.

The player raced toward them, grabbed up the ball, dodged an unseen pursuer, and was about to run back when he noticed the two men squatting against the wall. He dodged again and then dribbled the ball over to them, his free hand groping down the neck of his rust-colored sweater.

"Time out!" he yelled and dropped to one knee, downing the sodden ball. Then he carefully withdrew the hand from his sweater, pinched thumb and forefinger delicately in front of his mouth and said, "Light."

The gray-haired man jabbed both hands into his coat pockets, rising slightly till he found the matches. He struck one, leaned toward the player, leaned back and flipped the match away.

"Hell, you aint got nothing to light. Here—" He pulled out a pack of Wings, shook a cigarette half out and held it forward.

The player, his eyebrows lifting in pleased surprise, dropped down on both knees, returned to his shirt pocket the inch-long butt he had been holding and took the offered new one. Then he reached for the matches, tore one out, split it lengthwise with his thumbnails, put one of the pieces back in the folder and lit his cigarette with the other.

"Man, you sure waste matches," he said accusingly.

"Keep 'em—go ahead," the other said. "I got more. Here, you might as well take these cigarettes too—seeing as I'm being such a big shot."

"Thank *you!*" His grin showed a row of wide-spaced teeth. "I sure picked a live one today. Thanks." He started to rise, changed his mind and, twisting his body, threw the ball back across the yard. "Game's over."

"You're pretty good," said the man in the top coat. "Zach and me was watching."

"High school," said the kneeling youth. He looked closely at his cigarette, took a long puff, squinted at it again, pinched off the burning end, blew through the butt and eased his hand down inside his sweater.

"That's another good trick," he said, looking at the man who had not spoken but whose eyes had been fixed on him since he split the match. "You blow out the smoke that's left—keeps it fresh till next time."

He settled back on his heels, his toes tucked under like a child at prayer, and stared up the side of the wall. "I was captain. Only colored on the team—so you know I was good." Then: "I'm Lonnie James."

"Faulcon. Henry Faulcon. And he"—nodding toward his silent companion—"is Zach."

"Isaac L. Zachary," the other man said from between the

24

upturned collars of his new mackinaw. He stood up and reached down to shake the boy's hand. "I'm proud to know you," he said gravely, and then hunched down again.

"F and B's?"

Faulcon grunted. Then he laughed. "Zach here don't know that jailhouse jive." He turned toward his friend: "What's a F and B?" The other shook his head. He asked again: "What's a A and B then?" When Zach remained silent he said, sternly: "Listen: F and B is fornication and bastardy—you know, knocking up a woman—and A and B is assault and battery. There's a lot more of 'em you got to learn. See"—turning back to Lonnie—"I told you he don't know." He lowered his voice to a mock whisper: "He's just a big old innocent country boy."

Lonnie smiled at the big man's embarrassment. "You guys are dressed so sharp"—pointing to their trousers which still had a crease and then looking down at his faded dungarees which were inches short in the legs—"well, I just naturally thought you were F and B's."

He stared at them: the smiling old man, short and heavy-set, who had given him the cigarettes and the other who was forty, maybe fifty, tall, broad-shouldered, much darker than his friend and solemn-looking; except for his hard hands he could be taken for a preacher.

"Hey!" Lonnie said, loud with his discovery. "Now I know . . . they had your pictures in the paper. It was *you* wasn't it?"

"That's us," Faulcon said, nodding and smiling. "That's why we got all dressed up—we knew we was going to have our pictures took."

"But wasn't there another colored fellow?"

Faulcon pointed across to the little door. "Inside. Missed our first day out. Had a visitor. That's Paul Harper, about your age he is—your complexion too."

Squinting against the morning sun, Faulcon examined the boy carefully: his head, outlined under the knotted silk stocking he wore, was squarish whereas Paul's was rather long, but his smooth dark skin, drawn tight over high cheek-bones, had the same glow of underlying rosiness that Paul's had; his eyes, too, which were large and deepset, reminded him of Paul—the alertness, the glint of roguish humor.

"In fact," Faulcon said, "you and him could be kin."

"What about the rest—there was a mess of 'em—they here too?"

"Twenty-six all told. Only seven besides us in this jail. Four white fellows—they aint in our block else you could meet them too, and three women—but naturally they're on Women's Side."

"Well, are you—" but a whistle, whirring like a stone from ambush, startled them silent.

They looked up and saw a white man standing in the center of the yard; he was pointing at them. His trousers were the official blue serge but he had on a gray sweatshirt and a baseball cap. He dropped the whistle from his mouth and jerked a thumb over his shoulder.

"All right now, you guys, get moving. Exercise or get back in," he shouted at them. "Get going!"

They got up quickly and then he shouted something else, but it was lost in the loud burst of laughter that came from the broken circle of marchers.

"What did he say?" Faulcon asked Lonnie who was walking with them over to the line.

"I didn't get it either. Something about Moscow."

The three found a place in the Negro contingent at the rear and fell in step with the silent plodders.

Faulcon moved closer to Lonnie: "Let you talk?"

"Yeah, if you want to. Only not loud."

Lonnie saw the big man smile for the first time. "Now that's a good thing," Zach said, "else Brother Henry here would just naturally die. Talkingest man you ever did see."

Now they were passing the man in the center. He looked at them sharply but did not speak.

When they had gone another twenty yards, Faulcon said: "We don't know him but he sure seems to know us."

"Oh, him," said Lonnie, "he aint nothing to worry about. That's Dan Rooney, charge of the yard. Must have just come out. Told me yesterday that we could start baseball—softball, that is—in a couple of weeks. Snow just melted, that's why there's all this water around. Call *this* exercise? . . ." He snorted loudly and went on: "But we had some damn good ball games last summer. I was here all summer waiting court. Then no football—not allowed—and now that bastard won't let us play basketball any more. . . ."

"*You* was playing," Faulcon said. "How come you could play?"

"Yeah, I was." Then after a long pause: "Maybe I'll tell you about that some time."

The whistle blew again.

"Here we go in," Lonnie explained. "See you guys tomorrow?"

"Yeah, we'll be around, won't we Zach. Tomorrow and the next day too. And Paul—he'll be playing ball with you-all, I guess."

"OK. Take it easy Pop—be seeing you."

Faulcon chuckled. "Watch that stuff—calling me Pop! Just don't let this gray head fool you—it *could* have been F and B at that!"

Then they were through the door. No talking.

(3)

The inmate who held the post of rangeman and the one called Army were playing checkers in the rangeman's cell when the men from D got back from the yard.

Zach nodded in to them and went past; Faulcon stopped.

"How come you guys didn't go out?" But they did not answer.

The rangeman, a stout froggish man with a wild shock of hair, was sitting on a folding chair, his eyes on the board. He leaned over to the bunk on which it rested and moved his king.

His opponent, a brown-skinned young man wearing a woolen khaki shirt and matching trousers, who was sitting beside the board, shook his head sadly. "*Now,* you rascal," he said, "*now* you dirty dog, I got your big fat rusty-dusty now!"

"Got your *mammy!*" the other retorted. "Move!"

"Man, *tell* this joker something,"—Army looked up to Faulcon who had stepped inside—"Go ahead and tell him something cause he sure don't know."

Faulcon's eyes traced a criss-cross pattern on the board; he nodded slowly. "Yeah, you got him all right."

"That's *shit!*" said the rangeman, turning to him. "Where he got me?" His eyes were narrow under the overhanging fat.

Faulcon looked doubtfully from him to Army, but the latter waved his hand. "Go ahead man, I can't tell him nothing." He lay back on the bunk to show his complete lack of interest.

"Well, OK," Faulcon said. "Look . . ." He outlined the rangeman's inevitable defeat in four more moves.

The rangeman stood up and snapped his chair shut—the chair that was one of the prerogatives of his office. "How can a man ever win around here with every jailbird on the range butting in the game? Now get your ass offen there so I can get my rest."

"That's five straight today," Army said, yawning and stretching his arms before he got up. "Catch you again tomorrow."

"Catch your *mammy!*" The rangeman rolled onto the canvas and they heard his heavy sigh as they left.

"How was it out today?" and then Army remembered Faulcon's question: "I was hanging around expecting a visitor."

"Your wife?" asked Faulcon as they started down the range.

"No man, Jesus Christ no! If she—no, I thought my brother would come. See if they can't have my hearing before court's over, else I'll be stuck here till September. Not that I'm going to get out, but the workhouse is sure better than this dump. Got mattresses and sheets for one thing, feed better too. See you. . . ." They had reached Cell 7 and Army went in.

Number 8 was Zach's; Faulcon's was 9; Paul Harper's the next.

He was on his bunk writing, when Faulcon entered. His gangling, loose-limbed frame and the too-large hands and feet made Paul look much younger than his twenty-seven years.

"What you know, son? What Charlene have to say?"

"Just a second," Paul said, folding the ruled sheet into the envelope. "I want Zach to hear it too—no, don't get him yet. I got something to tell you first." He stood up and cleared his throat the way he always did before taking the floor at meetings: "Henry, I guess you know you're not in Moscow now?" It was more accusation than question.

Faulcon looked at him for a moment. "Paul, what in the—" Suddenly he remembered. "So that's what the son of a bitch said out there!" He laughed and shook his head in wonder: "News sure travels fast around here—who told you? Not Zach, he didn't hear him either. Boy, that black dispatch. . . ."

"I don't see a damn thing funny about it." Paul looked at him hard. "I don't blame Zachary, but an old-timer like you! You know what they said about keeping discipline—you were at the meeting—about how we were going to act. Not have any trouble in here. Not to give them any excuse."

Faulcon started to break in, but the younger man cut him off: "You especially, Henry—you were in here once before."

"Twice," the other corrected. "Twice—in Thirty-three and again in Thirty-five—and that's just what I'm trying to tell you. Last time they let you sit around if you didn't feel like exercise. And man, let me tell you, these bad feet aint got any better since then." He looked down at his shoes, noticing that they needed a shine.

"Just the same, you're wrong and you know it. Well, OK, how about getting Zach in? Not that there's much you don't know already, but Frank sent a message."

"Paul . . ." Faulcon had stopped in the door; one fist was softly punching the rolled-up coat on his arm.

"What?"

"Paul, I accept your self-criticism." Then he grinned, his eyes sly under the bushy gray brows, and added: "Not that I were wrong. . . ."

He returned with Zach and they sat down beside Paul on the bunk.

"Well, comrades," Paul began, "the new district organizer hasn't been sent in yet, but Charlene heard he should be in by next week. Frank—you don't know him, Zach—Frank Stanich from up around Turkey Run, he's in charge. He's acting-D. O. and acting everything else too, almost. Took off from the mine and came in. Anyway, Frank says that they ought to raise enough money for the appeal by early April. And you know what they're doing? Listen to this: everybody is giving a day's pay—*every week!*"

Faulcon whistled. "Man! Good thing I'm in here. Sure couldn't afford that on what I were making!" And after they had stopped laughing: "You mean that, Paul? *Every* week?"

"That's what she said: a day's pay every week till they raise enough." He took a final drag on his cigarette and, reaching his hand under the bunk, dropped it into the toilet.

"Now that is something really fine," said Zach. With a sudden movement, he threw one arm around Faulcon's shoulder and squeezed hard. "That's something really *fine!*"

"Look out, Zach!" Faulcon cried, breaking free. "You don't know your own strength."

Zach smiled at them. "I was just thinking about that old Judge Rupp. Thought he'd just go ahead and throw us in jail and that's all it would be. . . . How much do it take, Paul?"

"I don't really know, but plenty. Be surprised how much it costs to appeal—just the printing alone, and it was over sixty days' trial don't forget, and that's a lot of words—and a lot of money."

"How's Charlene?"

"Fine, Henry, just fine. Sends her love to you both and—how'd she put it? Oh, yes—said while I'm in here with you Henry I shouldn't pick up any of your young ideas about women, so that when I got out . . . Say, Zach, when's your wife coming?"

"Next week. I knew she couldn't get off today. They always give her Thursday afternoons off but she's going to change that to Wednesday mornings."

The bell rang for dinner: it was eleven o'clock. Breakfast was six-fifteen, supper four. They got their cups and found a place in the slop line which had already formed, waiting for Range D's turn to go down.

"Those damn bells," said Paul. "Reminds me of stories the

30

old folks down South used to tell us kids about slavery days. They had bells for everything too. One bell at four—I mean four *a.m.*—that meant get up. Two bells in five minutes—get out and work. Three bells at eight—eat. All day long, bells ringing. That's just what the old folks said."

"Four a.m., huh," Faulcon said. "Well, let's see—here they ring you out at six, that's two hours better. Who says Aunt Hagar's chillun aint making progress? I'm telling you we're really moving up, no fooling! Just look at this jailhouse now: last time I were here Negroes had the bottom ranges only, but now we got the bottom ranges and the next row up too! Take a look over there."

Like a reflection of their own cell block in an enormous angled mirror, they could see the entire side of the block opposite them; the sheer steel walls, painted gray, were softened by the enclosing trellis-work of bars. Now it looked like a great ocean steamer, riding high in the water and converging upon them, with all passengers lining the five long decks, facing forward, eager for port.

The top three levels were white men, but directly across, running the length like a waterline, the row of faces was dark; and on the next range down which was the bottom. The men on D could see only this one side of Cell Block Two, but they knew that the color line marked this level exactly on each of the five structures.

A thousand men on fifty ranges were standing and waiting—the young and the old, the crippled and whole, the tried-and-found-guilty and the yet-to-be-tried: the F&B's, the A&B's, the drunk-and-disorderlies, rapists, riflers, tinhorns, triflers, swindlers, bindlers, peepers, punks, tipsters, hipsters, snatchers, pimps, unlawful disclosers, indecent exposers, delayed marriage, lascivious carriage, unlicensed selling, fortune telling, sex perversion, unlawful conversion, dips, dopes, dandlers, deceivers, buggers, huggers, writers, receivers, larceny, arsony, forgery, jobbery, felonious assault, trespassing, robbery, shooting, looting, gambling, shilling, drinking, winking, rambling, killing, wife-beating, breaking in, tax-cheating, making gin, Mann Act, woman-act, being-black-and-talking-back, and conspiring to overthrow the government of the Commonwealth by force and violence.

A thousand men were waiting for their keepers to feed them.

The bell jangled again, and now the men on the top ranges began moving forward to the stairs that zigzagged steeply down the end of the cell blocks. When the last had gone out, the second range was opened and they followed the others down. At the bottom a pan was passed in through the bars to each man; into this, food was ladled from one of the large containers wheeled out from the kitchen by the serving gang. A second server handed each his ration of bread while a third filled the outstretched cup with coffee. Then the line doubled back, the men carrying food up to their cells passing those going down.

> REGULATION 61 (a): ANY INMATE DROPPING
> HIS FOOD ON THE STAIRS WILL BE DEPRIVED OF
> FURTHER MEALS ON THAT DAY AND/OR SUCH OTHER
> PUNISHMENT AS THE WARDEN MAY DIRECT.

B-6 (going down): *"The hell I won't, Whitey. Tomorrow, breakfast."*

A-4 (coming up): *"Yeah, you just look at my slop pan and we'll both go to the hospital—me so they can get my foot outta your ass."*

C-2 (to server): *"Hey, Joe, how about fishing out a piece of meat, something I can chew on this time. . . . Whaddya mean—two butts and two matches? Are you nuts? One butt and two matches, or one butt and two True Detectives—same as always. . . . OK, OK, you lousy robber—but it better be a hunk I can see!"*

D-10: *"You better quit flushing it down the toilet. You'll lose that bay window sure."*

D-9: *"Paul, I'm telling you the truth; any man love good*

32

food as much as me ought to have sense enough to stay out of jail."

E-21: "How come we got to be last all the time? Why can't they start feeding from the bottom some times and let them pecks wait? Time we get ours aint nothing in that garbage can but greasy water."

E-11: "Well, you know what Confucius say—child born of dark parents will see dark days." (They laugh.)

CHAPTER 3

"You don't have to wash it, Zach."

The big man turned from the washbowl and smiled shyly at Army, who had stopped to look in upon his new neighbor.

"I know, son," he said, briskly swinging the battered aluminum pan to dry it, "but it do seem more like a meal, me doing the dishes. Always did 'em for Mrs. Zachary—twenty-two years come July we been married."

"Twenty-two years, man! Well, maybe *you* was lucky." Army took a quick step backwards and looked to his left up the range. "Better hurry, or they'll take the pans away and then you'll be messed up for sure."

They walked rapidly toward the front where the dirty pans were stacked by the gate.

"See this?" said Zach, swinging his pan sidewise in a wide semi-circle. "That's called highball. Railroad signal, means let's go!"

The other grunted. "Yeah? Well, swing it again man, maybe he didn't see you."

They stood for a moment at the gate, looking down at the kitchen gang who now were wheeling the food cans over to a long steel-wire cage that was built against the far wall. Into this stockade, known as Bum Side, was dumped the human wreckage that was collected throughout the county; in bitter weather it also served as an overnight shelter for homeless men whom the other Charities could not accommodate.

Bum Side lay like a broken-off spoke, separated from the cell blocks which joined at the Hub. The separation was more than structural: Bum Siders were excluded by Regulations from the community life of the jail. No mail could be sent from the stockade; no mail came to it. Yard, bath-house, dispensary, barber shop, library, laundry—all were barred to those in the cage; lacking even souls to be saved, Bum Siders were also banned from Tuesday night prayer-meeting and Sunday morning chapel.

Frequently it happened that among those brought in of a night there would be one or two who could not be awakened in the morning. These, no longer eligible for Bum Side, were carried away to the County Morgue; but the others had to be fed, and whatever was left after the inmates had eaten, they could eat. And now as Zach and Army watched, they were moving forward, wary as mice, to the opening through which the food would come. They formed no line, nor was there pushing. Singly, the bolder ones first, they approached the servers and then darted back with their pans into the shadows at the rear.

"Goddam bums," said Army. They turned away.

The rangeman was lying down, looking through an old copy of *Peek*. The two large cardboard cartons which held his supplies were stowed under the bunk; on the opposite wall a clipboard was hung; next to it was a cigar box, fastened like a shelf, on which was crayoned OUT-GOING MALE.

"How about another game?" Army asked him.

"Maybe later—now I'm busy." He raised his head from the pillow, which like the chair was his privilege, and stared suspiciously at Zach who was reading the printed card, faded and yellowed at the edges, that was glued to the wall.

"*You* aint never gonna get the job—even after I go," he said. "That's one thing sure. Not them other guys with you either."

Whether Zach heard him or not he gave no sign; nor did he turn from the card until he had finished.

REGULATION 117

Rules For Rangemen

(a): THE RANGEMAN WILL KEEP THE ROSTER WHICH WILL BE CHECKED DAILY AT LOCK-UP BY THE GUARD ON DUTY.

(b): HE WILL ASSIGN ALL INCOMING MEN TO A CELL AND LIST NUMBER OF SAME ON ROSTER.

(c): HE WILL COLLECT AND TURN IN THE BLANKET, CUP, AND SPOON FROM ALL OUT-GOING MEN.

(d): HE WILL ISSUE ALL AUTHORIZED RATIONS OF PAPER AND ENVELOPES, SOAP AND TOILET PAPER TO IN-MATES.

(e): HE WILL COLLECT ALL OUT-GOING MAIL AND TURN IN SAME, TOGETHER WITH ALL POSTAGE MONIES, TO THE CHIEF GUARD AT 2:30 P.M. DAILY EXCEPT SUNDAY.

(f): HE WILL REPORT IMMEDIATELY ANY DISORDER OR VIOLATION OF RULES BY INMATES.

Underneath, in the margin, someone had pencilled: *THIS MEANS YOU JACK!*

Zach started out, turned back. "I do need another bar of soap, please."

"Yeah? What you do with the one I gave you?"

"Used it up. That place was a *mess.*" Zach had spent his first day scouring out his cell—the walls were caked with dried tobacco spit and the canvas, stretched over the metal frame of the bunk, was black. Now there were only the rusty urine stains on it.

"Look, man, *I'm* running this range." He heaved his bulk to a sitting position and swung his legs down, his feet finding the ragged carpet slippers on the floor. "I give out soap Mondays.

35

That's right, Mondays is soap. Not my fault if you people too damn lazy to get up off your ass and come get it."

"I need soap," Zach said.

His words, soft spoken and low, seemed to enrage the other. "You need soap!" the rangeman mimicked. "That aint all you need, but I aint giving you *shit*. No sir, not today. Cost you money you want soap today. Yes sir, gonna cost you some *money*. . . . Tell you what I'm gonna do, you want soap so bad. Tell you what: you give me—" he squinted up at the big man— "you give me three cent and I'll let you have a piece. Three cent *cash*—I don't trust my own mammy."

Zach found a nickel in his watch-pocket and the rangeman reached under and brought out a small bar of brown soap which he handed to the other.

"Look," he said, "you need soap so bad. Tell you what I'll do. Aint got no change so here's another piece and you owes me a penny. See, now I'm gonna trust you. You-all just act right around here and we be friends. See?"

They left him and walked back to Cell 8.

"Come right in," said Zach. "Have a seat."

Army sat down beside him on the bunk, propped one foot against the bars, slapped his chest, found the makings and rolled a cigarette. "Smoke?" When Zach shook his head, he returned the little sack to his shirt pocket, pushed in the yellow drawstring so it wouldn't show, and buttoned down the flap. "These guys see you with tobacco and you can't get rid of 'em. Course I'll have some money when my brother comes, but right now I got exactly six cents. Bull Durham costs ten cents in here, just double the price outside. But what the hell— warden's got to get his too. Can't let the rangeman get it all."

He exhaled hard and watched the smoke roll up the wall across from them. A scalloped border on the gray paint marked the height Zach could reach when he washed it. Now Army looked around the cell, examining it critically. Except for the cleaning job it was exactly like all the others: five feet wide, ten feet high, seven feet deep; a small washbowl, with a steel shelf over it, on the inside wall; a toilet, made without a seat and shaped like a spinning top, was set in the other inside corner and under the bunk which was suspended the full length of one wall by two angled chains. For the toilet to be used the bunk had to be swung up. Its location determined, better than any regulation could have, that the inmate would sleep with his head at the other end, next to the bars which, with the barred sliding door, formed the front of the cell. The fourth wall was bare except for a single clothes' hook. In the center of the ceiling was a small unshaded light-bulb.

"You really got this place looking like something," Army remarked. "Expect to pull all your time here?"

"Can't say," replied Zach. "First they got to decide if we can't have bail until the appeal comes up. But Lord, what kind of sorry people was in this cell before? No excuse for any man to be so trifling."

Army nodded and said it takes all kinds. "Take Slim—you know, down the end in Twenty-five?—doing two-to-five for manslaughter. Well, you'll never meet a better guy, I don't care where you go. Didn't even ask him and he lent me a quarter when I came in broke, so I could write out. Talking about Slim, I was telling him this morning about you-all, only I couldn't remember the name of the charge."

"Criminal syndicalism."

"Yeah, now I remember. Never heard of that one before."

"Me neither," Zach said, "but it means scheming to overthrow the government." He rubbed his chin, the bristles making a sand-paper sound. "I really don't know if they have a law like that down home, Mississippi that is, leastwise I never heard tell of it. But they tell me they aint hardly used this law since it was passed—along about 1919 I think it was."

"Oh, no wonder. I wasn't hardly born then. What's the maximum you can get on that rap?"

"Ten years. That's what he give six of our men, the main leaders that is. Paul Harper is one of them. Rest of us got three to five."

"Heck, man," Army said, "you-all got a *break*, you and what's his name—Faulcon. Let's see now—it's 1941 and sup-

37

posing they turn you loose in three, that'll be 1944. Aint half bad, Zach." He punched the other lightly on the shoulder. "Big man like you can pull that easy."

Zach was forced to smile at the boy's encouragement. Then his face became solemn again: "Son, we *all* can make it. All twenty-six of us, we can make *fifty* years if we has to. Just naturally wear this old place down. That's right, just naturally wear this old place down!"

The other nodded gravely. "That's what I got to do. And I'm really going to do it this time. Made up my mind." He started to throw his butt on Zach's clean floor but checked himself; instead he pinched out the fire, opened the paper, blew the grains out through the bars and balled up the paper between thumb and forefinger. "I wasn't at Custer long, but that's *one* thing I learned—the hard way. Threw a butt down, one time—man what did I do *that* for? . . . That's where they got me, Camp Custer, good old Michigan."

Zach made a clucking sound. "Why did they—say, what is your Christian name anyway? I like to call a man by his name."

"Harvey. Harvey Owens."

"Well, Harvey, why did they arrest you, if you don't mind me being so nebby?"

"Same old thing—alimony. Same as last time. See, I paid for a year, the first year, paid regular each and every week. Then one day I jumps salty on account of what she's doing and I tells the man I aint gonna give that bitch another cent. So what they do? That's right, put me right in that old workhouse. Year and a half. Then I get weak, see, and say OK I'm going to pay from here on out; and so naturally they turn me loose and I'm back in the mill and catching up on my payments. OK, especially since she's settled on this one guy, practically living with him, and I figured she'd go ahead and get married and I'd be through. *Shit!* They weren't *thinking* about getting married, just laying back and waiting for the check that the court sent every week. Then I really gets hot, see, but this time I use my head. Grab a bus dead up to Detroit and I'm working in Ford's. Nobody knows where I am, don't even write to my own brother. OK, I'm doing swell, all draped down in new togs, paying on a car, living—I mean really *living*, and then *wham!* the draft board gets me. One of them real low numbers that jumps up first thing. OK, I'm a selectee. I'll pull my year for Uncle Sam and then back to good old Detroit and freedom. What the hell, the Army couldn't be worse than workhouse. Only one thing I forgot about—what do you think?"

Zach said he couldn't imagine.

"Fingerprints! And the first thing you know the Provost Marshal calls me in and here's this dick, standing like here, see, and they ask me are you Harvey Owens and naturally I say no I aint Harvey Owens, I'm Harvey *Brown*. But there was the stuff from here—pictures, fingerprints, everything—right there on the desk. The Army guy says he can't keep me, if it was just alimony that would be different, but I'm a fugitive from justice, see? And here I am. Three weeks tomorrow and I aint heard a thing: no hearing, no brother—he's my only kin—no nothing. OK, but like I was telling you before, I want my hearing before court's over so I don't have to be here till Fall. That's the only thing I'm worrying about now."

"I don't understand—Harvey. Why you so sure they going to put you back in the workhouse. If you start paying, then—"

"You're wrong, man," Army broke in. "First thing, they *got* to give me some time for running away. That's first. And on top of that I aint going to pay. Not a cent. That's right, I'm going to tell the man he can put me up there from now on—I still aint gonna pay. Lock me up and throw away the key—I still aint gonna pay. I made up my mind that this time—"

Zach put a warning hand on Army's knee, but when Army looked out the patrolling guard had already passed by, silent as a cloud on his rubber soles.

Army jumped up. "Come on, Zach, let's walk," he cried, and the big man followed him out of the cell. A few men were pacing the walkway of Range D, but most of them were still inside; some napping, others writing, reading magazines, playing checkers—no cards were permitted by Regulations. Faulcon was not in his cell; he must have found a game somewheres, Zach said. Paul waved out to them from 10 and then turned back to his reading; it was an enormous leather-bound volume he had gotten from the library.

They walked to the back end, to the gate the guard had come through, turned around and retraced their steps. Back and forth they paced, 150 feet from gate to gate, while Army told his story. Listening and saying nothing save for an occasional murmur of sympathy, Zach could tell that the story had often been told; but the bitterness had not worn smooth, the wound had not scarred over.

Harvey Owens had become a man suddenly; maybe, as he said, too soon. When his aunt died he quit school and went into McGregor Sheet & Tube, into the chipping department where his older brother worked. Claude still worked there, and why he didn't come to see him, or even write, Harvey couldn't imagine.

He had got married when he was eighteen, and what did he do *that* for! Everybody in the Hollow knew she was a tramp, everybody but Harvey. He didn't know. He only knew he loved her and wanted a real home, a real home that he never had. In six months he left her, but he didn't take it hard. Hell, anybody can make a mistake and he was still a man and drawing a man's pay every two weeks at the mill, and the girls kind of liked him. So what. And when she asked for a divorce he didn't give a damn one way or the other. Claude thought maybe he should get a lawyer, but what for? Why should he give his money to some old lawyer to get up and say what everybody knew? Let her say anything she wanted to, her and her lawyer both.

The uncontested divorce was granted, and then the legal paper came to the place where Harvey Owens was rooming. *Alimony*, goddam. Alimony, my ass! He threw it away and thought no more about it until the laws came, two of them, in one of those black Chevvy coops the county dicks ride around in. Parked at the curb, waiting for him to come off shift.

He told them, and he told *all* of them right over there in the Cathedral of Justice, told them she was no good—everybody knows that. Just ask anybody in the Hollow. He argued;

man, how he argued! He pleaded, he insisted. But they wouldn't listen. Start paying they said, start paying now or you go to the workhouse.

So he started paying, and that wasn't all. Now he got a lawyer and started paying him too, but that didn't do any good either.

"It wasn't so much the money that hurt," Army said. "And you know I wasn't stud'n bout Hortense any more. It was just that it was *wrong*. All wrong. But every week, each and every week for a year, when I took the fourteen bucks to Family Court I told them white people what she was doing, what everybody *knew* she was doing, but they wasn't no more interested in me than a fly."

OK, he wouldn't pay.

They sent him to the workhouse.

"You mean they can just put you in there for that and keep you?"

"Me and a whole lot more. Man, you just don't know. People don't know. . . ."

For a long time they walked in silence, the dark, broad-shouldered man in his new serge suit, the young man in khaki. Back and forth from gate to gate. From Cell 1 to Cell 25 and back again. Sixty paces up, sixty paces down. The bell rang at noon for Block Three to go to the yard, and an hour later for Block Four. The bell must ring five more times before the day could end: at two o'clock for the last cell block to go out for exercise, at two-thirty for the rangemen to turn in the mail, at three for the workingmen to return to their ranges, at four for supper, at six for lock-up. Then the tier-walk lights would go on and the radio would be turned on until eight; and then nothing more from the Hub till morning.

(2)

Zach and Army were going down the range when the screaming started. They turned around and ran to the front gate where others had already clustered to see what was happening.

The screams were coming from somewhere down below, coming up in roman-candle bursts, rising, spreading, falling and rising again, higher and higher until the whole place was flooded and quivering with the agony that welled up from Bum Side.

Then they saw him, a scrawny little man pressed against the stockade wire. His arms were outstretched wide, his fingers gripping the mesh, his body lunging up with each desperate yell. A huge black overcoat, spread open, hung from his arms to the floor; outlined against it, his shirtless body was a startling blue-gray, gaunt as a new-hatched sparrow. His head was thrown back and up, the thin red neck corded and straining with each shrieking burst.

No one was near him. The other Bum Siders had scuttled away at his first outcry.

To the watchers above it seemed like a long time before a guard came running to order him quiet; but the pulsating rhythm of screams continued unbroken. Soon another man in the dark blue uniform ran over to where the other stood outside the cage. They were shaking their fists at the screaming one, and they seemed to be shouting to him but it was lost in the shrilling din. Then both of them beat at his clutching fingers and finally he backed a step away.

The silence was sudden, as if a switch had been thrown.

The Bum Sider took another step back; then, with two flapping motions he swirled the great black coat around him like a toga and jutted his sharp blue chin over the collar toward the guards. As he stood there, glaring, defiant, the men on the cell blocks could see that he was quite old; his hair a yellowed gray, his face a grimy spider web.

They must have said something else to him, because now he swooped upon them, stopping just short of the barrier. Then he jerked his head high and back and let out a piercing yell, but this time he was screaming words. Louder and louder, until they could hear it on the topmost ranges:

"... for this is the day of vengeance ... and the sword shall devour ... yea, the walls of Babylon shall fall. ..."

The words were coming in bursts, as the screams had come;

but the agony and despair were gone; now it was ecstasy and overwhelming triumph. His eyes were squeezed tight; one arm extended overhead, the pointed finger stabbing the air with every shout.

". . . *thou shalt be cut down, O Madmen . . . the sword shall pursue thee . . . and no city shall escape . . . the valley also shall perish . . . and the plain shall be destroyed. . . . Woe be unto thee O Moab! . . . make bright the arrows. . . . Behold, I am against thee. . . . I will roll thee down from the rocks. . . . I will make thee a burnt mountain. . . ."*

The guards were running now to the far end of the cage; a third man joined them as they neared the gate. His trousers were regulation, but he wore no jacket and his white shirt-sleeves were rolled up to the elbow.

"That's Steve," Army whispered to Zach. "Steve the Chief Guard. . . . *Now* you'll see something."

All men on D were out of their cells and crowding the gate, held by the drama unfolding on Bum Side, waiting the inevitable end.

Now they had him, the two in uniform twisting his arms high behind his back. But his yelling was louder, bolder, all-conquering: *"O repent, ye sinners, the hour is nigh . . . the time of my vengeance is upon thee. . . ."*

His body doubled forward as they rammed his wrists higher up his back, the thin red neck stretched taut from the ruff of his coat. He continued to cry out, but now the words were a muffled squawking against his straining chest.

Swinging his fist like an axe, Steve brought it down hard on the bowed-down head. Then, when the squawking went on, he smashed a looping uppercut to the face. The force of the blow drove the Bum Sider erect and staggered the two who were holding him. One pinioned arm broke loose and he pointed it high, and he lifted his bleeding face, and he cried in a loud voice: *"Behold, I will punish the multitudes!"*

Steve's fist caught him flush on the mouth and the upraised hand flopped down and was seized again. He opened his mouth to shout, but now it was neither screams nor scripture that came welling out, spattering the Chief Guard's shirt.

43

They held him erect while Steve hit him again, again; now a crossfire of hard-driving blows till the features were lost in the crimson smear. Once more: a chopping hammer blow to one side of the battered head. And now the little man hung limp in their arms.

Steve reached over and raised the drooping head. Gently cupping the chin in his hands, he peered closely at the mangled face, then let it fall and motioned them to take him away. Half carrying, half dragging, they pulled him inside, the great black coat trailing the ground like a fallen banner.

The Chief Guard looked at his knuckles, licked them, then picked the sodden shirt away from his paunch. They could see him unbuttoning it as he walked away.

"Steve by a knockout!" said one of the watchers on D. He studied the back of his bare wrist for a moment. "Let's see— in exactly two minutes and thirty seconds of the first round."

"You wrong, Jack," said another. "Wrong as hell. That was second round—you gotta give the first to the little old bum."

As they left the gate, Army turned to Zach and said: "Man, what did I tell you! That Steve—he's really something. If it wasn't for politics—him being a hunky—he'd a been warden or at least deputy warden a long time ago. Anybody been in here much can tell you that. In fact, if you want to know the God's honest truth, he's the one who really runs this place anyway."

(3)

When the screaming started coming up from Bum Side, Crazy Peterson ran into his cell to hide; but Lonnie James and the other two inmates of Murderers' Row watched it all.

Though they stood beside him at the gate, Klaus and Reardon did not speak to Lonnie: hatred hard and chill as the bars they clasped separated the white men from him. Klaus, a bald, middle-aged man who was waiting trial for the hatchet-slaying of his invalid wife, had been friendly to Lonnie before young Reardon came to Range C; but now the small blue eyes that had smiled at Lonnie were icy cold. Reardon had protested loudly against being put on Murderers' Row because, though he had blackjacked a pawnbroker to death, every one knew that the rap would only be manslaughter. But worse than that was the indignity of Lonnie's presence on the same range. Steve had been deaf to his demand that either the dinge be removed at once or he, Aloysius Reardon, should be moved to a white man's tier: the chief guard had been sympathetic but firm in his refusal and he gave no sign of his pleasure at the chance to make this brother of an Irish cop suffer.

Watching the strange contest below between the rebellious Bum Sider and the punishing guards, Reardon's boyish face was now frowning, now smiling, as his feeling of bitterness against Steve clashed with his admiration for the professional job the official was doing on the lousy little bum. But at the end, when they dragged away the fallen prophet, no trace of the frown remained. Boy, oh boy! Warm with the glow of victory, Reardon pulled out his cigarettes and offered one to Klaus. He was conscious as he always was of the nearness of the Negro and now, as he bent his face to Klaus's match, he peeped at Lonnie out of his narrowed eyes. The dark face was impassive, a mask in the presence of enemies. Reardon's hatred flared at this silent challenge to his own good feeling and though he was bound by his determination never openly to notice Lonnie he desperately sought for some way to retaliate against him.

O God, he prayed, if I could only smash this nigger one! And smash him again and punch him and kick his teeth out till they would have to drag him out of here like that bum downstairs and then— He grinned suddenly at the thought that came and turned to Klaus. "Bible crap didn't help *that* bastard none, did it Otto?"

He said it loud and slow so that not only should Lonnie hear it but he should know too that it was meant for him. For the Negro inmate often read his Bible—each cell on C was furnished with one—and he was the only man from the range who went to chapel.

Klaus started to laugh but when the meaning became clear

he choked it into a cough; he could feel the tingling pink spreading up to the top of his pate and he knew that Lonnie was looking at him. "Come on, Al," he said abruptly and he had almost reached his cell before Reardon caught up with him.

Lonnie loosened his grip on the bars and slowly exhaled. Then he turned and walked back to Number 11 where Carl would be crouched and trembling. He would talk to the poor dummy and try to calm him. Nothing to be afraid of, man, he would say; nothing to be afraid of. And maybe he would somehow believe his own words and forget the crushing truth that Reardon had swung like a club: that the Bum Sider's faith had fallen with him, that the Word had been drowned in his blood.

Everything is a long time coming. Everything except lock-up time. When the bell rings each man runs to his cell, pauses to take a last look out the walkway, shouts a final word to a friend down the range, and steps inside to close his self-locking door.

A shattering burst of thunder rolls around the jail, echoing and re-echoing from the high-vaulted walls as a thousand steel-barred doors slam shut; the rumbling mounts to a roar, to a soaring roaring booming crashing, a thousand kettle drums pounding, a thousand cymbals clashing; the thunder rolls away, rumbling over the stone horizon, and all is still; then into the heavy silence steals the sound of violins singing, soft as angels winging; then there is light, and from on high a mighty voice is heard intoning: *And now we bring you the sweetest music this side of Heaven.* . . .

46

CHAPTER 4

The tower clock was slowly striking off the hour. He looked up from his book: it must be midnight. He counted half aloud, waiting for the answering sound that would come muffled and distant from high above the Cathedral of Justice. . . . Nine—*bong* . . . ten—*bong* . . . eleven—*bong* . . . twelve—It was like going down the last step of a staircase only to find with a jolt that no step was there.

Only eleven o'clock. Paul Harper closed the book and got up to fix his bunk for sleeping. First he took some newspapers from a pile in the corner and spread them over the dirty canvas; then he unrolled the thin gray blanket from the foot of the bunk and covered the paper with it. Next he took off his overcoat and laid it on the blanket; he folded his jacket carefully and placed it at the head for a pillow. He washed, took off his shirt, socks and shoes, opened the top buttons of his trousers—they had taken his belt away—climbed under the blanket and, reaching a long arm up to the switch, snapped off the light.

Damn! The light from outside his cell was glaring in upon his face. Cell Number 10 on D is midway in the row of cells and like its counterparts on tiers A, B and C above and on E below, it is brightened at night by a bulb in the runway ceiling. For Lonnie James above him, the light was a steadfast friend; but to Paul it had been from the first an unwinking enemy.

Now he closed his eyes tight, but still the light stabbed at them; he covered his face with his hands. He had been reading steadily since lock-up and the dim bulb and fine print had hurt his eyes, though he had not noticed the pain till now. They ought to shade that light out there so a man can sleep. He got up suddenly and took another newspaper from the pile; folding it lengthwise, he wove it between the bars half-way to the top where the light shafted through, and lay down again. That's better.

Sleep did not come and he re-lived the day: the first visit

from Charlene, the news about the appeal money, Faulcon and Zach almost getting into trouble out in the yard, the way they beat that old guy on Bum Side, the book he had found in the library.

There were maybe a hundred volumes in the bookcase that stood on the far side of the Hub; the books were not arranged in any order and for awhile it looked hopeless—*Recollections of Brig. Gen. Cyrus T. Ames, Vol IV* and *Vol VII; Beginner's Guide to Good Cooking, Black Oxen, Collected Poems of Abigail Stockbridge, It, Never the Twain Shall Meet, How to Write Better Business Letters, State Papers of Warren Gamaliel Harding, My Garden and How it Grew, Unchanging China, The Businessman's Guide to Christ, The Story of Old Glory For New Americans, Over the Top, Rufus and Rastus or Two Dark Knights in Dixie. . . .*

The gold lettering on the torn leather binding was faded, but when he opened the heavy volume it was like finding a comrade in a company town—*Les Miserables*. It was 1,229 pages and that made it even better. But he was reading it too fast . . . maybe after awhile they would let books be sent in, but meanwhile he should make this one last.

He tried to fall asleep, but a sense of uneasiness tugged at him; he had forgotten something, something he ought to do. . . . He remembered and smiled, nearly laughing at the thought: his "To Do" list for tomorrow. Marty had taught him that—Marty with his thin, pockmarked face and narrow shoulders and his earnest lecturing way of talking. "You make up the list every night, see. That's number one. Then you follow it through the next day—number two. Number three: next night you check up on yourself and see what you have carried out, and put down all unfinished tasks and new assignments for the next day, see?" Marty was three years dead, in Spain, but Paul had faithfully followed the simple rule just as he had practiced so many other things Marty had taught him.

His "To Do" list—that's funny. Before, there never was enough time for all the things he planned to do, for all the things he had to do as Communist Party section organizer in the Hollow. Let's see: section committee on Monday, branch organizers' meeting every other Tuesday, two classes at the Workers' School on Wednesday, section new members' class on Thursday, district bureau meeting Friday morning, open-air meeting Friday night (in winter, open forums at Douglass Hall), Co-ordinating Committee for Employment, Saturday afternoons at the Y; sometimes Sunday would be free after morning distribution of *The Worker*. Then there was the work with the Negro Congress and the Steel Workers' Organizing Committee, and writing leaflets, cutting stencils, visiting contacts, planning fund-raising affairs, dances, picnics; and always a quota to be filled—membership drive, subs, tickets, literature; and special campaigns: Free Angelo Herndon, Save W.P.A., Lift the Embargo on Loyalist Spain, End Jim Crow in Sheffield Park Swimming Pool, Miners Strike Relief, Break the Ban on Negro Teachers. . . .

There was never enough time. Now he had nothing but time and nothing to do.

No, there was one thing—the weekly discussion meeting. Faulcon and Zach agreed that while the three were together, as long as their good luck lasted, they would have a meeting every Sunday to talk over the news of the week. Paul would be the discussion leader, and piled on his shelf now were the items he had torn from the Iron City *American* during their first seven days in jail.

The battle-front news was not much, that week in March, 1941, despite the roaring headlines (GREEKS SINK ITALIAN SUB, BRITISH DRIVE TO ENCIRCLE ADDIS ABABA), and most of his clippings were of things happening at home.

Item: "Washington.—An early end of the war was seen as a result of Congressional action yesterday approving Lend-Lease. With the U.S. now emerging as the arsenal of democracy, informed observers on Capitol Hill predicted the speedy collapse of the Axis powers despite stepped-up support to Berlin and Rome from their Russian partner."

Item: "San Francisco.—Harry Bridges, head of the CIO

longshoremen's union, was released here today on bail. Bitter about the new action taken against him by U.S. Attorney General Robert Jackson, the alleged alien Red remarked to reporters: 'How many times must a man be cleared on the same charges before they leave him alone?'"

Item: "Washington.—The largest marble building in the world has been donated to the Federal government by former Secretary of the Treasury Andrew W. Mellon. Erected at a cost of $15 million, the National Gallery of Art, together with art masterpieces valued at over $50 million, is the largest gift ever given to a government by a private individual."

Item: "Atlanta.—A cablegram wishing him a speedy recovery was received here today by Eddie Rickenbacker, World War air ace (26 planes) from Ernst Udet, German war ace (62 planes) who is now the directing genius of Luftwaffe production and design. Rickenbacker, president of Eastern Airlines, is convalescing in a local hospital from injuries sustained in a recent plane crash."

Item: "Iron City.—Trustees of the Adam T. McGregor Foundation announced today that the sixth annual survey on underprivileged minorities in the U.S., sponsored by the Foundation, has been completed at a record cost of $500,000. The findings, now being prepared for publication, will contain a special section on Negro infant mortality which is said to be the most exhaustive study yet made in this field."

The clock was striking again, and the young man in Cell 10 began to count. This time the last step was there—twelve! Now he made believe he was racing down an endless staircase; and now he was dancing again, dancing on down, light as a feather, his toes tapping out the intricate rhythm, never missing a beat, down and down, faster, faster. . . . Charlene was smiling and clapping her hands. . . . Now they were all cheering him, clapping and whistling, louder and louder, roaring their applause—

Later he was not sure whether he had fallen asleep or not; but here was the guard shouting at him, flashing a light in his face.

50

"Get up out of there! *Stand up!*"

He climbed out quickly, trying to understand what had happened.

"What's the idea of that paper? Get it down! *Get it down!*"

Paul pulled the newspaper from the bars and, squinting into the glare, said something about the outside light shining on his face.

"Too goddam bad about your face." The guard was silent for a moment and when he spoke again his anger was gone. "What are you worrying about your face for?" He laughed abruptly. "Afraid maybe you'll get a *tan?*"

Paul said nothing. The beam was still fixed on his face.

"What's your name?"

"Harper." (*Don't ever give a cracker your first name, son, not if you can help it. And if I ever catch you grinning to a cracker—I don't care who he is—I'll skin you alive! Remember that, Paul—sure as you're born I will.*)

"When did you get here?"

"We came in a week ago."

"We. . . . Oh yeah, the Reds. One of *them*, huh?"

No reply.

"One of them Hitler-loving Reds—what do you know about that. Say—here's something I'd like to know." His tone was pleasant now, almost confidential. "How did you colored boys get mixed up with that bunch of foreigners?"

No reply.

"I'll bet you can do plenty of hollering on a soapbox, but now you can't say a goddam thing. Well, if I ever catch you pulling something like this again, I'll put you in a place where you won't see light for a week. And don't forget it."

The man was gone: his footsteps made no sound.

Now he couldn't go to sleep for sure. He lay there thinking about what happened. His anger at the guard went quickly—after all, that's how they are; what can you expect? But his feeling of shame for being so dumb about putting up the paper—well that was different. Keep on pulling such boners and first thing you know we'll be split up, and then no discussion meetings or nothing. Still, he hadn't let himself be provoked; that was one good thing. And besides, how was I supposed to know—

"Paul!"

The whisper came like a shout.

"Paul! You sleeping?" It was Faulcon to his right.

"Sh-h!"

"He's gone, Paul. I seen him when he went out the gate."

"You saw him go out? How could you?"

"Never mind about how, but I seen him."

"How come you aren't sleeping, Henry. Old man like you ought to get his rest."

"I *were* asleep till you and the guard started that big political discussion. And another thing, *Comrade* Harper—you got some self-criticism coming from *me!*"

Paul said nothing; they could talk about that tomorrow.

"Hey, Paul—when he asked you how you got mixed up with the Party, I was wondering if you was going to tell him about the chamber-pot."

"Go to sleep—*boy!*"

Faulcon's low chuckle seemed surprisingly near. "OK. Goodnight—you *Hitler-lover!*"

Paul fell asleep trying to figure out how Faulcon, locked in his cell, could see the patrolling guard when he went out the end gate.

(2)

Paul had seen Henry Faulcon once or twice at city membership meetings of the Party, but it was not until the indictments and trial that he came to know the old man. Faulcon did not live in the Hollow, nor did he belong to the organization in that section; he was a member of the waiters' branch. As for Isaac Zachary, Paul had never met him before the case started: Zach lived in Kanesport, twenty miles up the valley, where he worked as a laborer in the tinplate mill.

On their second day in jail they had talked about all the things that had brought them behind bars; and each had told how he happened to come into the Communist Party. Paul's was the story of the chamber-pot, as Faulcon called it, though there was a stove in the story—the stove was an important part; and people. The people were important, too.

Paul was eighteen then and he had been working at Peerless Casting for over a year. His father had gone into the foundry at Peerless ten years earlier, after he had brought the boy up to Cleveland. That was in 1922. Moses Harper had planned to come North when his son finished grade school, there being no high school for colored in Bibb County, Arkansas; but when his wife, Mattie, died in the spring of that year, there was nothing more to hold them there.

Two months before Paul's class at Dunbar High graduated in 1931, his father suffered a stroke which left him bedridden. There was no money: Moses Harper had been working but three days a week—it was the Depression and the older men were put on stagger-time first. Paul had to quit school and they took him on at the plant: he lied about his age, saying he was nineteen. (He had forgotten about that until the trial when the Prosecuting Attorney, with a dramatic flourish, confronted him with a photostat copy of the employment application and forced him to say yes, he had made the false statement; yes, that was his signature. The judge was shocked, the jury horrified, the press outraged: the Iron City *American's* headline that afternoon roared in war-scare type—*RED LEADER ADMITS LYING.*)

The two had agreed that as soon as the father got well enough to get around a little, Paul would go to night school for his diploma. But months passed and still Moses Harper lay helpless, an arm and a leg totally paralyzed. Neighbor women looked in on him during the day and gave him lunch, but after work Paul had to hurry home to fix supper and stay with the invalid.

Sometimes, after his father had fallen asleep, young Harper would go out for an hour or so, but seldom farther than across the street to the Lucky Tiger Recreation Parlor & Barber Shop to shoot some kelly pool. Usually he remained at home, reading. At first he read because he had nothing else to do; but then books became a passion and on his off-days he took home all the library would lend.

He was coming home from work that day. It was early May and a cold wind whipped in from the lake front. The rain had been coming down hard when the second shift came off at Peerless, but now it had almost stopped and the sky was an old gray mop, dripping.

Paul saw the crowd when he swung down from the Scoville Avenue streetcar; it was two blocks away on the street that led to his house. A siren sounded from far off and he started to run. Maybe it's a fire!, though he saw no smoke. A sudden fear fluttered deep inside and he ran faster. He lived a block past the place where the people were crowding the sidewalks and street, but the houses in this section were rickety old frame buildings, standing but a few feet apart; they were dry as tinder and a blaze could spread like sheet lightning.

But there was no fire. Panting from his sprint, he stood across the street, where the crowd was thinnest, to see what was happening. A meeting of some kind. A short, light-skinned Negro youth wearing a gabardine raincoat was standing on a step-ladder and shouting something to the people.

"What's up?" Paul said to the man next to him.

"Wait till the laws come—you'll see."

The speaker too must have been expecting the police, because from time to time he would jerk his head around toward the avenue, but without breaking the angry staccato of his shouting. A few words could be heard from where Paul stood: ". . . crisis . . . relief . . . down to City Hall . . . mobilization. . . ." The crowd was noisy and people were going through holding up newspapers, crying, "Get your copy now! Only two cents a copy!" The vendors, like the speaker, were very young and some of them were white: one of these, a girl in a worn leather jacket, pushed a paper in front of Paul but he shook his head no. ". . . every night at the Unemployed Council," the speaker was yelling. "So don't forget. You know the place—the old U.N.I.A. Hall."

Paul knew where it was: when his father and he had first

come to Cleveland, Paul used to watch the Garveyites parading out of that hall in their green and black and red uniforms, plumes and swords. (*Plumb foolish, son. I swear they aint got the sense God gave a billygoat. If they had, stead of talking so much about going back to Africa they'd take them swords and some forty-fives and head straight back to Georgia where they came from and run them crackers out of there. Cause that's the best land there is, Paul—right down home.*) Then the Elks had the building for a while; still later it was a church; then a dance hall.

Now the young man on the ladder raised one hand and cried out: "All right then, how many will help?" A great shout went up and there was a rustling sound as many arms were lifted. Before the shout died down the young man leaped from the ladder and was lost in the throng. Some of the spectators drifted away and now Paul could see across to the other sidewalk. Furniture was piled in front of three of the houses. There were tables, chairs, lamps, rolls of linoleum, bedding, dressers, barrels, boxes—all kinds of stuff; a dressmaker's form, its chest proudly outthrust, was standing in the gutter, bravely protecting a glittering white object at its feet. The people were swarming around the furnishings: there were a hundred, maybe more—men, women and children.

Eviction. Paul had seen it before, though not on this street and not so many families at once. He started to leave—Dad would be plenty mad if his supper was late—but a movement across the street held him. On one of the long flights of stairs that rose steeply on the front of each building the furniture was moving up. Then on the second stairs—now on the other. It was almost dark and as he stared across it looked like a fountain, the furniture flowing up in three thin jets from the disordered pile below. Paul looked back the way he had come, the way the police would come, but there was no sign of the law. He crossed the cobblestones to the other side to get a better look.

He saw now that the shiny thing he had noticed was a gilded chamber-pot leaning on its side; the ornate cover was pressing against the bosomy dressmaker's form as if the pot were ashamed to be seen so naked on the street. Paul stared at the thing for a moment, but a shout from behind drew his attention. The flow at the corner house had halted. A massive parlor stove had been dragged to the bottom of the stairs and was blocking the way. The people were struggling with it, but it would not budge. Paul saw a slender young white man trying to lift it by the rear base while some other men tugged from the other. But the stairs were very narrow and not enough of them could get a hold.

That skinny guy is going to rupture himself sure, Paul thought. The white man was squatting, his knees far apart as he strained up against the weight. "Hey!" Paul shouted. "Hey there!" He pulled at the upturned collar of the man's jacket. "You're going to hurt yourself that way. Get away from there."

The young man got up and turned angrily on Paul. His narrow face was very ugly; the eyes were small and close-set, the skin blotched and badly pockmarked. "Goddamit," he yelled, "why don't you *help* instead of standing there talking. Cops'll be here any minute and then. . . ."

The others had looked around the stove—three Negro men; they were breathing hard and staring at him. Now they were yelling at him too.

"Look," said Paul. "Get out from behind there and I'll show you how to do it. You aint doing a damn thing that way." He looked around and saw a girl holding a folded ironing board. He snatched it from her and laid it lengthwise on the steps, smooth side down. "There," he said. "Now rope." He shouted behind to the crowded sidewalk. "Rope! Don't just stand there—get some rope!" When an old man brought him a length, he turned to the others around the stove. "Now shove her over. That's right, shove her right over onto the board." He mounted the stairs to pull from the ornament on top. There was a splintering sound as the stove crashed down and there was a woman screaming and pulling at his arm.

"Now look what you done! Just *look* what you done! O Lord," she wailed, "you done ruint my ironing board." She was an elderly brown-skinned woman; a brown kerchief was knotted atop her head, the ends hanging free. Her teeth on both sides were missing and as she shrieked and clawed at him, her drawn-back lips showing two large front teeth, she looked like an angry rabbit. Somebody pushed her away and the men turned to Paul. Now what?

"More rope," he demanded. "Lots of rope. Get me some more." When they could not find any, Paul jumped down from the steps and joined in the search. A small boy tugged at his trouser leg: "The clothesline! The clothesline! Here—" and led him around the side of the house. There, zigzagged across the narrow space between the buildings, was the line. "Here y'are," said the little boy, pulling out a jackknife. "I couldn't reach."

Paul hacked it down, all of it, then ran back around to the front. "Now tie that stove down," he ordered. "That's right, with that short piece. Just wrap it around the board—tight." While they were doing that, he made a noose with the clothesline and looped it lengthwise over the stove, between the feet at the bottom and the flanges which flared out from the middle. Now he doubled the rope for greater strength and as he pulled against it, testing it, the screaming woman was back at him and angrier than before.

"My line! My good clothesline! Brand new and now look at it. You're going to break up my stove too. Just messing up everything, that's all. Just messing up *everything!*" She was crying now, the tears following the wrinkles down her face. "Everything messed up . . . everything gone . . . gone. . . ." She struggled against them as they hugged her away.

Paul looked at the upturned faces and waved his hand. "All right now, I want all you men. Come on up here and grab ahold." A dozen of them climbed up and held the line, each man settling himself on a step. "Now don't pull till I say pull. All right, all right . . . easy now, don't jerk. Goddamit, I said *don't jerk!* Easy now . . . easy now . . . easy."

A hush fell on the crowd as the stove began to move. Slowly, slowly, its shiny black bulk rising like a monster from the sea. If only that rope will last. . . . The slender strands were twisting, squeaky taut as guitar strings. But the stove con-

57

tinued to rise, inch by inch, slowly . . . slowly . . . sliding
up smoothly on the ironing-board skid. Suddenly it toppled
forward as it reached the top. A great cheer went up from the
strained silence, and then there was laughing. And the furniture began bobbing up the stairs again.

Coming out of the room where they had dragged the stove
and set it up, Paul saw the young Negro who had been doing
the speaking. He was up on his ladder again, but this time
he was doing something else. When his eyes became accus-
tomed to the darkness of the narrow hallway, Paul saw what
it was: he was prying open the electric meter box to re-con-
nect the current the company had shut off. Paul had forgotten
about the police until then: he hurried down the stairs. It was
dark now and the street lights were on; all was quiet. The
people were gone; the furniture was gone too. No—here's
something they forgot. Small stuff, they don't need me for
that. It was a carton of dishes, a broken hatbox and off to one
side near the curb was the chamber-pot. Naked and alone.
He took a closer look.

"That was it," he said when he told the story to Zach and
Faulcon. "That little old chamber-pot. Up till then I wasn't
thinking much about it being an eviction and what that means
to people. Too busy showing them how to get that stove upstairs. And showing that skinny white guy—he was Marty
Stein who recruited me a few weeks later—that I knew how
to do it. You see, that's how we used to snake up those great
big machine foundations from the casting pit at Peerless. Slide
'em right on up—that's how come I knew. Well anyway, there
was that chamber-pot. That kind must be fifty years old, all
fancy and everything, with roses and leaves on the top and
gold-painted doodads all around the sides. All the time we
were working on that stove, in the back of my mind I kept
thinking about that pot being out on the street where everybody could see and laugh at it. And something else—personal,
I guess you would say."

He laughed. "You see, that was one of my first chores when
I was a kid down home—Elco, that's in Bibb County, Arkansas

—emptying that big old pot my folks had in their bedroom. That's right, and I used to hate it but I had to do it. And I was ashamed when we packed up to come North and Dad brought it along—I knew it was too countrified for a big place like Cleveland where people had toilets inside. But he wanted it, said it belonged to his father before him. Kept it in the attic till he took sick, then had me bring it down for him. Every morning I emptied it, just like before, and if I hadn't known ours was at home I would have swore that the pot setting out there was the very same one. Exactly."

He decided to carry the things to the top of the stairs; then he started for home. Before he had gone far, he heard somebody running behind him, yelling. But it wasn't the law: it was a small boy and when he caught up to Paul he clutched at his legs. "Gimme back my knife!" the boy cried. "Man, gimme back my knife. I *know* you got it, so give it back!" He was in overalls and wearing a brimless hat decorated with pop-bottle caps.

"Oh, *you*," Paul said. "I clean forgot." He found the jack-knife in his coat pocket.

The little one snatched it from him. "Forgot my ass!" he said. "You was *stealing* it" and he ran away.

Going home, as he told them, Paul couldn't get the sight of that chamber-pot out of his mind. But he did not tell Zach and Faulcon how, suddenly, he began to cry—bawling like he had not done since he was a kid. Or how a great wave of self-pity rolled over him and he thought of himself dead, maybe cut in half by one of the foundry cables snapping— that could happen to a man—or maybe being run over, or getting double-pneumonia, and him dead, and people saying Paul was a good boy it's a shame he died so young, and nobody to pay the rent, and Dad being thrown out into the street, bed and all, and the chamber-pot that had belonged to his father and mother, and to his father's father before them, standing all alone on the curbstone. . . .

"Well, anyway, comrades," Paul said, "it was seeing that old chamber-pot a-setting on the street that made me see things right. You know how it is. You can't explain something like that to somebody else, not like it really was—but you know how it is."

The two had nodded slowly at the wonder of such a thing; and Paul told them the rest of the story.

Moses Harper's body hardly made a mound under the Rose of Sharon quilt Mattie had made for their wedding. But the eyes in his thin, dark face could still flame with that terrible fury and when Paul came into their bedroom his father glared at him and then to the brass alarm clock that was ticking loud and angry from the dresser top.

"Couldn't help it, Dad," he said, humble before the silent rage. "There was some trouble up the street."

"Trouble? And didn't I tell you to keep away from trouble!" There was a rustling sound from the bed, like dry leaves rubbing on a winter tree, as the old man tried to sit up.

Paul moved over quickly and pressed the straining shoulders back to the bed; he avoided the angry eyes. Again there was the dry rustle from the corn-shuck mattress they had brought from home. "Take it easy, Dad. I'll fix your food and then I'll tell you what happened today and you'll see I wasn't being bad."

He brought his father supper on the tray, propping him up against the headboard. "How come neckbones and black-eyed peas always taste so much better the second day?" he asked, making believe nothing was wrong; and when his father did not reply he returned to the kitchen to eat by himself.

After the dishes were done, Paul sat in the rocking-chair beside the bed and told what had happened. Moses Harper's eyes were closed; he said nothing, asked no questions. The only sign he gave that he was listening was to grunt when Paul said that he was the only one who knew how to get the stove back in.

When he had finished, Paul braced for the outburst that was sure to come; the bitter how-many-times-must-I-tell-you, the rush of words crackling and beating against his head like somebody punishing a puppy with a rolled-up newspaper.

But there was only silence from his father. The minutes ticked away and now the stillness was worse than a word-lashing.

"That wasn't really bad, was it, Dad? Not really bad? . . ."

There was no answer. One thin black arm moved from under the covers, the curving fingers finding the light-string tied to the post.

Paul sat for awhile in the darkness, but when his father remained silent he went out to the kitchen, to his books. He had read for an hour, maybe longer, when he heard his father call. He hurried inside and reached under the bed, but the hand on his shoulder stopped him.

"I don't need the slop-jar, son. Not now."

He stood up, waiting.

"Paul—" The eyes were still closed tight.

"Yes sir. I'm here."

"Paul—you wasn't bad. I just wanted to tell you. You done right. To tell you the truth, son, I don't reckon I could have done better myself. That's right—couldn't have done better myself."

That was how he said it, as simply and easily as that, as if it were not the first time in his life he had ever praised the boy. Long into the night, and through all the days to come, it was a shining glory to Paul—these last remembered words of his father.

CHAPTER 5

Morning is best. The new day knocks on every door with a small clicking sound as the master switch is thrown. The cell gate slips open an inch and a man may look up from his bunk and smile, knowing that with a push of his hand the bars will roll away, his cell will be opened; or he may jump up, without waiting, and slide the door wide, and walk out and back and out again, and know that though the range gate is locked and all the other gates and doors between him and freedom are locked, *this* gate is surely open.

Morning is best. A man may talk to other men, look into their faces and, hearing them and seeing them, know that he is no longer alone. One more night has passed; one more day has been pulled. Or if he has not yet been tried, it may be that his name will be among those called for Court this morning; and no matter what happens there it is better to know, better than waiting.

Four men stand waiting at the range front gate. Two of them are dressed in dungarees and blue denim shirts; another wears a starched white shirt, split down the back, and carries his suit jacket over his arm; the fourth is dressed in khaki.

Slim and J. C. are workingmen, waiting for the eight o'clock bell that will open one more gate for them. Because there are a thousand men and less than a hundred jobs in the jail, few of these are given to the men on the bottom ranges. A workingman does not earn much—a pillow, an extra blanket, two shaves and baths a week instead of one, a pack of tobacco, working clothes—but nevertheless the jobs are eagerly sought after. That work itself is a blessing and labor its own reward may be a debatable proposition in the Iron City outside, but not in here. Slim put it this way: "There's nothing like a job to help a man pull his time and keep from blowing his wig"; and J. C. added: "Best thing about it is getting tired enough to sleep nights." Slim, who has served more than a year of his two-to-five for manslaughter, has the best Negro job in the place: he is janitor in the warden's office. J. C. works in the bath-house.

The bell that calls the workingmen out is also the signal for Court. The keyman comes to the gate with a list of names of those who are to be taken across the bridge to be given justice. Every morning for two months and seventeen days Old Pete has put on his white shirt and waited at the gate for his name to be called. And every day he has returned to Cell 20 to hang up the shirt he would wear at his trial. They call him Old Sneaky Pete because he is seventy-two years old and because he is charged with the illicit manufacture and sale of spiritous liquor. Whether he is guilty or not the accused does not say ("One thing sure, I never made stuff that would hurt a man"), but it is certain that he could not have been a large manufacturer since he did not have the fifty dollars to pay the bondsman.

Men who have received mail will not be called out until eight-thirty, but when a man has waited three weeks for word that someone knows he is in jail there is some satisfaction, at least, in being the first in line. The rangeman may laugh and say again: "Army, I'm telling you the truth—one a these days I'm going to write you a letter myself!" but the joke is not funny anymore. Army does not even turn to smile.

At the clang of the bell Henry Faulcon came out of his cell and looked toward the gate.

"All workingmen out! Say—" he turned to Paul and Zach still sitting on his bunk where they had been talking, "what's the matter with you fellows—aint you workingmen? Specially you Zach, big and strong as you are, what you doing loafing in my cell when it's time to go to work?"

Zach smiled but said nothing, and Paul's face still had the grim look that had come when they talked about him and the guard last night.

"That's what I always say about you colored people," Faulcon went on. "Just plumb lazy. No ambition. No git-up-and-go about you at all. Look at that—only two men from this whole range going out to work and just look at the rest of you! Reminds me of that man singing on the radio the other night—all about lazy bones and how you speck to make a dime that way. That's right, and that's why you aint never going to *have* nothing. Just sitting around and poking out your lips and talking about the white folks still on top and never hitting a lick of work yourself!"

Looking out of the corner of his eye, he could see Paul winking to Zach.

"You *know* I'm right, so what you want to argue with me

for? Just look at the kitchen here! A great big old kitchen and a lot of Negroes all around and not one of 'em cooking or washing dishes or mopping. Just laying back and eating up the white folk's food—I swear, I don't know what the race is coming to!"

Now they were calling out the names for Court and when it was over Faulcon went back in and sat down with the others.

"Wonder what Old Pete's name is anyway?" he said, and from the way he said it they knew that the old man had gone back to his cell once again to hang up the torn white shirt.

It was Zach who finally broke the silence. "Now with Army it's different," he said. "Says he's *got* to get some time for running away. Just hates to be in here all summer before his hearing and worrying about his people not knowing where he is. But Pete was telling me he looked to get a suspended sentence, this being his first offense and him being so old and all. Now if he misses this Court. . . ."

Paul nodded. "You know there's something in the Constitution about a speedy trial and that a man—"

"Get out of here, Paul, you and your Constitution!" Faulcon said. He shook his head sadly as he laughed. "I been trying to tell you about that, trying to tell you that them judges don't know nothing about no Constitution. First thing you know, you'll be telling me and Zach here that they can't put a man in jail for what he *thinks* and then you and me is going to have a terrible argument."

"All right, Henry," Paul said after they had stopped laughing. "Maybe I've been telling you too much anyway. Like yesterday—" He turned toward Zach. "Yesterday I was giving Henry hell about getting in wrong out in the yard, not marching when you should have been, and then last night it was me. My father used to tell me all the time he wanted me to do right, but it looks like I can't no more than any one else. It's like outside—I read somewhere that there's a law against *everything* and that no matter how hard a man tries to do right they can always get him for something. That there's no man they can't put in jail if they want to bad enough, and I guess that's right."

He stood up and went to the door.

"But let's do the best we can. Especially now with the question of bail not settled and them looking for any excuse to rule against us. And besides, we want to stay together as long as we can, and it's a cinch if we get into trouble they're going to say we are trying to start a revolution—you know, we're not in Moscow now—and separate us."

"You got something there," said Faulcon. "Not so much about the bail because I just can't see them letting us out before they turn down the appeal, but about us being together. That's important. Before when I was in here there was white comrades sentenced too, but I were the only Negro. Now I got me some company and it's a whole lot better. Course there's one thing I bet you never thought of, Paul, or you neither, Zach. As long as they got this Jim Crow it's better for a man to be on this side of the line than with the whites. No, don't laugh, Paul—I aint joking this time and don't come accusing me of nationalism, but I'm telling you the *people* here are better. That's right. Look—we only been here a week but still you aint heard nobody Red-baiting us have you? No, the only ones we got to worry about is the guards. But up on those ranges it aint like that. All kinds of reactionary bastards up there—Coughlinites, Jew-haters, fascists and everything. They're not in for being that, of course, but they're there just the same and I bet the white comrades—Jack and Leo and Smitty and Tom, up there—is catching hell from them right this minute. No sir, if there's going to be Jim Crow, please put me right in with my people!"

"I don't know about that, Brother Henry," Zach said. "Just two minutes ago you disowned us."

"That's the truth," Paul added. "You sure did. Said we aint got no ambition, never will amount to nothing. That's *just* what you said."

"Well," said Faulcon, "I might have said that and maybe I did disown you colored folks some, but that don't worry me

65

none. Time I'll be worried is when the colored folks disown *me!*"

(2)

> REGULATION 49 (c): THE GUARD IN CHARGE
> OF THE YARD WILL ESTABLISH SUCH RULES AS HE
> MAY DEEM NECESSARY TO MAINTAIN ORDER AND
> PROVIDE FOR ORGANIZED RECREATIONAL ACTIVITY.

This month the rules were simple: keep walking, keep in line. If you want to lean on something, stay inside. The guard in charge had decided that the basketball season ended with February and that baseball should not start until April 15 and for the weeks in between the organized activity would be marching. Every damned man must march. During the playing seasons it was better: those inmates who were unwilling or unable to take part in sports could do as they please for their hour in the yard. To do as they please, that is, as long as they did not break the Ten Commandments of God and the Two Commandments of Daniel F. X. Rooney: Do not raise your voice. Do not lower your rear. Some of the inmates loved God on Tuesday and Sunday. All of the inmates hated Rooney —every day.

The sky was dreary gray, like the asphalt beneath and the high granite walls, but it looked good to Paul on his first day out. Even the sulphur smell of the smog was good.

"They really got the mill going full blast nowadays," he said to Faulcon, abreast of him in the line of marchers. "Looks like the recession is over."

"Sure do, that's Defense. Aint been like that since the world's war."

Henry Faulcon was short and round and he seemed to be even shorter now, walking beside Paul who was over six feet tall. He looked up at his partner and said: "Bet you don't know I used to work in the mill. Well, I did—open hearth— all during the war."

"Ducking the draft."

"Ducking nothing. I were no slacker. Course, I can't say I were *mad* at anybody, and I did want some of McGregor's good money. No, I were too old for Uncle Sam."

Paul looked at him closely. There was not a line on the full-moon face; the light brown skin was firm and clear under the gray stubble.

"Too old! How old are you anyway, Henry?"

Now the eyes under their bushy gray brows had that sly look again. "Well, Paul, seeing as there is no women around, I'll tell you. On my next birthday I'm going to be sixty-three. That's what I said, sixty-three. Mrs. Jenny Faulcon's boy Henry were born right here in Iron City on the twenty-third day of August in the year of our Lord, 1878."

"Damn—they almost got you in the *Civil* War!"

Faulcon snorted. "No, son, I aint *that* old. But there were a Henry Faulcon that helped Sherman whip hell out of Georgia —my father. I got one of them big old swords he brought back up in my attic right now. But I *were* big enough to soldier when the war with Spain come along and man, I wanted to join up so bad it hurt me. That's a fact. Here comes the Ninth Cavalry through town, before they went to Cuba, and they had this big parade. Lord! All of them fine black troopers, lean and loose as their bridle reins, and the horses just a-prancing and a-dancing, and their swords just a-flashing, and all them pretty little brownskin gals just a-twittering and a-twisting. . . . Whooooeeeee! And then when I ran down to the post office, ran *all* the way down town, and they told me the quota for colored was filled up—well, Paul, I like to *died*. Guess I would have too, except along about then I fell in love and—"

But there was Dan Rooney, leaning against the wall, one foot propped under him, his face a thin shadow under the jutting brim of his baseball cap. He had not seemed to notice them today.

The marching line angled sharply to the left and now they could see the basketball player again. He had finished his one-man game and now he was shooting from the foul line.

He scored eight times without a miss but then the marchers came between him and the wall and he waited for them to pass. His chest was heaving under the tight sweater, his square dark forehead shiny with sweat. His half-opened mouth widened to a grin as he recognized Zach and Faulcon.

"Hi, Pops—and you other F and B," he called. "See you later." And then they had passed him.

Faulcon started to tell Paul about their meeting Lonnie the day before but Zach's finger jabbed him hard in the back. He looked around and the big man motioned for him to change places. The guard was now obscured by the men in front. They shifted quickly, Faulcon dropping back to Zach's place beside the young man in khaki.

"Look, Paul," Zach caid. "I been talking to Owens—Army— and seems like we ought to be able to help him. He's going to send his brother another letter today but he don't have much hope. So maybe if you was to write your missus to go to that place—maybe he's moved and she could find out where. That boy is just about sick with worrying about nobody knowing he's here."

"Sure thing," the other replied. "Sure. I'm writing her to-day, soon's we get back in. She'll do it, too."

"Course she will," Zach said. "Like I was telling Mrs. Zachary, your missus is a wonderful woman. The way she took everything—the trial and all that mess."

Paul laughed. "That's funny, Zach. Of course Charlene is all you say, but I was just thinking about how *she* had said just that about *your* wife."

The big man smiled but said nothing. Paul lit a cigarette and they marched for a long time without speaking. They could hear Faulcon behind them, talking to Army who was glumly silent, and they knew the old man was talking to hear himself as much as to cheer the other. Damn!, thought Paul, I forgot to ask him about how he could see the guard going out the range gate last night and him locked in his cell. Soon as we get in. . . . Now he heard Faulcon saying, "That's the other one I were telling you about yesterday—Paul Harper. Hey, Paul!"

He turned around and saw a third man with them. It was the basketball player.

"Paul, this is Lonnie. Lonnie—Paul."

They smiled at each other and then Lonnie moved up beside Zach and Paul. He nodded to Zach and asked Paul for a light.

"Hey," Paul said, when the butt was lit, "won't that guard give you hell? Said we got to stay in twos."

Lonnie made a flicking motion with his hand. "Dan aint going to mess with me. Not any more. We got that settled a long time ago."

Paul shook his head slowly. "Maybe so. Anyway it sure looks like you got one hell of a drag around here." He looked at the other who was an inch or so taller than he, noting the too-short dungarees, the kind they gave the workingmen, the ragged sweater that was inches short of the long dark wrists. He sure doesn't look like a big shot.

"Drag, hell," Lonnie said. "You just don't know me. Drag! You must be thinking about the way they used to drag me to the Hole, that's what you must mean. Twenty times, I bet. But now the bastards don't never mess with me. And as for *that* mother-lover—" he thumbed in the direction of the guard— "I really do believe he's scared of *me*. Really do. But I aint scared of none of *them*, not a damn one. No, that's a lie—there is one: Byrd."

"Who?"

"Byrd. Wait—you'll see him in a minute. I swear, that old son of a bitch scares me. I mean gives me the creeps. I remember one time last winter I woke up screaming, that's right, screaming—thinking he was after me." He smiled and bit his underlip, the wide-spaced teeth gleaming bright against the skin. "So they all came running to my cell, thinking I was raising hell again, and throwed me in the Hole. I never did tell them what it was. There—take a look up there, by the door."

They were nearing the center court that made the middle stroke of the hollow E of the yard. The old guard was sitting there beside the door, tilted back on his chair. The pale blue-white skin was stretched tight over the upper part of his face, outlining the shape of his skull, and puckered in folds around the small mouth as if pulled by a draw-string. He was bald except for a wispy fringe of silky white hair around the sides; his ears were long and parchment-thin, and over his folded hands the thick blue veins were crawling and twisted. His eyes, deep-sunk in the large hollows, were closed.

"Byrd," said Lonnie and he grunted. "Name ought to be buzzard, cause that's just what he looks like. Or maybe a buzzard's skeleton. This is his last year—thirty years in here—and he's going on pension. Bet they just carry him out on that chair and bury him. Ugh!"

Paul said he looks like he's sleeping.

"Oh, no—don't let him fool you. That old bastard aint asleep." And Lonnie told them how it had happened many times that when a prisoner was doing wrong behind Dan's back—maybe matching pennies or something like that—Byrd's whistle would shrill and a long bony finger would be pointing out the offender.

"No, don't ever think he's sleeping," Lonnie warned. "Why I can feel him looking at the back of my neck right now." He shivered and hunched up his broad shoulders.

Paul smiled past him to the big man on the other side. "Hear that, Zach? Got to watch that old guy."

"I watches them *all*," Zach said, and he didn't smile.

Paul winked at Lonnie. "Me and Zach won't let him get you."

Lonnie frowned and stretched himself up to his full height. He was taller than either of them, though slight compared to Zach's powerful build. "Guess I'm as big as you guys, and twice as bad I bet." He nudged them each in turn with a sharp elbow. "Hell, the only thing you guys were trying to do was overthrow the government—and there must have been twenty of you. Me, I been trying my damndest to overthrow this *jail*—and all by myself!"

They laughed at that and then he said, "Watch—in ten more minutes the whistle blows. I've got so I'll never need a watch. Always know exactly how much time is left. Except in the

70

Hole. There you can't tell nothing. You think it's nighttime and it'll only be noon."

He told them something of how it was to spend a week in solitary confinement. "And men, let me tell you," he concluded, "the range sure looks good when you get back out."

"Hey, Lonnie!" It was Faulcon from the rear. "You got some good checker players down there on E?"

"Can't say," said Lonnie. "I aint on E."

Paul glanced at him sharply. "What do you mean—you're not on E? You've got to be on Block One or you wouldn't be out here." He grinned and grabbed Lonnie's hand, comparing the color with his own dark brown skin. "Don't tell me you're upstairs with the white boys. Black as you are—don't tell me you're *passing!*"

"No," said Lonnie. "I aint passing. But I am the only colored on C, less one of them others is passing."

His tone was casual, bantering even, and perhaps that added to the shock and confusion that came over Paul Harper. Row C was Murderers' Row.

"I'm sorry," Paul said, not knowing what to say.

Lonnie slapped him across the chest with the back of his hand and said, "Now don't *you* be sorry about that. Just let me be sorry. Hell, it aint so bad. Except it does get kind of lonesome up there with nobody much to talk to."

Zach put his large hand on Lonnie's shoulder. "How many is there on C?" he asked.

"Only four of us now. The other three are waiting trial. They never come out here—I don't know why. Of course Peterson in the cell next to me—I'm in 10—he's nuts. Crazy as they come, but he's all right. Those other two—Reardon and Klaus—well, they still hate anybody who looks like me. So the only one I can talk to is poor old Peterson."

When they remained silent, Lonnie went on: "Funny thing, when you think of it. That Peterson—he's off in the head but he's really all right in here." He struck his chest with a fist. "Funny thing—first decent white man I ever met, and he's crazy."

"White folks isn't all bad," Zach said softly.

71

"That's *just* where you're wrong. And that's why you guys are in here today—getting mixed up with them. Don't tell me! Didn't I read all about your trial every day for a couple of months, all about them stoolpigeons testifying against you? And one of them used to be a big shot in the thing himself?"

Paul tried to tell him about Ronald Johnson, the Negro who had been one of the star witnesses for the Commonwealth, but Lonnie cut him short.

"Sure he's a rat, but the thing is: who was paying him to spy on you? *Who?*" he demanded. "No, don't come telling me about white people. I *know*. But look, not to change the subject, but how come you-all never heard about *me*—Lonnie James?"

When they didn't answer, he added: "I was in the papers too." He had been arrested in May, 1940, nearly a year ago, and his trial came five months later. "It only took them a day to find me guilty, and one week later Judge Rupp gave the sentence."

"Rupp!"

"Sure, him. Same one you-all had. Of course I wasn't on the front page, but still, it looks like people should have heard." His tone was bitter now for the first time, almost accusing. Then he smiled. "I've got all the clippings inside," he said. "So if you want to see, I'll bring them out tomorrow. It doesn't tell much but I—"

The whistle silenced them, but Paul jerked his head up and down: yes, they would like to see. His lips formed the word: tomorrow.

As it happened, however, it was a week before they saw the newspaper clippings that reported how Lonnie James, age twenty-three, had been tried by a jury of his peers on the charge of first degree murder and had been duly sentenced by Judge Hanford J. Rupp to be hanged by the neck until he was dead, so help him God.

CHAPTER 6

REGULATION 117 (f): THE RANGEMAN WILL RE-
PORT ANY DISORDER OR VIOLATION OF RULES BY
INMATES.

Paul Harper was writing when Army came
into his cell that afternoon. "Don't want to bother you," he
said, "but here's my brother's address." He held out an envelope. "This makes five letters to Claude, but maybe this
time. . . . Gee, that's a swell thing you-all are doing for me.
And I sure hope your wife finds out what's wrong. But you
better hurry," he added as Paul copied from the envelope,
"mail goes out soon."

"One minute I'll be through," Paul said. "And don't thank
me—it was Zach that thought of it."

Army waited until he had finished. "Here," he said, "give
me the money and I'll take yours up with mine." Paul gave
him the two pennies and the letter to Charlene. Army started
out the door. He stopped abruptly, with a gasp as though he
had run into the bars. He stood rigid for a moment, then
opened his hand slowly and stared blankly at the coins in
his hand.

Paul came over and touched his sleeve, but Army's eyes
stayed fixed on the pennies; the two dark coppers on the pink
of his palm were like eyes staring back at him.

"Hey! Army! What's the matter?"

Army looked up at Paul, but his eyes were unseeing; only
the muscles of his jaws were moving. Then he nodded and
released his breath in a great quivering sigh. "That's it," he
said softly. "That's just what he did." He went out quickly
and Paul saw him hurrying, almost running, to the rangeman's
cell. Then he came out and Paul saw him go into the next cell,
Number 2. That's funny—that cell is unoccupied. Maybe Zach
is right about him getting ready to blow his top.

He started into Faulcon's cell to tell him, but the old man
was sitting on his toilet.

"Oh, excuse me," Paul said, backing out.

Faulcon grinned up at him. "I wasn't really expecting company," he said. "But you're welcome to stay."

"Oh no! You need to be *alone* now." Paul waved his hand and stepped out into the corridor.

The bell rang then and the keyman came to let the rangeman through the gate with the out-going mail. The keyman too was an inmate, the highest ranking of all the workingmen. His key, which was given to him at the first bell and taken away at lock-up, could unlock the range gates but not the gate in the bars that enclosed the stairs on the end of the block. At the cry of *Block One!* he would run to the gate on the Hub level to see what the chief guard wanted. There he would be given the names of prisoners to be brought out for Court, or to see a visitor, or perhaps a lawyer, or to call out those who had received mail. It was he who opened the gate for the workingmen, and for the block to go to the yard, and for each range in turn to go down for slop. He was an important man, this prisoner with a key, and he could make money by carrying messages between any of his ten ranges.

The rangeman went out the gate, and then there was no one else on the runway except a couple of men playing Spanish pool in front of Number 6. Paul decided he ought to tell Zachary about the strange way Army was acting. Zach was the soldier's friend and maybe he should talk to him before something happened. Had Paul waited outside for another second, he would have seen Army come out of Number 2, look around to see if anyone was watching, and then duck into the rangeman's place; and seeing that, Paul would have acted. But he went into Zach's cell and for the next seven days he would regret it.

Army watched him closely for a sign, but the rangeman's face was as blank as the cell-wall when the soldier handed him the four cents postage after putting his letter and Paul's into the box marked OUT-GOING MALE.

"Boy, you know you aint allowed to send out two letters at once," he said. "Fact is, you really aint supposed to write more than one a week. But seeing as me and you is pals, I'll ask the keyman to slip one to one of them other rangemens so's he can hand it in with hisn. Steve wouldn't notice."

The jail administration, in this case Chief Guard Steve Kovach, had long ago ceased to enforce the regulation that restricted the inmates to one letter each per week. The constantly changing jail population—short-timers being released, others being sent daily to the workhouse or penitentiary—made it too difficult to keep the mail tally for each man. But since Steve was required to read all mail, he made certain that the weekly ration of official stationery was limited to one sheet of paper and one envelope for each man on a range. Some men seldom if ever wrote letters and these would sell their ration for a penny or a cigarette. And often a man would fail to collect his ration from the rangeman—there were many such men, some simple-minded, more who had never been taught to write—and the sale of extra stationery was the largest single source of a rangeman's graft.

"No, don't bother yourself," Army said. "Only one of the letters is mine." He yawned and stretched wide his muscular arms, the joints making a cracking sound. "Well, guess I'll just go on back to my bunk and get me a little shut-eye. Can't seem to sleep nights."

The rangeman shook his head sadly. "You worries too much."

"Yeah, reckon I do. Well, so long. Catch you later—for a game."

But instead of going down to his cell, Army slipped into Number 2, next to the rangeman's.

Catch you *now*, he thought, sitting in the darkened room. His knees were shaking and he pressed his tight fists down to steady them. Jiving me about it too—me waiting like a fool every morning for word from Claude and you always saying Army if you want a letter so bad one a these days I'm going to write you one myself, and me missing yard every Wednesday waiting for Claude to come and you just sitting back laughing inside your fat face, laughing at *me* and me in here for three weeks and sending out five letters and nobody knowing I'm here and no hearing set and Hortense and that guy she with just having themselves a ball out there. . . . O Lord! *Rangeman, I'm going to kill you, kill you dead!*

He sat there on the sagging canvas, tensed to spring from the cell at the sound of the rangeman's toilet flushing. *There!* —no, that's from down the range somewhere. O rangeman! *O God!*

The bell. And finally the keyman. The steel on steel. The squeak of the gate opening. "Hi ya, Fats." "Man, *you* got everything." The clang of the gate. Key turning. Now they must be gone.

He stood up and peered from the doorway. Gone. And down the other way—nobody looking, just Willie and Tuxedo squatting over their checkerboard on the floor of the runway. Quick. And he was in the rangeman's cell.

Only a couple of minutes. But it's got to be here. In here. He glanced into the toilet. No. He ran over to the door and snapped on the light. The bunk—he snatched off the blankets. Not under the pillow either. He slipped his hand inside the greasy pillowcase; it was tight and he ripped it open. No. The boxes underneath his bunk—the soap and toilet paper. He dumped the cartons over. It took a lot of time looking through it all, but not in there either. Now where? *Where?* He knocked the things from the washbowl shelf—not in that junk. He looked into the toilet again, bringing his face down close. It ought to be—*yes!* He plunged his hand to the bottom of the waterless funnel where he had spied the bit of paper, his fingers fishing around in the narrow end slippery with filth. *Ah!* He pulled out his hand and wiped the paper on his trousers. It was the corner of his envelope.

> *After Five Days Ret*
> *Harvey Owens D-7*
> *c/o Cathedral of Ju*
> *Iron City*

He was still staring at the trembling piece of paper when the rangeman walked in.

The man's eyes darted from the littered floor to the torn-up bunk to the soldier's face and then to what he had in his fingers. He opened his mouth as if to speak, then closed it. As Army leaped forward he turned and ran out. *"Keyman!"* but the keyman was gone and he raced down the range.

There was no way out, but he ran. Then he smashed down against the concrete floor as Willie, who had looked up from the checkerboard at his scream, shot out his foot and tripped him.

Army dived at him, his fingers squeezing through the rolls of fat around the rangeman's neck. The rangeman was quick, despite his bulk; he rolled over, drew up his knee and pushed. He scrambled up but Army's fist caught him under the ear and he staggered against the outer bars. Now Willie was hitting him, and then it was Tuxedo. Army tried to push them away, but there were more now: a dozen of them crowding in, hitting and kicking at their cornered enemy. *Report this!— you low-down rotten dirty stool!*

"Harvey! Harvey!" It was big Zach pulling at him. But Army swung at him and plowed his way through the others, pushing and clawing to make them give way.

The rangeman had fallen and they were all kicking and stomping him. The toe of Army's heavy shoe crashed into the man's face. He kicked again and suddenly there was room. *Now!* The rangeman's chest heaved high as he struggled for breath against the strangling pressure of Army's desperate fingers. *Now!*

It took all the strength of the four guards, two pulling on each wrist, to save the rangeman's life. Army fought back like wild. *Let go! Let go! I got to kill him! I got to kill him!* But now there were more of the men in blue and they dragged him away. *No! No! I got to kill him! I got to kill him!* Until finally the men on D could hear him no more.

The rangeman was taken away on a stretcher to the dispensary where they counted up his injuries. They would now enter another charge against Harvey Owens: Aggravated Assault and to that, possibly, Mayhem too. But Army, crouched in the blackness of the Hole, was not thinking of that. He too was counting injuries. Over and over he said it: *ten pennies, five letters, three weeks! Ten pennies, five. . . .*

It was Steve who called them all out of their cells on Range D an hour later. The six uniformed men who were with him pushed them all against the bars near the front of the runway. There were twenty of them, shoulder to shoulder.

Steve looked at each dark face before he spoke.

"All right," he said. "Who were the others? It was more than Owens. We know that."

No one answered.

"All right," Steve said, and he looked at his wristwatch. "I'm going to give you one more chance. One minute. *Who were the others?*"

There was a movement in the line and a man next to Faulcon stepped forward. It was Pee Wee, a frail little man with a withered arm who was in for writing numbers.

"I was just watching," he said. "Never left my cell, but I saw it happen." His voice became stronger, eager. "I saw it *all*—right there from Number 14."

"Fine." Steve walked over to him, pulling a pad and pencil from his hip pocket. At the gesture Pee Wee backed up.

"Give me the names."

The little man blinked. "I—I don't know all they names."

"Well point them out—go on!"

Pee Wee turned to face the others. "Well . . . I . . ." and he looked again to Steve. "It was *all* of them!"

"What!"

"Yes sir. I think—" He turned quickly to face the men again. "I know it was. I saw it. All of 'em. This one and that one and that next one with the sweater—that's right. *All* of them was hitting him."

Steve's face was flushed and he put away the pad. He was angry, but he knew the informer was too frightened now to change his story. And it would not be possible to press charges against them all. Too damn much work anyway for just one dinge getting a beating.

"What's your name?" he yelled at Pee Wee.

"Not me! I was right down there in my cell. See—down there in Number 14? That's where I was. . . . Ask anybody— I swear it wasn't me!"

"*Shut up!* I said what's your name?"

"I—Tom Holmes. But I swear it wasn't me—just ask any of 'em, they'll tell you it wasn't me." He was crying; the tears two glistening lines on his thin face.

Now Steve was grinning. "Tom, I'm going to make you rangeman. But next time you better give me some names—or it *will* be you."

Pee Wee stood there, trying to smile. Finally he managed to speak: "I sure will, captain. I sure will. Thank you! Thank you *sir!*"

Steve backed away a pace and looked at the lined-up men. "Maybe all of you will go up for this, I don't know. But anyway you are going to stay on this range for a week. Every man. No bath, no shave, no chapel, no visitors, no yard."

He turned on his heel and waved for the guards to follow him out. The men on D could hear them laughing as they went up the stairs to the Hub.

Paul Harper never forgot that day—the day he met Lonnie in the yard, nor did Henry Faulcon or Isaac L. Zachary. No doubt the rangeman-thief would always remember and so would young Army. After he got out of the Hole, and after they had sentenced him for his new crime, he commemorated the occasion with these lines which may be seen scratched into the paint on the wall near the toilet (to your left as you enter) in Cell Number 7, Range D of the Cathedral of Justice:

> *Rangeman stole all my money*
> *Tore up all my mail*
> *They put me in the hole ten days*
> *And a solid year in jail.*
>
> *Lord if I ever get lucky*
> *And get out of here free*
> *It will take a mighty pretty woman*
> *To make a fool out of me.*
> *H.O.—1941*

CHAPTER 7

"Henry, I been meaning to ask you: Were you lying about that?"

They had not been talking, just sitting there, the three of them together on the bunk; and now Faulcon looked at Paul and pondered over his question.

"Well," he said, "I might have been but now I really don't know. Specially since I aint got *no* idea what you're talking about." His smile reflected the warmth he felt for the tall black youth beside him. Our Paul—long-headed, long-limbed, hound-lean and eager. Got a long run ahead of him, but if any man can make it young Harper can. Kind they call a *bad* nigger and there aint nothing Cap'n Charlie can do with him except to kill him—and that kind is even hard to kill.

"Besides," Faulcon added, "it aint exactly polite for you to be calling a man a liar right here in his own home."

"You know what I mean, old man," Paul said. "Couple of nights back you told me you could see the guard going out the end gate. I been forgetting to ask you, so much been happening around here." He turned to Zach, who had been looking at them with the half-puzzled, half-amused look he always had when the other two were fussing, and explained what had happened.

Faulcon's face was round with innocence. "Well, I *did* see him, but I aint going to tell you how cause it's secret."

"You're lying," Paul said.

"Oh no I aint. Now look here, son. You has read a lot of books, I know that, and you got a whole lot more schooling than me. All right. But still there's a lot of things you don't know and I know. Look: you don't know, and Zach neither, how come we got put in three cells right here all together. And me in the middle one so's I can talk to any which one of you at night when I want to talk. Well, it cost me a lot of money to fix this up for us—with the rangeman when we came in. Fifteen cents, and come to think of it, you-all owes me a

nickel apiece. But about that other—" he shook his head—
"no, that's secret."

"Still, you ought to tell us, huh Zach?"

The big man nodded. "Talking man like him can't keep a
secret nohow."

"Oh, I can't, hey?" Faulcon jumped up and took a pencil
stub down from his shelf. Then he unrolled a length of toilet
paper and folded it into a pad. "Look," he said, easing himself
down between them, "I'm going to show you people something.
Right now I'm the only one what knows that secret—one
man." He made a big numeral one on the paper and showed
it to them. "See that—*one*. All right, now supposing I go ahead
and tell you Paul—which I aint, this is just supposing—" He
drew another vertical stroke and held the paper up. "Now
how many knows it?" he demanded.

"Why, two of course."

Faulcon groaned. "You can't even read good. That aint no
two, that's *eleven!* See? And if I go ahead and tell Zach too—"
now a third stroke on the tissue—"well, that aint no three.
That is exactly *one hundred eleven!* And you know damn well
that any time that many folks knows something it sure aint
much of a secret."

There was no doubt that he had scored, and his laughter
was louder than theirs. Still glowing with his triumph, he
pushed Paul aside and ran his hand into the rolled up blanket
on the end of his bunk.

"Now let me show you-all something else. Look!"

It was his spoon.

"Take a good look at that. No, take it—here!" he pushed
it into Paul's hand.

The spoon, larger than a tablespoon, was the kind they were
all given and which they kept, together with the tin coffee
cup, in their cells. Paul examined it carefully, then passed it
on to Zach. The only thing they could notice was that it was
new and that the eating part was flatter than it ought to be.

"Got you again!" Faulcon exclaimed, hastily before they
might guess. "See that spoon? Well, it's brand new and I

traded five cigarettes for it. Use my tooth-powder on it and that keeps it shiny. OK. And see how it's mashed in? Well, I put it between the blanket and stomped it like that. Now give me it and come over here."

They followed him to the front of the cell.

"All right. Now Paul you get on out there in the hall and Zach you too. Here I am in my cell, let's say I'm locked in, and I can't see down the range and if I say I can, well I'm a no-good liar."

Now Faulcon stretched himself out on the bunk, with his head toward the front of the cell. He rolled onto his stomach and with one hand poked the spoon out through the bars.

"You looking? No, not at me—look up the range. But maybe you people can't see so good. Maybe you-all better get you some eye-glasses. But me—I can see everything." He squinted into the spoon. "Sure. Down in front of Number Three it's Tuxedo and the new one that came in this morning—playing checkers. And let's see what else—there's two, no, three—that's right, three men standing by the gate. Now look around to the back." He twisted the spoon in his fingers. "Well, if it aint poor old Pete! Sticking his head out of Number Twenty and wondering if it aint just about slop time."

Paul and Zach went in to try Faulcon's periscope for themselves. After he was sure they were fully satisfied that it worked, Faulcon said, "Now, gentlemen, just sit down and let me say this: the Lord in His mercy have allowed Jenny Faulcon's son Henry to live for a long time and don't you-all ever get to thinking that all I can show for it is this here gray wool. No sir!" He winked at them and lowered his voice to a conspiratorial whisper. "Don't go telling anybody else about that spoon—you hear? And don't forget either how I showed you about keeping a secret!"

(2)

The Lord in His mercy allowed Jenny Faulcon's son Henry to live for a long time, but He took her other two boys away from her that terrible August in 1883. People called it the summer fever, and only the hardiest child could survive the sickness. Henry was her youngest and her favorite and not even the Almighty could stand against the fierceness of her will that the five-year-old boy must live. "No, God," she warned Him, "not this one. Not this last one. *Don't You dare!*" And there was no power above or below that could prevail against the fury of this little brown woman whom an earthly master had named Jenny.

It was the only name she had and it was all she had when they finally crossed over to Freedom. Many had perished along the way, and among them was Jenny's mother. They buried her in the swamp where she died and they sang their song about the many thousand gone. Sang it so softly that their sentinel, on the moonlit road outside, could only hear the crickets singing. And their leader, the great, gaunt black woman who was their Moses, led them in one more song. Not for the dead, this last one, but for the living and the long hard way that still lay ahead.

> *Keep a-inchin' along*
> *Like a po' inch-worm*
> *Jesus will come by an' by*
> *If'n you gets there befo' I do*
> *Jesus will come by an' by*
> *Tell all-a my friends I'm a-comin' too. . . .*

Whether it was the herbs and the roots and the bark from the juniper tree she ground up together and made him swallow, or the syrupy onion tea, or the brown-bottle medicine the peddler brought by, or whether it was the healing power of her tiny work-worn hands ceaselessly stroking his burning forehead, no one could tell; but Jenny Faulcon nursed her youngest back to life just as she had done for big Henry when he had come home from the march to Savannah, sick near to death with the swamp fever.

Afterwards she used to tell the boy: "Li'l Henry, the good Lord just didn't want you up there a-trackin' in mud all over them golden floors and a-flyin' round like a jaybird, gettin' into all kinds of devilment. And Satan wouldn't have you neither—cause boy, you *so* bad!"

Actually he was not bad at all; he did not have time to be bad. "My mother," Faulcon would say, "were the first Booker T. Washington there ever were. I don't mean she were a handkerchief-head like him—though it's a fact she always had one on her head—but I mean about believing that work were the salvation way for our people. She weren't in no position to handle the *whole* race, but Lord, she did have this one small Negro which were me and she had me working when I were *this* big."

There was always a lot to do in the house his father built for them in Willston, which was then a separate town from Iron City. It was a large frame house; big Henry, who had done most of the building work himself, fashioned it into the image he had seen in a thousand flickering campfires when Sherman's men had sung of peace and home. The carpentering, lathing, plastering and painting were the skills by which he had earned enough to buy himself free from his Louisville owner. He had wanted to frame the manumission deed and hang it over the mantlepiece so that all might know that Henry Faulcon had been his own emancipator; but Jenny said no: slavery was not something to be remembered and she would have no talk of it in her house nor should the children be thus reminded that their father had once been owned by a white man. So he kept the freedom paper carefully folded in the parlor Bible and after young Henry had taught him his letters, he would take it out and read it over and over again until he knew every curving flourish of the fine Spencerian script. *I, Jno H. Whitcomb Esq., for the sum of eight hundred Dollars paid to me this date by my negro man Henry, have and by these presents do hereby manumit and set free, now and for all time, my said negro man Henry as witness my hand and seal this 7th day of June, 1858. . . .*

After he came North to Iron City, big Henry came to know that there was more to freedom than his hard-bought deed. He was free forever but he was black forever, too; and he never was permitted to work at his trade again. From the

84

time he got married until he died in 1903, he drove the station hack for the Hotel Royale.

> Henry Falcon, a negro who died today at the age of seventy-four, will be fondly remembered by many distinguished residents, including some of Iron City's oldest families, as the coachman for the Hotel Royale.
>
> During his thirty-seven years' employment at the fashionable hostelry, Henry, a former slave, was never absent a day from his proud duties.
>
> It is recalled that when President Grant visited this metropolis in 1874, Henry was chosen to drive the President's landau from the station to the McGregor mansion where the Chief Executive was guest of honor during his stay.

The report might have added that the Hotel Royale's coachman also drove Republican presidents Hayes and Garfield and Democratic President Cleveland to Adam McGregor's castle when those statesmen came to Iron City. Young Henry had regretted that omission, as he regretted the misspelled name, at the time he cut the item from the *Monongahela Argus* and tucked it away in the big book beside his father's manumission paper and mustering-out certificate; but later he came to feel that it would have been more important to tell how the former slave had had to work at his proud duties eleven hours a day and six days a week for his five dollars' pay.

Little Henry was the only man around the house long before he was a man. The usual chores other boys did would not have been so bad—bringing in kindling and coal, taking out ashes, blacking the stove, cutting grass, fetching water from the pump. But Jenny Faulcon wanted her home to look as fine as anybody's, as fine even as the big house in which she had worked on the plantation down South. So every

Saturday was waxing day for little Henry. Every inch of every floor, closets, stairs and all, had to be done on hands and knees. The furniture had to be rubbed and polished, rubbed and rubbed, until the dark old wood gleamed like satin. Even the parlor had to be done like that, though it was never used except on Sunday nights for Bible reading time. There were seldom any visitors: all of their neighbors were white and while they were nice enough, they never came a-visiting and Willston was too far out from Iron City's Hollow for colored friends to come often.

But of the people who did come, not even the nebbiest female could have climbed up to see if the mouldings near the ceiling were dusty and the boy saw no reason at all for having to keep *that* so clean, but of course he dast not ever say such a thing to his mother. The curtains always looked stiff and spotless enough to him, but every two weeks they had to be taken down and washed and starched and stretched and put back up again.

Jenny Faulcon made her own soap, made all their clothes, baked all their bread, put up all their fruit and vegetables, jellies and jams. He could never remember her idle until the time, long after he was grown, she took to her bed and died as quietly and neatly as she had lived. And while she worked the boy worked with her. She had him washing dishes in their fancy cast-iron sink when he was still so little that she had to tie even her shortest apron around his neck.

The white people had to say there was nothing like Jenny Faulcon's garden for miles around. And every tiny weed in the large plot was Henry's enemy which he must seek out and destroy. Every little red potato bug must be picked off by his hand, though she told him often enough that he really didn't have to be squashing them all like that with his thumb—just throw the nasty things into the pail with the coal oil; but he hated them all and did not want them to live for an extra minute.

While she was ironing it was his task to bring her a hot iron and put the other back on the stove lid; and later she taught him how to do the ironing himself. When he was ten she taught him how to cook. ("*Seeing as there aint no women comrades around to be calling me something for saying it, I can tell you-all this: Aint no woman I ever met could beat me when it comes to cooking. And that's the truth!*")

The hardest part was seeing the other boys playing outside while he was working. He learned all their games just by watching them: Hit the Stick, Simon Girty, Run Sheep Run, Red Rover, Redlight, and all the others. Best of all was when the big yellow waterwagon came along the dusty street and all the boys and girls running along barefoot and barelegged splashing through the spray and squishing their toes in the muddy puddles it left behind. But he was always too busy to play and even on Sundays when he had almost nothing to do he could not get out to play because then he was dressed up in his shiny stove-pipe pants and the sissy starched collar he better not get mussed.

Young Faulcon finished school—it was only six grades then —when he was twelve but it was not until he was sixteen that he worked for anyone but his mother. He started in the kitchen at the Royale and he was there ten years before one of the old waiters finally had to quit and he became a first-class dining room waiter. In those days, around the turn of the century, all of the service employees in Iron City were Negroes; even the cheapest and meanest places had colored help. And of all the jobs there was none that ranked so high as being a waiter in the magnificent Hotel Royale. Not even the butlers in the biggest houses on Bessemer Boulevard had the social standing in the Hollow that these men had. But more than the prestige and the swaggering figure he was with the girls (no man before had ever achieved that rank in his twenties), Henry treasured the opportunity the job gave him to join the Waiters' Club. Only men from the quality houses were eligible.

The old waiters he met there were the best informed men in the community; they knew more than any of the preachers and of course they talked about a lot of things that preachers were not supposed to know. It was at the Waiters' Club that Faulcon followed the heated debates about who was right, the dangerous radical Du Bois or Booker T. who had even been invited by Teddy Roosevelt to eat in the White House. No topic of current interest was ever missed and all the old ones were gone over, time and time again. Did Frederick Douglass do right by marrying a white woman after his first wife died? Could Peter Jackson have knocked old John L. Sullivan bowlegged? How could Reconstruction have been saved? Was Douglass thinking about starting a new party before he died? Did old man McGregor make a deal with Count Cassini to get him to marry his daughter Jane or was it really love at first sight the way the papers said?

History, politics, literature, religion, women—everything was discussed and Henry Faulcon was a member three years before he dared take part in the learned disputes. It was in the Club library that he first saw the works of Negro writers—Chesnutt and Dunbar and Mrs. Harper—and the Negro newspaper that came all the way out from Boston. It was there that he first learned about Crispus Attucks and Phillis Wheatley and Martin Delany and Henry Garnet and Richard Allen —not one of whom had been so much as mentioned in his *Potter's Standard American History for Boys and Girls.*

"I guess you could have called me a race-man," he said when he recalled those years. "But aside from arguing down there at the club I never did much about it. Voted straight Republican, of course, but to tell you the truth I were more interested in good-timing than in worrying myself with politics and such. Good-timing and good clothes, I should say. My box-back coat were the most box-back in town and talking about peg-top pants—you should a seen mine! To look at me now you might not guess it, but every year when the Iron City Imperials gave their big Easter ball them other boys was hoping I'd break a leg or something so one of *them* would have a chance at the cakewalk prize.

"But I better skip a lot and come on down to what I'm supposed to be telling you about—how I come to get in the Party. You might say it were the church and it were in a way, or you might say it were the women and that might be right too. One woman anyway.

"Now I never were real religious like Zach here is, but

whereas Zach aint never been a churchman that's exactly what I were. I mean *all* the churches. I been baptized so much I know my soul is *got* to be straight by now, cause I been baptized every which way there is—sprinkled and dunked and re-sprinkled, dipped deep and dipped lightly, and *one* of them must be the right way. Never did get into any of the arguments about the Bible though I did like to read it sometimes. There's a lot of true things in that old book if you don't bother with the parts that say the opposite. Like Pa used to say, that's what really brought on the Civil War: folks down South showing where the Good Book says the slave must be faithful to his master and the Abolitionists up North pointing to where it says that slavery is a sin and abomination before the Lord, and first thing you know they was up and throwing everything at one another and came damn near tearing up the whole country before the argument was over.

"No, it weren't on account of religion that I were such a big churchman—it were the singing part I liked and the women all pretty looking and smelling so sweet. Anyway, I been a M.E. and a A.M.E. and a A.M.E.Z. and a Baptist of course and a Church of God and one time even, when I were really eating high up on the hog, I thought I'd get real hincty and join the *Episcopalians!* That's right, but I were wrong. Why them colored Episcopalians couldn't sing any better than the white ones—oh, it were so sad and draggy and the preaching so dusty-dry you'd want to run right out and get a drink of hard liquor to clear your throat and you know damn well that aint something a churchman ought to be doing on Sunday.

"But to get back to my story. Here I were this particular Sunday—summer of 1930—and on my way to the Baptist church in the Hollow where I sing lead tenor in the choir. And there, standing in front of one a them storefront churches were the cutest little brownskin woman you ever saw in your whole life. I mean she—now look, Paul, I got the floor and I'm going to tell this story in my own way. Trouble with you, son, is you're too damn *political*. Anyway, there she stood all dressed up so pink and pretty and I just had to cross over the street and tip my new straw hat and say howdydo ma'am.

"She just looks at me all sniffy—you know how they do—and I says: Don't you remember me no more? And she pulls herself all up like this and says: Why, I didn't know you the *first* time! You must be getting your womens mixed up. And besides, she says, I'm a respectable widow-woman and I'm sanctified too and I can stand right here and look into your rolling eye and know you might be something else but you sure aint sanctified!

"Well, I jived along with her and I thought I saw something in *her* eye that made me think that if I did go ahead and join the Sanctified Church—and the way she switched on into that church, well from the way she were built it might have been just a natural body movement but I just had to be sure so I followed her right on in and joined that Christian band!

"Mmmmmmmm mmmmmmm—*sweet* Lucy Jackson! She were built about this high and about this round—well maybe not *quite* that much—but she were *hefty*, know what I mean?, and I love a hefty woman. Maybe I'm just an old reactionary but I like a woman to be all woman and lots of it. Like that old-time song the boys used to sing, though they was mostly too old to mean it:

> *Says a skinny little woman*
> *Is like a cob with no corn,*
> *But a big-legged woman—*
> *Great day in the morn!*

Faulcon courted the widow Jackson for over a year, but all his smooth talk and winning ways did not win her. "Henry," she said, "I'm *so* glad you joined the church and you brought a good voice along with you to our choir, but man, your heart aint right and you aint redeemed. You been proposing to me: Lucy, let's us go on the boat ride, or, Lucy, might I just come in to rest my feet. Yes, you been proposing to me all kinds of things and Lord knows what you *meant*, but Henry, you never yet proposed marrying and I can see now there aint no marrying in you. I don't really know what I would say if you asked me for my hand, but until you do, *just don't ask me about nothing!*"

But every one knows a woman can change her mind and a man can wait till she does. Of course, a young man might not wait so long, but Faulcon was no longer young. Not that he would admit to being old, but he certainly was, well, *settled* was the word he used. Too settled to be thinking about getting married and settling down. At any rate, Faulcon stayed with that church, and the singing was better than at any of the others. One thing that hindered his progress with the widow, he thought, was that she was so busy all the time. There was the Ladies' Aid Society and the Missionary Society and the Busy Bees and the Building Committee and everything else.

Mrs. Jackson was indeed *the* rock of the Old Rock of Zion Church and that is why, when the people came to the Ladies' Aid with the petition papers, she took ten of them to fill out though the other members took but one. Fifty names were to be signed to each of the petition lists which were addressed to the Supreme Court, and on each line there was a space for contributions. She had filled all but two of the lists when she thought to ask Henry to help.

"Brother Faulcon, here is something I want you to do for *me*," she told him. "Of course, it's not really for me but for them nine poor boys who will die in the chair down in Alabama less'n people can stop it. Now let me see you put your slick-talking ways to some good use—just for once. And I don't want to see your face again until you bring these back all filled up with names and money too!"

It had not been difficult for him to get the hundred signers; one night at the union hall and it was done. But when he brought them back to her he was dismayed to find she had ten more petition blanks, and all for him.

"I went over to the Communist people's hall," she explained, "and got twenty more of these papers—seeing as I got me such a good helper." Never had she smiled so warmly upon him.

"But Sister Jackson"—no more Lucy, it was Brother Faulcon and Sister Jackson between them now—"I swear I don't know where I can find that many people. Aint these two enough?"

"Enough!" she said, and he knew then it would not be. "What if you was one of them Scottsboro boys—would you say it was enough? Now look here: you been asking me for the longest to go out walking with you. Well, I'm saying *yes*. You and me going to do some walking now! All over this Hollow to people's houses and we are going to get *everybody's* name. Everybody—even the Methodists. That's right, we're going to all them churches you used to belong to but not for foolishment this time. And we're going to go to all them sinful places, bars and poolrooms and such. It won't hurt *you* none to go in, and besides I'll be waiting right outside to see that you do come out."

They did not get everybody's name, of course, but they collected thousands; and every time they were finished Mrs. Jackson knew where to get more petitions.

"Me on my bad feet all day working," he shuddered as he told Paul and Zach, "and me on my bad feet walking—I mean each and every night. And Sundays—most of all on Sundays. I'm telling you that woman could walk like my mother could work—Lord! Walked me so much I couldn't even *think* of sweet talk no more."

One time she took Henry to the place where she got her endless supply of blank petitions.

"This is the man I been telling you about. Mr. Faulcon is his name and if it wasn't for him I don't know *what* I would have done."

There were about twenty people, Negro and white, at Douglass Hall that night and some of them were calling for the meeting to be started. But a tall elderly Negro held up his hand for them to be patient for another minute and came over to shake Faulcon's hand.

"My! You really can collect signatures," he said. "I'm proud to know you. My name is Bob Wylie. Mrs. Jackson's been telling us about you. Says you just won't let her rest before you send her up here to get some more to be filled up."

"Why—" but Sister Jackson cut him off.

"One thing I didn't tell you," she said, "about Mr. Faulcon here and maybe I should. He's a real good talker, he sure is, and when he tells the people about Scottsboro—why no preacher could do better."

The tall man had been delighted. "That is just what we need most right now, and as you can tell, my own voice is near about wore out. Did you ever speak at a street-corner meeting, Mr. Faulcon?"

Henry said no, but before he could add that that was one thing he would *not* do, the other had gone over to a large calendar on the wall. He ran a long finger over the dates and stopped at one. "Next Friday," he called over to them, "next Friday at eight. Corner of—" He looked back to what was written there. "Corner of Twenty-fourth and Jay." He moved back to Faulcon to shake his hand again and say, "Don't forget—eight o'clock sharp. We only got a permit for an hour there. But you'll have to excuse me now—got to open the meeting. You-all are welcome to stay."

But Faulcon was too tired to stay and it was a long trolley ride out to Willston.

"Did you speak at that street meeting?"

Faulcon's chin rose and his eyes rolled heavenward in the look of terribly wronged innocence he had learned from Judge Rupp at their trial; all of them, and the jury too, had come to watch for that expression from the bench whenever the cross-examination was making it plain that the Commonwealth's witness was lying like hell.

"Of course, I did, Paul. Why? Do you think I weren't going to?"

Of course, he did; and, of course, he had not meant to. He had intended just to stand outside the crowd and watch. No sense in me acting the fool at my age!

It was sticky hot that August night despite the drizzle that made the paint bleed off the cardboard signs they were holding up. The large crowd was strangely quiet under the shouting placards: STOP THE LYNCHERS! FREE THE 9 INNOCENT SCOTTSBORO BOYS! BLACK AND WHITE—

UNITE AND FIGHT! There was only the creaking sound of the arc light swinging up above and the idling mutter of the policemen's squad-car drawn up to the curb.

A young man came out of the bar where Faulcon stood. "What's the matter?" he said. "Reds scared of the cops?"

Someone said no: they're waiting for the speaker.

The young man spat through his teeth. "That's *shit!* Speaker must be scared."

"That's a lie," Faulcon heard himself say. "He's not scared."

"Don't go calling me no lie. I say he is! Besides, how do you know he aint?"

"You want to know how I know? Well, just watch." He was as surprised as the other to see himself pushing through the crowd, climbing up the ladder and shouting aloud: "Brothers and sisters!"

Two of the small group of Communist Party members who had been waiting for him at the speaker's stand were old members and they were somewhat shocked to hear him begin that way instead of the right way which was "Comrades and fellow workers!" But that was nothing compared to what he did next.

"First off," Faulcon said, "how many of you-all knows that good old church song, 'I Been Tramping'?" Nearly all did and as they raised their hands he began to sing it. They joined him; and by the time they got to the refrain the crowd was a choir, singing in parts, with even a couple of bassos coming in with "home, home, home."

When it was done, they laughed and applauded him and he applauded them and said: "You sopranos especially—that were mighty sweet. But look: I don't know about you folks but me—I really been tramping! Not so much in trying to make heaven my home—my head might be gray but I'm only fifty-three and I aint *thinking* about moving nowheres yet. No, I been trying to help save them boys from being lynched. That's right, Sister Jackson and me been tramping all over this Hollow getting signatures for to be sent to the Supreme Court and I think I see some folks here in this congregation what signed. All right, but first I got to say something to them and the rest of you-all can listen till I get around to you.

"Maybe you're figuring: well, I signed and I gave a quarter too and that's enough. Enough! But what if *you* was one a them boys—would you be saying it were enough? But I were as bad as you and I said I done enough when I collected a few names and when you say you done enough already I know *just* what you mean. You really mean *it aint no use to do any more.* That's what you mean and don't come telling me no different! But let me tell you what I know: when you aint doing nothing you can't help feeling them boys got to die sure enough, but once you really start to doing something you get to feeling them boys *can't die.* And then the more you do and the more people you talk to and the more papers you get signed and the more money you collect, well then you know for a fact that the Scottsboro boys *aint going to die!*"

The rest was easy, and he always said later that his first speech was the best one.

After that he was speaking every night, at street-corners, at lodge meetings and union meetings and churches. Soon he was going on speaking trips out of town to the mining camps and company steel towns. He had but one subject: Scottsboro. And one day when someone remembered to bring along an application blank he signed it and became a member of the Communist Party.

Since then, of course, he had spoken on many topics and he told them now that if he could have kept on speaking for another six months in the campaign to get Negro teachers into the Iron City schools, "Well, Paul, your Charlene would be teaching here same as she did up in Cleveland. If only I was out there talking. . . ."

"You're doing plenty of talking in here," Zach said.

"That's just where you're wrong. I *were* talking but now I'm through. Anyway, that's the story of how they roped me in."

"Who did that, Brother Henry? You mean the Party?"

Faulcon looked at him hard: "Zach, I swear, you're getting to be bad as Paul. I'm not talking about no Party. I'm talking about them Alabama lynchers—*they* roped me in!"

CHAPTER 8

Dan Rooney told them he did not like the way they had been marching lately; he was sure he had never seen such a lousy performance of Organized Activity as yesterday.

"Looks like we might be getting into the war one of these days and maybe Uncle Sam might use some of you jailbirds when you get out, though I doubt it. But if you do get drafted, well, by God, you'll have to drill then! So you might just as well start now."

The men from Cell Block One were backed against the wall and the guard stood some twenty paces away, facing them and stiffly at attention the way he thought a general would stand when addressing his troops. That *they* should be at attention and *he* should be at ease instead of the other way around was something he had not yet learned.

"Today we're going to do it different. I'm going to divide you into squads and I want a space of ten paces between each squad. Ten paces, like this—" He walked forward, knees rigid, counting out each stride up to ten. "See? OK. Now Range A will be Squad A, and Range B will be Squad B, and Range C will be Squad C—get it? And here's something else: If I see any squad just fooling around and walking instead of marching, well, anybody from that range who comes out tomorrow won't have to march—they'll have to *run!* All right Range A— I mean *Squad* A—get in line two by two."

After he had finished arranging the white men from A and B, he turned to the Negroes who had been snickering at some secret joke. The peak of his baseball cap lifted in surprise when he saw Lonnie James.

"Not practicing today?"

Lonnie shrugged, the movement showing a strip of dark skin under the too-short sweater.

"Well, OK," Rooney said. "Only you got to be Squad C all by yourself since you're the only one out from C. That means you got to march by yourself."

"And what if I don't want to?"

But it was the guard's turn not to answer and he moved over to line up D and E. Then he marched out to his original commanding position and came to attention again.

"All right, march," he ordered. "Get moving!"

Before they had gone the length of the yard, Squad C turned around and walked back to join Harper and Zachary, who, because they were the tallest men from D, had been placed at the head of that contingent.

"Where's Pops today," he said, slapping Paul's shoulder.

"Pops?" Then Paul grinned. "Good thing he can't hear you say that. Faulcon's hot enough already cause Rooney put him back with the short men. But look, aint you going to get in trouble—coming back here I mean?"

"Trouble? Boy, you're talking just like Booboo the fool. I told you last time I aint stud'n bout Rooney." Lonnie frowned and pounded a fist into his other palm as though he held a baseball. "I'll tell you how that is. Now if I had said right out I wasn't going to march by myself, well he would have *had* to send me in. But now he can make out like he don't see me and he won't say nothing. It took me and Rooney a long time to understand one another but now we do. Even so, I might have given him some more lip back there but I been waiting to see you guys for a week. Fact is, you should have been out yesterday."

Paul said that that was right: the rangeman got beat up a week ago last Thursday and the seven days' restriction was over yesterday, Friday; but nobody came to let Range D out to the yard and none of them knew why.

Lonnie sniffed loudly. "Suckers, that's what you are. Probably on account of Steve being so busy all the time he just forgot about it. You-all should have raised hell. Like me when I was in the Hole. Every time my ten days was up I started hollering and banging on the door so's they'd know damn well *I* knew the time was up. Otherwise, maybe, a man could be in there two weeks. But you'll learn—least you'd better learn."

Paul wondered whether he should tell this new acquaintance that it was not because he and the other two Communists were lacking in militancy but that they were being extra careful because of the pending court decision on bail and that twenty-three others were involved. But before he could decide, Zach said *shh!* They followed his pointing finger till they saw it too.

It was a sparrow, bouncing along in front of them in the space where the one-man Squad C should have been. After each leap, the little brown bird turned a frantic eye behind and then, seeing them still moving relentlessly upon it, leaped desperately ahead again. Finally, remembering its wings, the sparrow took flight and their eyes pursued it till it was over the wall and gone.

Paul and Zach kept their gaze uplifted until Lonnie's laugh brought them back.

"Uh uh," he said. "That's another thing you better learn. Forget about out there. Make believe that part aint real—only this." He waved his arm to take in the walled enclosure and the two projecting structures of the jail. "In *here*. That's where you are till they turn you loose."

They made no comment to that, and they had circled the yard five more times before Lonnie broke the silence.

"Maybe it was a sign!" He clapped his hands together at the thought. "The sparrow," he said, seeing their bewilderment, "the sparrow! Right where I was before." He pointed to the open space ahead of them. "The same spot!" His eyes were large and bright with his sudden excitement.

When neither of them replied, he dropped his arm; and when he spoke again his voice had fallen too.

"Guess you-all don't believe in signs," he said.

Paul would not say no, so he kept silent; and Zach merely sighed and nodded his head gravely as though he were considering the matter.

"Well, I didn't use to either," Lonnie said. "But now I got to. A man in my fix has got to believe in *everything*. That's what I been trying to tell that crazy old Peterson on my range. Hell, I keep telling him he aint even been tried yet, much less sentenced, and that he's white and maybe they'll give him a break and that him being crazy might help too. But he just don't seem to understand that if you don't believe— well, you're dead before they. . . ." He shook his head. "Not me!" And then as though they had not heard he repeated it: "*Not me!*"

Lonnie clapped his hand to his chest and then reached down under his sweater and brought out an envelope which he handed to Paul.

"The clippings. Now you-all can read about me. And for Christ's sake don't *lose* them whatever you do."

Paul said oh no, they certainly would not lose them.

"I would have sent them down to your range after the key-man told me about D getting restricted, but that bastard wouldn't trust me in front for the nickel he charges, so I had to wait till you guys got out. You see, I won't get my next money until Tuesday."

He went on to explain how, after his trial and sentence— he still had not told them what the sentence was—the jail chaplain had brought a colored minister to see him. Reverend Digby had insisted that all he could offer was spiritual con-solation, but finally Lonnie had convinced him that if he could not help in other ways it would be good if the preacher helped him to reach out to others. Postage money would be a great consolation to a man with such a tough sentence; and tobacco money too.

Reverend Digby, a plump man of middle age, had explained that his church was small and quite poor. They certainly could not send him money for cigarettes or anything else wicked like that, but he thought they might supply him with stamp money. He would ask the deacon board about that. "But my son," he added, "you can't reach your Maker by writing letters. So let us pray: O Heavenly Father, remember Thy only begotten Son who forgave the Good Thief nailed up alongside Him at Calvary, and look down upon Your sinful servant, and soften his heart. . . ."

"I'd have softened his fat *behind* with my foot," Lonnie told

99

them, "excepting for the promise. Good thing too I didn't."

The deacon board had acted favorably and since then Lonnie had received a dollar in every other Tuesday's mail.

"Sometimes I cheat on them people when I get real hard up for a smoke, but mostly I use it all up in writing."

Zach spoke then for the first time. "Brother James, who you been writing to?"

Lonnie lit the cigarette Paul gave him, inhaled deeply and let the smoke curl slowly out of his flaring nostrils. He smiled his thanks to Paul and then looked over to Zach. Lonnie noticed again the solemn bearing of the big man, the stern unsmiling face, the slow dignity of his speech.

"Preacher-man," he said, "I been writing to everybody. The President and Mrs. too. And the governor and the mayor of Kanesport. And my high-school principal over in Ohio. I've written to the N.A.A.C.P., the Y.M.C.A., the Urban League, the C.I.O. and everybody else including Father Divine in New York. Oh, there's lots I can tell you if you really want to know but first you ought to read those clippings."

"Soon as we get in," Zach said. "But look, son, don't come calling me no preacher. I aint one and besides"—he seemed near to smiling—"you might start kicking *my* behind—and you might break your foot."

"OK, Mr. Zach. I sure don't want to be breaking anything now with ball-playing coming soon. Say!—" Lonnie jabbed Paul with his elbow, "that guy Army in the Hole—maybe they'll make him do time here. And if he is half the catcher he claims to be, well, we got us an all-star battery!"

"How come?" Paul said. "Who's the star pitcher?"

Lonnie faked a punch at him. "Man, you really don't know *nothing* about me, do you?"

(2)

It was nothing yet everything about Lonnie: NEGRO TO HANG. The two-paragraph story under that heading was from the Iron City *American* of October 13, 1940. The other two clippings, of earlier dates, had given the public the facts.

100

From the Iron City *American*, May 22, 1940

NEGRO ADMITS MURDER GUILT

KANESPORT, May 21.— Police Commissioner James J. Toomey announced today that a Negro had admitted his guilt in the slaying last month of Waldo Thornhill, a local businessman.

In a statement signed here this morning, the burly suspect, Lonnie James, alias Slim James, age 23, confessed that he fired the fatal shot while attempting to rob the victim's drugstore on Cottage Ave.

After his capture, James, a former laborer in the Tin Plate mill, led police to his room in the Goat Hill section where the murder weapon was hidden.

Commissioner Toomey, who expressed his gratitude to the County Police for their help in solving the crime, said the Negro is being held in the County Jail at Iron City.

From the Kanesport *Morning Eagle*, October 7, 1940

FIND NEGRO GUILTY IN LOCAL SLAYING

IRON CITY, Oct. 6—Lonnie James, 23, a Kanesport Negro, was found guilty today of the fatal shooting of Waldo Thornhill, white, also of that city.

A verdict of murder in the first degree was returned by the jury of seven women and five men after two hours' deliberation.

The trial which began this morning in Criminal Court at the Cathedral of Justice was marked by clashes between the defendant and Clement B. Coxe, one of his two court-appointed attorneys.

James, who repudiated his previous confession and pleaded "not guilty," interrupted the proceedings several times by angry outbursts. On each occasion he was admonished by Judge Hanford J. Rupp, visiting judge from Meade County, and when the Negro insisted upon speaking to the jury after closing arguments had been made by his counsel and Prosecutor Stewart McKee, the Court called upon the marshals to restrain him.

Following the verdict, Judge Rupp, who has been called in to help clear the crowded docket, thanked the jurors and ordered the convicted killer remanded to the County Jail to await sentencing next Monday.

Court attaches pointed out that while the death penalty is not mandatory, it is usual in such cases. Defense counsel indicated that an appeal would be filed.

———

The family of the late Mr. Thornhill refused to comment on the verdict, but public sentiment locally expressed satisfaction with the trial outcome.

Herbert T. Wills, Negro, industrial secretary of the Kanesport branch of the Negro Improvement League and Goat

101

Hill civic leader, visited our offices this afternoon and requested that the following statement be published:

"I am grateful to the Editor and Publisher of the MORNING EAGLE for the opportunity to make a public statement in behalf of the law-abiding colored citizens of Kanesport.

"We are happy that the fiendish killer of Mr. Thornhill has been convicted and hope that he will be given the supreme penalty under the laws of this great Commonwealth.

"By his dastardly crime Lonnie James brought disgrace and shame upon all law-abiding colored citizens, but we are co-operating with the Police in every way possible to control the dangerous element in our group who have come here from other cities.

"The law-abiding colored citizens are doing everything we can to uphold all the laws and preserve our democracy, Free Enterprise and Defense Program and we want all our friends of the majority group to know that we consider Lonnie James a traitor to our race and we respectfully hope and ask that the fine spirit of toleration and good will that have always been so outstanding in Kanesport race relations will continue."

Paul carefully folded the two clippings and put them back in the envelope with the first one he had read, "Negro To Hang." His eyes lifted to the ceiling of his cell: Lonnie was up there, directly overhead. "You ought to be glad I'm not on C. . . . Murderers' Row," he had told Charlene. He thought of that now. Here I'm in D 10 and he's in C 10. Same judge, same jail, same block—nearly the same age. Paul tried not to feel glad that the tall young Negro up there was not he, but the feeling would not stay down. *I got ten years to pull and even if they make me do it all, I'll only be thirty-seven. I'll still be alive.* . . . The envelope crackled in his clenched hand; he looked down at it and frowned. *Happy—* that is what the Kanesport Negro leader had written to the paper! Paul's feeling of his good fortune was lost now in the burst of anger that swelled within him.

Now, a cotton-mouth snake will bite you till you're dead,
Cotton-mouth snake will bite you till you're dead,
But just don't turn your back on a lowdown handkerchief head.

That's one of them all right—Herbert T. Wills of the Negro Improvement League. Talking about somebody else being a traitor to the race—you no-good back-stabbing Uncle Tom!

102

Faulcon was wiping off the bars and crosspieces in front of his cell when Paul came to give him the clippings.

"Saturday," the old man explained. "Mrs. Jenny Faulcon's son Henry is still cleaning house on Saturday. But let me show you something I found—look here." His stubby finger pointed to a place on one of the flat crossbars.

Paul looked closely at the curious ridges on the gray paint and finally he made out what it was: raised letters cast on the steel beneath.

"McGregor Steel," he said.

"Aint that a bitch," said Faulcon. "Half the guys in here, including me and Zach, have made McGregor steel. That's a fact, we made this here jail for them to put us in." He shook his head at the wonder of it. "We sure did."

"Yeah," Paul said. "And to put *me* in. But look, where's Zach?"

The round shoulders heaved in a shrug. "Don't know. Probably down the line somewheres listening to some guy tell him his troubles. Beats me the way everybody tells him their business. Maybe it's cause Zach acts so much like some old country preacher."

"I don't know about that, Henry," Paul said with a smile. "Maybe they'd tell you something if you ever stopped talking long enough to listen."

Faulcon tried his best to look hurt. "Now, son, you know that aint right. Why just this morning I were listening to a guy down in Number 17 where we was playing checkers and he was giving me a brand new theory about race. You ever see those books where some Negro is proving that half of the great men that ever lived—King Solomon and all the rest— were Negroes? Well that guy in 17 goes him one better. According to him, *everybody* is really a Negro. That's right, says it were like that in the beginning but then some of the tribes wandered off from Africa and their skins got faded from black to brown to light brown to yellow to white. They kind of went to seed, see, especially the real white ones—just aint got the blood and strength that we got. Us hundred per cent Negroes, I mean."

103

Paul sniffed. "Don't tell me you believe that stuff?"

"Who said anything about me believing one way or the other? I were telling what *he* said. Still, I kind of like that idea—everybody being a Negro only we are the best ones. Aint *that* something! Why, do you know what that means? We should be up there on A and B ranges and *they* should be down here on D and E. And let me tell you something: E is worse than here and not only cause they get the last in the slop-can. It's cold down there and damp all the time on account of them big old ventilators blowing in on them. I ought to go get the warden right now to put us up where we belong!"

"Yeah," said Paul, "and what if we were up there? Come out here and let me show *you* something."

When Faulcon had followed him out to the runway bars, Paul pointed up and across to the top tiers on Cell Block Two.

"Maybe you're getting so old you can't see so good any more," he said, "but those sure look like bars up there to me. Meaning we'd still be in jail just the same, just like the white workers in the mill are still exploited even if they do get a better break than we do. And furthermore—" He stopped, noticing that Faulcon, while pretending to look up, was peering at him from the corner of his eye. He pushed the other away. "Old man, you ought to quit that jiving all the time. Damn near had me giving you a lecture that you know better than me! And making me almost forget about giving you these clippings about Lonnie. Here—and be careful with them. You can read them tonight and let Zach have them tomorrow and then we can talk about it after we have our current events meeting. Which reminds me—I'd better go into my place now and look over the papers, seeing as it's my turn to lead the discussion."

Faulcon put the clippings into his shirt pocket and told Paul that he'd better start cleaning up his cell for Sunday inspection.

"I know," said Paul. "But I'm going to do that after lock-up—on company time, not mine."

104

(3)

Dear Annie Mae:
I am well and so are we all. Mr. Harper and Mr. Faulcon
are in the same part of this place with me and that is good.
I am sorry that the white Comrades got put in another part
and we cannot see them even in the Yard. Your letter came
today and that was very nice too and I was happy to hear
that Mrs. Logan have said you could be off Wed. morning
instead of the way it was before so you can make a visit. Now
listen Annie Mae I am surprize that you are worried about me
being in this place with a lot of bad men the way you said.
Because that is not right at all. There are some very good
People in here as well as the other kind and even the ones
that are bad are

Zach sighed and looked up from the ruled sheet. From high
up on the wall across from Range D the radio was roaring the
Hut Sut song for the third time that night; but he did not hear
it. Even in jail where there was little else but time Isaac
Zachary had no time for foolishment. He stared at his pencil
and then back to the letter he was writing: ". . . and even the
ones that are bad are—" What?

Not really bad? No that is not what he wanted to say. He
could not mean that, for in these first ten days in jail he had
learned that a man can become so bad that even while he is
talking to you your mind cannot accept the fact that he is a
fellow man, cannot believe that anything human is left in the
rottenness. This knowledge had come to Zach with an overwhelming shock: there seemed to be nothing in all his experience with which he could relate the incredible things he
had learned.

He thought now of the one called Tuxedo. Just today, before
lock-up, Zach had sat in the man's cell and heard his story.
Many of the words were hard to understand and his ideas were
even more confusing. If ever a man was low-down bad this
one was, and yet he had talked of what he had done with no
sign of shame, with no thought that Zach would consider him

105

less than other men. Perhaps that was the most puzzling thing about it: Can a man be so completely evil and not know it at all?

Tuxedo did not look evil. He was a handsome man of middle age, and his large brown eyes reflected the warm good humor that seemed to be a part of him. His face was smooth and unmarked except for a small upcurving scar at one corner of his mouth that accented his habitual smile. His low-pitched voice was strangely gentle and pleasant even when his words were most foul and bitter. He had exchanged how-de-do's with Zach each day but they had never talked together until today.

Tuxedo had begun by asking Zach why he was in, but more because it was the custom rather than from any real interest. And Zach had not said much before Tuxedo waved him silent and said: "Politics, sure, sure. I know. Well, anyway, you won't be in for long. That stuff don't mean a thing. Me—I only got five more months to pull before I hit the street. But come on in and set down awhile and we can talk."

Zach followed him in and was pleased to see that the cell was as spotless as his own: the washbowl and toilet were gleaming white, the concrete floor freshly scoured.

"Ready for Sunday inspection I see," Zach said, seating himself on the bunk.

"Oh, I aint studying none about that," the other replied. "By rights a man ought to keep his own place clean all the time."

Zach had agreed with that; and afterward he would always marvel that the man could say such a thing.

"Yes, sir," said Tuxedo, as he settled down beside his guest, "five more months and I'll be right back out, and right back to that sweet little woman. You got an old lady?"

Zach nodded, half-smiling at the thought that the expression could refer to Annie Mae: "Mrs. Zachary and I been married going on twenty-two years."

"That's fine. Man, that's really mellow. Here—" With a sudden motion Tuxedo pulled out his wallet, flipped it open and handed it to the other. "That's her," he said, and there was no missing the pride he felt.

Zach nodded his appreciation, though he could but dimly make out the photograph under the yellowing plastic panel.

You might say I was guilty all right, Tuxedo began, and naturally I copped a guilty plea in court. Sure. But I was framed just the same and that's the onliest part that really hurt me. Hurt me *bad*, worse than the working-over they gave me. You can't hurt a man but so much no matter how much you beat him. But something like this—well that's different. Last summer it was, long about August, and everything was really all right. Sure. Defense has got the mills going full swing and down on 17th and Rambeau it's three shifts too. Lots of new studs flocking into town and the place is really jumping. Law can't see a thing—everything's *straight*, know what I mean?, everybody getting theirs and the suckers can't wait. Things never was so good. So there I was on the corner that evening, waiting to catch the 11 to 7 shift coming off. Payday, too, it was. And man you should have seen me—stacked to the bricks! I got me some hard-cutting drapes, thirty dollar shoes, a red ruby ring big as a stoplight and my time is strictly Lord Elgin. Really straight, see, and my ass-pocket is loaded down with nothing but twenties. Bet I must have had close to $300. Anyway, here comes this gray tipping up on me and he wants to know where he can get him some trim. He's a big old guy, red face, beer belly, panama hat and smelling like the House of Seagram's. Seems like he's an all-right sport so I carry him on up to my place. Sure. And while I'm waiting, I goes on into the kitchen for a shot of java. Then after a while I hear them arguing about something inside and then Marie starts to screaming and I run into the bedroom and here's this big old gray slapping her around. She aint really hurt none except for a bloody nose, but she's yelling like somebody's killing her. Shut up, I tell her, and then I say to this guy: Now look, why can't you act like a gentleman and get your clothes on and go on home like a sport and go to bed? I talk to him nice, just like that, but no—he don't want to do right. Says he's going to sleep right here. Well, that wouldn't have been so forty any time, but on payday night—. I'll be damned if you're going to sleep *here*, I tell him, cause that is my bed and that is my wife and now you get the hell on out of here and go on back where you belong—by rights you aint got no business being in this part of town in the first place. So there was a big argument but I finally cuffed him a couple of times and got him out without much trouble. I was glad about that cause the laws don't want that kind of stuff, especially with a white man. You know *that*. Only I was wrong this time cause he's one of the laws himself. Sure, a dick. Well along about five in the bright and I had forgotten all about this guy and I'm just climbing into bed myself when bam!—him and three more dicks come busting in and they got me. First he claims that I rolled him, says I took ten bucks from his pants whilst he was laying up in bed with my old lady. All right. Naturally they banged me around pretty bad down to the Precinct and naturally they took all my dough, and my ring and my watch too. Sure. But then what did they do? I figured at most it would be a disorderly conduct maybe, and maybe a fifty fine or a nine-o in here. But no, them rotten sons of bitches made the rap felonious assault and I better not squawk about my roll or it's going to be armed robbery. Judge gives me a year and it just goes to show you how dirty some people can be. But don't you be feeling sorry for old Tux. I'll be back on top and me and Marie will start all over. You'll see—I'll have me some sharp threads again and a Elgin watch and a ruby ring and plenty of scratch in this here wallet too. . . .

He reopened the billfold to gaze at the picture, the scar on his cheek curving high with the smile. "Best old lady I ever had," he said. "Fine as wine, Jack—really fine!"

Zach picked up his pencil again. He knew he could never find the words to tell what he meant, not even to Annie Mae. So now he finished the sentence by saying: *"and even the bad ones are no trouble to me so don't you be thinking nothing like that."*

108

*It will be good to have you visit me and when you come be
sure to come early because sometimes it gets crowded with all
the folks who want to see their People in here. Now I will close
and God be with us while we are absent one from the other.*

Your loving Husband,

Isaac.

Annie Mae would come early next Wednesday; he knew
that. But he could not know, of course, that he would miss
her visit.

CHAPTER 9

Sunday is worst. Faith may be pumped
from the little chapel organ and be lifted on hymnal wings to
the soaring dome, but Hope, like Chief Guard Steve, has the
day off. (Charity, of course, is admitted to Bum Side only,
and there only in bitter weather.) A man might not receive a
letter on any other day, but on Sunday he knows he will not.
A man might not be called to trial on any other day; on this
day there is no reason even to wait at the gate.

In the annex to the Cathedral of Justice, Sunday is a day for
communion and a day for penance; a time for soul-searching
and a time for cell-searching. Holy Mass is celebrated at 6:00
A.M. and Interdenominational Chapel is held at 10:00. Few
of God's children on the bottom ranges go to mass—for one
thing, they are not used to celebrating anything so early in
the morning—but they are grateful for the extra hour of morning sleep: because of mass, the first bell does not call until
seven. There are some, more impious than the sleepers,
perhaps, or more worldly or more gluttonous, who mumble
against mass, saying: How come some folks got to wait a
whole extra hour for coffee just cause some other folks get
religion early in the morning?; but these bigots are few in

number and they better not mumble too loud lest, waking their sleeping brethren, there be some *hell* raised in here this morning!

The two lower ranges are closer to Chapel: these all-Negro tiers are located below the level of the Hub and it is in the open space beneath the Hub that the Interdenominationalists congregate on folding chairs. Despite this proximity, however, not many of the Negro inmates attend.

Chaplain H. C. Jerricote is nice enough, they say. He is very young, very earnest and he greets each man with a rosy-cheeked smile and a hearty handshake. There is nothing holier-than-thou about him: he sincerely believes that though their sins be as scarlet they might be washed white as snow. And though he does not say so, it is plain that he holds out the same hope for the colored worshipers in the rear row. Nor is he an old fogey: once each week he distributes to each range mimeographed sheets that list the Bible Quiz of the Week. "How many plagues did God send upon the Egyptians? Who was punished by being made to eat grass like the oxen? What did the Handwriting on the Wall say?" After each query was given the book of the Bible where the answer could be found, and all inmates were cordially invited to the Tuesday night prayer-meeting where the Quiz Contest would be held and where all might volunteer for one of the teams. In his Sunday sermons the young minister used man-to-man words whenever he could. Thus when he told how Noah drank overmuch of the wine from his vineyard, Reverend Jerricote used the terms "Home-brew" and "pie-eyed."

But still there was something lacking for the A.M.E.'s and the A.M.E.Z.'s and the Baptists and Church of God followers among the Negro inmates. "His name might be Jericho, but there aint no Jericho in him when it comes to preaching. Sure aint." The hymns too were lacking in juice and when it came to beating something out of the tiny carpet-pedaled organ that was rolled out for Chapel—well, Reverend Jericho was strictly a square from nowhere. I mean *nowhere,* Jack!

Inmates who do not attend are locked in their cells while the services are being held, but there is nothing punitive about that rule. Quiet is ensured by not permitting the stay-at-homes to gather upon the runways and there is another good reason: modesty. From time to time choirs come to sing at chapel and frequently among the singers there are ladies. There being no regulations as to what, if anything, an inmate must wear on the ranges, and since the ranges are visible from the Hub, the possibility of scandal is avoided by the lock-up rule.

Henry Faulcon was one of the few men from D who went to Chapel.

"First place," he explained, "I always were a churchman like I told you. Second place, I do not like to be locked in and can't talk to nobody. But the real reason is the singing. Even bad singing is better than no singing and far as I'm concerned if you don't count the slop and being locked up and them no-sleeping bunks—well, not being allowed to sing is the hardest part about being in jail."

"Maybe so," Paul Harper said. "But I can stay right up here and enjoy myself just as good, even read in peace if you-all don't sing too loud. Funny thing, though. I always thought that singing was one thing you could do in jail if nothing else."

"Son, you been seeing too many movies, that's what. Every time they show a prison here's a whole gang of Negroes, faces all black and shiny and sad, and what are they doing? —*singing*. That's right, singing spirituals all day long and when they aint a-moaning and a-humming they're a-praying! Shucks, talking about 'couldn't hear nobody pray'—well, whoever wrote them words must have been in jail cause what I hear around here sure aint nothing like prayer."

The bell for Chapel rang then and Faulcon hurried toward the gate.

"We'll be listening for your lead tenor," Paul called after him.

> *The God who made both heaven and earth*
> *And all that they contain*
> *Will never quit His steadfast truth*
> *Nor make His promise vain.*

The poor and all oppressed by wrong
Are saved by His decree;
He gives the hungry needful food
And sets the captive free.

When Faulcon returned to Range D from Chapel that day, he found the others still locked in. The guard was late in coming to throw the master lever outside the gate. The old man's cell was locked too and he regretted not having the chance to go in for his usual midmorning nap. Not that he gave any sign of his discomfiture, for here, surely, was a situation to be made the most of. He pretended not to notice Paul or Zach or to hear their welcoming words. He began to pace energetically in front of their cells, swinging his arms about freely and all the while talking loudly to himself.

"Man, oh man! It sure do feel good out *here*. First, all that *fine* singing and now all this *fine* freedom. Mmmmmmmm *mmmmmmmh!* Sure would hate to be locked in and all cooped up in some little old cell on such a lovely Sunday morning. That would make me feel awful bad, it really would. And I *got* to feel sorry for anybody who can't come out. Why look up there—just look at all that wonderful sunshine coming in at the top! And the air—just smell this air out here! I swear it smells like the first day of spring. Say—" his voice dropped to a loud whisper—"did you hear what they said? About them sinners who don't go to church going to be locked in all day Sundays starting *today!* Oh la lalee, oh la lalee and sets the captive free."

The loud *whack* that came when Paul snapped shut his big book stopped him.

"Henry," Paul said. "How come you don't cut out all that signifying? I'll bet those bad feet are killing you right now and you can't even get in to lay down. Talking about something feeling good: how come it is that these bunks are hard as steel at night and a man can hardly sleep but come daytime they feel *so* soft? *Ah!* Sure glad I'm in here and at least got a place to rest my bones and not be locked out like some people are."

112

There was no pretense in Faulcon's weary sigh. He eased himself down to the concrete floor and rested his back on the outside bars. He was facing his cell and from that position he could see both of his friends.

"You aint lying, Paul," he said. "And you Zach—supposed to be such a good Christian and not a hypocrite like you call me—you ought to quit grinning at me that way. If there's one thing that's mean it's for somebody to be laughing at somebody that's down. And that's what I am—*down*. Bet I didn't get more than two hours sleep last night and now these people got me cut off from my bed. What won't they do to Henry Faulcon next—locking me *out* of jail now! And that singing. . . ." The gray head shook weakly. "That singing, it really gets me down. These people sing the way they walk around the yard—a-slouching and a-slumping and nobody in step at all! And then I'm thinking about dinner. OK, they give you a solid piece of meat on Sundays and what is it all the time—*sheep* liver. Gentlemen, I swear, these capitalists will do anything to a man. Furthermore, they aint got no gratitude at all. Just look at me: a man that worked hard all his life and what were I doing for forty-seven years? *I'll* tell you. Ten years I helped fix food and for the rest of the time I served food and to who? That's right, the capitalists! Delmonico steaks this thick, and filet mignons and porterhouse steaks and breast of pheasant and baked squab and baby roast pig—oh, it hurts me just to think of all that fine food I served them. I know all them people from the McGregors on down and if I was to tell you all I know about them—why you'd be shamed. Fact is, when I read in the Communist Manifesto where Marx says their greatest sport is messing with each other's wives—well, right there and then I figured he really knew what he were talking about, no fooling! Anyway, to get back to my point, after I do all that for them, what do they do to me? I'm not talking about putting me in jail cause that's how the class struggle goes and it's been going like that all through history. Aint that right, Zach? They throwed Joseph into jail and Samson into jail and the Apostle Paul too and when all the jails got filled up the only thing they could do was throw 'em to the lions. All right, so I'm not talking about that. I'm talking about what they give *me*—sheep liver! And I'd talk about them other meals too but *nobody* knows what's in that stew."

"Poor old Henry," said Zach, who was still smiling, "you just aint living right."

Faulcon looked up. "Isaac Zachary," he said, "that's just what Lucy Jackson used to tell me all the time, but when you say it now, it's the truth. Lord knows it's the solid truth."

Like a small boy's stick against a picket fence, the clicking sound ran down the row of cells as the lever was pulled and each lock was opened. Faulcon heaved himself up and went into Number 10 to give Paul the note from Lonnie James.

"Slipped it to me at chapel, said to give it to you. Say, that boy can really sing—you know that? Why he's almost as good as me and—"

But Paul was not listening; his long dark fingers were carefully unrolling the tiny ball of toilet paper, then smoothing it against the cover of *Les Miserables.*

SEE ME ON SICK CALL TOMORROW. 8 A.M. SHARP. BRING CLIPPINGS.

"Sure wish we could do something for Lonnie," said Faulcon when he too had read it. "Last night I was reading what the papers had about him and—what do you think, Paul? What can we do?"

Paul did not answer right away. First he tore up the note and flushed it down his toilet. Then he turned around sharply and his face had a hard and angry look.

"Goddamit, Henry, you talk like a fool! What the hell can we do about anything in here? Nothing, that's what, and you know that good as me."

The old man sat down and began to turn the pages of Paul's book. "Can I have this next?" he said softly.

"Sure," said Paul, looking down at him. The anger was gone as quickly as it had flared.

114

"You're going to see him tomorrow anyway?"

Paul nodded slowly and smiled. "You know that too," he said.

(2)

Cell search comes after Sunday dinner. At the sound of the bell each inmate enters his cell and locks himself in to await the coming of the guards. Nothing will happen to him; he is sure of it. He has nothing to hide; he knows that. In the hours that pass he will tell himself again and again: What do I care? Let them look—there's nothing in here. But why do his eyes keep returning to the cigar box on the shelf until he must jump up from his bunk and look again at the things he knows are there. A couple of letters, a pencil, a toothbrush —nothing wrong about that. And why do his hands continue their restless search, patting his pockets from the outside, slipping in again to make sure? Foolish, of course, and he knows that too. They can always find something if they really want to—a deck of cards, a pair of dice, or even a Jim Kelly, as the inmates call a pocketknife in memory of the old guard, long gone to his reward, who never got through a Sunday search without finding his pearl-handled jackknife in some man's cell. No, it is not that—not the chance of a petty frame-up with maybe a week in the Hole.

But the man is afraid. *The searchers are coming and there is something here that must be hidden.* A sudden panic flares within him at the clash of the key in the range end gate. They are coming! One by one each cell in turn is entered and the murmur of voices draws nearer to where he is trapped. Now his eyes are desperate in their darting search . . . only a moment is left to conceal that which must be kept from them. Now they are crowding into this place that has become a part of the man, and now he stands before them—naked, defenseless, alone.

They find nothing. The secret self of a man, elusive even to love, is forever locked against the men with the keys. Only for the truly damned is there no hiding place.

The three guards who came through Range D that Sunday afternoon were in an amiable mood; and Pee Wee, the new rangeman, who trotted behind them with his clipboard roster, was grinning widely at their high good humor. Their searching this time was little more than a glance within each cell and a snatching off of a few blankets: the only thing they seemed to be looking for was an answering smile to their friendly joshing. They asked Slim where he was hiding that great big ol' razzah, and of Willie, naked except for his socks, they observed that by George this boy could really give some high yallah a good time—now, couldn't he, Pee Wee? One of them asked Paul Harper, with a wink, if the volume by Hugo had some good hot spots in it, and somehow Faulcon reminded another about the one they tell about the old darky preacher and this time he had Mandy up in the hayloft, catch on?, and. . . .

They were still laughing at that when they entered Isaac Zachary's cell.

Zach stood up quickly and turned to unroll his blanket for them, but the one who had told the joke said, "Nah, don't bother with that—guess there aint nothing in there but your smell." He was about to leave when his eye caught the strange markings on the prisoner's back. He whistled sharply through his teeth, then motioned for the other two searchers to come in. "Jesus Christ, look at that!" he said, pointing.

The big man did not turn to face them; now he leaned over the bunk to roll up the ragged covering. They could all see it now—the spatter of scars that streaked like a comet's tail across the dark expanse of his skin.

"Looks like he zigged when he should have zagged."

"Bird-shot, eh?"

"Bird-shot nothing! Wouldn't make holes like that. Looks more like buckshot to me."

"Bet he didn't come back so quick to *that* henhouse. I bet you that."

Zach still had not turned around to smile at their attentions.

"Hey you," said the guard who had come in first.

The broad back seemed to stiffen slightly, but Zach continued with his bed.

"I'm talking to you, nigger—hey!" He nudged the prisoner with his toe.

Zach turned so quickly they barely caught the motion. Facing them now, his eyes were narrow slits, his features drawn tightly immobile except for the quivering nostrils.

"*Don't do that!*" He let his breath out slowly. He had not spoken loudly and when he spoke again his voice was strangely calm. "I don't want no trouble with you-all. No trouble." He shook his head. "But just don't touch me, that's all. Just don't touch me."

They had drawn back a step at his sudden movement, and now they faced him in silence. The silence filled the tiny place and flowed out through the bars and down the length of the range, flooding the other cells so that even the prisoners who had not heard were engulfed in the surging stillness. Pee Wee stood rigid outside Zach's cell, his grin now a grotesque mask of panic. No man can measure such a moment, for time itself is caught and held in the trap which grips them all.

The guards continued to stare at the man in the cell, blinking against the hatred and fear that seemed to blind them. Abruptly, as though obeying a secret command, they backed out into the runway and one of them motioned to Zach to come out. He hesitated for a second, then strode forward.

"All right," he said quietly. "But just don't touch me!" Then he followed behind as they hurried toward the front gate.

There had been no sound of their going, for Zach's feet were bare and the guards wore rubber soles; and Faulcon and Paul could not be sure that he had been taken away until their cells were opened and they went into Number 8 to find it empty. Only his clothes were there and the letter, propped on his shelf, addressed to Mrs. Annie Mae Zachary.

"Better take his things so they won't get stole." It was Slim, the warden's janitor, and he drew Paul aside to whisper: "You can give me that letter. He aint allowed mail privilege now, but I'll see it gets out."

When Paul gave him the envelope, Slim licked the flap and closed it; and that was strange too, for only the Chief Guard was permitted to seal out-going mail.

The events of the day had left no room for the current events discussion they had planned; too much happening right in here that we got to talk about.

"No, I'm not mad at Zach. Of course, the decision was that we be especially careful to keep out of trouble while the bail question was still up, and I was kind of sorry when it happened that one of us three was the first to mess up. But I guess it had to be one of us instead of the white comrades. A man can't take but so much—and they put so damn much on us." Paul glanced at his friend and a smile broke through the worried look on his lean dark face. "To tell you the truth, Henry, I thought sure it was going to be you. When they were in your cell and telling that joke about the darky preacher, I said to myself: Here it comes—and there goes old Henry to the Hole."

Faulcon chuckled. "Uh uh," he said. "You're forgetting about that old-time song about how 'De ol' sheep, dey know de road—Young lambs must find de way.' Shucks, if you had waited on as many white folks as I did in my days, you'd a heard so much of that stuff you'd never pay it no mind. Oh, I admit there was times when I took exception and mixed a little dirt or maybe a little spit into their soup—not being so politically developed as now—but other than that. . . ."

They looked up to see Slim standing in the door. "Five more minutes," he called and then he was gone before they had a chance to thank him. They jumped up and went out to the walkway where the other men on D were already moving about to stretch their legs and socialize in the last few precious moments before lock-up.

"You know," said Faulcon as they strolled toward the front, "I don't think they're going to allow bail anyway."

Paul nodded. "All we can do is hope for the best and expect the worst. But you may be right."

And Henry Faulcon was right, for twenty minutes after

118

the lock-up bell jangled through the County Jail, the warning buzzer sounded on the giant presses of the Iron City *American,* just four blocks away, and the first morning edition began to roll through, carrying on Page 23 the announcement that the Court of Appeals had approved the ruling of Judge Hanford J. Rupp that the twenty-six convicted Reds were too dangerous to the community to be permitted out on bail pending action on their appeal.

(3)

Sunday is a slow day, a day when even the grapevine is slow in getting around from range to range, and it was nearly lock-up before word came to Lonnie James that there had been some trouble down on Range D. It came as a surprise because Murderers' Row was directly above D and if there had been a ruckus down there Lonnie should have heard. But more than the surprise was the worry, for the keyman who brought the news said that the Reds had started raising hell and got thrown into the Hole.

"That's a lot of crap," said Lonnie. "Whitey, what do you want to tell me a lie like that for?"

"Aint lying," said the keyman, a towheaded boy of about eighteen who was doing time for armed robbery; he was standing outside the end gate of Range C, resting a freckled hand on the bars while they talked. "I aint lying," he repeated because he was. "Didn't I see it myself?"

"You sure?"

"Sure I'm sure."

"You're a liar," said Lonnie, for he did not want to believe it.

The white boy was not offended; but now he had lost interest so he said, to end the conversation, "Oh kiss my ass."

Even as he said it Lonnie's hand shot forward and grabbed the keyman's hand. Whitey grinned as his arm was pulled through the bars.

"I ought to break it for you," said Lonnie. "Go ahead and dare me."

"OK—I dare you."

Lonnie smiled now for the first time and let go of the imprisoned arm. "Bet you think I was scared to. Well you're wrong. It's just that I'm going to need you back on first base pretty soon. Remember last year? We really had us some tough games didn't we?"

The keyman nodded, then squatted down to look at the big clock across the middle of the Hub. "Minute more," he announced.

"Hey, Whitey," Lonnie called as the other started down the stairs. "Did they really put all them Reds in the Hole? No kidding now—did they?"

The keyman paused, his head and shoulders showing above the steel bannister: he looked up and now he was frowning. "Just like I said. But what are you worrying about them for anyway."

The bell rang then and Lonnie had to shout after the disappearing head: "I aint worrying about them and you know it, Whitey. I aint worrying about nothing!"

He said that again to himself as he walked from the gate. I aint worrying about a damn thing.

That was not true, of course, no more than was the keyman's eye-witness report; but each had had to lie to the other. Whitey because a keyman is supposed to know everything that goes on in the jail and Lonnie because he must never admit that he was worried: it would show a lack of self-confidence which is never so precious to a man as when no one else has any hope for him.

Crazy Peterson was fast asleep in Number 11 when Lonnie looked in to say goodnight. His wasted cheek, blue-white with the stubble, was pillowed on praying hands; a thin smile marked his idiot's dream. Lonnie grinned, thinking of the old jailhouse joke of unhooking a sleeping man's bunk chains to spill him to the floor.

And I ought to do it, Carl. I really should. Just look at you—sound asleep already, not a thing to bother you. And look at me—now I'll be awake all night wondering if that guy

120

Paul is really in solitary and won't be there to meet me on sick call. Remember how I told you about him and the other two Reds and you said maybe they could help me? Only a fool like you could think of something like that—and them in jail the same as us. Just like last week you said that my lousy no-good lawyer would finally get around to see me and I was crazy enough to believe you. Waiting every day, hardly sleeping nights . . . OK, Carl, I'm going to believe you this one last time and if Paul isn't there in the morning—well, I—

He frowned, not knowing how to end the thought. He closed the door of Peterson's cell, gently, not to waken the innocent murderer who was his friend, who could only listen to him, understanding nothing except their common sorrow, as guiltless of crime as he was of saying the words of hope with which Lonnie had just now charged him.

Then Lonnie James walked into his cell and quickly closed the steel-barred door. Quickly but not in time, for he knew that another long night had slipped in behind him. Another long night that would wait up with him—waiting for another day of life.

CHAPTER 10

"You're late," said Lonnie when Paul Harper came over to where he was sitting. "Jesus Christ, man, I said eight *sharp!*" His whispered words were savage with the rage that was meant for the keyman. Whitey had lied all right, and if the sleepless night had been bad, the ten despairing minutes that he had waited for Paul to come on sick call had been almost unbearable. "Sit down," he ordered.

The long backless bench was set against the whitewashed

bricks of the basement passageway: there were about ten other inmates seated on the end nearest the locked door that was marked DISPENSARY. As Paul sat down beside him, Lonnie stared at him for a moment; then he smiled, recalling how Faulcon had said that Paul and Lonnie looked enough alike to be kin. Reckon he was right.

"Boy, you had me worried," he said. He shook his head sadly and slumped back against the wall.

"I came as quick as they let me out of the range," Paul said.

"Oh, I don't mean about that. It was just that—well, I heard you got thrown into the Hole"—he jerked his thumb toward the end of the corridor. "Keyman told me yesterday."

"No, that was Zach." Paul started to explain what had happened but Lonnie cut him short.

"You can tell me about him some other time," he said. "You got the clippings?" And when Paul gave him the envelope, he added: "We might have a lot of time here to talk—maybe an hour seeing that it's Monday and Doc is always drunker than usual over the weekend and gets in later than other days —but I got a lot to tell you. By the way—when you go in to see him just say 'stomach' and he'll hand you a big white pill. But don't take it unless you want to die, cause they tell me it's strong enough to clean out a stopped-up toilet bowl." He slapped his palm with the envelope. "Did you read this stuff?"

Paul nodded. "Faulcon too. Zach didn't get a chance."

Lonnie was silent for a moment; when he looked again at Paul the appeal was plain on his face: "You never saw it in the papers—I mean before?"

"No, and Faulcon didn't either. Seems like we should have, but I guess we weren't following the papers much last May except for what they had about us—and that was plenty. That's when we all were indicted. Then in October," he added apologetically, "we were busy getting ready for our trial. Conferences with the lawyers, raising money, holding mass meetings, getting out leaflets—all kinds of things."

"Sure," said Lonnie. "That's all right. I wasn't front-page news anyway. Besides the most important things weren't

122

in the papers. The way I was framed, I mean. They didn't even say when I was arrested—bet you didn't notice that, did you?" But Paul said yes, and now the frown was reversed as Lonnie's eyebrows lifted in pleased surprise. "You did? Well I'll be damned. You're the first guy I showed these clippings to that noticed it! And that's one of the most important things—when was I arrested? Maybe I wouldn't be here today if that had come out."

And maybe he would never have been in jail at all if he had gone straight home after getting his one good suit from the cleaner's. Actually there were two suits in the case—the one that belonged to Lonnie and another that did not belong to Leroy Flowers. Leroy, of course, was in the story that Lonnie now told to Paul; but three months would pass before they would learn about the other suit.

A sign in the fly-specked window of Sam's Fancy Tailoring & Dry Cleaning Shop said PRESSING WHILE U WAIT, but Lonnie seldom wore his English drape since he got laid-off at the mill: the $4.20 weekly relief check did not allow much sporting around. He had only a quarter left that evening but there was another sign tacked to Sam's counter: NOT RESPONSIBLE FOR UNCLAIMED GOODS AFTER 30 DAYS; and Lonnie made sure to claim his most valuable possession.

On the way to his room at Mrs. Spencer's he passed the Hi-Life Pool Parlor on Beech Street where Cliff Parker was lounging in the doorway. Cliff, who had worked in the chipping department with Lonnie, pistolled a stubby finger at him and said: "What you know, Slim?" and Lonnie had given the usual reply: "Nothing much. White folks still on top."

"Shoot you a game of fifteen-point," Cliff challenged; but Lonnie held out his free hand, palm up, to show that he was broke. "That's OK," Cliff said. "I'm flush. Come on in."

That was about nine o'clock and it was after twelve before Cliff's half-dollar was spent. Be seeing you, they told each other at the door; Cliff went down toward the Bottoms where he lived and Lonnie climbed the steep hill homeward.

He had walked four blocks when he heard a car whining in low gear up the cobblestones: he did not turn around until the spotlight found him. He stopped, then faced into the glare: he heard the squeak of rubber on the curb as the car swerved in. He could not see past the light but he knew that it was a black Chevrolet coupe and he walked toward it even before the County detectives called Hey you—get over here!

"And that's how it started," Lonnie said to Paul. "What's my name. Where did I live. Where did I work. Where did I steal that suit. Hell of a time to be getting clothes from the cleaner's. . . . I told them it was only three more blocks to where I was rooming, that Mrs. Spencer would tell them I was straight, that they could go to Sam's in the morning and ask him about the suit. But no soap. They made me get in and first thing you know we were tearing across the bridge into Iron City and there I was at headquarters."

There were more than fifty others who were picked up that night of May 4, 1940, in various parts of the county. Most of them were Negroes, but it was one of the white men who told Lonnie not to worry: It was just a lot of bullshit for the papers by McKee, the new crime-busting D.A., and in the morning they would all be turned loose again. At worst it would be ten days on Bum Side for those who had no visible means of support or no pull. But if you're on relief like you say—and here the bookie's runner wrinkled his nose in disgust—well that shows you're a square for real. Forget it, kid—you're a cinch.

In the morning Lonnie was the last to be called out, for of them all he was the only one of whom they had no record. He was photographed, weighed, measured and fingerprinted; and it was late afternoon before they asked him any questions. They did not want to know anything about the suit: it was nowhere in sight. ("Damn *good* suit it was. Best I ever had. And I never saw it since the night I got picked up.") But if they had no interest in that, they did have an interest in everything else about him. Every detail of his life was gone over. It was not much and the main points were pecked out on the typewriter.

Name of Accused: *James, Lonnie no middle initial*

Address: *347 Beech St.   Kanesport*

Date of Birth: *January 15, 1917*

If Foreign-Born Give Country of Birth: (blank)

Sex: *M*   Marital Status: *S*   Religion: *P*

Color: *Black*   Hair: *Black*   Eyes: *Brown*

Weight: *178½*   Height: *6/1*   Marks: *None*

Place of Employment: *None*

Previous Employment: *McGregor Tin Plate at Kanesport. Chipper. From Aug/37 to Dec/39. Laid-off.
Now on County Welfare.*

Name and Address of Nearest Relative: *None*

Date of Arrest: (blank)

Charge: (blank)

Circumstances and Arresting Officer(s):   (blank)

Comment: *Accused states that he was raised at Sheltering Arms Home for Boys, Castle Ferry, Ohio.
Mother died when he was infant. Father killed
in mine accident when boy was 4. No brothers or
sisters or known relatives. Graduated 1935 from
Lincoln HS same city. Worked at odd jobs until
1937—came to Kanesport said year for mill work.*

Recommendation: *Check with Castle Ferry. Also
landlady Mrs. Catherine Spencer address above.
Also McGregor's. Also H. T. Wills former company man for negroes. Also Welfare Dept.*

125

"Now are you going to turn me loose?" Lonnie asked the one who had questioned him. The detective gave no sign that he had heard; he turned to watch the other rip the card from the typewriter and Lonnie saw him mark the answer in large red crayon letters across the filled-out form: H O L D.

"But I've been trying to tell you about the suit," Lonnie cried in alarm. "I can prove it's mine. I can even show you where I bought it!"

The shirt-sleeved man at the machine spoke over his shoulder. "What suit?"; but before Lonnie could reply the other pulled at his arm: Let's go.

"Wait a minute. Wait a minute *please!* What are you arresting me for? Why can't I go home? Why can't I call my landlady about getting me a lawyer? Please—loan me a dime to call, I'll pay you back. Just let me talk to her for a minute. One minute, that's all. Why won't—"

"*Shut up!*" The seated man swiveled around and looked at Lonnie for the first time. "Keep your mouth shut till we ask you something. You aint arrested and you don't need no lawyer. OK, Jim." He nodded for the other to take him away.

The records at the Detective Bureau show that Lonnie James was arrested on May 20, the day before he signed the confession: a certified copy of the form giving that date is appended to the proceedings of *Commonwealth vs Lonnie James*. There is nothing to show that he was held for sixteen days before he was arrested, and now, in telling the story to Paul Harper, Lonnie spoke more strongly about that matter than of the fact that he was innocent.

"That's the truth," he said. "For sixteen days—yes, and sixteen nights, they worked on me. And every day they took me to a different police station. It was bad. So bad I can't even tell you how it was. They beat me. Sure, they beat me—bad. But that wasn't the worst part—the beatings. No. It was the way they hammered at me all the time. Never let me rest. After a while I didn't know what day it was, or if it was night or day. All I knew was that they were after me. . . ."

126

It was a week before they asked him about the murder of the drugstore man in Kanesport. Until then it was about a hold-up in Glenmere, and a watchman who had been shot in an Iron City warehouse, and—a dozen murder cases from the Unsolved File. For two days they had concentrated on the Lovers' Lane Case, as the *American* called it:

"You killed that guy, didn't you?"

"No."

"And then you raped his girl and killed her too."

"No."

"You're lying, you black sonofabitch you!"

"Wait a minute, Jake"—this was the Good One now—"Let me ask him about it. He's tired and you're being mean to him again. I told you not to talk mean to him. . . . Now look at me, Lonnie. No, open your eyes. See?—this is Jim, your friend. Attaboy! You didn't mean to kill that kid did you?"

"No."

"That's right, Lonnie. You didn't."

"No."

"You just were walking through the park and he called you a name. You asked him to stop but he kept right on and then he took a poke at you. You didn't mean to kill him. Just wanted to defend yourself. And then the dame—hey! wake up kid. This is important. I can't get you out of this jam if you don't listen to me."

"No."

"And then the dame started running and screaming and you just got scared. Figured just because you are colored they wouldn't believe you, huh?"

"No."

"But you didn't mean to kill her either. That's how it was, wasn't it, son?"

"No."

And then it was only the Kanesport case. Lonnie did not remember where he was on the night of April 10. He may have heard about the killing of the drugstore man but he did not remember that either; and when he finally said yes, he would sign the confession, he was not even sure whether it was the filling station attendant in Willston, the warehouseman, the couple in the park or Waldo Thornhill of Kanesport that he had killed. But he signed, and they let him sleep.

He slept for eighteen hours before they woke him up.

They were all friendly then, like the Good One. They gave him cigarettes. They did not call him names. They talked with him about the coming fight between Joe Louis and Arturo Godoy while they drove him out to Mrs. Spencer's rooming house. He stayed in the car: they did not need his help to find the fatal murder weapon, a 38-caliber Smith & Wesson revolver. It was hidden, they would testify, under his shirts in the second drawer of his dresser.

"Funny thing," said Lonnie. "I didn't know where I was on the night that guy was killed until I had been in here for a month. That was in June sometime and France had just surrendered to Hitler. So the paper printed a little piece giving the different dates of big things that had happened in the war. Timetable of Conquest—you know, something like that. Anyway the date jumps right out at me—*April 10*. It says that that's when the Germans invaded Norway and Denmark. I never saw anything so good in my life because then I knew where I had been. . . ."

It was at Big John's. A bar and grill it was called, though the only tables that were used were in the gambling part in back of the green curtain. The curtain did not hide much, but it looked better that way: not even Big John Cummings who was Republican ward chairman of Goat Hill could afford to be too open about the crap-table and the slot machines.

Only Lonnie and his friend Leroy Flowers were at the bar that night, nursing along the last of their beers, when Big John turned on the radio on his side of the bar to get the eleven o'clock news. It was all about the latest Nazi invasion that had been reported all day—*unconfirmed reports say Oslo has fallen unconfirmed reports say Oslo is strongly resisting*—and Big John grunted his disgust and snapped it off.

It was Leroy who spoke first about the news: "That guy

128

Hitler is really *rough*. Bang bang and they all fall over dead.

Lonnie had agreed: he just got too much stuff. Dive bombers and those panzer tanks that come on like Gang Busters. Wow!

Leroy again: "Tell you one thing I sure would like to see. No fooling. Supposing old Hitler came over and dropped a bomb on Georgia. Just one, that's all I want. Mmmmm *mmmmmm!* Be more crackers running every whichaway you ever saw. I'm telling you, Slim, I sure would like to see it. Right smack on old Talmadge's ass."

Lonnie had agreed with that too. But not Big John.

"Now look here," he said. "You-all aint buying enough beer to drown a flea. But I'm not kicking about that cause I know you're broke and you can loaf in here all you want to. Just the same I aint going to allow that kind of talk in here. Give this place a bad name if people was to hear you saying things like that. Besides it aint patriotism."

Leroy told Big John' where he could shove his patriotism and the whole damn state of Georgia too, and Lonnie had been amused at the long argument that followed between the two. At one part in the debate Big John threatened to throw them out, but finally Lonnie had suggested a basis for mutual agreement. Hitler was no good and neither was Talmadge. One was bad as the other. Furthermore colored people might get killed by the bomb on Georgia and—Leroy conceded this—it wasn't likely that Hitler would bother to tell the colored people what he was going to do so they could get the hell out of the way.

They were there until twelve o'clock when Big John closed the bar and went into the back room. It was not possible for Lonnie or Leroy or Big John to forget the argument or the war news that had started it; and it was during that hour that Waldo Thornhill was shot to death in his store on Cottage Avenue on the other side of town.

Paul had listened in silence to all that Lonnie told him, but now he interrupted as Lonnie knew he would.

"The same time! Well, then you got two witnesses! How—"

"No," said Lonnie, "it was like this: there was a man on

129

first and only one out. First I throw a fast one, see, high and on the outside because he's a pull-hitter and—"

Paul looked up startled and then he saw the guard who must have just come up to where they sat.

"And then I give him a low-breaking curve that he grounds to short, so it's six-to-four-to-three, double play and the side is retired and we win again."

"You did just right," Paul said. "You sure did. Don't ever give a pull-hitter a good one up close or it's goodby and gone."

The guard waited until the last man had been treated and Lonnie could whisper only one more word: Yard.

(2)

No one, of course, had any use for him; but remembering the fate of his predecessor in Cell Number 1, Pee Wee Holmes was trying desperately to win some friends on Range D. Now, when the keyman opened the gate for Paul Harper to come in, Pee Wee rushed from his cell to greet him.

"How you feeling, fellow?" he said anxiously. "Doc take care of you all right?" When Paul brushed past without speaking, the rangeman hurried after him. "Look, fellow," he cried, "I'm sorry about what happened yesterday to your friend. Honest I'm sorry but there was nothing I could do. You can't blame me at all, can you? No sir, you sure can't." He was nearly running now, trying to keep up with Paul's long-legged strides down the runway. "And remember this—anything I can do for you just let me know. . . ."

"OK. OK," Paul said to get rid of him; then he went into Number 9.

Faulcon was not in his cell. Maybe he is playing checkers with Tuxedo; but that cell was empty too. Number 7 and 8 were vacant of course, for Army and Zach were in solitary— but where is everybody else? Pee Wee must have gone back to his place and there was no one on the runway now. He listened but there was no sound from any cell. No, there was a choking noise from one of the far-end cells and as he walked toward the rear he suddenly realized why the range was so

130

strangely deserted. Of course—it's after nine and Cell Block One goes out to the yard from nine to ten. Lonnie would not have forgotten that, so he meant I should see him out there tomorrow. Paul stopped and was about to go back to his cell when he heard the noise again.

Eighteen—no. . . . 19—no. . . . It was Sneaky Pete in Number 20. The old man was sitting on his bunk; his head, shiny bald except for a fringe of gray, was bent to his folded arms; his tiny body shook with the uncontrolled sobbing. Strewn on the cement floor were shredded pieces of cloth—the white shirt, so carefully saved for his long-awaited trial, now carefully torn to bits.

"Hey, Pete," Paul called from the doorway. "Pete! What's the matter, old man?" But the sobbing did not cease, nor did he look up, and Paul tiptoed away to his cell.

He tried to read the Hugo book, but the words kept slipping away: he had not finished a page before the clang of the gate and the rush of feet gave notice that Range D was back from the yard.

"How did you make out, Paul?" but before he could answer, Faulcon ducked into his next-door cell and returned with the morning *American*. "Bad news. Nothing but bad news today. But first about Zach: he got ten days in the Hole for insubordination and threatening the guards. Fellow who works on the Hub told us out in the yard. And then there's Sneaky Pete —he were called for court right after you left and got back in half an hour. Poor old guy—he's over seventy you know— judge gave him a year on the liquor charge. They say he were really rough this morning—gave everybody at least double the regular sentence. And here's the worst—" He handed Paul the folded newspaper, one finger pointing to the heading:

COMMIES STAY IN
CLINK SAYS COURT

Surprisingly, for Faulcon knew that the young organizer was a stickler for detail, Paul read only the first paragraph of the half-column report on the Appeals Court's decision upholding Judge Rupp's ruling that denied their release on bail.

"What's the matter?" Faulcon said. "Acting so unconcerned. Did somebody tell you?"

Paul shrugged and shook his head no.

"Well, don't it bother you none that we'll be stuck in this rathole till Fall and then if our appeal is turned down. . . ."

But Paul was slow to answer him: he stared up at the ceiling, resting the back of his long head against the steel wall. Finally he spoke, but in a strange low tone that Faulcon could barely catch: "Anyway, whatever happens, we'll still be alive."

"Oh," said Faulcon softly, "I forgot." He sat down now, glancing up at Paul's ceiling which was the floor of Lonnie's cell. "Did you see him on sick call—get a chance to talk?"

Paul nodded. "I didn't hear it all, but I'm to see him again tomorrow outside. But Henry—"

"What?"

"He didn't do it. No more than you or I. He is innocent. Framed and forced to confess and now they want to kill him. I'll tell you how they did it—much as I know, that is—but first: Do you remember how that first clipping said that the police commissioner at Kanesport announced that Lonnie had signed the confession and he thanked the County cops for their help? Well that was because the Kanesport police had nothing to do with it at all. That commissioner didn't even see Lonnie till after they'd made him sign!"

He went on to tell the story that Lonnie had told him. When he had finished he looked square at Faulcon and said: "Henry, I was wrong yesterday. Wrong as hell."

"What about, son?"

"About Lonnie. Remember—just before lock-up it was—how I jumped salty when you asked me if there was anything we could do for him and I said there was nothing? Well, how can anybody sit here and see them getting ready to kill an innocent man and not do something to stop it!" His words were harsh and he jabbed an accusing finger into Faulcon's bulging middle.

Despite himself the old man had to smile: his eyes were sly again under the thick gray brows. "Now don't go hollering at me again—you're supposed to be mad with yourself not at me."

"Well, I mean it for the both of us. Here you and I have fought for years in cases like this—Scottsboro, of course, and Willie Peterson, and more too. We didn't know them, but we knew it was legal lynching and we did everything we could to save them. So now it's Lonnie and what's the difference? OK, we're in jail. That's right. It's harder, sure, but here we have met him face to face. How can we do nothing?"

Faulcon nodded his agreement, but slowly and his eyes were doubtful. "I know, Paul. I know. But who is left out there to do anything?"

The young man jumped up and began to pace the cell. Suddenly he whirled on Faulcon. "Who is out there?" he demanded. "I'll tell you—*everybody but us*. The whole population, that's who! Look: Were you in the Party when you started to work for Scottsboro? Was the woman who gave you the petitions and made you fill them out—was she in the Party? No! You didn't join till afterwards and she never did. But isn't she still out there—and a lot of other women too? And men? And the guys in your union who signed for you? Besides there's the rank and file of the Party—do you think they ran away or disappeared? There's the members of your branch and Zach's, and there's Charlene and Mrs. Zachary and others too. Why look here, Henry: If you really believed nobody out there gave a damn about anything, *why are you in here?* You could have ratted and gone free like Ronald Johnson and so could all the rest of us. So I know you don't really mean that."

Sure, but what about leadership, Faulcon wanted to know. There has to be somebody to take charge of such a campaign and the small membership of the Party is already terribly over-burdened with the fight to free the Twenty-Six.

But Paul had an answer for that too. "Henry," he said, "I was thinking the other day that here in jail I got all the time in the world and nothing to do with it. But I was wrong about that too. Maybe we don't even have enough time for what we got to do. Leadership? Why can't *we* still be leaders? Aren't

133

we the Communist Party of Range D, Cell Block One? That's right, you and me—yes, and Zach when he gets out of the Hole. It won't be easy, but this is something we got to do. We got to do it, Henry. You and me and Zach are going to be the first three members of the Lonnie James Defense Committee!"

PART 2

He delivered Daniel from the lion's den,
Jonah from the belly of the whale,
An' the Hebrew chillun from the fiery furnace,
An' why not every man?

CHAPTER 11

Morning is always good, but the new day is best when it comes as a surprise, suddenly, fresh and bright, not tired from a long night's waiting. Lonnie James was startled: he had slept the whole night through. He marveled: surely this was a happy sign, for he could not remember when the lonely hours of darkness had not touched him.

Crazy Peterson was standing in the doorway and now, as Lonnie looked up from his bunk, the white man's face was sharp with worry.

"Good morning, Lonnie."

The young man sprang to his feet. See! It *is* a good morning. Even this poor dummy knows it's something special. Oh, Carl—I almost believe you now. I almost believe you. For there was something about that guy yesterday—he only listened, but . . . Lonnie had fallen asleep last night trying to put into words what it was that had been so strangely moving in the way Paul Harper had listened to his story. Now it came to him with the shock of the cold water he splashed upon his face: *He believed me.* Didn't say it, but that's how it was—he believed me! And there was something even more wonderful: he seemed to *know*. I didn't even get a chance to tell him about the trial—but he seemed to know how it was. Oh, Carl —do you think . . . ?

He dried his face on the ragged huck towel and turned from his washbowl to speak to his friend who couldn't think at all.

"Good morning to you, Dopey. How's everything today?"

Like a slowly opening curtain, the deep-etched furrows on Peterson's cheeks parted into a broad smile; the pale blue eyes glowed bright with the fierceness of his pleasure. For it was only when Lonnie was feeling good that he called him names like Dopey. That was not often, of course, but somehow, to Peterson in the numbness of this cold hard place of steel and stone to which they had dragged him, these moments of reflected happiness were shivering warm, filling him with a bursting joy that overflowed into tears. Of all the fears that gripped him there was only one that he could name: that this tall dark boy who was his friend would be taken from him. With the guards who came through the range a dozen times a day there came a panic that squeezed his heart; it did not seem to beat again till they were gone. And whenever Lonnie went out to the yard, the quivering fear came again and the only comfort he could find was to wait in Lonnie's cell for his return. Lonnie was the only human he knew: all others were shapes of terror. He remembered nothing—nothing about himself and nothing about his son, the hulking half-wit son whose head he had battered to pulp with a piece of the junk they were gathering. Was he mean to you? Lonnie had asked him once, but Carl's eyes had been blank as the answer: Who?

It was a good morning for real. For the first time in six weeks Lonnie's lawyer came to see him—the sorry one, as he said afterward when he saw Paul and Faulcon. So sorry, he was, that the newspapers had not bothered to mention his name in reporting the trial. ("Honest to God, that guy is a joke sure enough.") The *American* had told only of Clement B. Coxe whose name was frequently in print and was usually followed by the phrase, "the distinguished counsellor." He looked distinguished enough, Lonnie recalled, though Lonnie was even more bitter against his chief attorney than toward Judge Rupp himself. Attorney Coxe was tall, silver-pink handsome; his bearing and his dress were impeccably proper. To the aging ladies on the jury he was Lewis Stone-of-the-Movies and they had fidgeted with excitement at his elegant charm: they did not miss a single broad "a" just as they did not miss something that was even broader and more impressive—that he had nothing but cold contempt for his Negro client. In his few, impatient interviews with Lonnie before the trial he had made it clear that while his service as court-appointed counsel was a matter of *noblesse oblige* and the highest ethical code of the profession, he was a very busy man: Lonnie should not repudiate his confession and since a death sentence was not mandatory under the law, a plea for mercy might be granted. Especially, he implied, if Clement B. Coxe asked for that favor. But if he had been politely bored by Lonnie's account of the illegal detention and forced confession, Mr. Coxe was outraged by Lonnie's stubborn refusal to plead guilty. The accused lacked all the proper virtues of the poor and lowly: he was shrill in asserting his innocence, loudly abusive of the authorities, and—worst of all—*ungrateful.* Even when Mr. Coxe had emphasized that Lonnie was receiving his high-priced counsel at no cost, that the pittance the Commonwealth would pay the lawyers was really nothing for the time involved, Lonnie had slapped the table with his black hand and cried: "Now don't give me that crap about your time. It's *my* life and I tell you I'm innocent! After what I've been through I'm not thankful about anything. *Not a damn thing,* you hear me? And I aint going to plead guilty—not for you and not for anybody else!"

The other lawyer had sat in silence through the stormy interviews, dreading to bring upon himself the chilling look of his distinguished colleague or the hot, accusing glare of the defiant young Negro. It was the scrupulous justice of the Law and the pitying charity of the Bar that had brought Arnold Winkel into the case of *Commonwealth vs Lonnie James.* The Law required that no less than two attorneys be appointed to defend an impecunious defendant in a capital case, and the Bar was aware that the $250 fee would mean a lot to Winky who was shamefully poor.

Arnold Winkel was a failure. He had always been a joke, as Lonnie called him. He would have been a joke even if Franz and Hilde Winkelried had not named their puny infant son after the fabled Swiss hero. But that served to point up the jest, and whenever he appeared his schoolmates would never cease to shriek: "Make way for Liberty! he cried—Make way for Arnold Winkelried!" The very thought of this timid wretch advancing toward an enemy phalanx, boldly drawing the cruel spears into his narrow chest, was always good for howling laughter. He fled from their sneers and snowballs as he would always flee from everything. Somehow he got through law school and somehow he got past the terrors of the bar examination, but he had never risen higher than a clerk with the law firm to which he had clung for twenty years. Fallon, Erhardt, Schwimmer and Ross kept him, for he was more reliable than the brash young fledglings who normally did such work and his mousy presence was less distracting to the staid old partners. He seldom appeared in court and it was a standing joke of Iron City's legal profession that the only case he had argued and won was his petition to have his name changed from Winkelried to Winkel. There were some who thought that more than compassion was involved in giving Winky a murder case; there were hints of a sly jest to be chuckled about over the scotch-and-sodas at the Club. He wouldn't have to do more than carry Coxe's bag, so to speak, but still when you think of that Winky in a case like this— Why, I'll bet you money that when old Rupp sentences that boy to hang, Winky will *faint!*

Arnold Winkel had not fainted; he had even tried to smile encouragement to Lonnie when he spoke to him about the appeal that would be filed. It was to be a simple routine job —there was little enough on which to appeal—and Mr. Coxe had left the matter to Winkel who had handled the few things that had had to be done before the trial.

Now, as he talked to Lonnie at the long oaken table provided for that purpose on one side of the Hub, Arnold Winkel seemed to fumble among the brief-case papers for some comforting word for his client. His reddish hair, thinning on top of the too-small head, was streaked with gray; the fierce bushy moustache, copied from his father's, vainly tried to hide the timorous cast of his face; only the large blue eyes were appealing, though they seemed always to shift from Lonnie's stare.

"Oh, no, Mr. James, we have certainly not forgotten about you. Of course not! Mr. Coxe, as you must know, is frightfully busy but he said he would try to see you—soon, that is." It was a lie, of course, and seeing the disbelief hard in Lonnie's eyes, Winkel bit his lip in shame that he had not been able to make it ring true. "And as for me, Mr. James, well, I. . . ." He smiled helplessly. Had nothing to come to see you about? Dreaded to face the desperate hope of a doomed young man?

"Skip it, Mr. Winkel. Tell me something about the appeal. And how about Leroy—have they found him yet?"

"The appeal? Well, the status of that matter is precisely as I wrote in my last communication to you. It has been properly filed and argued as you know, and is now under advisement by the Supreme Court of the Commonwealth. We expect— Mr. Coxe and I, that is—we expect that the judgment will be rendered, let's see, yes, sometime before summer adjournment. That would be, well—April, May or June, perhaps. Within the next three months, that is. And of course—we—Mr. Coxe and I—are expecting favorable action." As soon as he uttered the words of hope he realized that that too had been a mistake, for his voice had belied the statement, so he rushed to speak of Leroy Flowers, the missing witness.

"We have received every assurance from the Kanesport police, Mr. James, that they are doing everything possible to ascertain his whereabouts. You may have every confidence that as soon as he is located we will secure from him a supporting affidavit to the appeal. I am sure the local authorities are doing their utmost."

He really believes that, thought Lonnie; and for a moment he almost felt sorry for Mr. Winkel.

(2)

"He aint nothing at all," Lonnie said to Paul as they marched around the yard an hour later. "But still it was good to see him. He's the only lawyer who ever comes to see anybody here so early in the day and that's because he's scared to be late for work! Anyway, he aint nothing like that son of a bitch Coxe—the other one. You should have seen the way Coxe cross-examined those County dicks after I made him bring out about how they had given me the works for more than two weeks before they made me sign. Butter wouldn't have melted in his mouth, the way he asked them questions. And you would have thought that the old lady who was the only eye-witness against me was his grandma! No, he wasn't hard on anybody but me. But I'm supposed to tell you first about *my* witnesses. . . ."

Leroy Flowers and Big John Cummings could tell that he had been with them at the time the murder was committed and Mrs. Catherine Spencer could tell about Lonnie's disappearance sixteen days before it came out in the papers that Lonnie James had confessed. She could not, unfortunately, verify Lonnie's testimony that he had not shown the officers where the pistol was hidden, that they had not let him out of the car: Mrs. Spencer had been shopping downtown when the searchers had come to her rooming house.

Leroy and Big John could prove him innocent. But Leroy had not been found and Big John's memory had failed him. The County detectives had come twice to find Leroy Flowers: the first time he had not been home to receive the subpoena and the next time his landlady said he had moved, she didn't know where.

Now why would Leroy do a thing like that? Somebody around there must know why he left and where he went: Lonnie had insisted that his lawyers do more than had been done to find him. You got to find him! *He'll* tell you I'm not lying! Finally Mr. Coxe told his associate that if he could find the time Winkel might run out to Kanesport to talk to the landlady himself. Winkel had gone but he had barely seen her: Mrs. Bailey had opened her door only to the width of the safe-guarding chain. At his first knock she had called out that she did not want to buy any—whatever you got; and when he had bravely rapped again, she had peered out at the suspicious-looking white man and said no to everything he asked her about Leroy Flowers.

There had been no difficulty in finding Big John Cummings: Yes I know the boy. Not very well, you understand, but just from seeing him around. He's not one of our local boys—may be one of them floaters that always come around looking for some good pay from the mill and then don't like it cause they have to do a day's work to get a day's pay. But this here place I got is run right, decent and no rough stuff, and I never allow no bad characters to loaf around my club. You just go out there and ask anybody and they'll tell you that! . . . When Winkel told him what Lonnie had said about the argument between Leroy and Big John that had been started by the war news and that Lonnie had been present that night, the club-owner pursed his lips thoughtfully: Maybe so, and maybe not. . . . He was not sure then whether he remembered; but when he took the stand at the trial he was quite sure. Positive, in fact. He did not remember. Mr. Coxe had seen no reason for calling him, but Lonnie had insisted upon that too. Big John couldn't sit up there in court, right in front of my face, and tell a lie like that!

With Cummings, Mr. Coxe had come closest to being sharp in his questioning. To Lonnie it seemed as though this time his attorney was actually trying to shake the witness' story. But Big John would not budge: I don't remember seeing him that night; I don't remember any argument at all—don't allow a lot of arguing in my place nohow. . . . The tipstaves and marshals who outnumbered the few curious spectators in the courtroom had admired the way the famous counsellor made the pudgy Negro witness sweat, but they whispered among themselves that Coxe had been wrong to mention that part about the two boys wishing a bomb would fall on Georgia, for Judge Rupp had looked dismayed and the members of the jury had imitated his outraged expression.

It was while Big John was on the stand that the defendant had made his second outburst of the day. No one had noticed him stand up but their heads snapped around at his cry. Nor could the witness, who had not once looked at him, keep his eyes away now. *"You are lying, Big John! They are making you lie!"*

143

("Boy, you should have seen them!" And now Lonnie could laugh about it. "Old Rupp damn near fell out of his chair and Big John jumped like I had stabbed him. But then the marshals were all over me like white on rice and I couldn't see anything. I'm telling you it was really something!")

The judge had gavelled a recess until order was restored and then Mr. Coxe had apologized to his honor and the jury for the intemperate conduct of his client. He was quite calm this time nor was his handsome face as pink as it had been earlier when Lonnie first disrupted the workings of justice. For then it was Clement B. Coxe himself whom the defendant had abused. It had happened during the cross-examination of the clerk-detective who testified as to the date and circumstances of Lonnie's arrest. He had said nothing about the confession, for since the accused had repudiated it, the confession could not be mentioned though, of course, it had been in all the papers.

Q. And are you quite certain that no force was used against the defendant when he was questioned?

A. Yes sir.

Q. No threats or intimidation?

A. None. That would be against the regulations of the Detective Bureau.

Q. Thank you. That is all.

Lonnie's heavy oak chair crashed backward as he sprang to his feet and pointed a long finger at Attorney Coxe. "I told you," he cried, "they beat me! They kept on beating me! They never let me rest! He knows what they did—*and so do you!*"

Paul asked him now why he had not refused to have Coxe continue as his attorney—you could have, you know.

Lonnie snorted. "Sure I know it—now. But then I was dumb. Didn't know and nobody told me. Don't forget—I was just a kid then."

Paul started to say that it was less than six months ago, but he checked himself and was glad that he did. Less than half a year! How long is that when you are sentenced to hang by your neck till you're dead? And maybe the nine young

Scottsboro boys had grown into men by the time we heard the first report of their trial. . . .

The three of them were walking together: Faulcon had sneaked up from his place with the short men in the rear and now he stood between the tall young men, hoping that they might shield him from sight. He and Paul waited for Lonnie to resume his story and they were startled when his next words were: "I could kill that guy!" They thought he meant Attorney Coxe until they saw that he was looking toward the old guard, asleep on his tilted chair against the door. "Byrd," said Lonnie, forgetting that he had told them before. "The old buzzard—I hate him so bad. Never said nothing to me, but man, he sure gives me the creeps. I always say I won't ever look at him but still I always do. I wish he'd go away and die and never sit there no more."

But now he took up his story again: "Mrs. Spencer—" he smiled—"she sure was nice." Her smooth brown face had beamed at him from under the flowers of her Sunday hat as she sat in the witness chair. But her black eyes had flashed with anger and her lips drew tight when the prosecutor seemed to suggest in his cross-examination that Lonnie had not been missing for two weeks before his official arrest as she had testified.

Q. *Are you sure beyond any doubt that he did not return to his room in all that time?*

A. *I told you once and that ought to be enough.*

The Court: *Answer the question. Mr. McKee is asking if you are certain.*

A. *Well I ought to be sure. It's my house. But I'll tell you once more: No, I never saw him again until today.*

Q. *Had he ever stayed away before? Not even overnight?*
A. *No sir.*

God bless you, Mrs. Spencer, for telling a Christian lie like that! She smiled at Lonnie as she said it and he knew she was remembering the times she had fussed with him about staying out all night. "Shame on you, Lonnie," she had said. "Tomcatting around like you do! Why don't you do like I tell you

145

—come to my church and meet some of those real nice young ladies and marry up with one of them and settle down?" And he had laughed and hugged her ample waist and said that he sure would do it if he thought that one of those gals would be as sweet as you, Mrs. Spencer. How come you never married again yourself?—why you can't be a day over forty! She had said shame on you again, Lonnie, and me going on sixty; but just the same, she had been pleased.

"I guess it didn't help me none, because the prosecutor showed the jury that her testimony didn't prove that the cops had had me and as for her saying that she never saw the gun in my room, well I could have hid it from her. But she tried to help me, she tried her best, and she was the only one. She still writes me pretty regular and she would come to see me if they let her but nobody can visit guys on Range C except their lawyers and close kin, and of course I don't have any people at all."

The gun? It was not Lonnie's; he never had a gun; and look— "You guys don't know me very well, but can you imagine me being so simple that I'd keep the gun in my room for nearly a month after I shot a man with it? I'm not Crazy Peterson! And anybody that had read as many detective magazines as me would know that every gun makes different markings on the bullet. And that brings me to something else: Until that part came up I thought those dicks really believed I'd done it. I figured they had asked me about all those other killings just to trick me before they sprung the Kanesport charge on me. But when they claimed they found the gun I knew they were out to frame me for real. Guess what—at the trial here comes the ballistics expert from the Detective Bureau and he's got two bullets with him. One of them, he says, is from the body of Waldo Thornhill and the other is from the revolver they found in my dresser. OK, and he's got photographs—magnified big as this—of the two pieces of lead. Sure thing—both have got the same markings! So Coxe calls in another expert from the University to examine the evidence and of course he says they're exactly alike; both were fired from the same barrel. That was bad, terribly bad for me, worse even than the witness who said she saw me."

Somehow, to Lonnie, Miss Martha Hightower was not important at all, though she had been the star witness for the Commonwealth. Miss Hightower was tiny and very old but her voice was young and strangely gay; there were moments while she was testifying when everyone in the courtroom held their breath in fear that she would giggle. She lived two blocks from the Thornhill Pharmacy and on the night of the murder she was on her way to the store to buy some liver pills. (The jury had tittered when she added at that point: "—they really do me so much good, you have no idea!") She had reached the intersection of Cottage Avenue and Van Buren Street—she jabbed a bony finger at the diagram held up before her—catty-corner from poor Mr. Thornhill's place of business when she heard the shot and saw a tall black man run out the door. For an instant he was silhouetted against the neon glow of the main display window as he sprinted in the opposite direction from her. She knew beyond the shadow of a doubt that the shadowy figure was a colored man. She was positive that he was Lonnie James. Her eyesight was perfect, she exclaimed in triumph, for she could read all but the itty-bittiest words without her reading glass!

At the Detective Bureau where she had been taken after the long thrilling automobile ride from Kanesport, she readily identified Lonnie as he stood manacled between the two men in uniform. "That's the one!" she cried, pointing. She would have been sure of it even if they had not told her of his confession. As she stared, fascinated to face the dangerous young man, Lonnie had seen her eyes grow bright with excitement, her withered cheek fevering to pink.

"Damndest thing you ever saw," said Lonnie. "Here she was standing there, this little old white woman, wearing high-laced shoes and a black silk shawl, pointing her finger at me and saying she saw me that night, and yet she looked like—you'll never believe it but honest to God fellows—*she looked like she could go for me!* Not like some old whore neither, but like some hot young gal. I'm telling you it was the damndest thing I ever saw in my life!"

Rooney's whistle shrilled and the yard guard called to the straggling marchers: "One more time around and then line up at the door. Let's make it snappy this time—move up there, Squad E, this aint no funeral!"

"Quick," said Paul. "What's the address of your lawyer so I can tell Charlene—my wife, she's coming tomorrow—where to find him?"

Lonnie gave him the name of the firm in the Iron City Law Building. "But if you forget all those names—Fallon, Erhardt and so on—well, Arnold Winkel's name is in the phone book."

Hastily, for there was little time, Paul Harper told him of the Lonnie James Defense Committee that had been started the day before. "Me and Faulcon and Zach, when he gets out of the Hole. Zach and his wife can do a lot—they're both from Kanesport just like you. And we'll get a committee started outside—lots of people. You'll see! But be sure don't tell a soul till we get started. . . ."

Lonnie had not been surprised. He did not even thank them. "That's swell," he said. It was all he said. The flood of words, racing and tumbling through the bursted dam, came later as he told Peterson about the miracle come true. It would have been safe to say the words aloud to the crazy man, but they had said no—the Reds who now would lead the fight that he had led alone. *Oh Carl—they're going to save me!*

CHAPTER 12

He jerked erect at the sound, not believing what he had heard. No!—there it is again, louder and longer this time: the distant shunting of a switch-engine making up a train of box-cars. Now it was unmistakably clear: first the muffled crash as it jolted into the string of empties, and then the reverberating *boom boom boom boom* as the shock rolled down the line and faded away into the distance. Now the driver would be staring out of his cab, waiting to see the brakeman's lantern bobbing up and down like a tiny dancing star in the blackness; and then the snub-nosed yard engine would brace itself against the drag, snuffling and snorting as it strained backward, and the long grumbling line of cars would begin to roll—then faster, clicking lightly on the rails, no longer stubborn against the bossy little engine now chuffing along so scornful-like and bragging with its bell.

But these sounds did not come, of course, and Zach smiled at his own foolishness. Lying there in the darkness of the Hole, he had thought that by now it was late night, but the far-away rumbling showed that the time was only six o'clock when all the cells were slammed shut at lock-up. Only five hours had passed since they had brought him here: it was hard to believe. Morning would be a long time coming.

They had heeded his warning: they had not touched him, their only abuse had been words. In the morning, they told him, he would go before Steve and Steve would give him ten days solitary and that will teach you not to threaten an officer you black bastard you. Then they had closed the door and were gone. For a long time he had stood there, leaning against the solid steel, exultant that it had been so easy. *I sure messed up all right, but not real bad: they didn't make me fight them.* All along the way they had led him—down the cell-block stairs and through the narrow arched passage in the basement that ended at the row of solitary confinement cells—he had told himself that he should not fight them. He had repeated it in his mind, over and over, insistent, pleading: *Isaac Zachary, don't you be no fool. No matter what—don't you be no fool!* But he knew he would if they laid hands on him; and when they only cussed him it was all he could do to keep from laughing. Laughing like that Abed-nego in the story old Deacon Ransom used to tell in Sunday school. . . .

Now, way back in them days—way before slavery it was— that old Nebuchadnezzar was the King of Babylon and he had no use for the children of Israel. No use at all. That was the

149

time they went and put them three boys in the fiery furnace.
Shadrach, Meshach and Abed-nego. Good mannerly boys
they was, like you-all ought to be but aint; but he threw them
in just the same cause he was poison mean and wicked and he
had the power. He fetched all the coal-oil he could find and he
poured it on the fire. Hot? Whooeee! Hotter'n a two-dollar
pistol on the Fourth of July! But them boys wasn't studyin
bout them Babylonians nor the King neither. Just sat around
a-spittin and a-talkin till they opened up the door and turned
em loose. Shadrach he said, shucks, didn't even scorch my
collar, and Meshach he said, I do declare, seems to be turnin
mighty cool around here. But Abed-nego—now he was really
somethin, that boy. Didn't say nothin. Just looked around at
all them white folks and laughed!

The people always called it the Goin' Straight to Glory,
though the right name for the railroad which lurched and
rattled across that part of the state was Great Southwestern &
Gulf. The people said that in fun, but to Isaac it was the glory
train for real and long before he ever saw it. Because he was
the youngest of Tom Zachary's nine boys, he was fourteen
and near man-grown before he was allowed to accompany
his father on the seven-mile buggy ride to Laurelton where
the train came through. He saw it then, and it was a shining
day in the years of his dream—the dream that had first called,
plaintive and urgent, mocking and far away, to a small black
boy on a Mississippi farm.

Every day at noon the whistle had come, hooting and laughing like a crazy jaybird. The boy would haul back hard on
the reins and say: "Hear that Dan'l?—and you, Queenie? Oh,
I'm going to drive that devil one a these days. I will, *I will*.
Drive him straight and hard, straight and hard and *fast*. Clear
acrost to Georgia I'll drive him, maybe far as Atlanta even—
you'll see. Just you wait and see. Now *git!* you no 'count
rascals—don't you-all be laughing at me too." And at night
he would lie awake until it came again, crying low like something lost in the swamps, rising and falling. . . . Then he
would scrounch down into the hollow of the corn-shuck

150

mattress to dream about the railroad until he fell asleep. There were other things too besides the noon and midnight whistles. There was the calendar picture pasted on the wall behind the parlor stove, with the great locomotive roaring head-on at you, real as life, and the smoke racing back and forming into letters against the blue blue sky—*GULF GETS YOUR FREIGHT THERE FASTER!* And on Sundays there were the songs they sang down at the New Hope Baptist church. Yes, get on board little children—and all you grown-ups too, but you better hurry cause Isaac Lee Zachary is sitting right up here in the engine and he sure aint going to wait for no stragglers. Yes'm, this is the Glory Train and you better climb on fast lessen you want to get left behind with all my no 'count brothers. That's right, I aint taking a one of them excepting maybe Benjamin—he's the one next to me—but none a them others not even if they gets down on their knees and *begs.* No! Don't come crying to me now, specially you Jacob and you neither Levi—always signifying and poking fun and saying I aint never going to drive nothing more'n some ol' jug-haid mule. I been warning you-all and now it's too late. Says I'm going to leave you right back at the station with all the hypocrites, back-sliders and sinners what aint allowed on.

> *This train is bound for glory, this train*
> *This train is bound for glory, this train*
> *This train is bound for glory*
> *Everybody ride it don't has to worry*
> *Cause this train is the through train, this train!*

> *I said this train don't carry no jokers, this train*
> *This train don't carry no jokers, this train*
> *This train don't carry no jokers*
> *No moonshine-drinkers or cigar-smokers*
> *Cause this train is the glory train, this train!*

And no pimps or whores or gamblers, no tobacco-chewers or midnight ramblers like the song says—not on my train. And none of you other boys except Benjamin and he can ride right alongside me in the engine. . . . Ring that bell! Choo! Choo! Get offen that track cause we're coming through— just a-reeling and a-racking, just a-reeling and a-racking, reeling and a-racking. . . . *Whooooooooo whooooooooo*, great God-amighty—I'm a-rolling through!

But Jacob and Levi and the others were mostly right, for Isaac never did get to be an engine driver in all the years he worked for the railroad. He started as a call boy when he was sixteen, at Locust Grove which was a division point on the GS&G's main line. There were few telephones in those days and it was the call boy's job to find the crew-men who were posted for duty and when he had found them, in boarding house, barbershop or saloon, he must make sure the order was read and signed for in the book. The hours were better than on the farm, only from six to six; and the pay was big, $12 a month; and best of all Isaac was a railroad man at last. Back and forth he ran, from station to all corners of the town and back again, call-book tight under arm, flying legs gray in the swirling dust, just a-reeling and a-racking, reeling and a-rack-ing, *whooo whooo*, chug chug STOP! The Lucky Horseshoe, and I know Mr. Colby just *got* to be here cause it's only four days after payday. . . .

Two years passed before the day he was called to the Big Office. I aint done nothing bad, he told himself; but still he twisted his cap in nervous alarm while he stood there waiting outside the wooden railing. They aint got no cause to fault me—no, but white folks is queer; can't never tell about them. Mr. Greer, the super, was talking to Mr. Folsom who was foreman at the roundhouse. They talked for a long time while he waited outside the railing; but finally when they had noticed the broad-shouldered young Negro, the super jerked a thumb toward him and said: "That's the one I was telling you about, Jim. He's a right good boy but you can have him."

That was another great day, for now he would be an engine wiper and he would have a brass badge and a number; and

152

even better than that—he could now learn all about the mighty locomotives he would some day drive.

The roundhouse crew were all Negroes—the wipers and tenders and hostlers, and even the mechanics, though these were called helpers because they drew a helper's pay. All of these were black men's jobs and it had been like that since way back.

The brakemen on the GS&G were all Negroes too and so were most of the firemen. There was a time in Mississippi when no white man would lay a hand to the fireman's shovel, but that was before the panics of '93 and '07 when jobs got so scarce a man had to take anything. But of course no Negro was ever promoted to engineer: not in Mississippi, not anywhere in the South—no, not even up North, the men told him. Never did and never will, so you can stop that foolish talk right here and now. Course, if you get to be a hostler you can drive a engine here in the yards, just moving them around and into the roundhouse, but not out there on the high iron, not on no regular run. Never. No son, not so long as your skin is black. And just remember this as long as you're black and live in Mississippi: there's three main things Cap'n Charlie won't 'low you to do, and that's mess with his women, vote in the elections, or drive a railroad train.

Perhaps those were the main rules, but there were many other things to know about being black in Mississippi and young Zach learned them all while working in the roundhouse. Back home on the farm there had never been much talk about white folks one way or the other, but here with the roundhouse gang it was the constant topic of conversation. Even if the talk started on something else it had to get around to the same old thing—Cap'n Charlie and what he's up to now, and how poor ol' Ned is still catching hell.

For the most part they spoke of these bitter things in a jesting way, for otherwise a man is liable to get to feeling mean and acting bad, and first thing he knew he would find hisself dead. And when a man started to talk that way, the others would caution him, saying: "Look out now, brother, else when the flag comes down you'll go up!" For it was the

153

custom that each morning Old Glory was hauled to the top of the tall white flag-pole that was set in the star-shaped bed of flowers on the lawn in front of the Big Office, and at sundown it was lowered. Every evening when the gang went off they could see the knotted loop at the bottom of the halyard slowly rising on one side of the towering mast as the flag came down in solemn majesty on the other. Never did they watch the descending banner of freedom; their eyes stayed fixed on the inexorable, jerking rise of the rope on the other side. And thus each working day of their lives the railroad's patriotic ceremony came to remind them of the supreme law for the black majority of Mississippi's people.

Young Zach listened in wondering silence to all their talk, his eyes now smiling shyly, now near tears, but always brightest when they re-told the old-time legends of the railroad men: tales of reckless rides, thundering wrecks, washed-out bridges and narrow escapes; of Railroad Bill, the baddest Negro there ever was, so bad that when he blew into town the birds grew quiet and the people all rushed inside to bolt their doors and slam their shutters, the sheriff locking himself into his own jail for safety. . . .

Young Zach was a good worker and so he was well liked by the other men despite all his peculiar ways—never drinking, smoking, gambling or cussing like a regular railroad man should, and always calling the older workers "mister" the way his father had trained him, and always pestering them with more questions about the engines than any man could rightly answer. From the first they had joshed him about being a country boy, though nearly all of them had come from the country too; but after a while they ceased to scoff at his crazy ambition to be an engineer. There was something in the quiet way he said it, something so terribly deep and strong and fierce, that it touched even the hardest of them: it made them afraid and sad too, and somehow, at the same time, strangely proud.

In later years, whenever he remembered his schooling, Zach would not think of the white-washed one-room shack they called a school at home; he would recall instead the five

154

hard-working years in the Locust Grove roundhouse where he had learned about engines and, even more important, about people. Things he could never come to know about in the cut-off and isolated life in a back-county community. Back home he could only know his folks and their few neighbors; here he got to know his people. Here he became drawn into a greater family, the rough brotherhood of workingmen, no longer tied to the soil, talking and thinking of more than crops and weather, birthing and burying, boll-weevil and Bible; linked now, however remotely, with the turbulent, surging currents of industry that vibrated down to the Deep South through the slender shining rails. Here were men who could tell of life in far-away places, of Birmingham, Atlanta, St. Louis and even Chicago. Footloose men, many of them were, boomers as they were called, who worked on one line for a while and then were gone along their restless way. Other men came to take their places, strangers with strange new thoughts and ways of speaking, and with new things to talk about. Men from Alabama and Georgia, Louisiana men and West Virginians. It was a boomer from Florida who told them about the union the men had started there and how badly it had scared the company before it was smashed. A union for black workers!—surely that was a thing of wonder to hear about, for none of the regular Brotherhoods, of course, would admit Negroes to membership.

The roundhouse was his home and these men were his brothers, but when Zach got the chance to be a brakeman, he left them, just as earlier he had left his kin back home: a man must make his own way and brakeman was the next rung in the ladder.

It was lonesome work for him after the years with the roundhouse gang but with him always for company and comfort was the glowing certainty that one great day he would be on the other end of the lantern's signals. It was dangerous work too, for the freight-cars were still equipped with the outlawed link-and-pin instead of automatic couplers. To couple two cars the brakeman had to stand between them and with his hands guide the link on one car into a slot on the other, and then drop in the iron which fastened them together.

Hardly a week went by in the Locust Grove yards without accident to one of the shacks, as the brakemen were called. If the man was fortunate, it would only be a finger or two missing, but often it was a hand and in the two and a half years Zach worked at this job the link-and-pin claimed the lives of eight of his fellow shacks. Perhaps because of his exceptional agility Zach escaped injury, but maybe it was just luck; and as the gambling men said, there's only one thing sure about luck—it changes. They said that about Georgia Skin, their favorite payday game, but it must be true, Zach figured, about human skin as well. But in one way the dreaded link-and-pin helped Zach: in a safer yard it would have taken him much longer to accumulate the necessary seniority to be promoted to fireman, but here, with the high turn-over caused by accidents and men leaving the job, he soon got to the top of the list and then it was only a matter of waiting for a fireman to quit or be fired.

His first regular run as a fireman was 120 miles northward to Ellamar, the next division; and he was to stay on that run for thirteen years.

The first years were the best—before the war and during the war—before the trouble started. The engineers with whom he worked were friendly, though, of course, he never got to know them except in the cab. Most of them would freely answer his many questions about the rules and regulations of their trade, though he could not miss their secret smiles of amusement that a black man should want to learn all about a white man's job. But he was a skillful worker and a good man to have along on the upgrade pull to Ellamar; and there was warmth in their Good evening, Zach, to his Good evening, Mr. Bonner, or Mr. Chadwick, or Mr. McDonald or any of the others to whom he reported for duty. The famous Rule G for railroadmen all over the country that prohibited the use of strong drink while on duty was seldom observed by either the white or black men on the GS&G, and though the engine drivers would often bait Zach about his strait-laced ways they came to respect him for it: he was punctual, alert, energetic and they could testify that he was a man of good moral character, though they would not have used those words. But even a "good nigger" could never be their Brother, for the constitution of the Brotherhood of Locomotive Firemen and Enginemen provides that for a man to be eligible he must be "white born, of good moral character." The white-born requirement comes first.

Young Zach could not know it then, but his working with the engineers was to be one of the main signals that lighted his way along the road he would travel. For the relationship between white engineer and black fireman was significantly different from that of other white men and Negroes in the South. Here black worker and white worker worked side by side; not as equals, of course, but nevertheless together. There was much master-and-man in the partnership, but they were fellow workers too and each had his part to play in making the run. In the long miles of pounding the rails there were even fleeting moments when the engineer, glancing across the cab, might see in the flashing light of the opened firedoor a fellow man and not remember that he was black. And sometimes a close attachment, even an unacknowledged friendship, grew between engineer and fireman, the white man taking the other along with him whenever he changed runs or was transferred to another division.

Once, during his first year, Mr. Chadwick asked him to go along with him on a different run, but Zach declined: he had already met Annie Mae Bolton, a member of the family that kept a boardinghouse for the Negro railroaders who laid over at Ellamar; and because she was as shy as he was, Zach stayed on that run for three years before they got married.

O Annie Mae, Annie Mae . . . eight more minutes to Renfrew, and then it's East Point, Chickasaw, Acropolis, Seminola, Alcorn, Sharpsville and Ellamar—one hour and thirty-two minutes and I'll be home! O honey lamb!—the whistle spilled his happiness over the jack-pine forest, flashing blue in the moonlight, and the pounding of the drivers was his heart just

157

a-reeling, was his heart just a-racking, was his blood just a-racing . . . *whoooooo whoooooo*, I'm a-coming through and home to Annie Mae!

A man needed a woman like Annie Mae: a steady-going woman for a steady-going man. She was a small, gentle brown-skinned woman, but strong with the strength of John Henry's people, beaten strong by sun and wind and sorrow, leathered by the lash, steeled by the very chains that bound them. And the women strong as the men.

> *John Henry had a little woman,*
> *Her name was Polly Ann,*
> *John Henry took sick an' couldn't get to work,*
> *Polly Ann drove steel like a man,*
> *Lawd, Lawd, Polly Ann drove steel like a man.*

But she was woman-soft, too, and tender in her quiet love: he would never be lonely again. Her eyes would shine with the knowing when Zach spoke of that great day when he would come driving up to Ellamar, easing the big engine into the station and swing down from the cab and wave goodnight to his fireman, all careless-like to hide his terrible pride. And Annie Mae would be waiting there and he would kiss her lightly and they would walk together homeward through the sleeping town, hand in hand like children, solemn silent with the wonder and the glory of their triumph. Sometimes, however, her eyes would glisten brighter with the unshed tears of sorrow and longing for a child to mother. The sadness too was a bond that drew them together, though the want of a child was harder on Annie Mae, alone when Zach was gone on the road. For that reason more than any other Zach was determined not to change his run; she had her parents in Ellamar, though they lived near the yards on the other side of town, and she dreaded the thought of moving to another city where she would have no one when he was away. But Zach was not transferred, and through the years he became as much a part of the Locust Grove-Ellamar run as the rails that connected the two divisions. A steady-going man, and it got to be said by the old-timers that even if you tore up all the track and signals too Isaac Zachary could still fire a locomotive on through to Ellamar and tell you exactly where you were every minute of the way. Wouldn't need no engineer neither—though it was only the Negroes who would add that, and only among themselves.

But he did not get to be an engineer. And somehow, slowly and against his will, against all the strength and passion of his dream, he came to see that he would never drive an engine until—no, not like the roundhouse gang had said: as long as you're black and live in Mississippi—for his skin would always be black and he did not intend ever to leave the place that was his home. No, that was not right: he would never believe that. But this he came to know: no one man could make it by himself. No matter how much he knew, no matter how hard he worked. He, Isaac Zachary, would never drive an engine until Negroes had the right to drive engines. A simple, easy truth; but it came hard. Later he would wonder why it had taken him so long to learn such a simple thing, forgetting how he had shut his ears against the jeers of his brothers and the doubts of his fellows, forgetting how the very brightness of his goal had blinded his eyes. He knew all the rules in the company's book, but this was a rule so big and plain that no one had ever bothered to write it down. Once he had asked Mr. Bonner about it: he was a tiny, silver-haired man, soft-spoken and friendly; he had given Zach a ten-dollar gold piece for a wedding present. But even with him Zach did not dare to speak directly. The old engineer had been talking that day about all the changes he had seen in his life on the road, going way back to the time of wood-burning engines and tallow lamps, and wondering about the marvels that were still to come.

"Mr. Bonner," Zach said, "I aint thinking about our time of course, but do you reckon there'll come a day when a colored man will drive an engine?"

The old man had studied his face, as Zach knew he would; then he shook his head slowly. "Zach, look here. Don't you ever be thinking or talking about nothing like that. I'm your friend, Zach, and I sure would hate to see you getting in trouble. But seeing as you asked me, I can tell you this: that day will never come. Wouldn't allow it. Company wouldn't allow it and the Brotherhood neither. Never."

"Thank you, Mr. Bonner. I'll remember what you said."

I'll remember what you said, but remembering aint believing. So far as the company is concerned—well, maybe they won't allow it. But they wouldn't allow you-all to have the eight-hour day, but here you just got through telling me how you beat the company down on that, and on a lot of other things too. The company wouldn't allow no union—but they signed the contract just the same. And the Brotherhood could beat them down on this thing too, but as you say the Brotherhood would never allow it either. . . .

One track leads into another, and learning goes along the same way. One Negro could not make it alone, no, and the black workers could never make it without the white. As long as the Brotherhood said never—well there would be no driving through. That was as plain as a headlight coming head-on at you, as plain and as fearful. But what power could change the hearts of the white railroaders and bring them into a unity of will with the black men with whom they shared the unity of work? No man could tell him, and as hard as he figured and as long as he figured Zach could not find the answer. You live and learn, the old folks used to tell him, and that was right for most things; but not for this. Here was something that must be found; but what could guide a man in his quest? Where now was the pillar of fire by night and the cloud by day that had led the Children through the wilderness of Sinai?

But the times of trouble came after the war was over, times when a man would forget what he was looking for. Folks had said that after Kaiser Bill got whipped things would be better for everybody; but that wasn't right either. Not for the railroaders. Hundreds of men were laid off—from the round-house and shops, maintenance of way and train crews too. White men and black men without work, pinching and borrowing and going broke, scratching and scrambling and getting hungry. That was all bad, but it was not yet the trouble. Not the bad trouble that was to come when the God-given advantage of being white wasn't worth a damn against the man-made rule of seniority. Nothing was more precious to the Brotherhood men than seniority: no gain had been harder won, more jealously guarded; it was the sure ladder to the top. But now everything was going down and the man with the longest service could bump the man off the next rung down and take his place. That was the rule and it was fair enough until a terrible thing was noticed: more white men were being laid off than Negroes! A black fireman could never be promoted to engineer and as a result most of them, like Isaac Zachary, had more seniority than the white firemen and more than many of the engineers; and because of that, too, the black brakemen under them had a firmer grip on their places than the shacks who were white. The law of the land—North and South and East and West—decreed that Negro workingmen be last hired and first fired, yet here—in Mississippi!—the law was being nullified. Surely nothing so evil had happened since the days of Black Reconstruction; and now there arose a muttering and a murmuring and then a roaring outcry so loud and dreadful that its rumblings could even be heard far north in Chicago where the board of directors of the Great Southwestern & Gulf held their quarterly meetings.

Now, gentlemen, we are not unmindful of your—ah—sensibilities, and we can appreciate how you men and the other good people of Mississippi feel about this unfortunate situation. But surely you must see that our hands are tied and—well, we hesitate to bring up old scores, but it was you who forced this rule upon us. . . . Of course, no one knew better than the company men that rules can be broken, but involved here was something infinitely greater—the Highest Law, more sacred even than White Supremacy which is subordinate and auxiliary to the law of profit. For the black railroaders were lower paid; and no wail from down the river could be as loud as the silent sound of dividends piling ever higher. . . . Furthermore, gentlemen—and we would not mention this had you not brought it up—but isn't it on record that the differential in pay was something you wanted too?

161

But there came a day when the directors of the GS&G would cease to smirk at the delegation of Brotherhood chieftains. Now it was an ultimatum: the strike vote had been taken, the date was set. And this time, thank God, the whole state is with us—even the biggest planters are backing the unions this time: here are the editorials, the speeches in the *Congressional Record*—strong words and dire threats. Race war it would be, and nothing like that little old riot you-all had up there in Chicago last year. There was no strike: and finally out of the conferences of Labor and Management and Government came an equitable agreement—the Fifty Fifty Rule as it came to be called. After the formalities of signature and seal, the new order was posted on all bulletin boards and it was there that Isaac Zachary and his fellows first learned of it.

Nowhere in the long columns of fine print was the word Negro mentioned: but to the black railroaders reading it every word was doom. Effective in thirty days not more than fifty per cent of the employees in any Operating Department could be other than Brotherhood members. That was disaster, but there was more, and worse. All subsequent vacancies were to be filled by members in good standing of recognized railroad labor organizations. There was much more to be read, of course—*pursuant to . . . and under the provisions of . . .* but all the big words meant nothing more or less than this: nearly half of the Negro firemen and brakemen were now to be fired; and after that, whenever a Negro quit, was retired or disabled, his place would be taken by a white man. Fifty-fifty now—all and nothing soon. . . .

There was no hope for those on whom the axe had fallen, but after the first stunning shock the older men who remained came to believe that something might still be saved: if the company could be made to recognize a black workers' union along with the others, then Negro replacements might be provided under the Fifty Fifty Rule. It was desperate hope rather than true belief, but when the organizer came down from Atlanta they joined the Grand Alliance of Firemen, Hostlers and Brakemen which had already been formed among Negro trainmen in Georgia, Alabama and the Carolinas.

Isaac Zachary was a charter member of the Ellamar lodge and vice-president too, though he was one of the youngest of those who were left; and now his dream to become an engineer was lost in the struggle to stay a fireman. And the struggle like the dream must be kept secret from the white men: more secret, for many men and their families were now involved. Even among themselves the members never spoke of their union outside of meetings, and the Ladies' Auxiliary, in which Annie Mae was active, had no other name than that. Nor was there need for any of the lodge members to reveal themselves: no bargaining was possible in Mississippi; only the Alliance representatives up North could speak for them to company officials—if they could get in to see them. But still there was a great deal that had to be done locally: every man that was left was precious and when a man got sick or was injured his bills must be paid, his family supported until he could return; women from the Auxiliary must nurse those who had no women-folk to tend them. For a man gone was a job gone—forever. Only when the Alliance was recognized would there be hope of Negro replacements, and that was slow in coming. All through the years of Coolidge prosperity they worked and prayed for Recognition, and tended their sick and bolstered the weary and scrimped and scuffled to keep something in the treasury.

But if Recognition did not come the Great Depression did and with it the most terrible trouble of all. It had been an uneasy peace for the beleagured black railroaders: now it would be war. For again there were Negroes working while white men were jobless. Fewer, of course, this time, for the decade under Fifty Fifty had taken its toll even before the lay-offs started: death and dismissals had thinned the ranks of the black firemen and no nursing can return a brakeman who has lost an arm or leg. There were hardly any jobs for anyone, but still there were some black men at work; and if one of these were gone a job would be open for a white man. Threats, not even in Mississippi, were enough to scare the Negroes into quitting: they had fought too long and too desperately for spoken hints or anonymous letters signed KKK to move them now.

It became a shooting war. A strange war, secret and implacable, that raged throughout Mississippi on all the railroads from 1931 to 1934. The newspapers never heard of it, the companies were indifferent, the Brotherhood chiefs disclaimed any responsibility and the law knew nothing about it either; but shotguns roared in the night at McComb and Durant and Aberdeen Junction and Vicksburg and Natchez and Brookhaven and Canton and Water Valley—and black men fell. Twenty-two Negro firemen and brakemen were killed or wounded or shot at; and of the ten who were killed two had been previously wounded. For the black workers there was only one way to fight back—to stay on the job. A man quitting now was more than a job gone: it was a battle lost, a betrayal of those who had fallen. They did not quit.

Two brakemen had been shot at in the Locust Grove yards and old John Givens, the senior Negro firemen on the division, had been killed the year before; but in the spring of 1932 Isaac Zachary was still firing on the run to Ellamar. It was not so bad when he was on the day run, but recently he had been put back to nights though the super must surely have known that night was most dangerous. Zach did not worry much for himself, but for Annie Mae, waiting at home, these were nights of terror. He knew it even though she never said a word; he would have known it even if he did not see the look in her eyes each time he got home. Her mother and father had died long ago—the Flu that had taken away so many after the war; and now she had only Zach.

It could happen to him anywhere—on a side-track when the red ball freight roared through, or at any one of the lonely places where they took on water, or when inching up a steep grade where the black man in the cab would be silhouetted against the firedoor's glare, or from behind a board fence as he made his way home through the unlighted streets of the Negro quarter. Or at the very moment he opened his front door to the lamp-lit parlor where Annie Mae was waiting up in her rocking chair, facing the black marble clock he had given her on their wedding anniversary.

The blast came from behind the flowering lilac bush planted

164

beside the porch, and the big man crashed to the floor, half way through the doorway, and by the time Annie Mae reached him the carpet was thick with his blood. Had it come squarely into his back, the buckshot would surely have killed him; but it was a grievous wound. No ambulance could be called, for there was no colored hospital in that county to which he might be taken; and Isaac Zachary was near to death from the bleeding when the company doctor, for whom the neighbors ran, finally came many hours later.

A steady-going man, a strong man: somehow he lived. And with him, through the long tunnel of pain and darkness that was the seventy days and seventy nights he lay helpless in the brass-knobbed bed, was Annie Mae, nursing him now as she had nursed so many others whom the railroads had laid low. Now you are only mine, she thought, and after you be all well again they can never have you back. O Isaac, they tried to kill you dead and you're all I got and I love you so, I love you so. Don't have nobody but you, nobody but you. . . . But she knew in the bursting flood of her tears—the mother-tears so long unshed that came so quickly now—that he would go back. She saw it in the look on his face when his union brothers came, awkward and ill at ease in their Sunday serge, to sit in silence beside his bed. She saw it too by the yellow glow of the kerosene lamp when the midnight whistle of Old 44 trumpeted from far away that Zach's train was pulling in. *Hear that Dan'l?—and you Queenie? Oh, I'm going to drive that devil one a these days. I will. I will. Drive him straight and hard, straight and hard and fast. . . .*

And with the dream that returned so urgent and compelling to Isaac Zachary the forgotten question came back too. But now more than ever the answer was lost in the dark swirling fog of hatred that was lighted only by the stabbing flash of shotguns. What power could change their hearts? What force could bring the day when the men in overalls, the white and the black, would truly clasp hands in brotherhood and grand alliance? No one who came could tell. But it was something to think about in the long dragging hours while his torn muscles were slowly healing. All men are created equal—yes, the wise men said that long ago and *they* were white. All men are brothers—yes, the Good Book says that and it must be in theirs as it is in ours. But there is something more a man must know and though his mind may trace through all the turnings as his eye follows the pattern, twisting and twining, on the bedroom wall, there is no path he can find from the maze.

There are many things a man can't figure out, but this he knows: a man must work and a man must fight. And so, on the first day he could walk from the house, Isaac Zachary reported back for duty. (*"Bet he didn't come back so quick to that hen-house, I bet you that!"*) The very first day he could.

But now there was no work for him: no cotton and corn for the trains to haul, for who could buy it? Above the cloud of strife and hate and hunger that covered the Magnolia State was the greater pall still spreading across the Land of Plenty. Root, hog, or die—but what could a jobless workingman do? What could a black fireman do when the great engines, lined up on the rusting rails, stood patient and still like elephants trunk to tail? Back to the farm, some of them said as they packed up to leave; back to the farm—at least you can always eat. But Zach could not go back: there were already too many mouths to feed on Tom Zachary's farm and even through the good years he had had to help out from his pay. Many were heading North and while people said things were better up there, Zach did not want to go where a Negro could never get a job as brakeman or fireman.

But he had to go, for there was nothing here at all. His brother Benjamin, who had worked since the war in the steel mill up in Kanesport, wrote that Isaac and his wife could stay with him while Isaac looked for a job. That was in August of 1932 and along the way they could see through the grimy windows of the Jim Crow car the billboards with the pictures of the two men America must choose between: one fat-faced and grim in his high choking collar, the other lean and smiling at his coming victory.

The voting was something for white folks to study about and there was too much for Zach and Annie Mae to see and learn in the northern city for them to think about it one way or the other. Kanesport was the largest place they had ever seen, its population of 75,000 surpassed even the greatest city in Mississippi; but Benjamin laughed at the marvelling greenhorns—Kanesport aint nothing but a big old company town, wait till you see Iron City down the river a ways; more than a million people there. And with all the wonders of streetcars and tall buildings there was much that was like down home, especially in the Goat Hill section where the colored people lived. Most of their houses, perched along the steep-rising banks of the Monongahela, were no better than down home and some of them, Annie Mae noted with triumphant scorn, were worse than any in Ellamar. Course we got outhouses like these, she told Benjamin who always acted like he had never seen the South, but Lord, not so many people has to use the same one!

Isaac was lucky and got a job in the tinplate mill where his brother worked; and though that was a wondrous thing these days, Benjamin was strangely unimpressed. For—and he never did tell Isaac about it—he had fixed it up with Mr. Wills, the Negro Service Representative for the steel company. Later, when Herbert T. Wills left the company to become Industrial Secretary of the Negro Improvement League and folks said he was still on the McGregor payroll, Benjamin would only sniff and say to himself: Don't know nothing about that, but I won't never forget how that rascal got a month's pay from me!

In the hard days of work and new ways of life where a man must learn how to live while being black in the great Commonwealth of coal and steel, the same and yet different too from Mississippi, his old dream and the search for the way were buried in the slag-pile of the past, with only an occasional wisp of smoke rising to tell of the long-gone fire. Not even the whistles of the speeding trains could recall it: their thin shrill pipings were lost in the roaring rumble of the mill and the imperious big-voiced blast that called the men to work.

But though a great dream may die, it can rise again like Lazarus and walk the earth once more to claim its own. And so, one night, the dream came back to Isaac Zachary and with it, this time, the long-sought answer. It came as such a dream must come to a company town ruled by the Coal and Iron police—under cover of darkness, secretly, slipping under doors locked against the hostile streets of law and order.

It was still pitch black outside when Zach got up that morning to make the 3 to 11 shift and saw the corner of the folded paper peeping from under the front door. BUY NOW it would say, BUY NOW AND PAY LATER! Washing machines or 3-way lamps or used car bargains or GENUINE simulated GOLD watches or Paris fashions CHEAP at Hoffman's Big Downtown Store. He had no mind for such foolishness and no money either, and he would have tossed away the handbill had he not seen the pictures of the two men. He had no time to read it then, but he folded the paper into his mackinaw pocket until he got back home from work when he and Annie Mae could study it together.

The photographs of the two men running for office were printed side by side: the white man and the Negro, William Z. Foster and James W. Ford, for President and Vice-President of the whole United States. To the man and woman but a few short months up from Mississippi, this was something that belonged to the world of fantasy they could enter for fifteen cents and see Douglas Fairbanks with a towel wrapped around his head and wearing Bible garments ride through the clouds on his magic rug—a thing of wonder and nice to see, but make-believe and something serious-minded folks wouldn't study about for a minute once they emerged into the hard sunlight outside the Bijou.

The revelation was in the tiny printed words beneath each picture. First they read about the Negro: born in the South . . . grandfather lynched . . . worked in the Birmingham mills . . . came North . . . then a union leader. The other was also a workingman and—here was something that had to be read slowly and carefully, and read again and still another time until the words were lost in the blinding flash of glory, in the burning rush of tears. The white man had been a brakeman and a fireman! *A white railroader side by side with a black man!* For unity, it said, for equal rights, for brotherhood of all. Not hating each other, not killing each other—what man could believe that day would come? But Zach had believed it, had always believed it, and here was the way. Here was the Way and the Truth and the Light, as it was written long ago.

Here was the through train for real, and now that Isaac and Annie Mae had found it they would ride it all the way. Through everything—through good times and hard times and times of trouble, through towering granite walls and through the deepest Hole, through darkness and danger, through side-tracks and crossings, on and on . . . to the great day a-coming when all people shall stand together, hand in hand like Zach and Annie Mae, with clean hearts and seeing eyes and loving one another. . . .

O Shining Day when all America shall ride that Glory Train, just a-reeling and a-racking, just a-reeling and a-racking, reel-ing and a-racking—*whoooooo whoooooo*, goin' straight to glory —Zach a-driving on through!

CHAPTER 13

"D ten—visitor!"

Paul Harper rushed from his cell at the awaited call from the keyman but Faulcon grabbed his arm in front of Number 9. "Don't forget she should tell Mrs. Zachary—she's coming too —that he's all right and she should come back next week." Paul nodded impatiently and pulled away but Faulcon ran after him: "Another thing, Paul—tell your gal I'm still sweet on her and quick as I get out of here—"

"Go to hell, old man," said Paul as he hurried through the end gate.

Charlene! It was three weeks to the day since he had kissed her, a short kiss for such a farewell, but the steel on his wrist had jerked him away. Two weeks since her first visit, and last Wednesday they had turned her away, for Range D was being punished for beating up their rangeman. In another few days it would be five years since he married the pretty young school teacher up in Cleveland. I only did it, he used to tell her, because I couldn't recruit you any other way; and she always had an answer for that one: All right, Comrade Harper, but from now on you'll have to limit yourself to getting men into the Party and let somebody else who is not so conscientious sign up the women!

In 1937, a year after their marriage, the young couple had moved to Iron City: an additional Negro organizer was needed for the C.I.O. organizing drive in Big Steel and Paul had been picked for the job. No Negro school teachers were employed in Iron City, but Charlene had found work as a stenographer in the regional office of the South Carolina Mutual Benefit Society, a Negro insurance company. High society we are, she would tell Paul, and not common labor like you steel workers. Even if we do get only sixteen-fifty a week—still we're *executives* and don't you forget it! But in the laughing and loving that was her life with Paul she was not really unhappy that she could no longer work at her profession.

There were several cubicles for visiting hour, and in the one to which the guard directed Paul, another inmate was already talking into the screen which extended the six-foot length of the wall. He was a white boy; one arm, in a plaster cast from the elbow, was cocked like a boxer's: he was yelling to his visitor and she was shouting back. Even though Paul and Charlene pressed their mouths to the screen at the opposite end from the other two, they could barely hear each other above the angry voices. . . .

"Run that middle part over again."

The man from the Detective Bureau settled back into the leather easy chair in the Deputy Warden's office to listen once more to the second disk of the recording that had been made an hour earlier.

"I can't help it, Paul. I was sure they would overrule Judge Rupp at least about the bail. All of us and the lawyers were sure—"

(You're just a bum, that's all you are!
Never nothing but trouble. Always . . .)

"Well don't cry now, honey. Can't hardly hear you as it is without you crying. Keep that up and you'll make me sad too."

(You're somebody to talk, Ma. What did
you ever do for me except always telling
me I aint no good. Tell me that, huh!)

"All right, Paul . . . I didn't order those books from the publisher's because I was thinking—but I'll do it now and you should get them soon."

(Well you aint no good or you wouldn't
be a thief and be in jail again.)

"That's fine, because I'm almost through with Les Miserables. It's a wonderful book, honey, and I copied out a part from the preface to put in my next letter but if you want I'll read it to you now. OK?"

(You're a fine one to talk, Ma. You never
gave me nothing and now I bet you're
glad. That's what you are—glad!)

"Sure. I'd rather for your letters to be more—you know."

"About love and stuff like that?"

"Uh huh. Why not?"

(Sure I'm glad. What do you think I am?
My only son in jail — a dirty sneaking
purse-snatcher. . . .)

"OK. I'll try to write more romantic. Anyway, here it is — and now a word from Victor Hugo: So long as there shall exist, by reason of law and custom, a social condemnation, which, in the face of civilization,"

(Well why don't you laugh then? You can
laugh for the next three years I'm in this
stinking place! Go ahead . . . laugh!)

"artificially creates hells on earth . . . so long as the three problems of the age—the degradation of man by poverty, the ruin of woman by starvation, and the dwarfing of childhood by physical and spiritual night—are not solved; so long as ignorance and misery remain on earth, books like this cannot be useless."

171

(*Shut up mister no-good bum! That's all you are and the only thing I'm glad about is your father being dead and not be shamed like me.*)

"That's beautiful, Paul. It's true, it's true. I try to remember things like that and not to cry. It's only now. . . ."

(*Shame? What shame you got you stinking whore! Think I don't know about you, huh!*)

"Sure, I know. But look—I'm going to write you an important letter soon and I want you to do exactly what I tell you in it."

(*Oh, Bobby, Bobby! Why did you do it? Why were you always so bad . . . I tried. I tried—God knows I did, son. . . .*)

"About what, Paul?"

"Can't tell you here. Too important."

"OK. Shut it off. That was the part I wanted again." The detective got up and walked over to the massive glass-topped desk; he picked up the pen from the holder and scratched a memorandum for the Deputy Warden: *Have copies made of all out-going letters from Paul Harper and forward same in triplicate to Detective Bureau, marked attention Confidential Squad.—Lieut. P. J. Kennedy.*

(2)

REGULATION 126 (b): NO INMATE SHALL BE KEPT IN SOLITARY CONFINEMENT AND/OR ON LIMITED DIET IN EXCESS OF TEN CONSECUTIVE DAYS.

Army had been returned to Range D while Paul was away for his visit; and now they were kidding the young man in khaki because he had been in the Hole for thirteen days although he had been sentenced to only ten. You must have liked it in there, they told him. He smiled to the welcoming circle of faces, his eyes still blinking against the light of day.

172

"Well, one good thing about it," he said, embarrassed with his secret, "was that I didn't have to see so many ugly Negroes all around me every day." Nothing could have made him tell them that the three extra days had been given him to reconsider his stubborn refusal to name some of the others who had joined him in assaulting the rangeman. And after that, when he still refused to tell the guards, Steve had ordered his release. It's one thing, Army thought, not to be a stool, but I sure would hate for these guys to think I was being noble!

Army was surprised to hear that Isaac Zachary had been sent to the Hole too. "He's the last man—quiet as he is—that I'd figure to ever get in trouble around here. But don't you-all worry about him—if I could make it all right, well, that big guy can do it standing on his head."

Paul gave him a hearty handshake and then nodded to Henry Faulcon to follow him to his cell.

"I changed my mind about telling Charlene anything about Lonnie or asking her to see his lawyer. Maybe I'm being too careful and I know we got to move fast on this business—but still that place might be tapped. Don't forget, Henry, that you and me are conspirators and they might want to find out where we keep our bombs. Come to think of it, old man,"—and now a boyish grin broke the serious look that Paul always assumed at meetings—"you'd be right funny-looking wearing whiskers. With that gray hair, people would take you for a sepia-toned Santa Claus instead of a real Bolshevik!"

Faulcon had to smile, thinking how he would look; he ran his fingertips around his chin-stubble and said: "Maybe so, son, but leastwise I could grow my own whiskers and not have to buy a set like *some* folks I know. But now let's get down to business!" The phrase was Paul's, and Faulcon was pleased at the chance to use it against the other.

"That's right," said Paul. "Guess I was just feeling good after talking with Charlene. Anyway, something tells me that in a cold-blooded frame-up like Lonnie's—well, if they knew what we were going to do they'd break it up fast. Move him, or more likely move us—to another block so we couldn't see him or maybe even transfer us to the pen. And it would

173

be all over, I guess, for Lonnie then." He went on to tell Faulcon what he had said to Charlene about the letter he would send.

The gray head shook vigorously. "How can you be so dumb —with them censoring our mail? I can't see that at all less you mean you got a code or something."

"No, of course not. And I don't have a code. But I was thinking about something last night when I couldn't fall asleep: Remember last Sunday after Zach got put in the Hole how Slim took his letter to mail? Well, that's what I've been counting on. Slim is janitor in the Warden's office and he must have some way to sneak out letters. So all we got to do is wait for three o'clock when the workingmen get back in here and then I'll ask him. Now you get out of here and let me start writing it.—Hey, wait a minute, Henry. Did you see Lonnie out in the yard? What did he have to say?"

"Nothing much," said Faulcon from the door. "Just asked me if your wife had come and when I said yes, he ran like hell out of ranks and started to play his one-man basketball game. Boy, you should have seen him play!"

The instructions at the top of the jail stationery warned that the inmate should write on only one side of the sheet; Paul ignored that now, for the letter must not be too bulky. The words were printed so that if the message were intercepted they could not prove that he had sent it. There was no room, of course, to include all the details of Lonnie's story, but the main facts were there. The words *innocent* and *frame-up* were heavily underscored as were the repeated phrases, *the organization must, immediate action, complete mobilization*. The letter was written as if the sender were outside and the jail was referred to as "the place where they sent your husband."

In addition to the main message which was obviously meant for the new District Committee that had been set up to replace the jailed leaders, the letter instructed Charlene personally to see Attorney Arnold Winkel. She must tell him none of the plans, but as someone who is interested in the unfortunate youth, she must learn the true state of affairs con-

174

cerning the appeal and any other legal angles she could. But when all the plans for the conference of organizations were completed (the conference was the first action he had proposed for the suggested Provisional Committee to Save Lonnie James) the lawyer should be asked to participate. It would be better, he wrote, if Winkel could be included earlier, but there was doubt as to how far he could be trusted; and the other lawyer, who seems to be an accomplice in the frame-up, should not be seen at all. Another thing Charlene must do: get Mrs. Zachary, and anybody else we know in Kanesport, busy trying to find out what happened to Leroy Flowers and why Big John refused to remember about Lonnie. Also: what about Herbert T. Wills of the Negro Improvement League—what's his part in this? And don't delay a minute, he warned her—the courts may rule on Lonnie's appeal any day. He printed the words "A Lover of Justice" for a signature.

Next? The call for the conference, of course. He might just as well do it himself so they could rush it to the printer after they set a date and arranged for a hall. After all, he thought, I seem to have appointed myself Executive Secretary anyway. The call should be short and urgent:

A CALL to all Trade Unions, Churches, Clubs and Fraternal Organizations:

SAVE LONNIE JAMES!
Defeat the Legal Lynching in Iron City!

Lonnie James, a young Negro steel worker of Kanesport, was arrested last year for a crime he did not commit. He was framed-up by District Attorney Stewart McKee and the police of Monongahela County. He was cruelly beaten for many days to make him confess. He was denied a fair trial. Last October Judge Rupp sentenced him to be hanged.

HEAR THE SHOCKING FACTS
BEHIND THIS BRUTAL FRAME-UP!

Elect delegates to represent you at the Mass Conference to Save Lonnie James to be held on (date) at (place). Don't fail. Only MASS ACTION can free him. Remember: We saved the lives of the 9 Innocent Scottsboro Boys of Alabama! We

175

saved Angelo Herndon from death on the chain-gang in Georgia! *WE CAN SAVE LONNIE JAMES FROM THE GALLOWS IN IRON CITY!*

Signed: Provisional Committee to Save Lonnie James.

Address: (blank)   Secretary: (blank)

"For Christ's sake, don't scare me like that!" But under the angry flare-up was the warm relief that it was Faulcon who was looking over his shoulder at what he had written.

"Paul," said Faulcon after he had finished reading the Call, "I want to take back all I ever said against you. Boy, that's *fine!* It makes me feel good just to see it. But what I came in to see you about is Slim—he's back in his cell now. Guess you was too busy to notice the time."

(3)

Slim looked up and frowned when Paul came into Number 25. Slim never visited with the others on the range nor did he ever join the bull sessions at the front end of the runway. From three o'clock when he returned from his job until lock-up he never left his cell except for slop-call; whenever any one passed they would see him busy making his belts or studying his paper-bound book. The belts were a jailhouse hobby, but the *Spanish For Beginners* was for his time of freedom to come.

"That's pretty," said Paul, staring down at the nearly completed creation on Slim's bunk. The belts were made from the wrappers of toilet-paper rolls and from the cellophane jackets of cigarette packs: the wrappers, bordered in gay colors, were carefully torn and folded into tiny strips, then wrapped tightly into the cellophane that provided a strong covering. The strips were woven and fitted into a belt complete with slot-buckle and loops, and all so cunningly joined that no one could tell that it was made from hundreds of tiny pieces and that no glue or thread was used to hold them together. The color design, artful as the weaving, resembled the intricate mosaic of a gleaming snakeskin.

Slim's frown at the intrusion still held, but his voice sounded

176

pleased at the compliment; he stroked the belt lightly with a large hard hand. "Yeah—you really think so? I kind of like this new one myself." No, he didn't make them to sell and he indicated a dozen of them laid across his shelf. "Takes me a long time to make one of 'em," he said, "and I just like to look at them once in a while. Course, I do give some of them away sometimes. . . ."

Paul explained that he did not mean to bother him by barging in like this, but this was something very important. He had barely mentioned his request when Slim stopped him.

"Nothing doing. No sir! I know what you mean—about last Sunday and your friend's letter. I don't know why I did that myself," he said, "—guess I was crazy, that's all." He knew of course; he knew why he had taken the risk just as he knew that he would never have stood up against the baiting guards as Isaac Zachary did. *Don't touch me!*, the big man had said. *Just don't touch me!* The words had come to Slim's cell as though they were meant for him: That's how a man talks if he is really a man and not an old coward like you, Slim! You never did that—not once in your life, not even outside, not a single time when the color of your skin had marked you for abuse or insult. . . . And with the accusation had come a surging thrill of proud kinship; here was a man as black as Slim, as outnumbered and as unarmed, who could face them down. *Just don't touch me!*; and they did not dare.

"I guess I was crazy, that's all," he repeated softly.

When Paul insisted that this was much more important, Slim got up to face him—this man, this inmate, he could stand up to and show his anger and warn him not to touch him. "Important? What's important? I'll tell you what. *Me,* I'm important! Even in here where I got the best job open to colored. But I don't mean that so much—it's this!" He reached under the pillow they gave to workingmen and brought out the precious book. "Here—look at that. Go ahead and count them!"

On the fly-leaf, painstakingly precise as his weaving, were blocks of tiny lines—four down, one across; four down, one across. "Just look at them," he demanded. "Every mark a day. Every mark a lock-up. I don't have to count 'em—not me. I

177

know: six hundred and seventy—one year and three hundred and five days—locked up like a dog and for what?" An accident that could happen to any man. An argument, a fight, fist on chin, head hitting the curb—manslaughter. He was guilty, he admitted it, though of course he had not meant to kill the man. The sentence was two to five years in the County jail.

"Two more rows, twelve more blocks, sixty more marks and I'll be free! June it will be, the grass will be green and everything so nice." Slim would go back to the garbage truck and then after exactly forty-eight pays he would have saved enough to go on to the greater freedom of his plan. South America! A new life—he was only thirty-nine and that's not too old is it? "I don't know exactly where, what country it'll be, but it don't matter none because they tell me that down there people don't care what color you are. It's only what you are that counts. And I'm not a crook and nobody there will ever know about this. I got some money in the bank and with a little bit more I'll be gone for good. Yeah man!" He smiled now for the first time: "I mean, *Si señor!*"

But his visitor persisted. "Just one time, Slim. I won't ask you any more. It's not for me—if it was I'd tell you what it's all about, but you got my word—"

Slim blew a scornful blast through tight-pressed lips. "Your word—aint *that* a bitch! And who do you think you are? Army told me what you're in for—*politics*. A two-timing politician, promising everything—'I give you my word'—till you get your man elected and your hands on a piece of graft and then to hell with us suckers. And now you come around trying to trick me into losing all my good time and maybe have to pull another year or two years or even the whole five!" The fear, always pressing against the levee of his life-plan, was rising now in chilling flood and with it a terrible anger against this insistent intruder. His eyes focussed on Paul's good suit, baggy now but clean and nearly new.

"Think you're better than the rest of us, don't you? Wearing those fancy clothes to jail and acting like a big shot! Think cause I'm in dirty dungarees that I don't count—maybe I still stink from the garbage—huh? Well, just leave me alone that's

178

all. And when I leave this goddam jail and get out of this goddam country if anybody comes asking me about white folks or colored people either I'm just going to grin in their goddam face and say: Me no savvy! No, I aint doing nothing for nobody—just for me, Slim Gaither, hear me? Just for me!"

(4)

Faulcon had brought his slop-pan into Paul's cell where they ate together. Paul did not touch his food, only the coffee, bitter-black as his disappointment. When they were finished they emptied what was left into the toilet and washed the battered tin cups and the spoons in Paul's wash-bowl. Faulcon polished his periscope-spoon, blowing upon it, then rubbing it carefully with toilet paper. After he was satisfied that it could gleam no brighter, he wrapped it in tissue and returned it to his shirt pocket. The old man had made no comment while Paul was telling of his failure with Slim: Whenever there's food, eat!, Jenny Faulcon had taught him—you can always talk some other time. Now he settled back on the bunk and opened the top button of his trousers.

"Paul" he said, "only this morning I took back all I ever said against you. But now I got to charge you with something else. How come you got to be so quick all the time to judge people? Now this guy Slim—he's an 'escapist.' Why? Because he wants to get away from what's bothering him, that's all. Shucks, that aint no different from most people—everybody's trying to get away from something best way they know how. And when you get my age you'll understand that good as me. Escaping—pooh! Why look at me: forty years I been escaping matrimony and the first time I ever felt safe was in here! I hate to be a-bragging about it, but I sure had some mighty close calls!"

There was a hissing sound as Paul flung his cigarette into the toilet.

"And here's something else," Faulcon went on. "Don't be so sure Slim won't change about that. He did it for Zach and nobody even asked him to. Maybe if we told him about Lonnie

—Oh, I know it's best not to trust anybody right now if we can help it, but what else can we do? Just like that deep philosophy you were handing me the other day: Freedom is based on necessity."

Paul could not let that go by: "Freedom is the *recognition* of necessity—that's what I said, or rather that's how Engels put it."

"Sure, that's what I just got through saying. Meaning we got to take a chance with Slim."

"And what if he turns the letter in? I told you how he said that he's only out to help himself and don't give a damn about nobody else. Turning in that letter would really put him in solid with Cap'n Charlie—maybe they'd even let him out before June."

Faulcon eyed the younger man for a moment. "Paul," he said, "you're being subjective. Yes, you—I mean you and that's one of your own favorite words—*subjective.* Meaning you're hot cause Slim cussed you out and said some reactionary things as well as turning you down about the letter. And as far as our clothes is concerned I even agree with him. Not for his reason, of course, but now that we aint going out on bail we better have some old clothes sent in and save our good suits. But about Slim—I vote we tell him."

Paul said he was not sure; he would think about it some more.

The tower clock struck one. For the third successive night Lonnie James did not hear it: now that someone knew, now that someone was helping, he could rest on Murderers' Row. Down in the Hole, Isaac Zachary was sound asleep on the narrow plank that is the bed in solitary: he had nothing to worry about until they turned him loose. But on Range D two men were still awake. The man in Number 25 was reading, his lips forming the words: *Yo tengo una pluma*—I have a pen. *Yo tengo papel*—I have paper. . . . The other, in Number 10, was wrestling with the hard decision he must make.

"I'll sleep on it," Paul Harper had told Faulcon; but now he could not sleep. It won't be easy, he had said when they first agreed to fight for Lonnie's life; but he had not thought it would be so hard from the start. Before lock-up he had gone to look at the rangeman's roster: it confirmed what he already knew—old Pete had been the last man on the range waiting trial; there was no one else who might carry the letter out. And the chart showed something else: it would be sixty more days before the nearest man pulled his time and even that would not be definite until the parole board acted upon Slim Gaither's appeal.

No, only Slim can do it now. Would he do it if I told him about Lonnie? Or would he betray us all? The man's words came back to Paul: *Important? What's important?—I'll tell you what. Me, I'm important!* Man, you don't know how right you are. I hardly knew you before today but now, far as I'm concerned, you're the most important man in the world!

Henry is right, of course: we got to trust Slim. We can't delay, can't wait for something else. Every day counts. While Lonnie is alive, before they get to kill him. But still, if I give Slim the letter and he gives it to the Warden—what then? The front door opens for Slim, the trap-door for Lonnie. That's one thing sure, everything else is a chance. It could be me up there, but it's Lonnie—it's his life we're talking about, his life we'd be risking with Slim. But if we don't—if a movement doesn't get started outside right away? The frame-up will be completed: Lonnie will die.

Slim must get the letter out. He must be told. Tomorrow.

CHAPTER 14

In vain the tower clock strikes out the hours of night: time, caged in with a man behind McGregor steel, cannot move. To Do begins at six when the door clicks open for impatient time and man to rush out to the runway, to the main street of this iron city of life and men and struggle, linked by visible and secret ties with the greater iron city beyond the walls.

After breakfast there would be only an hour left before Slim went off the range to report for work. Time was desperately short. In the long hours of making up his mind, Paul Harper had been seized with the idea that the letter must go out today. Delay would be worse than unbearable: it would be disaster. The thought was relentless: *It must be today.* Every word of his appeal to Slim was carefully rehearsed; he had gone over it again and again till there seemed to be no possible opening for Slim to elude him. It was a stirring, impassioned appeal that would move a heart of stone—but Slim never heard it.

When he walked in to see the man in Number 25, Paul had the Call in his hand. Without a word he gave it to Slim; he did not speak until the man had read it through.

"You know Lonnie," Paul said.

Slim did not answer; he did not even look up.

"I can tell you how they framed him, if you'll only listen."

Slim shook his head. He would not listen. He got up slowly, deliberate with his decision, and walked over to the book on his shelf. He opened it and though Paul could not see, he knew the man was looking at the record of his days.

"Give me the envelope," Slim said abruptly. He turned around. His face showed nothing.

Paul and Faulcon watched him when he went out the gate. Going out with him was J.C. who worked in the bath-house.

"See how easy it was?" the old man said. "I was right about Slim."

"Henry, I hope so. But we had to tell him." We had to tell him—he said it again to himself, defending himself against the accusing finger of doubt. "Maybe it was too easy," he said aloud.

An hour later, as they waited in line for Range D to go to the yard, they debated whether to tell Lonnie what they had done. Faulcon was firm against it: Wait till we know for sure. No use worrying him. Bad enough you got me worried now. They were still whispering about it when the keyman's high-pitched voice came calling:

"*D nine and D ten—Steve wants to see you!*"

Whitey shrugged his narrow shoulders as Paul and Faulcon followed him up the stairs to the Hub. "Don't know what for—he didn't say. You guys aint been up to nothing have you?" When they reached the gate that faced the chief guard's desk, Whitey told them to wait there; he continued up the stairs on another errand. Behind them, through the inner gate, they could see the runway of Murderers' Row. Lonnie was down at the far end, talking with a little white man. That must be Crazy Peterson. *Hey, Lonnie! Please—turn this way. Look around, man, look around! We may never see you again. . . .* Paul coughed loudly, but Lonnie did not hear. He did not turn around.

Steve was short behind his high desk; they could just see the top of his round curly head as he bent over his papers. He glanced up now and saw them; his eyebrows lifted in question. When they said nothing, he stood up: "What the hell you guys doing there?"

The keyman said you wanted us for something—D nine and D ten.

He nodded and walked over to where they waited. One chubby hand held some papers, the other fished in his white shirt pocket for his pencil.

"Who's Paul Harper?" he demanded. His voice was angry. "Them goddam bums will steal anything. Now I got to do this job too!" He looked at the two Negroes as if seeing them for the first time and they knew that his anger was not meant for them. "Money," he said. "Two dollars for each of you in these letters. You got to sign for it."

The shocking happiness and relief that Slim had not betrayed them must have shone on their faces, for Steve grinned back at them. He looked at the printed return-address on one of the long envelopes. "International Labor Defense," he said. "Looks like your people remember you, all right. They write that you're going to get two bucks a week from them. And the same for your four friends over on Block Three—the white boys. Every week—not bad." He frowned now. "I'm the only one that has it bad around here. What do you think about these scum—the guards I mean: they been stealing so much money from the mail that Warden says I got to hand it out myself. As if I aint got enough to do already!"

He was still grumbling about it after they had signed and thanked him and turned to leave. "Wait a minute," he called. And when he spoke again his voice was barely a whisper, strangely confidential. "Maybe you can tell me your ideas— these Irish bums I work with don't read nothing but the funnies. About Russia: do you think it's right the way the papers say—about Russia letting the Nazis take charge of everything she got, the army and factories and everything?"

Paul Harper tried to hide his surprise and the suspicion that was even greater. They had all agreed not to let any of the guards provoke them by hositility or trap them into confidence—and this was the chief guard himself. Paul had only meant to shrug but the words came out despite his resolve: "The papers are lying!"

Steve winked and said he sure hoped so; then he thumbed them away.

It was a day of surprises, of sudden wonders, of things to talk about. When Slim came back he looked in upon the two conspirators and nodded; his lips formed the word OK, then he was gone. Faulcon wanted to follow after him, to share with the silent weaver their overwhelming joy, but Paul stopped him; this time he was the wiser. "Don't bother him now. He wants to be left alone. Some other time. . . ." And now the thought that had been forming through all the hours since morning came clear: "Henry, you were wrong about one thing. It was not easy. Not for Slim."

They laughed about how Steve had called the others Irish bums while holding in his hands the letters from the International Labor Defense signed by Patrick Emmett O'Flynn, the grand old man of the steel-workers who was president of the Iron City chapter of the I.L.D. Good thing Old Pat wasn't around to hear Steve make that crack—Sure they're bums, he would roar, but I'll be damned if they're Irish! And it was good to hear about the others, the four white Communists who were here under the same roof with them but whom they had not seen since they were all brought over from the Cathedral of Justice. They are on Cell Block Three—glad he told us: maybe we can send them a note some time soon.

Now they talked again about Steve. They recalled the day they first saw him, down below on Bum Side. His brutal fist smashing into the Bible-shouting mouth, his fingers picking away the bloody white shirt that clung to his paunch. Maybe he had complained afterwards because he had to attend to such details just as he had been displeased today about having to handle the incoming money. Yes, and it was Steve who had taken away all their privileges for a week when the thieving rangeman got caught. And it was Steve who had put Zach in the Hole for ten days, making no effort to find out what actually had happened. No, you can't trust a man like that no matter how friendly he speaks, whispering and winking at you, calling the other guards scum.

It was not until later, not until after that Sunday in June when the news came that Hitler's legions were rolling toward Moscow, that they would learn why Steve had spoken as he did about Russia. For he was a Slovak, and ever since Munich the members of the Catholic Slovak Society to which Steve Kovach belonged had come to the disturbing belief that Red Russia was now the last hope for a liberated Czechoslovakia. Chamberlain had said Munich meant peace, the papers had said that too, but the Russians had denounced the settlement which betrayed the homeland to Hitler: the Red Army had been ready to march if called upon by Prague. No one in the Society hated Reds more than Steve, but even he half-shared the secret hope that Uncle Joe's boys would some day rescue their cousin Slavs.

The letter and the Call had gone out, but there were other things that Paul and Faulcon could do while they waited for the answer. Lonnie must write a personal appeal that could be distributed by the committee to the press. To the Negro newspapers first, starting with the *National Chronicle*, published in Iron City and circulated throughout the country. "Maybe," said Faulcon, who had no use for that paper, "they'll manage to find some room for something worthwhile along with all that scandal stuff. Maybe—but it might take some pressure to get them to print it: Cap'n Charlie got a whole lot of strings tied to the *Chronicle* and that's the truth."

OK, but who will Lonnie mail it to? Not to any of our people—not yet. Not till there's a strong committee, with real backing. But it must be sent to somebody responsible, who would know where to take it without being told.

"Lucy Jackson!" Faulcon cried. "You reminded me about her just the other day. She's the one, and you couldn't want a more respectable address: care of the Old Rock of Zion Church of God in Christ!" He chuckled and slapped Paul on the knee. "Sure doesn't sound like the Reds, does it? But if Lonnie puts in a note to her saying she should take it to people who will help an innocent man condemned to die—well, she'll carry it over to our people at Douglass Hall for sure. Remember— that's where she got the Scottsboro petitions . . . and walked me near to death with them. Sweet Lucy Jackson!" and now he sighed heavily. "Sometimes I think I should have married that wonderful woman!"

(2)

April 7, 1941

"Dear Paul—

"Thank you darling for the wonderful, tender, loving letter you sent me on our anniversary. Now I know what you meant that you were sending me an important message. Oh, Paul— it was the nicest present I ever got. . . ."

There was more about his love letter and his eye skimmed over it in his search for the answer about Lonnie.

"And now about less romantic things. As you know we are terribly understaffed at the Mutual Benefit Society"—the Party surely!—*"for our normal work-load. (I hope you won't mind*

me talking shop, but I always used to tell you about such things when I came home from work.) Anyway we were all thrown into quite a turmoil last week by a Home-Office memo that outlined a big new selling drive for us. It said this added work must be started immediately. The acting office manager and some of the salesmen were dead-set against undertaking it at this time. We're not getting enough pay for what we're doing now"—they haven't raised all the money they need for our appeal—*"and the office is so short-handed. Some of the people insisted that we defer the extra work until the new manager is sent up from Charleston and some others said we should not rush into something new without knowing more facts about this type of insurance, schedules, etc. But finally it was settled and that means plenty of overtime work for us all."*

Charlene, Charlene—I love you! I know how you and the others must have fought for my plan against those who hesitated and doubted. Too much to do already, but you comrades understood that this job cannot wait for easier times, for stronger leadership to come!

"The day after tomorrow is visiting day, but I won't be able to see you this week. I promised to go shopping with Mrs. Zachary and that is the only time she can get off work. You should tell Zach not to expect her. You should have seen how excited she was last week after her first visit with him, especially after being unable to see him the other two times. We had a good cry together—she was so happy it made me bawl too. Darling, we'll be like them won't we?—loving each other after twenty years like the Zacharys. I know I'll always love you, Paul, and here's five big kisses and hugs for our anniversary. X X X X X!

Your Charlene

"PS. I bought a present for you: a subscription to the Chronicle. *The jail office told me that Negro newspapers are not sold in there and I thought you'd like to know what your people are doing. Let me know if you get it."*

It was a battle won—their first; and today the marching around the yard was a secret victory parade. Only Paul and

Zach were together; Faulcon was back in the rear ranks and Lonnie was playing his furious game alone. A few days ago Dan Rooney had said something to Lonnie which frightened them: "Watch out for those guys. I notice you've been talking a lot with them lately, but they're Reds and you ought to know it." So Lonnie must not be seen with them; they could only wave to him now when the guard was not looking. But next week it would be better: the tedious marching would stop, the baseball season would begin by Rooney's decree. Then we'll get a chance to talk without him noticing, Lonnie told them. Rooney will be too busy umpiring.

Now, by a vigorous nod of his head, Paul had signalled to the basketball-player that the letter and Call had been received; and his self-handshaking gesture of a winning prize-fighter had added the wonderful news that the plans had been accepted outside, the fight would begin. And Lonnie had let them know that he had heard from Lucy Jackson in response to his personal appeal: as Range D, now Squad D, swung around to where he was playing, Lonnie tried a long set-shot while loudly exclaiming: "Bless my soul Miss Lucy— did you see that!" The arching ball missed the basket-rim but Paul's broad smile and Zach's wink showed him that his message had sunk home.

It seemed to the four defense committee members that all of the inmates from Cell Block One were happier today. Even Rooney sensed that something was different for not once did he have to shout to the marchers to snap it up—this aint no funeral. It was Spring. Suddenly, today, the miracle had come. The velvet-soft smell of the new season filtered through the sulphur fumes that spread from the mill two miles away, and through the windblown, smoggy clouds patches of brightest blue could be seen. One day soon a robin would hop along the top of the wall, shaking the granite blocks with his feather tread, bursting with his song the cold steel grip of winter. Their joyous shouts would send the jail-breaker winging: they would feel no loss, for the redbreast's flight like his coming was testimony that the land still lived outside their tomb, that the birds and the bees and the cigarette trees and the lemonade springs where the bluebird sings might still be found in some big rock candy mountain.

Another Spring. It proved time could be pulled.

Isaac Zachary's only regret was that he had not been present when Paul and Faulcon began the fight for Lonnie. But Paul insisted that Zach was wrong about that: it was by Zach's getting thrown into the Hole that they had learned how Slim could send out an uncensored letter, and Paul was certain that somehow Zach's resistance to the baiting guards had won Slim to them even though he had later denounced them as two-timing politicians. Paul was right: in the long chain of events that began when Judge Hanford J. Rupp sentenced them to the jail where he had already sent Lonnie and through all that followed, Zach's stand that searching Sunday was a necessary link.

That Annie Mae too had her part to play was a great satisfaction to Zach: her shopping trip with Charlene would be the search for the missing Leroy Flowers. They would see his landlady and somehow they would try to learn what it was that made Big John Cummings, who could remember the names of all the voters in his ward, yes and their children's names too, forget about Lonnie and Leroy being with him that night. Was it only his fear for his gambling business, or was there something more?

The clippings had been returned by Lonnie for Zach to read; he was told the whole story. Although he lived in Kanesport, Zach had never heard of Lonnie; there had been some talk that a colored hoodlum had been caught running out of a shop where he had shot a man and had admitted his guilt, but neither Zach nor his wife had time for what they called scandal news. Zach and Lonnie had worked in the same mill, but there were ten thousand men in McGregor's and Zach was a laborer in Open Hearth while Lonnie worked as a chipper. Before he was laid-off in the recession that came before the defense boom, Lonnie was a member of the Kanesport lodge of the new steelworkers' union, but his dues were collected by the check-off; he had never attended a meeting where Zach might have met him.

189

Lonnie told them that maybe his joining the union would account for the letter Herbert T. Wills had written to the *Eagle* about him. For in 1937, when Lonnie first came to the mill town from Ohio, he had heard that only a recommendation from Mr. Wills, formerly the company man for Negro employment, would get him a job. Wills had already become Industrial Secretary of the Negro Improvement League and in this position the Wagner Act could not stop him from asking how a job applicant felt about labor organizations. Lonnie had promised not to join the union, but he had broken that promise when a work-mate asked him to sign—Everybody is signing up in the S.W.O.C. and you don't want to be a stooge, do you?

But Zachary, who knew of Mr. Wills, was sure there was more to it than that: Annie Mae and the members of Zach's Party branch in the tinplate mill must try to find out more about this man who is worse even than Judas of old times. Judas had gone out and hanged himself; Mr. Wills wanted rope only for Lonnie. "Makes me mad sometimes," Zach told them, "how our people go around always singing the blues about the white folks. Why can't they all see that Cap'n Charlie couldn't treat us like he do lessen he had old Uncle Tom working right with him?"

(3)

Great day—look! The first issue of the *National Chronicle* that came to Paul carried Lonnie's appeal. For once the big headline type was good to read:

> "*SAVE ME—I AM INNOCENT!*" *SAYS*
> *YOUTH FROM LOCAL DEATH CELL*

A box set into the text, which was printed in full, announced that a conference would be held in two weeks at the Old Rock of Zion Church to launch a mass movement to save the doomed young man. The temporary officers of the Provisional Defense Committee were named: Reverend T. J.

Buford, chairman; Mrs. Lucy Jackson, treasurer; Theodore Archer, secretary.

Bless *your* soul, Miss Lucy—you did it! And look at that, Henry—Ted Archer secretary! Archer was an old-timer in the Communist Party but in recent years he had grown weary; he would promise faithfully to come to meetings but he never came and finally they ceased to ask him. Paul, I got to hand it to your gal—she's brought the dead back to life again!

They knew Reverend Buford, and Paul was not too happy about his being chairman. "Of course, Reverend Buford is a good man, but that Rock of Zion of his is just a little old store-front church. Seems like they should have gotten Reverend Stackpole or Parker to head it up—one of the preachers from a big congregation."

"That's just where you're wrong, son," Faulcon exclaimed. "This man Buford will really work, and what did your Stackpole or Parker ever do except come around and make a big speech and a show after all the work were done! Stackpole —that faker. For your Jobs For Negroes Committee you-all got him for chairman and that were a good name for him—all he ever did were to warm a chair. Store-front or not, I hope they elect Reverend Buford official chairman at the Conference and with you being in jail this time maybe they will!"

Suddenly from the range above, they heard a shout. It was Lonnie. Then they heard him singing: it was against regulations but he sang out loudly so that they should hear him down on D. The tune was *Sweet Georgia Brown* but he had changed the words to sing of Sweet *Lucy* Brown. Soon there came the angry ringing of a key on the railing of the Hub which silenced him: another peep and he would have to do his singing deep down in the Hole.

He must have got the paper too, they thought; a few minutes later they knew it. The keyman, in exchange for the cigarette he was smoking so hungrily, brought them a note from Lonnie: *The colored paper! I'll let you see it later. I got to read it some more.*

The news was too wonderful to keep to themselves: others

must share their happiness and first of all Slim who had made it possible. "I'm glad for him," he said when they showed him the newspaper on his return that afternoon. I'm glad for him! Does he think it strange, this man who insisted that he doesn't give a damn for anybody else—does he think it strange that he should say those words? But Slim gives no sign of his thoughts; he returns the paper without another word; and the big hands, scarred by garbage cans, calloused by broom and mop, are busy again with their magic, creating from rubbish shining things of use and beauty.

The others—the four white Communists—must be told. J. C. who works in the bath-house where once a week each cell block comes to shave and shower can be their messenger. Cell Block Three, they tell him, giving him the names to ask for. Paul gives him the clipping from the *Chronicle*—Lonnie has another—with a pencilled message: "Get your visitors to help too!" J. C.'s hand with the rolled-up paper on it remains extended. He smiles when a dime is dropped into his palm. "Dime's too much—don't want to hold you up," says this hold-up man. "I'll give you a nickel back quick as I get change. Wouldn't charge you nothing if you was broke, but I know you-all is the richest men on the range. And me—well, I reckon nobody in this jailhouse is poor as me. Even old Sneaky Pete—at least he's got his Bible, but I can't even read!"

It was true: the two dollars a week each received, which they shared with Lonnie until the outside committee sent him an allowance made the three Communists the richest men on Range D. "Now if only I had something fit to eat I'd know what it feels like to be a capitalist," said Faulcon. Zach remarked that they'd all feel better if the people who ran this jail put mattresses on these hard bunks, but Paul said no. "That would be socialism," he said, "and what good would that be for us millionaires? We'd have to become working-men like Slim and J. C.!"

The newspaper which carried Lonnie's cry for help and the notice of the defense conference gave them another idea of how to extend the search for Leroy. The committee, of course, would issue a press release about the missing witness; it would be a central feature in all the publicity. But here was a way for the search to be mentioned in every issue of the paper; and it was Zach who happened to think of it. Reading through the rest of the paper he noticed the Help Me Find column where, for a small fee, those who had lost track of relatives and friends could tell of their search. It was an important column for a Negro newspaper with a nation-wide circulation and each week scores of missing persons were listed.

> SIMMONS, Fleming P. (father). Approximate age, 71. Last seen in Montgomery, Ala., 47 years ago. Home somewhere in Florida. Please contact his daughter, Mozelle Robbins, 409 W. 130 St., New York City.

> WOOLFOLK, Chester A. I was born in Gum Springs, Ark., on April 3, 1913, son of Victory and Clarence Woolfolk. Anyone knowing the whereabouts of brothers, Ozie, Marshall, Eulace, Fred, or sisters, Jessie, Clarice, Pearl, please notify me c/o Centre Ave. YMCA, Pittsburgh.

And now each week there must be a call to Leroy. It would not do, of course, to have it signed by Lonnie James or to give the jail as a return address—the office would be sure to destroy the letter if Leroy wrote. "He knows my landlady," Lonnie said when they told him later of this plan. "He'll trust her. She was always giving him something nice to eat whenever he came to see me—specially when he wasn't working. So use her name. And Zach, you have your missus tell her what to do if he contacts her."

> FLOWERS, Leroy. Age about 27. Light brownskin, freckles, gray eyes. Urgently needed by his brother Lonnie who is in serious trouble. Telegraph to Mrs. Catherine Spencer, 347 Beech St., Kanesport, or telephone collect McGregor 0697.

193

CHAPTER 15

Steve's day began at seven. He was never late and recently there had been many days when he got to work an hour early. That was on account of the lousy Deputy Warden who seldom came around any more: Steve's richest Slovak curses were saved for him and especially for his grandmother. It had always been taken for granted that the Warden's job was pure political gravy, but a Deputy Warden had work to do. Now the whole burden of jail direction fell on Steve and upon the chief clerk in the office out front. Scalise was crying too, but Steve had no sympathy to share with him: All you got to do is paper work, he told the clerk. But for Scalise it was an awful lot of paper. Two complete sets of records had to be kept, for example, on Purchases & Supplies—the real and the official. It was easy enough for the big boys to cut the daily food-ration for inmates from thirty-five to eighteen cents so that all concerned might get their fair share, but it was up to Scalise to make it look right. It was not easy. To Steve, the chief clerk was always just a wop; to Scalise, the chief guard was nothing but a hunky: the only thing they had in common was overwork, under-pay and no chance for promotion.

Today, as he stood before his cluttered desk, Steve bent his curly head to softly say his morning prayer: that the Deputy Warden should die a horrible death, a lingering, slow-eating death, so painful that his ancestors in Ireland should cry out in agony. Then he went through his litany, taking in the Deputy Warden's brothers and sisters and cousins, his father and mother and grandmother too. For good measure, this morning when the weight of all the steel and stone seemed too much for him to bear, Steve appended a tribute to the man's *great*-grandmother. Only when he had finished did Steve reach for his phone which had been jangling loudly all the while.

"Chief guard speaking."

"I have a message for Mr. James."

194

"Who?"

"Mr. James."

"Wrong number, bub. This is the county jail."

"Wait, please. . . . I'm *calling* the jail. Mr. Lonnie James is my client. You have him in your custody."

"I'll be goddamned!"

"Beg pardon?"

"If this don't beat all—say, who in the hell are you?"

"Winkel. Arnold Winkel. I'm his attorney."

"Yeah, you are, hey? Well, who ever gave you the bright idea that we deliver messages around here?"

"Mr. James told me."

"WHO?"

"Lonnie James. He said whenever I had an important message I should phone you and you would tell him."

"ME?"

"Yes sir. That's what he said. Just phone the chief guard."

"Ah—hold the line a minute." Steve's voice had sunk to a whisper: his last words had sounded almost cordial. He put down the receiver, got up to his seat on the stool that was his place of power, and buried his face in his short chubby arms. After a moment he reached for the phone again: he would not resign; they could not make him.

"OK, Mr. Finkel—this is the messenger boy. What shall I tell Mr. James?"

"It's *Winkel*—W like in Walter. But he'll know. Please tell him that I did not have time to write that I was coming to see him this morning, but I will be there within an hour for a conference with him."

"A conference?"

"That's correct. A little after eight. Thank you. Goodby."

"Hello—Mr. Winkel. . . . Hey there! *HEY YOU!*"

The line was dead. It was just as well, for the lawyer probably did not know a word of Slovak.

Lonnie James! That guy has broken every rule in the book and gotten away with it half the time. Just call the chief guard he says, just like that. . . . Why I ought to snatch him out of there and throw him into the Hole for forty days!

195

But Steve had too much work to do to be bothered with anything like that now. He did not punish Lonnie and as for delivering the unnecessary message—well how many last straws can a man take?

That morning Lonnie James was standing at the front gate of Murderers' Row: it was his favorite spot and by tacit agreement the two white men who hated the sight of him—Reardon and Klaus—never loafed at that place unless there was something special to see, like the beating of a bum down below. From here Lonnie could see the full circle of the Hub —the small door through which they had brought him from the courtroom in the Cathedral of Justice, the door to the visiting cubicles that he had never entered because he had no kin, and the long oak table where the lawyers came to see their clients. To Lonnie the lawyers looked like mother birds, fluttering in to feed their helpless young who leaned across the table, open-mouthed for any crumb of hope that might be found in the bulging brief-cases. He glanced at the table now and was surprised to see a man seated stiffly on the lawyer's side. So early—why nobody but that half-ass . . . it's *him*. By God it's Mr. Winkel for real! How come they haven't called me?

Steve's head was bent down. He'd show this little louse of a lawyer, this Finkel or Hinkel or Stinkel, that Steve Kovach was nobody's messenger boy! But the lesson was lost on Arnold Winkel: he was used to being made to wait. Finally a guard showed up at the desk. "Ryan, where the hell you been screwing off to?" but before the guard could answer, Steve said to go get James—C 10—his lawyer wants to see him.

It was a new Winkel today. His eyes no longer dodged Lonnie's open stare; they glittered cold like Mr. Coxe's. He rapped the table with his knuckles. His hand did not fumble within the brief-case; instead, with quick sure fingers, he drew out the pink-tinted page from the *National Chronicle* and slapped it down before Lonnie. His words were brisk and sharp.

"Mr. James, this is an outrage! Intemperate, ill-advised,

196

embarrassing. You had no right to do it without consulting Mr. Coxe or myself. You know that. By this rash act you have almost wrecked all of our careful efforts in your behalf. Mr. Coxe is prepared to step out now, once and for all. And I must warn you, Mr. James, that my own patience with you is near an end. You disrupted the court proceedings on several occasions. You antagonized the judge and the jury as well. And now by this reckless, ridiculous diatribe in the newspaper you are threatening the orderly processes of the high court itself!"

His finger stabbed at the concluding paragraph of Lonnie's appeal which asked the public to demand that the Supreme Court reverse the frame-up verdict.

"*Demand*, Mr. James! It is contemptuous, arrogant, foolhardy to say such a thing. Don't you understand what it means to advocate such action when a law suit is *sub judice*—under consideration by the best legal minds in the Commonwealth? 'Mass pressure'!" His voice quivered now. "Anarchy, that's what it is. Subverting justice, undermining the foundations of legality, propriety and . . . oh, yes—the whole social fabric." In his excitement Winkel had almost forgotten the third phrase that Coxe had thundered at him yesterday.

"Another thing. This element that is arranging the so-called defense conference—we have something to tell you about *that*, too. This man—let's see. . . . Oh, yes, Theodore Archer. He is a *Communist*. Don't smile, Mr. James. You are willful and obstinate but you can't laugh off documentary proof. We are quite prepared, you see, to support that allegation against this Archer fellow. We have been advised by very responsible sources that his name was included on a list of known Communists in this community. An official list, if you please, released several years ago by Congressman Rankin of the House Committee on Un-American Activities!"

"What's that name, Mr. Winkel?"

"Congressman Rankin."

"Where's he from—around here?"

"Let's see now . . . I have that here . . . somewhere . . . here! The Honorable John E. Rankin of Mississippi."

"*Mississippi!*"

"Yes. But I have no time for chatter." Mr. Winkel glanced hastily at his wristwatch and then looked up for verification to the big electric clock above Steve's desk. Poor bastard, thought Lonnie—worrying about his boss giving him hell if he's late.

"Here, Mr. James. I have no time. Please sign this document and I must go. It's a retraction and an apology. It may partially undo the terrible mischief. I'll leave an extra copy for you to read at your leisure—of which, I dare say, you have considerably more than I." He pushed the legal-sized sheaf of blue-bound papers across the polished oak and unscrewed the top of his orange-colored pen. "Three copies. Please sign them all at the places I have checked."

There was no time to read it all: Lonnie's eyes raced over the words on the crinkly tissue paper. *I, Lonnie James . . . deeply regret . . . misled . . . full confidence . . . distinguished counsel . . . freely repudiate and retract . . . impartial . . . mercy. . . .* His hand groped for the pen.

"At the bottom of the page, Mr. James."

But Lonnie flipped the papers over. The old-fashioned pen spluttered and scratched as he wrote.

"I know you'd be scared to tell him, Mr. Winkel," he said, returning the pen and document, "so I wrote it out nice and big."

Winkel stared in disbelief as he read the shocking suggestion addressed to Clement B. Coxe. And now, under Lonnie's fiery eyes, the new Mr. Winkel melted away. It was the old Mr. Winkel who flushed and stammered something about the whole social fabric but all the strength of Mr. Coxe's wrath was gone.

"I'm sorry, Mr. James," he said. "I'm terribly sorry." Whatever it was that he regretted, his weak smile and wistful eyes showed that now he was quite sincere. He glanced again at his watch and sprang to his feet, crumpling, in his haste, the document with the blasphemous scrawl as he stuffed it into his bag. He did not say goodby, nor did he offer his dead-fish handshake. He started to run, but remembering who he was and where he was, he slowed to a very fast walk.

Lonnie followed his flight around the circled walkway and out the door on the other side. Mr. Winkel was gone. Lonnie James would never see him again.

(2)

He could at least take off his hat, Steve thought as he stood before the Warden's glass-topped desk. But the Warden kept his hat on, the snapped-down brim shadowing his face. Nor had he removed his tweed topcoat: he would stay but a minute.

"This is important, Steve," he said as if it were not obvious that no trivial matter could bring him to his office. "The boys downtown asked me—" a movement in the far corner of the large room caught his eye. But it was only the janitor, polishing the panelled wall, his face barely discernible against the gleaming walnut.

"The boys downtown asked me," the Warden began again, "to check on something. Those Reds we got in here pending appeal—have they been seeing this dinge who's up for hanging—what's his name?"

"James. Lonnie James." Steve scowled, remembering the business this morning about the phone call.

"Yeh—that one. I don't know why they think it's so important but I got to report on this today. I'd have called you about it, but . . . well. . . ." They had told him he'd better get his lazy ass down to the jail and find out what's going on down there. You're supposed to be the Warden, you know. "Anyway, I decided to come. You can tell me, I know."

Sure, you bastard. Everything you want to know you got to ask me. But when I was up for Deputy—that was different; I couldn't tell you anything then. But there was no hint of bitterness in Steve's reply.

"Yes sir. I know all right. The Reds are over on Cell Block Three. So I know they haven't seen James. We aint giving them any of the jobs so's they can mingle around outside their range. And they go out for recreation at a different time from him. As you know—"

The Warden raised a warning hand. The door was opening. It was Dan Rooney who called in. "Steve—can I see you for a second?"

Steve whirled around. He could safely vent his churning rage on this subordinate. "Goddammit, Rooney—can't you see I'm busy? We're—we're in *conference!*" That lousy lawyer Finkel's word. "I'll see you when I'm done. Wait outside." The door closed as the yard guard withdrew.

"As you know, sir," Steve continued, "Murderers' Row is on Cell Block One, so James would never see anybody from Three out in the yard. And as you know too"—of course you don't even know this—"Block Three does not face One so they couldn't talk across to him either."

Fine. The Warden could leave this stinkhole now. "That's swell, and make sure they can't get to him. I'll report that everything's under control. Take it easy, Steve."

Take it easy—like you, you bum? "Goodby sir, I'll keep an eye on them."

Slim's heart had skipped a beat when Rooney looked in. If Rooney had been allowed to wait inside he surely would have told the Warden that the Reds did see Lonnie in the yard. Rooney would not have forgotten that, for he had already warned Lonnie against them; and he would have been pleased at the chance to show up the hunky chief guard before the Warden.

At eleven, dinner time, Slim rushed back to tell Paul and his friends about what he had overheard in the Warden's office.

Whew—that was close! The big shots must be burning up because the news about the frame-up has gone out. They'll be working on Lonnie hard to make him denounce the Provisional Committee and its projected defense conference. That's for sure. But what about Steve? Slim said that Steve must be in their corner for real—else why would he tell a lie like that?

Paul shook his head doubtfully; it didn't seem possible that Steve should have forgotten about the three Communists on Range D since only recently he had asked them the question about Russia and Germany. "But look," he told Slim, "there actually are some Reds on Cell Block Three—the four white ones—and maybe he was only thinking about them. Or maybe because we're Negroes he couldn't imagine we'd have brains enough to do anything by ourselves. We can't know for sure how it happened but there's one thing we can't ever forget— you can't trust a guard, not anybody who works for those who are pulling this frame-up. But still it's a wonderful break for us. A miracle, maybe, but we need every one we can get."

It was a wonderful break but it was no miracle: it was fashioned of many pieces of which they could not know. Had Steve not been so angry at the insulting phone call from Winkel, he might not have ordered Rooney from the room —but Coxe had terrified Winkel just as he himself had been previously alarmed by the peremptory demand from District Attorney McKee that the Red propaganda campaign about a legal lynching be stopped before it gets out of hand. You're on the spot too, Clem, the prosecutor had warned Lonnie's senior defense counsel. So Winkel had phoned Steve as Lonnie had told him to do if it was anything important. And had the Warden been on the job, he would have known about the three Negro Communists on Range D, directly below Murderers' Row: but according to the system the Warden's job was merely a political plum, though a juicy one that could be squeezed for graft—safe graft too, for no good citizen would worry about what was fed the crooks.

But still what about Steve? as Slim had asked. The chief guard was harassed and overworked, too many things on his mind to remember everything. That was partly the explanation for his unintentional half-truth, but there was more: Steve hated the Reds, of course, as he should; but it was not his fault that in his mind he always associated the word Communist with the word Jew. Father Coughlin was responsible for that: the Kovach family never missed his Sunday radio hour. Another thing, and this too could not be blamed on Steve who only carried out orders—the Jim Crow set-up in the Monongahela County Jail. Had the Negro Communists been put in together with the whites they might never have met

Lonnie to hear his story and start the movement to save him.

Coxe and McKee, Coughlin and Judge Rupp, the Jim-Crow jail and the boys downtown—of such was the miracle made! The enemy had blundered: it was the second battle won. The inside committee might function a while longer. Lonnie would not have to face the pressure alone.

(3)

Baseball was a blessing for all the inmates, for those who could play and for the others who would no longer have to march. To the inside committee it was a chance to function better; and to one of them, Lonnie, it was something more. Something as unique and personal as his being the only man among them all who was sentenced to die. He was enthusiastic about sports, for he was an extraordinary athlete—but it was not that alone which made the game so all-important to him.

All during the previous summer he had played the game as if his life depended upon his playing. It was all he could do except to pray and to write to people who would not listen. Each game became a symbol of his fight for life, just as the strength of his pitching arm, the power of his bat and his speed on the base-paths proved the glowing vitality that was he, Lonnie James. How can they kill me when I am so alive? Within each game there were a thousand secret signs and omens. OK—the count on this guy is three and oh . . . if I can strike him out now, well, that will be a sign. There must be such a sign every day to assure him that he would be believed at the trial. Winning the game—that was the best sign there could be, better even than hitting a homer. He pitched nearly every day, for the games seldom went longer than three or four innings in the time allowed. He fought to win every game. Three runs behind . . . well if I can only pull this one out Mr. Winkel will be here tomorrow with some good news. And that means I'll have won three straight games. Three runs behind, three straight games—*Hey* that ought to be something special for a sign—maybe even they'll catch the fellow who killed the drugstore man! Twice Lonnie had been thrown into the Hole for screaming a protest at the umpire: Rooney, who called the balls and strikes, did not know that the right to boo an umpire is inalienable to every American. He was the guard in charge and Lonnie was black.

Of course there were bad signs too, but a man must risk them. Like being banished from the yard for three days as penalty for hitting a foul ball over the wall. No one knew why Rooney had made that rule. The wall, close behind home plate, was forty feet high. Who could deliberately make the batted ball rise straight up and arch back over the top? And since it had to be an accident, why should the player be punished? Rooney never explained. The yard guard had made other ground rules, though none as mean as that one. Some of his rules could be evaded, such as the one about choosing up sides. The inmates wanted to have teams, the same men to play against each other daily—only that would give a thrill of competition to players and rooters alike. Rooney said no: he did not want it that way. But this rule was flouted every day before his eyes and no one knew whether they got away with it because he was indifferent to the result as long as the choosing-up was done or whether he was just plain stupid. Each day Rooney picked the same two captains—one of them was Lonnie—to choose their players. The captains invariably picked the same men who had played for them the day before—their regular team. Still, all of the inmates hated Rooney for the precious minutes that daily were lost when he had them all line up—two or three hundred men in all, including the aged, infirm, crippled and blind—and directed each of the captains alternately to choose a man, then another, slowly at his command, until the eighteen were finally selected.

Home plate was near the wall opposite the door they came out, the batter facing the jail building. Because of the two projecting wings of the structure which formed the hollow E shape of the yard, the outfielders played in separate courts— the cross strokes of the E: they could see the infield but they could not see each other. Covering the narrow slit windows at the ends of the projecting wings were vertical bars which rose to the roof: a short fly ball would hit against them, and often the ball would become wedged into the bars. Rooney's rules made that a home run, but it was so unfair the inmates ignored it. The black-painted scoreboards, one along the third-base wall, the other at first base would show the official score. If the bases were loaded and a batted ball lodged in the bars, the scorers would chalk up four runs. But only for Rooney did it mean anything. The secret rule of the inmates decreed that only one of the runs batted in might be counted. If no man was on base at the time, the hit was only a single and though the batter who made the fluke home run must trot around the diamond, the inmates pretended that he was still on first base. It was a complicated system, but without it the game would be as senseless as Rooney. All bets—matches, butts, pennies, comic books, true detective magazines—were paid off on the secret unofficial score which was kept by two trusted spectators picked for that purpose.

A legitimate home run could be hit over the far ends of the three courts which were the outfield: in right field and center the ball would land on the sloping roof of the jail; in left field, which was the farthest from home plate, the ball would drop over a wall. Jailhouse legend had it that no man had ever hit an out-of-the-yard home run to left field, not even Slats Dixwell, the fabulous slugger of the Iron City Black Giants, when he did a short stretch for reckless driving. "Every time I go to bat," Lonnie told Paul, "I'm levelling for the top of that wall. Bet nobody would ever forget me if I socked one over. But at the same time, whenever I connect solid and the ball heads out that way I'm scared to death it's going to be a homer! Funny, aint it?" He did not reply when Paul asked him why that was. Paul had noticed that frequently Lonnie said something as if he were talking to himself; it must be, Paul thought, on account of Lonnie talking so much with that crazy guy on Range C who never needs an explanation.

Baseball was not Jim Crow. The partisanship of rooters and players would not have it so. A man was a man on the diamond and no one seemed to think it should be otherwise. Whitey, the keyman of Block One, had no use for Negroes; but he was the star first-baseman on one of the teams and an influential man off the field. Whitey would have fought any man who tried to keep Lonnie from pitching for his team.

They called it baseball, though the game was actually soft-ball—the size of the yard and the asphalt floor made only soft-ball possible. "I wish it was really hard ball we were playing and I'll show you why," Lonnie remarked one day to Paul as they were waiting for their turn at bat. "Look straight out past second, at the end of center field—old Byrd sleeping on his chair. Bet you if we played hard ball I'd hit one on the line clear across to him and knock the old buzzard kicking. Fracture his skull and kill him. He's a bad sign that Byrd, a hell of a thing for me to have to see every day!"

Paul and Army were the only other Negroes on Lonnie's team this year; four others, from Range E, were on the other side that was captained by Stan Kuczinsky, the rangeman of A who had pitched for the rival team the previous summer. Army, who was almost as good a catcher as he claimed to be, was Lonnie's battery mate. Paul, the only other newcomer to the team, was put into left field. He had thought it would be better for him to play at third or short where he might openly talk to Lonnie about committee matters during the game while pre-tending to calm down the pitcher when he got into a jam. But Lonnie pointed out that that would not work, for Rooney did his umpiring from behind the pitcher's box and would overhear anything Paul said. "And besides," Lonnie added, "you can't be as good as the two white boys I got for those positions—and we got to win. That's me—we got to win and I play hard!"

Paul saw how hard he played. No other runner besides Lonnie ever charged in at full speed from third to home for fear of the wall: it was so close to home plate that the catcher, squatting in his position, could steady himself by touching the wall behind him. Yet Lonnie did charge in if the real score was close and the run was needed; and no one could understand how he was not knocked unconscious by his reckless collision with the granite. "You shouldn't do like that," Paul warned him, but Lonnie laughed it off. "Winning is the best sign there is. Last year a fellow told me not to do that and guess what he said? Lonnie, you might get killed! Fact—that's just what he said. To *me*—how do you like that? —and them out to kill me all the time no matter whichever way I run!"

The inside committee decided that Faulcon and Zach should try to be the keepers of Rooney's scoreboards. In that way they were sure to have a place near home plate where they might talk things over with Lonnie: it was the rule that before his turn at bat the player must stand along the third-base wall and after he has batted—unless, of course he gets on base—he must stand in place on the other side. It was another Rooney rule but one that could serve them. The two had no trouble in getting the job for no one else wanted to stand there chalking up the meaningless official score. Zach and Faulcon could keep an eye on Rooney: the guard could not sneak up behind them.

There was always something to talk about: new ideas for the defense campaign, information that came to the three from their visitors, letters which Lonnie received from the outside committee to be passed on to them. There were many such letters coming to Lonnie now, enclosing copies of leaflets that were being issued, press releases, petition blanks. No one, in those first weeks, had told Steve to stop Lonnie from getting this material: it was wonderful to see. Even the report that as yet no trace of Leroy had been found was welcomed. They were trying: no one had ever tried before.

It was Spring. A warming, hopeful, bursting, beautiful Spring. People knew now. People believed now. People were helping now. The committee inside. The committee outside. Working. Fighting. An invisible banner fluttering atop the wall McGregor had built. And above the roar of the mill and the blare of the Hut Sut Song a voice was crying out to Iron City—

LONNIE JAMES SHALL NOT DIE!

CHAPTER 16

It had become a Sunday ritual. When Henry Faulcon returned to the range from chapel he would reproach Isaac Zachary for his stay-at-home ways. "A good Christian like you, and I never can get you to go with me," and Zach would smile and say, "Brother Henry, it's like I been trying to tell you—I just aint got no use for a jailhouse religion."

This time Faulcon was even more holier-than-thou. "Shame on you Zach and Paul too. Today starts Brotherhood Week and you missed a fine sermon by Chaplain Jericho about how we must all act like brothers. Regardless of race, creed or color and things like that."

"Brotherhood Week!" Paul threw up his hands to express staggering surprise. "What do you know about that?—and me thinking all the time it was National Canned Peaches Week!"

That silenced Faulcon. Then Paul continued: "Fact is, Henry, while you were down there loving everybody I was walking my cell and cussing up a blue streak—and all on account of your Brotherhood Week. I was reading the Sunday *American* when I came across this story and—but read it yourself, both of you."

WOMEN HEAR WARNING ON RACIAL TENSIONS

Richard Canfield, noted lecturer and sociologist, last night warned the Women's Civic League that tensions among underprivileged groups threaten the security of the entire community.

Speaking to a large audience gathered at the exclusive Glenmere Country Club, Dr. Canfied presented a scholarly analysis of the causes of group maladjustment.

"We are confronted by fourteen million Bigger Thomases," he pointed out, referring to the central character in a recent Book of the Month Club selecion, "and we cannot evade our responsibility to get to the heart of the problem. Crime-busting drives such as the one launched last year by your own distinguished District Attorney Stewart McKee are necessary, of course, but we must do more if we are to cope with the critical problem of delinquency among certain ethnic categories."

To illustrate the root causes of the problem, Dr. Canfield referred to various laboratory experiments made with sheep and rats. When the animals, after having been trained to follow a certain path through a maze to get food, were baffled by a change made in the route, the results were comparable to the social issue under review.

"The rats," said Dr. Canfield, "were observed to become maddened by the imposed frustration. Frantic, confused, desperate, they battered themselves to death against the barrier. Sheep, who normally are docile and gregarious, became sullen, morose and solitary, pathologically warped by the continuous cycle of hunger-hope-frustration.

"This explains," the lecturer pointed out, "why we have among the Negro race both the destructive Bigger Thomas type and the helpless, hymn-singing passive type familiar to us all."

After warmly applauding the speaker, the League members voted to donate $500 from their treasury to defray costs of printing Brotherhood Week posters.

"See," said Paul. "Now you know. Me—I'm a wild rat and I guess that goes for Lonnie upstairs. And you Henry are surely one of those hymn-singing sheep. Far as you are concerned, Zach—well, if you aint a passive type I never saw one. A big old black sheep for real."

Zach sighed heavily. "I reckon," he said, "if I had as much school-learning as that Dr. Canfield, well maybe I would have known before just now what colored people are like without him having to tell me."

But Faulcon shook his head in disgust. "Paul," he said, "we was both wrong. It aint Brotherhood Week or National Canned Peaches Week neither. It's *Be Kind to Animals Week!* Now clear out of my cell and let this old sullen, solitary sheep take a nap."

(2)

The wild rat upstairs was having a visitor. But it was not Brotherhood Week that brought Chaplain Jerricote to Lonnie's cell after chapel. Crazy Peterson was sitting on Lonnie's bunk, shivering grateful that Lonnie had come back again. He jumped to his feet when the chaplain entered.

"Hello, Lonnie. I saw you at chapel again today and—I don't believe I've ever had the pleasure. . . ." His hand shot forward to clasp that of Peterson, but Peterson shrieked with alarm at the threatening gesture and broke past the visitor to flee to his own cell.

Lonnie tapped his head in explanation to the startled clergyman. "Oh, he's a good guy otherwise. Just scared of people. Reckon he don't trust anybody not to hurt him."

Reverend Jerricote glanced out the door through which Peterson had escaped. "Poor fellow. We must trust one another, for we are all children of God—brothers, as I tried to say in my sermon today. I'm sorry he did not attend."

Lonnie choked back a laugh at the thought of Crazy Carl in chapel. "Say, Reverend Jericho," he said, "that was a mighty fine talk you gave today. I been doing a lot of thinking about things like that lately and what you said was sure enough the truth."

The young minister's full pink cheeks grew riper. "Did you really like it? I'm glad you found some comfort in my poor words." He cleared his throat gently. "Mind if I sit down? Thanks." He offered Lonnie a cigarette and took one for himself. Nothing fuddy-duddy about him, the gesture showed.

"Lonnie," he began, after these preliminaries, "I know you trust me. You know that I am trying to help you in every way that I know how. You know that my report on your good conduct and faithful attendance at Sunday chapel and Tuesday night prayer-meeting was read into the record of your trial. And the record, as you are aware, will be carefully read by the Supreme Court. It wasn't much, perhaps, but—" He spread his soft hands to show that he had done what he could. "At any rate I want to talk to you now, man-to-man and as your spiritual advisor too, about something very important."

He drew from the inner pocket of his black suit coat a folded newspaper clipping. It was an editorial that had appeared last week in the *American*: Lonnie, of course, had read it; a copy of it was among the letters in his cigar box on the shelf. Entitled "Undermining Justice," the editorial deplored the hue and cry that local subversive elements had raised about a convicted Negro killer now in custody in the county jail. We had hoped, the editors wrote, that the jailing two months ago of the twenty-six Communist leaders would put an end to un-American activities in Iron City, but it appears that other Reds and Pinkos have not learned the lesson. Now they are challenging the most sacred of our institutions in their "defense" campaign of pressure against the judicial calm of the higher court.

"You must believe that," his visitor urged when Lonnie said he had already read that in the paper. "You must believe in the justice of the court. You owe it to yourself, to all of us who have your true interests at heart, to reject the support and activities of these people. They are only using you, Lonnie, for their own purposes. Your distress,

210

your suffering—what do they care about that? All they want to do is to use you for their propaganda."

Lonnie had resolved not to antagonize the young chaplain: he seemed to be a nice guy as far as his kind goes and he probably believed that crap in the papers. But Lonnie was stung by his last remark; he could not restrain the outburst that came now.

"Using me!" he cried, sliding away from the other toward the toilet end of the canvas bunk. "I get it. Me—I'm too dumb to know what's good for me! That's what you're saying—I can't think for myself, just a dumb Negro for somebody to use! Man, you talk just like Mr. Winkel—that piece of a lawyer I got—coming around asking me to apologize for fighting for my life. Sign, he says, you can read it later! Yeah, but know what I wrote to that Coxe who sent him? Well, I told him what he could do with that tissue paper. Told him straight out, that's what I did! Mr. Winkel never came back but he's writing me every day. That's right—he's got *plenty* to write me about nowadays and I got all his letters in that box to prove it." He jumped up and snatched the box from the shelf, but it was not to get Winkel's letters. In his haste to find the petition blank the committee had sent him, he threw all the other papers to the floor.

"Here!" He waved the petition before Reverend Jerricote's nose. "You're my friend. All right—take this out and get people to sign for me—a thousand people like Lucy Jackson done already and she's one of them that's using me. You and Mr. Winkel and the editors too—you're all so interested in me. If you don't like the names of the committee on the bottom, well go out and print your own! Maybe the newspaper guys will print them for free, they like justice so much. And if you don't like what's writ on the top—Save Lonnie James—well say it your way then. Help Lonnie James—Free Lonnie James—Turn Lonnie James Loose, or get him the hell out of Murderers' Row—I don't care how!"

The chaplain raised a calming hand and tried to say

something about no offense intended, but Lonnie would not hear him.

"Don't you tell me nothing! I *know*. Some people are trying to kill me and some people are trying to save me. Before, I didn't know why they framed me like this but I'm beginning to find out and the more I learn the more I hate them and the more these other people do the more I love them. That's how it is and if somebody told you to try to turn me against them, you can say I said no!" He was yelling now, the cords of the neck they wanted to break were swollen and jerking. "No, and I'll die saying no. *No!* Hear me? *NO!*"

Crazy Peterson had been peeking out of his next-door cell; when he saw the man in black go out the end gate, he hurried to Lonnie's place. The floor was littered with Lonnie's mail and the young man was busy now picking up after the storm.

"Is he a bad man, Lonnie? Did he want to take you away?"

Lonnie made no reply. He tried to wipe a heel mark from one of Mr. Winkel's letters. He gave no sign that he knew the anxious little white man had returned.

"Read it to me," Peterson urged. If Lonnie would not talk, the reassuring sound of his voice would come with the reading.

Lonnie heard him now, but he continued to gaze at the soiled paper in his hand. He shook his head slowly. Mr. Winkel's letter wouldn't make sense even to you, Carl. Not even to you.

But maybe I'm wrong about that, thought Lonnie as he carefully folded the papers back into the box. Maybe this Peterson would sense what was happening to Mr. Winkel even though he would not understand his words. Now that he thought of it, something about the lawyer's frantic letters reminded Lonnie of the unblinking terror that stared from Carl's colorless eyes. Mr. Winkel had not quit him: neither Lonnie nor the others of the inside committee could understand that. But it was plain that the lawyer was terribly afraid of something, and every day his panic was shriller through the precise, typewritten words—his appeals to make them stop. "They" were the members of the committee and others who were interested now in the case of *Commonwealth vs. Lonnie James.* Winkel had ceased to demand that his client repudiate the committee which was no longer provisional after the successful conference. The lawyer no longer ordered Lonnie to tell his friends not to harass him: now he pleaded—Please, Mr. James, it is becoming quite impossible. . . . It began that awful day when a young Mrs. Harper and a gray Mr. Archer came to Fallon, Erhardt, Schwimmer and Ross to see Lonnie James' junior defense counsel. "A colored woman together with a white man, and he was the notorious Communist, Theodore Archer, whom I warned you against. They asked for me," Mr. Winkel wrote. He had not described what a scandal that was nor did he mention the overwhelming threat that had been sounded when Mr. Ross cleared his throat when he saw the shameless pair talking with his law clerk. The intruders had even dared to suggest that Winkel speak at the defense conference! He told them it was unthinkable, and he rushed them out as fast as he could but not before he made a terrible blunder. "Please don't ever come here again—write me. And if you feel you must phone, please call me at home—any evening after seven." He gave them the number.

Now he wrote of the unrelenting avalanche that had descended upon him. Phone calls *every* evening after seven! And letters—more than half of the law firm's mail now came addressed to him. A communication came from one of the lawyers who had defended the Communist leaders; his name was brazenly printed with the return address for all to see. The receptionist, stenographers and clerks began to call him Comrade Winky now. It was not funny. Fallon, Erhardt, Schwimmer and Ross—McGregor's corporation counsel for over forty years—saw no humor in what was happening. Had he not shown them the carbon copies of his replies to all who wrote, they would long since have fired the incredible Mr. Winkel. Mr. Erhardt, his wattles quivering when he saw the firm's name mentioned in the papers in connection with the

James case, had insisted that Winkel be dismissed at once—now, *today*. But the faithful clerk was spared: Mr. Fallon called the editor of the *American* and said it must not happen again, his voice as imperious as it was when he repeated the words to Winkel.

"I shall not withdraw from your case," wrote Mr. Winkel to Lonnie when he sent word that Clement B. Coxe was through. "I consider it my duty to stand by you until the appeal is heard. But please, Mr. James, may I ask you again to urge your friends to cease and desist their constant calling and writing. I have told them repeatedly that I cannot speak at mass meetings, before church groups, labor unions or anything like that. Even if I did not strongly disapprove of their efforts, I would still feel that it would be highly unethical and contemptuous of me to participate in these clamorous gatherings. I have given them all the information I have. I can answer no more questions. Surely you can make them stop and I beg you to do so. Thanking you in advance for your help in this matter, I am yours truly—"

Shucks, Mr. Winkel, I don't know all them people who are bothering you. Besides, you're supposed to be helping me!

(3)

Lonnie's team had a slim lead in the standings, eighteen games to sixteen, when Army was lost to them. Harvey Owens —nobody called him by his right name except Zach—was going out. Uncle Sam wanted him back: he should never have been released to the civil authorities in the first place. True, there was now the added charge of aggravated assault and battery for which he had gotten a year; but it was a simple matter to get the sentence commuted. The loss of his catcher was a bitter blow to Captain Lonnie, for Army was a star on the team, second only to Lonnie himself as most valuable player. His throw to second was a bullet; his heavy hitting more than made up for his slowness on the bases.

In a different way his going would be sad to Isaac Zachary. The big man and the boy in khaki had become close friends: only lock-up separated them. Zach, who seldom talked much to anyone, not even with Paul and Faulcon, spent hours and days in earnest conversation with his young friend. And strangely, the others noticed, it was Zach doing most of the talking. "Looks like Zach found a brother," Paul remarked one day to Faulcon; but the old man understood it better. "I'd say it's more like he has found a son." But brother or son, and star catcher too, Army was going out today.

Of all the men on Range D only Pee Wee Holmes was fully happy to see him go: the rangeman lived in fear that he might some way offend the muscular young man and so meet the fate of his predecessor in Cell Number One. Through the grapevine the men had learned how Army had taken three extra days in the Hole rather than betray them, though they let him think they did not know of it. But even if they had not known, they would have liked him and missed him when he was gone. He battered them with curses and insults, but there was no sting to that. Beneath it all, unspoken but heard, was his feeling of comradeship; they had to smile whenever they saw him. His lamentations about jail and the Law and the ways of white folks had the swing of the blues: it made them feel better.

Now they are crowded around him by the range gate as he says his farewells. Jailhouse Willie, didn't you say you got a sister lives in Philly? Well, I might be passing through and . . . Sneaky Pete—so long, old man, and don't forget what I told you about not selling that stuff no more when they turn you loose. Drink it all yourself and stay happy. . . . Slim, I'm going to be so glad not to see your ugly black face no more I just won't know what to do! . . . OK, Tux, I'll watch 'em. I aint much for shooting craps but if I do I'll use my own dice sure. . . . In case I don't get to see Lonnie on my way out— well, Paul—let's shake on it. I only wish. . . . And you Henry, you old grayhead lying rascal—*I'll* take care of all the women while you're in here and that's a fact! . . . Well, Mr. Zachary, it looks like I got to leave you. But I'll remember all you said. You know I will and I just want to say that—well, you know what I mean. Goodby, Mr. Zachary and all you no-good jailbirds. The man says I got to go now. I'll write you all first chance I get, I sure enough will if I live and nothing happens.

Take it easy, Army. So long, kid. Don't forget about writing. Don't forget to duck. Watch out for them womens. And when the man says *retreat!*, well, just remember you aint trying to beat out no infield single. Goodby, son, I am proud to know you . . . just carry yourself like a man.

Goodby, Harvey Owens. You'll have your old serial number back instead of D-seven because you're a selectee again and you're a pre-Pearl Harbor too though you don't know that yet. After a while they will give you a yellow breast-ribbon for that and you can tell all the 'cruits that you are an *old* soldier, Man, I was in the army while you were still wearing Jodie clothes and worrying bout your draft board—and that's a fact! From Camp Custer you will go to Fort Huachuca way out in Arizona, infantry, you and a whole lot more; some will be dark chocolate brown like you and some will be almost black and some will be light brown and suntan and even white with blue eyes and blond hair, but they will all be Negroes just like you. All except from captain on up, that is. In a year you'll have a candy-stripe Good Conduct ribbon and be pfc too and you'll find out for yourself why Nogales is such a *fine* place to head for on a week-end pass. And you'll meet up with your buddy and when you see the photo of his gorgeous chick thumb-tacked over his barracks bunk you're going to say mmmmmmm *mmmmmmm!* and he will say Watch that mmmmmmm *mmmmmmm* stuff Jack! cause that's my gal, a brownskin Georgia peach I met when they had me down at Benning and she's really all right and I'm going to marry her too. Yes, she has a sister and she's really all right too he says and you write and she answers and then you see her on your furlough and it's love sure enough and not kid stuff like with Hortense back in Iron City. Man!

> Lord if I ever get lucky
> And get out of here free
> It will take a mighty pretty woman
> To make a fool out of me.

That's what you scratched onto the wall of your jailhouse cell, but this is going to be different, the real thing, and you and your buddy go down there for your last furlough before shipping out and it's a double wedding and she's so sweet and you're so proud in your new corporal stripes and thinking about the extra pay you can send home with the allotment and then goodby honey, goodby Georgia, goodby U.S.A.! The division pushes out to sea and you're gone to fight old Hitler and Benito too and that's a good thing to do if you have to do it and to fight for the Atlantic Charter and the Four Freedoms too and those are good words to hear. You'll like the Italian people, Harvey, and you won't be thinking you're better than the crummy Eyeties and talking about how poor they are and how dirty they are and how can anybody live so many to a house and no decent plumbing neither; you'll be welcomed to their homes and see what a good time they can have with no money, just a little vino maybe and some songs and a mandolin, just like homefolks except for the language but hell, man, anybody can pick up on this Italiano jive, and you sure will and you do all right and—watch that stuff Jack, remember you're a married man! And then you are going to get some more stripes on your arm and battle stars on your campaign ribbon and a purple ribbon to add to the row and even a Bronze Star medal for—well not very much but they say some generals get the DSM for doing less and it all counts up to points and you got a mess of points, man, when that jive comes out after V-E Day. So you and your buddy will be heading home, he's from Harlem and you're from Iron City but both you-all got Georgia on your mind, and it's two ruptured ducks winging South and the war is over and you're free at last; you can't see the South for living and neither can your buddy but the gals got a house and that's something these days. You will latch on to 52-20 and that's something too and maybe you'll start back to school up in Atlanta on the GI Bill but now it's a honeymoon for real. It's another Spring, five years since the season caught you inside the Monongahela County Jail and man, if there aint nothing else good about the South you got to admit that Spring really comes on like Gang Busters down here, it sure do,

Brother-in-Law! It is nothing but a little old town and before you know it you can walk into the country and the road is springy and the stars are big and heavy and the night is warm and young like the way you feel and your buddy and his wife a few steps behind just a-giggling about some secret they got but you and your wife got your own secrets too and you don't have to study none about them. Then it will be four cars stopping when the headlights find you and the white men getting out and you saying you aint done nothing wrong but they got shotguns and they'll line you up in the ditch and kill you. Four shotguns with both barrels. You and your wife and her sister and your buddy, and the red clay will be redder where your bodies are found. They won't bother to tell you though it wouldn't take long, just one word but they don't even say it. Uppity. You carried yourself like a man the way Mr. Zachary said to do, though he wasn't the one who gave you the khaki clothes and your purple and yellow and candy-stripe red, the ribbons and stars, the stripes and the bars. Four carloads of men—their families will know, maybe hundreds of people in Morrow County will know all about it, but the Law won't learn. Nor the FBI's when they finally come down to look around and ask the sheriff what does he know about it anyway. Your funeral, Harvey, is going to be bigger even than the double-wedding was; your brother Claude won't make it from Saipan but son, you could never imagine how many people you got: they will come from miles around, talking quiet, crying quiet—no sermon will be preached. Just the four gray coffins all in a row, you beside your gal and your buddy beside his, just like you walked, just like you fell; and the coffins will be closed because while the colored undertaker is a good man and learned his trade in the best school up in Cincinnati, he won't be able to do much with what the buck-shot left behind. But people won't stare through the coffin lid and the flags so silken shiny that the colored Legion post will bring to cover you with because you and your buddy were veterans; the flag of your country, Harvey, with the red for the blood and the white is right and the blue that's you; and one of the stars, the whitest of all, is for the great State of Georgia where your people came from and where you will die, you and your wife and your buddy and his wife too—in the great State of Georgia and under her shield whereon is written *Wisdom, Justice, Moderation*.

Goodby, Harvey Owens. We were proud to know you, son.

CHAPTER 17

In Charlene Harper's letters to Paul, there were times when Mutual Benefit Society referred to the place where she worked rather than to the Party. She complained one time that the "executives" who worked at the insurance company's branch office were so much wrapped up in their Bundles for Britain activities—which the *best* society people were doing these days—that they had no time for local civic problems (meaning the Lonnie James campaign, of course). But when, on the contrary, she wrote of the untiring work being done by Mutual Benefit people for Defense, it was clear she meant the Party. Her shopping trips with Mrs. Zachary had found no bargains—Leroy Flowers' landlady, Mrs. Bailey, did not know why he left or where he had gone. But once Charlene had something wonderful to report, prefacing it as usual with the remark, "you probably won't be interested, but—"

A Mutual Benefit worker who was taking an evening course at McGregor Tech had interested her class in a famous murder case which had become a *cause célèbre*. The case hinged largely upon the testimony of a single eye-witness and the class decided to make a trip to the scene of the crime—a bank hold-up and murder it was, Charlene wrote—in order to examine for themselves the conditions under which the witness had seen the accused. The instructor had been reluctant to give his assent to the excursion, but when a class member reminded him about how several years ago Theodore Dreiser, whom the instructor admired, had led a student delegation to investigate the Kentucky miners' strike, he agreed to go along with the idea and on the trip.

The results of the excursion, which became public a week after Charlene wrote about it, was a big story that even got mentioned in the *American* as well as in the Negro paper. The unanimous report of the McGregor Tech students (it was also signed by the instructor and for that he must soon sign a requested resignation from the faculty) found that the eyewitness' testimony was open to serious doubt. The lamp-post at the intersection of Van Buren and Cottage Avenue was on the corner where Miss Martha Hightower stood when she saw Lonnie James fleeing from the Thornhill Pharmacy. From that place and at the same time of night, the students had tested what they could see of one of their number who re-enacted the post-murder flight from the door, running past the neon-lighted display window away from them on Cottage. The mock-fugitive was supplied with two rubber Hallowe'en masks: one the ghostly white of a skull-face, the other a jet-black Sambo; two pairs of silk gloves, white and black, were to be worn with the matching color mask. The instructor and three of the students were posted within the store to make sure that the fugitive would alternate the masks and gloves on ten repeated runs, five times white-faced, five times black. At no time, the report stated, could the observers who were catty-corner across the wide street-crossing tell the color of the runner's hands or face; they saw nothing but a shadow against the glow!

Their report was now included in the Defense Committee's publicity: the question was asked—*Why was not such an investigation made before Lonnie James was put on trial?* The demand was made: *The Supreme Court must reverse the verdict!* New thousands of petitions were gathered, more telegrams flew to the Court, more organizations became affiliated to the committee headed by Reverend Buford, Lucy Jackson and Theodore Archer. Notable among the groups which joined now was the big steelworkers' local in McGregor's Iron City mill, defying their district director who said this was not a legitimate trade-union matter.

Charlene and Annie Mae had been unable to learn much more than was already known to the inside committee about Big John Cummings, but they did report more about Herbert T. Wills. Whatever had been his motives in writing the letter to the *Eagle* about Lonnie, the official of the Negro Improvement League was now making the case the subject of his speeches to Negro churches and other groups in Kanesport. If we want advancement, he told his audiences, if we want to be upgraded in the mill, if we want better housing—whatever we want, we must behave ourselves! Hoodlums like Lonnie James must be sternly dealt with! And somehow, too, he was connecting the case with the local swimming pool issue which was now getting as hot as the weather. Under the leadership of a Negro physician, a campaign had been launched to win for Negroes the right to use the municipal pool; but Mr. Wills strongly condemned the effort. Hoodlums like Lonnie James will only make trouble, he was saying. We all will suffer. No decent colored people will go where they are not wanted. The pool is public? Negroes pay taxes too? Well, the City Council had planned to build one for Goat Hill residents but because of Defense work it had to be postponed.

The walls which hold Lonnie James in Iron City must also buttress the black ghetto of Kanesport.

As it happened, it was the inside committee that learned more about Big John Cummings and his strange lapse of memory. The left-fielder of the opposing team was a man from the lower all-Negro tier, Range E, and Paul Harper who also played that position came to know him. One day during the choosing-up of sides, his opposite number said something to Paul about Goat Hill. Yes, he replied to Paul's question, he came from Kanesport and did he know Big John?—why if it wasn't for that mother-lover I wouldn't be doing time in here today! The rival left-fielder was a numbers man who worked for the Iron City syndicate that was branching out into the county—and that's what was wrong. He explained that

James J. Toomey was not only police commissioner of Kanesport, he was also, and more importantly, the head man of all organized vice in that town—whorehouses, gambling joints, book-making, numbers, pinball and slot machines, floating crap games—just as he had been head of the bootlegging ring during Prohibition. Big John Cummings was Toomey's lieutenant for Goat Hill; Big John's own joint was not so important in itself but because it was the collection center for all pay-offs that came from all the rackets in the Negro section. "Big John and Toomey are just like this," the numbers man told Paul, showing him with his fingers. "But of course Jim Toomey is boss and Big John got to do what he says—I should know." He had tried to fix it with Big John so he could write numbers for the Iron City boys. Big John took his hundred dollars but the next day the laws picked up the interloper. "So you see Big John got me coming and going, and if he didn't have all that backing—well, when I'd get out, his soul would belong to God but his ass would belong to me!"

It was not legal proof, of course, that Commissioner Toomey had told Big John to forget about the two boys who had argued with him the night of Thornhill's murder; and it would be hard to prove the secret link between boss and lieutenant. But still it was something for the outside committee to work on and they must be told. Because of the names involved—Big John and Toomey—the information must be smuggled out by Slim: he must take the risk again. He did, without hesitation, for he was now an additional member of the inside committee.

Leroy Flowers? Each week the notice appeared in the Help Me Find column of the Negro newspaper: *Urgently needed by his brother Lonnie who is in serious trouble*. Every issue of the *National Chronicle* now carried big headlines and stories about the case—big news, it sold papers. But every week too there was an editorial echoing the one on undermining justice that had been published by the downtown *American*. It was a curious thing to see—the news columns roaring the mass outcry against the legal lynching, the editorial page thundering against the protesters who were dupes of the nefarious Reds. The necessary link with its readers on the one hand, the pull of Cap'n McGregor's strings on the other. Two-faced! said Faulcon in his bitterness. Two-souled, said Paul Harper who preferred the exactness of theoretical formulations.

A clipping of the *American's* story on the students' report was brought to Range D by J.C., the bath-house sweeper, who had become the unpaid but willing-to-be-tipped courier between the Negro members of the inside committee and the white men on Cell Block Three who had joined it. Pencilled on the clipping was the message: WONDERFUL! WE ARE WITH YOU. Smitty must have written that, Paul said: he's always saying something serious in a joking way. Of course the white comrades are with us—in this jail and the ones outside too; and the white militants in the unions and middle-class progressives. "That's what I been trying to show you," Zach said to Slim. "And they're not *South* Americans either. Italians, Slavs, Greeks, Jews, Yankees, Hungarians— yes, even some Irishmens—all kinds, but they're white folks and doing as much as they can!" They told Slim that the girl student who had suggested the investigation was white; she was the only Communist there but the others had agreed and they were white folks too as was the liberal instructor who got canned.

The outside committee had realized from the first that any legal action was of minor importance. The defense campaign had officially started the first week of May; Lonnie James had been convicted the previous October. The appeal had long since been filed and argued—it might be acted upon any day now; it would surely come before the end of June. The main and immediate thing was to make the frame-up known to the public, to agitate and rally a mass outcry. It was late, terribly late. When the lawyer who had led the legal defense of the Twenty-Six saw for himself what kind of an appeal had been prepared by Winkel acting for Coxe, he was certain it would be denied: the appeal reflected the empty defense at the trial. The only legal action that could be taken at this late stage was to submit an affidavit from Leroy Flowers if

223

he could be found. The best of lawyers would be impotent now. Only the widest and strongest protest could affect the outcome.

(2)

"Don't go, Lonnie."

"Don't go! Man, are you nuts? Aint you satisfied that I been cooped up in here for three days and couldn't play on account of fouling over the wall and now we're trailing those bums by half a game! You must be wacky sure enough, but come to think of it I reckon even you'd do better in charge of the yard than that Rooney bastard. Me here wondering why nine o'clock won't come so I can go out to play and you sitting here hoping I aint going! OK, I'll tell you again—I'll be back here for sure if I live and nothing happens." He smiled now, surprised at the expression. "Hear what I just said? Funny about sayings like that. Fellow says to me a while back—just talking about something or other—says, Lonnie this will kill you. Or you take the way people say: You'll die laughing. To *me*. And now here I come saying if I live and nothing happens!"

He pondered about that, trying to decide if it was a bad sign. He couldn't make up his mind but he thought of something else. He grinned and turned to Peterson who was perched on his usual place at the head of Lonnie's bunk, his drawn-up knees wrapped tightly in his arms, his unblinking eyes adding to the picture of a wise little owl.

"Tell you a funny story about that saying, Carl. Colored people always say that—don't know why but they do. Well, anyway, it seems there was a light-skinned fellow, had a good education and everything like that but he couldn't get a job in an office downtown. OK, so he decides to pass. Course you don't know what that is so skip it and I'll tell you what happened. He got a job in a fancy place, maybe it was a bank even, but anyway he was working in an office and doing fine. Passing. That's all right till one day—maybe somebody saw him sneaking back home to Goat Hill—the boss gets

224

tipped off that one of his employees that he got working for him aint pure white. In fact, he's a Negro. Naturally the boss gets all worried cause he don't know which one it is and he don't know who to fire. But finally somebody tells him how to find out, and this time when everybody was punching the clock going off shift, the boss he shakes each one by the hand and says he hopes they have a pleasant week-end and be back safe and sound for work on Monday. Everybody's a little surprised but he's the boss so they say something back: sure . . . I will . . . thank you . . . same to you, things like that. OK, and here comes the guy that's passing. Hope to see you back bright and early on Monday, says the boss. Sure thing, says this guy, *if I live and nothing happens.* That's the giveaway and the boss fires him on the spot. Cause somebody told the boss that if you can't tell a Negro by anything else you can sure as hell catch him saying if I live and nothing happens! And I guess that old story is true cause here I come saying the same words myself. I sure did and I'm colored for a fact. Aint I, Carl?"

Peterson stared at him. Now the eyes blinked once and he smiled.

"I like you, Lonnie," he said.

"Oh, go to hell man," said Lonnie who never ceased to be embarrassed by the simple man's simple words of friendship. The bell rang and Lonnie skipped down the runway toward the gate. He pivoted sharply and ran back to his cell. Damn near forgot to take along the letter. It was another one from Mr. Winkel that had come in the morning mail.

Faulcon's scoreboard showed eight runs for Lonnie's team and Zach's had seven runs chalked up for Kuczinsky's side, but the real score was five to four against Lonnie—the Rooney home runs don't count. Two were out, nobody on; Paul Harper was at bat. "Get on man," Lonnie pleaded, for he was up next. "Just save me a raps. He'll walk ya—he'll walk ya!" But Kuczinsky was bearing down: the ball broke sharply across the plate. Rooney's fingers lifted with the count—no balls, two strikes. "Goddamit, Paul, what ya *doing?* Watch this one!" Paul's bat lashed out at the next pitch. Just topped it and the ball dribbled weakly toward third. Paul's long legs flew toward first. "Safe!" cried Lonnie even before the runner crossed the base. "*Safe!*" he screamed out to Rooney. The umpire must have thought so too for he gave the sign for safe.

Lonnie crowed his triumph as he moved to the batter's box, savagely pounding the painted spot on the asphalt that was home plate. "Don't walk me, Kootchy," he begged. "Put it over, man. Just once." Kootchy did: his first pitch came hard and true, straight across the middle. Strike one. Now Lonnie yelled his delight: "That's the kind I want—just wanted to see if you could do it. Once more, same place." He held out his bat to show where he wanted it, taunting his rival on the mound.

It came now, the same pitch, and Lonnie swung with all his supple power. The ball started out low on a line, just missing the finger tips of the leaping third-baseman; then it slowly began to rise, streaking up like a startled quail. Lonnie must have known even at the split second he started toward first: he stopped abruptly and stood frozen while his eyes followed the soaring drive over the left-field wall and out of sight. For a moment he stared in wonder and disbelief that he had done what no man had ever done before—hit a home run over that wall. Then the bat fell from his hand, bouncing on the hard pavement, and he started toward the door at the end of the center-field court that led inside to the jail. Hey, Lonnie! they all cried, where you going? But he did not answer; he did not look back. Past second base he began to run. Paul, who had raced around with the tying run, now ran after him and pulled at his arm. The thought had flashed that maybe Lonnie for some reason was running to attack the hated old guard Byrd who always dozed by the door but who was up now to bar Lonnie's flight. Rooney's whistle shrilled now, but it was not to halt Lonnie: he motioned to Byrd to let Lonnie go in. It was against the rule for any man to leave the yard before the hour was up, but the stupid Rooney knew what most of the inmates did not yet know; and afterward, when they found out, the men would say that it was the only decent thing Rooney ever did in his life.

The game was not resumed though fifteen minutes were left. The men walked aimlessly about the enclosure, the word spreading among them. It was Slim Gaither who told the other inside committeemen about the tiny court that was behind the left-field wall. "It's between our building and the women's side of the jail. Can't see it except from one window in the warden's office. Nothing in it now but that's where they do the hanging."

The jailhouse legend which told that no man had ever hit a ball that far had another part to it. The newcomers had not heard of it, for it was never mentioned whenever there was some one in here under sentence of death. *Any man who hits a ball over there will follow it some day: even if he pulls his time and goes out free the day will come when he will be brought back and hanged.* And now that the inmates heard it from the whispering long-timers they would speak of it no more—maybe silence would take away the curse, just as not mentioning the fact that a pitcher has a chance for a no-hitter is said to help him perform the feat. But despite themselves their eyes were pulled to the wall, to stare as if they might see, through the blankness of the granite, the gallows and the thirteen steps that people said led up to it.

"Imagine a guy like that," Paul said softly to Zach and Faulcon. "Always trying his best to hit one over and scared to death that he would! I guess of all the signs he ever saw this one is the worst. . . . Sure hope we get some good news soon." Now he remembered the letter that Lonnie had slipped him when they came out today. From Winkel, but they would have to wait till they got back to Range D to see what it said.

(3)

Everything was different about this letter from Lonnie's attorney. It was written by hand, neatly; the paper was not the thick crackling stationery of Fallon, Erhardt, Schwimmer and Ross—it was torn from a small notebook.

June 10, 1941

My Dear Mr. James—

I am afraid that I have fallen behind in my correspondence. I have not been feeling well and there have been many letters, more than ever, for me to answer. Now they come to me from all over the Commonwealth. This has imposed a great burden upon me since the facilities of the office are no longer available for this purpose.

However, I shall no longer ask that you try to stop them from writing for I have come to the conclusion that you cannot help me on this. There are too many letters, too many telephone calls, too many questions and requests—and as you said, you do not know these persons. You cannot help me. No one can. I know that now.

Mr. James, I wish to tell you something now which I have not mentioned to any one else for many years. I chose to enter the legal profession not to gain power, wealth or prestige, but because the Law is the age-old shield of the weak against the strong. Without that protection the helpless individual has nowhere to turn from the blows of injustice. In my own small way I desired to help sustain that shield. I still have faith that the Law is just, but I have come to doubt after all these years that I made the proper choice for my career.

I want you to know that whatever I could do in your behalf I have done. I did not withdraw my assistance even when I was firmly advised to do so by Mr. Coxe. But people persist in misunderstanding my efforts and draw the most damaging inferences as to my motives. There were many things that I suggested to your senior counsel, but after all he was in charge and I was merely his assistant. He was much more experienced in such matters than I. This is common knowledge and a matter of record as well.

Believe me, Mr. James. I want you to believe in my sincerity and loyalty. I hope and pray that the Court will render

228

a just verdict in your behalf and that you will soon be released from custody. The decision must come within the next twenty days.

Respectfully yours,
Arnold Winkel

Across the bottom margin Lonnie James had scrawled: *What do you think—is he getting ready to quit me?*

Before lock-up the answer came in the Closing Stocks edition of the Iron City *American*. Mr. Winkel had withdrawn from *Commonwealth vs Lonnie James*. He had quit Clement B. Coxe and Fallon, Erhardt, Schwimmer and Ross too, leaving the firm by way of the sixteenth-story window.

LAWYER DIES IN LEAP
FROM LAW BUILDING

Employee of McGregor
Corporation Counsel
Is Suicide Victim

The newspaper account dealt mainly with the spectacular aspects of his plunge from the skyscraper window, but it also mentioned that Mr. Winkel had left a note on his desk at the law firm—its name had to be mentioned this time—which said, "I am sorry." The message was not addressed to anyone; it was signed Arnold Winkelried which was his family name.

Was he sorry for the scandal that he would bring upon Fallon, Erhardt, Schwimmer and Ross? For the dismal failure of his law career? That this final flight would end a life-time of fleeing? One reader of the paper was sure he knew the answer. When he saw the latest sign on this day of doom, Lonnie James remembered that before he fled from his last visit to the jail, Mr. Winkel had said, "I'm sorry, Mr. James. I'm terribly sorry." There was no doubt in Lonnie's mind: Mr. Winkel knew there was no hope for me. He was saying goodby that day, though he did not know that he would go before me, that his fall would be deeper than

229

through a trap-door. He could not wait the last twenty days before my appeal would be decided. *Too many questions. . . . You cannot help me. No one can. I know that now.*

What would they say now at the Lawyers Club, the ones who had snickered over the joke about Winky being brought into a murder case? Poor Winky, didn't have much on the ball maybe, but he was a nice enough chap when you got to know him. Too bad, he must have been depressed by illness the way the paper reported. . . . There was little that could be said about the funny little man whose mangled remains on the sidewalk had been covered, not by the age-old shield which protects the weak from the strong, but by a mildewed canvas brought by the Police Department ambulance. Perhaps there were some in Iron City who still remembered the victim from schooldays and who would repeat the copy-book lines, the scorn now melted away like the snowballs they had hurled—

> *"Make way for Liberty!" he cried*
> *Then ran with arms extended wide*
> *As if his dearest friend to clasp*
> *Ten spears he swept within his grasp. . . .*

I'm sorry, he said before he died. Make way for Arnold Winkelried!

CHAPTER 18

Lonnie did not come out to play. Not the next day nor the one after that. Whitey brought back to Paul the reply to his note of encouragement and the assurance that the outside committee would provide a new lawyer. "Thanks," wrote Lonnie, "I'm all right." That was all. They desperately hoped that on the third day he would come to the yard, for the day after that would be Sunday when no one might go out. "We must talk to you," Paul wrote in another message; but there was no answer. And when the paper came that Saturday afternoon they were not sure they would ever see him again. There was no headline about his client as there had been for Mr. Winkel—the front page shouted the news that FDR had ordered all assets of Germany, Italy, and the occupied countries to be frozen. The news about Lonnie was buried on an inside page, in a series of decisions announced by the Supreme Court which was soon to adjourn for the summer. "The Court also upheld the conviction of Lonnie James, Negro, for the hold-up murder last year of a Kanesport businessman." Twenty words, and Mr. Winkel would not have had to wait for twenty days to read them.

REGULATION 245 (J): IF NEGATIVE ACTION IS TAKEN ON COURT APPEAL IN SUCH CASES, THE INMATE ON RANGE C WILL BE CONFINED TO HIS CELL UNDER 24-HOUR OBSERVATION. LEGAL AND/OR SPIRITUAL COUNSEL IS PERMITTED ONLY UNDER THESE CONDITIONS AND IN THE PRESENCE OF THE GUARD ON DUTY. . . .

There is nothing in the regulations which provides for the spotlight which is mounted on the outer bars of the cell block, its beam shining day and night upon the caged man. The light is a small matter, for what can add to the horror of the doomed man? But for Lonnie there was something that could. The terrifying shock of it broke through the numbness of his despair that Saturday night when he saw that the guard who would sit outside his cell till morning would be Byrd.

Now I know why I was always so scared of him, why I hated him so. He is a buzzard for real and I must have known it would be like this. He's been waiting for now. All the time he's just been waiting. Pretending to be asleep out in the yard but all the time he was watching for me. Waiting. "Get away!" he screamed. "I'll kill you! I'll kill you!" But the old man ignored him; he leaned his chair against the runway bars and closed his eyes. "Steve! *Steve!* Take him away!" The cry echoed through all the jail but the chief guard could not hear him: it was hours since he had quit for the day. Finally Lonnie remembered and ceased to call him. Now the only sound was the whimpering of poor Crazy Carl in the next-door cell.

I'll never be able to sleep again. How can I sleep with him watching? "You're not fooling me, you old buzzard!" He had not meant to say it aloud; the sound of his own voice startled him. But not Byrd. The eyes in the deep dark hollows of his head did not open. The thin fringe of silky white hair around the bald dome could not be seen in the glare of the light: it was truly a skeleton's head. "You're not fooling me a bit," Lonnie said again, deliberately now. "But I'll be watching you too. Don't forget that. I won't be sleeping." Lonnie stretched out on the bunk, covering himself with the blanket, then turned to face the wall between his cell and Peterson's.

Don't you be crying like that in there. I aint dead yet. Besides, I got friends, Carl—a lot of friends. And if I had had them before, even this much wouldn't have happened. They'll save me. You'll see they will. I aint in this alone no more. . . . *Do I believe that?* he asked himself, not Carl. *Can they save me now?* He no longer believed it possible but he could not say it to himself any more than he could to his friend in the make-believe talking through the steel. . . . No, Carl—I aint alone no more. Everybody knows that and it's true.

It was true: for the first time in his life Lonnie James had friends. In the nights that were to follow, sleepless nights again, that truth would be the only solid thing to which he could hold. Daytime was not so bad. Cahill, the guard assigned to that shift, was friendly. Lonnie had only to pull out his cigarettes for the observer to rise from his chair to give him a light. (Regulation 245-k did not permit the doomed inmate to keep matches. At night this was a great hardship for Lonnie who would not ask old Byrd for the favor.) And all through the day shift Carl Peterson squatted on the runway outside Lonnie's cell. Carl was happy, for now his friend never left the range and the crazy fear was calmed. Some other guard might not have permitted him to approach so close to the locked cell, but for loonies and men sentenced to die Cahill had a warm sympathy. Carl's steadfastness was a comfort to Lonnie; the irony of Carl's happiness was not bitter. It was good to see a happy man around.

Steve had been called to see Lonnie the Monday after he was confined, but there was nothing the chief guard could do about taking Byrd off the night watch. Regulations provided that the guards for this purpose be appointed by the Warden and the official had stopped in long enough to fulfill that duty. "Byrd asked for the job," Steve explained. "Claimed that it was easier to sit in here where it's cool instead of in the hot sun outside. What the hell—the old geezer only got to put in two more months to finish his thirty years for pension. So forget about him, Lonnie—just go to sleep and you won't even know he's there." Lonnie could not bring himself to tell the chief guard that with buzzard-Byrd out there he could not sleep: he would not show them his weakness. "OK," he said, "if you can't change it. But Steve—please—do me one favor. You tell him not to ever come in here. Not even come close to the bars. I swear if he does I'll grab him by that skinny red neck and it would take a cold chisel to cut my hands loose! I mean that, Steve."

"Sure, kid. I'll tell him what you said." The chief guard eyed him closely. "I bet you really would," he said slowly. "You got a mean streak in you, Lonnie. A mean streak."

That had been said about him before. Long before Mr. Coxe accused him of being arrogant, contemptuous, intemperate. Long before any of this had happened. In the wakeful hours of night, Lonnie would never allow himself to think ahead toward what would come. Over and over again, as his eyes counted the rosary of the rivets up the wall, his mind traced and retraced the pattern of his short life, going back to the earliest days he could remember.

He was alone even then, though he was one among seventy orphan boys in the Sheltering Arms Home in Castle Ferry.

There were few Negroes in that little mining town and Lonnie's was the only name on the list of young inmates that was followed by the letter C in parentheses. He did not know about that, of course, but he knew from the first that he was different. He was told about that and the words which the white kids used were pure American, though most of their fathers had come from far-away lands. There was nowhere for the slender black boy to run from their jeers and blows. He learned that truth after he had run away on two occasions only to be caught and returned Home. He had to fight, though he was always outnumbered and the punishment of blackened eyes, bruised ribs and bloody nose was sure to be followed by official penalty. But not before he had landed some blows on the enemy —and in time that made a difference. He was a black bully; he was mean; he was crafty too in catching a foe who had strayed too far from the others—but none of those names had the sting of the other kind and he was secretly proud of his bad reputation. His sheltering fists never became stronger than the Sheltering Arms, but by the time he was ten they seldom ganged-up against him. And because he was reckless and daring he won the front position in all the follow-the-leader games; but though they followed him he had only contempt for them. Any gesture of friendship was suspect—the proffered bite from an apple might be the wormy part, maybe they had spit upon the extra slice of bread smuggled from the refectory. None could be his friend.

Even in high school where he first came in contact with others outside the Home, the pattern was not broken although not once did he have to fight. He was even a hero now—captain of the basketball team, star pitcher in baseball, school record-holder in track; but a lonely hero who must return each day to eat the moldy bread of charity. At Lincoln High there were a few other Negro students, but he felt no bond of kinship with them. Their lives were apart; they had people and friends, real homes for refuge and love. One of these Lonnie hated from the bottom of his soul. He was dark of skin, though not as dark as Lonnie, and they called him Snowball. The boy did not resent it; he even seemed to enjoy the name and the

234

laughing. He graduated a year before Lonnie and in the yearbook, under his grinning picture they printed the nickname along with his scholastic record and achievements. Lonnie could never provoke him into a fight, and that was a keen regret. Lonnie had never fought a colored kid and when he thought of the pleasure of his fist smacking into Snowball's face, he wondered what the others would shout. For never had he heard anything but the old chant he learned when he was six—*A fight! A fight! A nigger and a white!*

By the time he came up to Kanesport where they said the mill was hiring, Lonnie had come to accept the fact that he would always be different, an orphan for life. Mrs. Spencer, his landlady, was friendly but she could never induce him to go to her church for social life. The workers in the plant were friendly for the most part: a white man showed him how to use the air-driven chisel that was used for chipping steel and the knowledge made possible his promotion from common labor to chipper. Lonnie was grateful, but he stayed aloof; he joined the union when the white man asked him but he would never go to meetings. The young fellows he knew—Cliff Parker, Leroy and some others—were never close friends. Just somebody to hang around with and shoot a game of pool. He liked them as he did the girls to whom he made love, but always he felt a barrier between his inner self and these others.

It was only Crazy Peterson who had been keen enough and persistent enough to reach the hidden Lonnie within, the motherless child, crying the secret tears of his boyhood. Lonnie struggled against the intruder whose simple words reached so deep and filled him with glowing wonder. *No, I aint no good, Carl. If you want to know the truth, I'm mean and that's a fact.* And sometimes when he first came to know the little man, his cruel knuckles had scraped across the addled head to make Carl feel that fact. But Carl refused to believe him and he had stopped trying to make him believe.

Funny, when you come to think of it. If I hadn't been all alone maybe they would never have framed me. But if it wasn't for that I wouldn't have so many friends now. Carl here, Paul and the others downstairs on D, the white guys on Block

Three, and all those people out there fighting for me. Not quitting like Mr. Winkel. Not even now. And besides they got me a new lawyer—a good one. . . .

Milton Cohen was an excellent lawyer—the profession conceded that fact though otherwise he was held in bitter scorn by the Club. Cohen was poor but there was nothing amusing about his lack of success as there was about Winky's. Cohen should have made money, they said; he could have won a position of respect even though his unfortunate racial background made him ineligible for Club membership. Winky was a fool: Cohen was worse. They called him an *idealist*. They also called him a Red though they knew he was not a Communist—but what else can you call a man who clings to the liberal philosophy of Holmes and Cardozo in the age of Martin Dies and John Rankin?

As attorney for the local Labor Defense, Cohen was as overworked as he was under-paid. A tall, heavy man of middle age, he always looked tired; but the dark fatigue that ringed his eyes was testimony that he was tireless. His work in the case of the Twenty-Six did not end with the trial; there was much more to be done. Yet when the outside committee asked him to assume this additional burden he readily agreed. And somehow he found the time now to visit Lonnie several times each week. He did not speak much about the legal matters, for what was there to say? That he had filed a motion for a re-hearing by the Court, citing the results of the students' experiment and the fact of Winkel's suicide, though of course there was no legal proof that the case of Lonnie James had any connection with the incident. That after Judge Rupp set the date of execution the Governor had the power to commute the sentence to life imprisonment. That pressure might compel him to take the action, thus giving the committee a chance to prove Lonnie's innocence. That there were no legal grounds for an appeal to the Supreme Court in Washington. There could have been, of course, had Lonnie's court-appointed attorneys laid the basis during the trial for an appeal on constitutional grounds, had they exposed the frame-up and the forced confession. But Mr. Cohen did not tell Lonnie the whole terrible record of the trial as it looked to an honest lawyer—no reason for that now. Mostly he reported in detail the work of the committee, the unceasing efforts of the mass movement, the plans for a large delegation to see the Governor. We'll win, he said; and Lonnie was sure his lawyer believed that, even though he himself had given up hope.

(2)

Paul Harper still played left field, though now it was only to try to get his mind off what had happened—and Lonnie under the light. He was restless now and more snappish than ever. His letters to Charlene now had an accusing tone: he could not understand why more was not being done. Why can't people outside understand how it is? Why don't they do something? He had flown into a rage at gray-haired Faulcon for nothing at all. "Damn it, Henry, how come you're always hitching-up your pants when I'm trying to tell you something?" Faulcon had not given the reasonable explanation—because I have no belt. "I'm sorry," he said. The old man had lost a lot of weight but his stomach seemed to bulge even larger and his trousers must be continually pulled up by his thumbs to keep him decent-looking.

Faulcon and Isaac Zachary kept their scorekeeping jobs, but now that there was no necessity for them to remain posted on opposite sides of home plate, the two committeemen would stand together and talk while an inning was being played. Seeing Paul play constantly reminded them of Lonnie: the two young men so alike in build and color, except that Lonnie's head was squarish and Paul's was long. The scorekeepers often talked about the resemblance and the differences too. "Paul's the older in years," Zach observed, "but he's still a boy, where the other is full man-grown." He admired Paul's learning, his ready answers to questions, but he admired Lonnie more. "That one—he's quick and sure and steady-strong. What an engineer he could be!"

Faulcon smiled at the highest tribute Zach could pay to Lonnie, but he felt that somehow Paul was being slighted.

237

"What's wrong with Paul?" he demanded. "I can't say he'd make a good waiter like me. Too touchy for something like that. But he's not filled out yet and he's going to be a mighty big man when he is. He's kind of awkward-like with his feet and hands too big and he's kind of like that with his ideas too. They're big and strong too but he can't always manage them just right—but he will. Looks like it hurts him to smile too much but that aint nothing—it's just that he figures he's got to look serious cause he is serious. But guess what Charlene told me during the trial—said not to tell a soul: before he became an organizer he wanted to be a *dancer*. No lie. And one time after lock-up awhile back I heard some shuffling of feet in his cell so I pushed out my looking-spoon and asked him what were he doing. Killing cockroaches, he says, but that were a lie. There aint that many bugs in nobody's cell!"

The ball games now were not the same. Kootchy's side had a big lead in the standings but there was no glory in that with the other team's star pitcher gone. Sometimes above the shouting of the players the inmates seemed to hear the missing man's whoops of joy when he struck a man out, his yelping protests when Rooney ruled against him. And always their eyes turned to the left-field wall from where one day soon would come the screeching of saws and the hollow beat of hammers.

The only honest excitement now was for the big fight coming soon. Each day the fever grew and for the first time before a Joe Louis fight the betting was heavy. Whole books of matches, full packs of cigarettes, stacks of comic books were wagered. In part it was because of Jimmy Williams' column on the *American's* sport page. Daily that expert predicted a victory for the challenger: the sullen, lethargic, slow-thinking tiger that was champ would be tamed by the clever, flashing fists of young Billy Conn. A new White Hope had risen in Pittsburgh who would surely dethrone the Brown Bomber from Detroit. Many of the inmates were firmly convinced he was right, but others were staunch for Joe. The arguments grew bitter and only the dread of being put into the Hole and missing the fight stopped them from backing their words with blows. Only for a heavyweight championship bout was the radio left on after ten o'clock, though too often the champion had caused it to be turned off a moment later by scoring an early-round kayo. But not this time, the Conn-men insisted. That Billy he's smart, a boxer, a fencer. And don't forget what Corbett did to John L. Sullivan and John L. was an Irishman too! Sure Joe's all right in there against some bum, but all you have to do is clout him one on the head—that's where he's weak.

(3)

Cahill had bet him a dollar on the fight and Lonnie was sorry that the genial guard was not with him tonight instead of old Byrd. The night guard had taken out his false teeth and put them into a gaping side-pocket of his uniform coat, opened the brass buttons down the front, settled back in his fireman's chair, and closed his eyes. He was not pretending to sleep, for one foot was tapping in time to the hill-billy music that floated down from the loudspeaker. He's waiting for the fight, Lonnie thought; waiting for the champ to get beat. Wonder how many men he's watched like he's watching me now—waiting for them to die?

Seven times in the past year Lonnie had listened to Joe Louis fights; and each time Joe's victory had been a sign. Not a great sign—nobody gave the McCoys and Burmans and Buddy Baers a chance against the great champion—but a good sign for Lonnie just the same. Regulations required that the inmates be silent after lock-up and fight-time was no exception; but when Joe knocked out Godoy the first month Lonnie was jailed, Lonnie had bellowed his joy for all to hear. The rugged challenger from Chile had previously gone fifteen rounds with Joe and because of that feat people said he might take away the crown in the second match. The cheering Lonnie had been hustled off to the Hole: he was kept there five days for the darkness to dim his enthusiasm. He would go to the Hole many times after that, but not again for that offense: since the punishment cancelled out the good sign, Lonnie controlled himself.

Tonight was different. No matter how much he yelled they would not take him from his cell; but that was of no importance now and he did not give it a thought. Everything was different tonight. The dollar bet with Cahill was but a symbol of the last limp shred of hope that he had somehow found and which he wagered tonight against himself. It surprised him to learn that he still had hope, but it must be true, he told himself, else why am I acting like this? Why should I care about some old prizefight when they got the light on me?

He could not stand still while he waited. He paced the four short steps from washbowl to door; he kicked softly at the wall with the toes of his sneakers; he pulled at the door. In his nervous excitement he almost put his hands on the place where many hands before him had worn away the paint, the place he never should touch. He wiped his hands on his shirt front: they were wet with sweat. The sweat on his face made highlights on the bony, square forehead and high cheek-bones. He was suffering for a smoke but he would have to wait till about eleven when the patrolling guard would come through on his second tour. Lonnie cursed the hill-billies: why wouldn't they get through with all that yowling so the fight could come on? And why should they torture us with that big-mouthed fool selling beer and making that guggling sound of pouring it? And me not tasting a drop since that night in Big John's with Leroy Flowers. Oh, Leroy—you'll be listening too wherever you are! Why don't you come back? Why can't the man who's going to announce the fight call for you instead of all that crap about Buicks and razor blades! You'd hear him. You'd come. I know you would Leroy. I know you would . . . *Oh shut up!* As if they heard him the twanging voices stopped and the beer-man said they'd be back tomorrow same time same station.

Lonnie's heart jumped in time with the *bong bing bong* of the network signal: ten o'clock! A squawking and squealing followed as the guard at the Hub desk twirled his dial to the

240

station that would bring them the fight. Now came the familiar roar of Yankee Stadium in New York packed with the thousands who were free to yell and cheer. Then sudden silence as the guard snapped it off so that all might hear the ringing of his key on the railing: the excited murmuring that had filled the jail must cease before he would turn the radio back on. Each man prayed for every other one to be quiet for Christ's sake or none would hear the long-awaited battle. Now all was still except for a muffled coughing as one man pressed his mouth to his blanket roll. The radio came back on. The introductions were over: it was the bell and Round One!

Through each round Lonnie would stand rigid at the door, his face pressed to the bars as he strained to catch each racing word of the blow-by-blow announcer. Between rounds he would resume the rapid pacing, pounding one hand with his fist as though to add power to the Bomber's punches, his lips moving in whispered advice to Joe—Watch him! Get him quick! Don't let him get away again! At the warning buzzer for the next round Lonnie would spring to his place as though the bell that would come ten seconds later was for him. This is what he had done for the other seven fights and he would follow the pattern tonight until the terrible third round. Joe is hurt! the announcer screamed. The dancing Billy Conn was grinning his scorn. The champ is dazed . . . confused . . . and the swelling roar of the crowd showed that something was happening. At the end of the round and through the rest of the fight Lonnie would not release his grip on the bars.

It came with the bell that ended the fourth round. KILL THAT NIGGER! The voice was not the radio. From one of the cells the words had flicked out like a snake. Lonnie flinched at the bite. "NO!" he screamed. "NO! NO!"

Now the jail was filled again with the murmuring hum from a thousand cells; but it quickly died away under the threat of the lowered volume of the loudspeakers. The fifth round and the sixth were bad for Joe. He's dazed, befuddled by the clever Billy; he's missing those punches . . . Billy slashes him again . . . and another left and a right! . . .

Again at the end of the seventh: KILL THAT NIGGER!

Lonnie was braced for it to come and now he was sure that the cold flat words had come from Murderers' Row and that they were meant for Lonnie. It was Al Reardon, eight cells away, though the voice was disguised. And now there were other voices shouting: it came first from Cell Block Three— "NO! NO! NO!" The radio clicked off and more voices joined the yelling: KILL THAT NIGGER! and NO! NO! NO! The rival chants clashed and swirled, the dome overhead echoing the clamor. Other voices could be heard crying out and after a while these merged into a third chant: SHUT UP! SHUT UP! RADIO! RADIO! Then came the clang of cell doors being opened and the scuffling of feet as the guards rushed men to the Hole. The third chant grew louder: all were shouting it in unison, marking the rhythm by banging their cups on the bars. Then the chanting stopped and all was still. . . . The silence was endless. What round was it? Had the fight ended? Who won?

Finally a distant sound came and Lonnie knew what was happening: the guards were huddled around the set on Steve's desk. They would hear the rest of the fight themselves; the loudspeakers would not be turned on. For the first time since the start he noticed Byrd. The watcher had not moved: his eyes were open and staring at Lonnie. Now all the locked-up fury in Cell Number 10 burst out at the guard. "Get up and turn on the radio!" Lonnie shouted. *"Turn on that radio!"* Byrd gave no sign that he heard. Lonnie shouted it again and other voices took up the cry. TURN ON THE RADIO! TURN ON THE RADIO! It was savage now, not pleading, and it seemed as though the granite walls would shatter from the pounding beat of the chant. Like a giant battering ram, remorseless, booming—TURN ON THE RADIO! TURN ON THE RADIO! Everything was in that outcry—the beatings, the Hole, the graft, the slop, the senseless rules, crooked cops, crooked judges —everything. Again there came the sound of opened cells and of men being dragged away, but this time the rebellion would not be crushed. There were not enough solitary confinement cells to hold them all. TURN ON THE RADIO! TURN ON THE RADIO! . . .

242

At last the Hub surrendered. The thirteenth round had already been ended by the knock-out, but the inmates would hear the solemn announcement. THE *WINNAH* AND STILL HEAVYWEIGHT CHAMPEEN OF THE WORLD—JO-O-OE *LOUIS!*

Lonnie released his grip and opened his eyes to look into the staring hollows of the skull outside. Deliberately he placed his hands where the paint was worn off the bars. He was no longer afraid of that. He laughed. He was no longer afraid of Byrd either. He stared back at the unmoving watcher.

"Old man, you lost. You got nothing to wait here for." Lonnie's voice was calm, but loud enough for his enemy Reardon and Paul and his friends to hear. "We won tonight. We won."

CHAPTER 19

The fight which rocked the walls of the jail was on a Wednesday night. On the following Sunday another battle began that would rock the walls of the world. Again there was the clash and swirl of two contending chants: a greater kill-the-nigger side was screaming *On to Moscow! Heil Hitler!* and two hundred million voices shouted *NO!*

Sunday, June 22, 1941. The Nazis against those the *American* had called the Nazi-lovers. One year to the day since the betrayers of France had surrendered their land to Hitler: this time the blitzkrieg would have a different ending.

For the first time in several months the current events discussion group in Cell Number 10, Range D, would have an additional topic to the case of Lonnie James. The *American* was cheerfully gloomy—the Soviets would not last six weeks. They had no chance against the all-conquering power of the master race even though, as *Time* magazine reported that first week, "the Russians have a childlike, Oriental faith in the un-answerable power of machinery and they have equipped their divisions to the ears."

More than machinery.

Steve Kovach's question—would Uncle Joe's boys fight?—was answered; but now he would have many more. The hopes of the Catholic Slovak Society members that their homeland would be liberated would rise and fall in the days to come, in the years to come before the turning point. No one in Iron City on the Monongahela could know, of course, that the fas-cist onslaught would break against the Steel City on the Volga. But Stalingrad was yet to come: Pearl Harbor would come much sooner.

Later, when they would remember those last few days in June, Paul Harper and the others would think that everything happened at the same moment, though actually the return of Leroy Flowers did not occur till the following Friday. The missing witness' reappearance was as casual as the search for him had been desperate. He had known nothing of the search or of Lonnie's trial: there was nothing of such matters on the sport page or in the funnies.

It was Milton Cohen who came running to tell Lonnie after he had telephoned the clerk of the Supreme Court. The story was a simple one. Leroy had come back to his landlady to rent a room: she called Mrs. Spencer even before he explained his absence. It was on account of the suit he had bought on time from Hoffman's Big Downtown Store where credit is given with a smile. But the smile had faded and the letters they sent him were angry. It would become a legal matter. Leroy had no money after he was laid-off from McGregor's, and worse—he had no suit. He had pawned it for five dollars, then sold the ticket for two. The county dicks had not found him the first time they came: he made sure they would not find him when they came back again. He had hit the road again, as he had done in the big Depression; and when he finally found a job it too was on the road—helper on an inter-state moving van. His bed was the bunk behind the seat in

244

the cab: the pay was little, but he saved enough to buy new clothes and to pay the back-rent he owed Mrs. Bailey and the twelve-dollar debt to Hoffman's. The Defense boom was on; he would get his old job back in the mill.

No one had said goodby when he left: thousands hailed his return. He was a hero; his picture was in all the papers. And Mrs. Bailey's blackeyed peas and neckbones were better than any fatted calf could be.

The Supreme Court would reconsider Lonnie's appeal when they returned in the Fall: a reversal was possible; at the least a new trial would be granted. Some people said the Court would have permitted a second hearing even without Leroy's coming back—the questions about Winkel's dramatic death were loud and insistent. No one would ever know for sure, but the inside committee and the outside committee would not have time to speculate about that. *To Do* was as urgent as ever. The death watch on Lonnie would now be removed but only the most determined fight could free Lonnie from Murderer's Row. The men behind the frame-up were relentless, powerful, rich. More people would have to be enlisted against them, more mass meetings held, more money collected, more leaflets issued, more petitions signed. Not only Iron City but the whole Commonwealth and all America must hear the cry: *Lonnie James Shall Not Die!*

"But what about you guys?" Slim Gaither asked Paul. "Your appeal comes up in the Fall too. Aren't your people outside going to do something to get you-all out?"

"Sure," said Paul. "They're working for us, trying to tell people what's behind our case. Lonnie's is an emergency and they had to do more on that for the past three months especially. But of course you got to see it another way too. The fight for Lonnie is part of our fight—the same people who framed him framed us. Look at me—I'm the same color as him: it could have been me. Or it could have been you up there on Murderers' Row—Merle Gaither, alias Slim. Like the papers said about him—a burly Negro, Lonnie James, alias Slim. But it's more than that: the papers call the Lonnie James Defense

Committee a bunch of Reds. They aren't all Reds, not most of them, no more than you are; but still people can see that nobody is working harder to save him than the Communists. And that helps those of us who are in here, because it's easier now to show the people that instead of advocating force and violence we are actually trying to stop it—third-degree beatings, legal lynchings. Reminds them of how we always have done that, Scottsboro and all the rest, leading the fight against the Coal and Iron Police terror and the company thugs in the steel and mining towns around here. Now it's against the law for McGregor Steel to have all the shotguns and tear-gas and clubs they used to use against the men, and people will remember how we fought for that law to be passed. And now when our Party can tell about how we started the campaign for Lonnie James in here"—Paul's gesture took in Slim as well as Zach and Faulcon—"well more people will know the truth about us. And that brings me to the last thing I want to say about this. When you boil it all down and whatever the Court decides about Lonnie or us or anything else—that won't be the end. The final say comes from the people and you can't fool them all the time. No matter if they fill up all the jails and all the Holes—somebody is always going to stand up and holler out the truth. It's always been like that. Of course I knew that before I came to jail, but there's something else I found out for sure in here—there will always be other people who will help spread the word. Regardless of danger, Slim. Regardless of anything. People like you."

(2)

Chief Guard Kovach had put Byrd on the night patrol, saying that the walking around would be better for his ailing kidneys than sitting out in the yard. Byrd did not like the change, but it would not last long: the veteran guard would soon be retired. Now he was passing through Range D, poking his light into every cell. He stopped at Number 9 and frowned at what he saw in the wavering beam. A smile lit up the

246

smooth brown face of the sleeping gray-haired man. He must be dreaming, thought Byrd—but what can an old Negro have to dream about? . . .

Maybe this is Jacob's ladder I'm a-climbing, Henry Faulcon said to himself. Reckon I never climbed so high before. . . .

But it was not Jacob's ladder, he realized now; it was the speaker's platform they brought from Douglass Hall to the corner of 24th and Jay in the Hollow section of Iron City. Overhead the sky was ragged gray like a jailhouse blanket, but dripping wet. The drizzle reminded him of the long-ago time he climbed up the platform on this very corner to make his first public speech—for Scottsboro. Looks like it's been raining ever since, he observed, his eyes on the weather-beaten red-brick wall of the building across the street. On the street floor a torn sidewalk-canopy, with pieces flapping in the wind, led to the dim-lit door of the Ritz Hotel; and next to it was the neon-lighted window of Bessie's Bar B Q. Seems like these old buildings around here should have melted away by now—*hey!* For with the thought a strange thing was happening before his startled eyes—the red-brick building and the three-story frame house next to it were going down, slowly crumpling and dissolving away like dirty snowbanks along the curb before the sun and rains of Spring. *Hey!* He tried to shout but no sound came from his throat; anyway, there was no one to be warned of the silent slow-motion disaster for now he saw that he was all alone. That's strange, he thought, stranger than the way all the houses in the Hollow were a-slipping and a-sliding to the ground. Never in all his life had Faulcon passed this corner day or night without seeing *some* of his people around. Now the fire engines and ambulances and law-cars will be coming, blowing their sirens and ringing bells and making such a fuss people won't be able to hear my speech. A hell of a thing.

The screaming red engines and snarling black coupes did not come. There was only the dreadful silence and all the buildings going down down down. Henry Faulcon was all alone but he was not afraid. Good thing I were fixing to tell these people the truth, cause I know what this is for sure. He hummed the tune softly.

You better mind how you lie
You better mind what you lying about
Cause you got to give account in the Judg-a-ment
You better mind.

That's it! From far away came the sound of Gabriel's trumpet. . . . Faulcon closed his eyes tight while he listened. Old Gabe is really in the groove to*night*: if I didn't know it were Judg-a-ment Day I'd swear that's nobody else but Louie Armstrong coming on with *Sunny Side of the Street!* I'll be damned. He had opened his eyes, then half-closed them again against the brightness. It was the sunny side but there was no street —everything was gone: the houses, the streets, the telephone poles. The sky was a brilliant blue and the Hollow was a green plush valley. The mountains around were no longer scarred and gray; they were covered with the great branching oaks and hickory-nut trees, the flowering richness toward which Jenny Faulcon's son Henry had yearned through the windows he was washing. Man, I got eyes like a duck-hawk! From his platform Faulcon could see the deer moving through the trees, their tawny backs dappled with the sun through the leaves. And the river—he had never seen it like that. A winding silver ribbon unrolling through a pass in the mountains, and his duck-hawk eyes could see clear to the bottom where the rainbow trout were darting across the pebbles. His fishing pole was at home in his attic, in the house his father had builded with the skill of his small black hands and his heart full of love for little brown Jenny. Faulcon sighed. Willston is going to be a long walk home for these bad feet what with all the streetcars being gone. But fishing could wait. His eyes took in the sweep of the broad valley that had been the Hollow. Lord, he said, what a place for a big labor picnic or a mass meeting even. Bet you could get a million people in here!

248

Now there were a million people seated before him on folding chairs. It did not surprise him even when he counted them a moment later and it came to 2,139,047 which was near about the whole population of Monongahela County. Shucks, he said to himself, I'm catching on to this jive *now*. All eyes were upon him and for the first time a panic rose within him. What if I forgot what I were going to say! And how can all these folks ever hear me? "Can you hear me way in the back there? Testing . . . one . . . two . . . three. . . ." A shout from the farthest row and the waving of hands assured him that they could hear him fine.

I'm a talking man for real, don't need no kind of a microphone neither. He noticed now that the speaker's platform was really a pulpit like the carved panelled one at the Old Rock of Zion, but much greater in size and the Book before him was larger than any he had ever seen. It was bound in leather with huge brass hinges and at a glance he took in the gold-engraved title: *The Good Book of the Brotherhood of Man, Science, Art, Literature, History, How to Make Periscopes From Spoons, Culture of Africa, Asia, North America, South America, Australia and Europe too; Music for Male Quartets, Female Voices and Songs for Children.* His hand stroked the great volume and then he knew what he must do before he started the meeting. He raised his hand high and brought his palm smack down with all his might upon the Book. It was a weak noise, he could hardly hear it himself, and people were jumping up and down, waving and shouting that they had not heard.

"It's that jailhouse slop," he apologized. "Guess I kind of lost my strength. But I know what. If you can't do something yourself get somebody to help and that's just what I'm a-going to do. I need me a strong man with a strong right arm—John Henry that's who. John *Hen-ry!* John *Hen--ry!* Get yourself on up here, man, so we can get this thing started right."

From the side where the Negroes were seated a tall black man arose. He was naked to the waist, the great muscles

249

rippling in the sun as he twirled his twelve-pound hammer lightly in his fingers as if it were Charlie Chaplin's cane. In two strides he was at Faulcon's side in the pulpit. "You can put that hammer down for a minute, John," Faulcon said. "Just give her a lick with your hand." John Henry nodded and smiled. He wasn't a big man at all. He wasn't even John Henry! "Well, I'll be switched if it aint old Reverend Buford. How you been Rev? Looking just the same." Reverend Buford had not changed since Faulcon had seen him last at the Widow Jackson's church. His thin dark neck was lost in the great white collar, his adam's apple jumping like a frog, his smile was still as golden. He winked at the speaker and said he'd give her a whop. He took off the rusty-black frock coat and Faulcon saw his patched white shirt, the wide purple silk suspenders and the pipestem arms. Faulcon shook his head doubtfully but he backed up to give the little preacher room. Reverend Buford took a couple of practice swings, stopping just short of the gold-engraved cover, and then he raised his hand large against the sky and smote the Book.

Great Godamighty what a blow! Dust jumped up like a windstorm and there was a great blast of light and pinwheels and roman candles and rockets and comets flashing and sparkling red and blue and green and black and yellow and orange and white and there was a crashing sound that filled the valley, a crumbling and crashing sound of all the walls of all the Jerichos a-tumbling down—a shattering burst of thunder rolls around the valley, echoing and re-echoing from the mountain sides as a thousand steel-barred doors slam open, and the rumbling mounts to a roar, to a soaring roaring booming crashing, a thousand kettle drums pounding, a thousand cymbals clashing—the thunder rolls away, rumbling over the green horizon and all is still . . . then into the joyous silence comes the sound of people singing, into the blue the dove is winging, and from all lands one voice proclaiming

PEACE! THERE *WILL* BE PEACE!

Reverend Buford, chairman of the Lonnie James Defense Committee, smiles shyly as Faulcon helps him into the old frock coat. "Thank you, Rev. That were a real good lick. Now I can start this meeting." He beamed down upon the first row: then came a sudden frown at what he saw. O Lord, I can't start yet. "Folks," he cried out, "please bear with me for one more minute whilst I get something straightened out. I just looked down at the best seats here in front and damned if I didn't see the Best People still hogging them places. There's old Adam McGregor the Second—and you know that aint right at all. He loses a half a million dollars over in Monte Carlo and then comes back to the Hotel Royale and tips me a lousy *dime*. Oh no, he got to go! Him and his eighteenth wife from Hollywood too. And bless my soul if it aint his sister a-setting there with him, hiding her face behind a *imported* lace veil so people can't see the marks of the Italian disease and the Greek disease and the French disease and Lord knows what else on her face. No, Countess Cassini - Princess Romanoff - Baroness Scarpatti - Duchess De Grass—you can't set there no more. And look—*oh oh oh*— Judge Hanford J. Rupp himself! Your Honor, don't you dare open your mouth or I'll say *objection overruled* even though I would let *you* say what the objection was before I over-ruled and I do believe that pained look on your face is sure enough real this time!"

The Best People made no move to go and Faulcon real-ized that he needed help again. He looked over the crowd. "Don't think I'm being nationalistic, folks, but it's just that I know my own people so much better. And now I want two of the baddest Negroes here to escort these people to the rear. I know who—Railroad Bill, he were the baddest Negro there ever was, and Stackalee cause he were even worse." Rail-road Bill and Stackalee came forward now. "Shucks, you boys aint bad," Faulcon said to Paul Harper and Slim Gaither. "Say, man"—he turned to Slim—"you sure got back fast from South America didn't you?" He faced the crowd. "Two of the best men you ever laid eyes on, both members of the inside committee, and they're going to move all that rich white trash to the back seats."

When that was done he looked over the great audience again but he still was not pleased. In one section were the steel workers and the coal miners—but just the men. "Oh no, no," said Faulcon. "That aint right. You left your women at home but now it's a different day." With his words came a great rushing sound, a rattle of dishes, a whisper of brooms, the swishing of mops and the crying of babies and lo and behold all the women from the steel towns and mining patches were seated beside their men. "That's fine," said Faulcon. "Fine. If you'll pardon me for saying so—all of you-all can learn something from my people on *that* subject, cause we gave America two of the greatest women that ever swung a broom against the worst dirt there ever was. Meaning Harriet Tubman and Sojourner Truth and now they're going to be in all the history books and everybody will see their beautiful faces." *AMEN!* came a voice from the crowd. "Thank you, Sister Jackson. And stand up for all the people to see the lady who collected the most signatures for Scottsboro and Angelo Herndon and Lonnie James too." They pushed Lucy Jackson to her feet and they all saw how tall and black and beautiful she was, and then it was Charlene Harper, and Annie Mae Zachary; and Catherine Spencer who lied like a good Christian for Lonnie; and old Mrs. Bailey—young-old black-brown plain-pretty fat-slender—beautiful all, strong and tall. Faulcon's eyes clouded when he saw that she was little Jenny Faulcon too. I'm going to put some roses on your grave, the roses you grew, first chance I get. . . .

When the cheers died away he saw something else that must be done before he could begin the speaking. "Brothers and sisters," he cried. "Also comrades and fellow workers—something else is wrong. You people came here just like you been living, the white on one side and the colored on the other and now you're setting that way and after awhile the photographers from the Iron City *American-Worker* are going to take our picture and people might think when they see it that this were a Jim Crow meeting. So I want you to scatter around, everybody together—course I don't want my people to get *lost* you understand, but this way you-all will get to know each other better."

It was done before he finished saying it. "And now, people," he said, "just one more thing but I know you'll be glad. I want you to meet somebody you all know but never seen. *Lonnie James,* come on up here and meet your friends!" Lonnie ran forward to smile upon them all. "*Our* son," said Faulcon, "and a mighty brave man. And I'll tell you something else: He's going to be a thirty-game winner for the Iron City Stars and with him doing the pitching we aint never going to be last in the League no more!" The cheers went on: everybody was clapping and whistling for Lonnie standing there so proud and free, his arm around the shoulders of his first friend, Carl Peterson, who had sense enough to be here on this great day. The whistling grew louder, the millions of tiny blasts merging into one great whistle blowing. . . .

All men could hear the mighty thunder of the great locomotive racing across the land with its drivers just a-flashing and the wheels just a-rolling, just a-reeling and a-racking, just a-reeling and a-racking . . . *whooooo whooooo*—the Glory Train, and Zach a-driving her through!

O Shining Day!

Faulcon bowed his head with the weight of unbearable joy, and when he raised his eyes again there was no sound except the singing birds. The seats were empty. All had boarded the Glory Train. He was sad to be left alone, so he sang aloud:

> *This train have left the station, this train*
> *This train have left the station, this train*
> *This train have left the station*
> *This train takes on every nation*
> *Cause this train is the best train, this train.*

253

And here I went and missed it! Everybody riding but me and I never even got the chance to make my speech. He shook his head sadly and stared out over the rows of empty chairs. *No!* His duck-hawk eyes had spied a lonely figure far to the back. Shucks, let that old train go, cause I see Lucy Jackson! He hurried from the pulpit and walked down the long green aisle toward where she sat. On and on he walked, faster and faster; his bad feet no longer hurt but he did not even notice that wonder.

"Sister Lucy Jackson!"

"Brother Henry Faulcon!"

"You sure are looking pretty."

"Thank you, Brother Henry. I was so proud of you. That was such a fine speech—the best one you ever made."

"Sister Jackson—Lucy, I mean—I'm glad you liked that little talk but right now I got a song on my mind. Remember how we used to sing it in the choir—*Just a Closer Walk With Thee*"?

"Oh, no, *Brother* Henry. I told you about that foolishness before. Said I wasn't going walking with you, or nothing else, till you asked me for my hand in marriage and that goes for now too!"

"Now look here, woman. Seems like nobody today is giving me a chance to say *anything*. And I got all the words right in my mouth."

But he never said them: he took her in his arms and kissed her full on the lips. "Mmmmm *mmmmmm!* Sweet Lucy *Faulcon!*"

Slowly, for he was very old, Byrd climbed the steel stairs from Range D which he had just patrolled. His key trembled in the gate lock of Murderers' Row; then he was inside. He sighed, remembering the easy job he had had on this range only a few weeks ago. Just sitting and watching the condemned man under the spotlight. . . .

Now there was neither watcher nor light outside Lonnie James' cell. The guard looked in on the young Negro. He was sleeping: his breathing was strong and steady. How peacefully these bad men sleep—and me not having a good night's rest in years!

Byrd turned away from Lonnie. Then on he walked, this old old man with death on his face, flashing his light in the gloom, slowly, painfully making his way toward the other end of the tier, to the gate through which he must pass.